Euanie MacDonald was [...]
of Scotland and spent [...]
She took a First in Socia[...]
later complemented by [...]
university she moved to Ayrshire (the home of her favourite
poet, Robert Burns) to do post-graduate research, then lived
in various parts of the UK, working in education and management training. Later she moved to Scandinavia, where
she set up a management consultancy.

As a wandering Celt with roots in Scotland, she has no difficulty in regarding Europe as her workplace. At present she
and her Swedish husband live in a village in Languedoc,
France with their (trilingual) son and two (trilingual) dogs.
She combines management consulting and writing fiction
and non-fiction. Her first adult novel *Steelworker's Row* is
also available from Piatkus. In her spare time, Euanie enjoys
gardening and walking with her dogs.

Also by Euanie MacDonald

Steelworker's Row
Catch the Moment

Kirkowen's Daughter

Euanie Macdonald

PIATKUS

For more information on other
books published by Piatkus,
visit our webside at
www.piatkus.co.uk

Copyright © 1997 by Euanie MacDonald

First published in Great Britain in 1997 by
Judy Piatkus (Publishers) Ltd of
5 Windmill Street, London W1T 2JA
email: info@piatkus.co.uk

This edition published 2001

The moral right of the author has been asserted

A catalogue record for this book is available from the British Library

ISBN 0 7499 3246 5

Printed and bound in Great Britain by
Cox & Wyman Ltd, Reading, Berkshire

To Helen

'Fate still has blest me with a friend'
Robert Burns

Contents

(Chapter titles from the poetry of Robert Burns)

Chapter 1
Kirkowen's bairns are bonnie

Kirkowen, December 1880

'For God's sake, man, have ye not a scrap of pity? Don't throw them out in this!' The old man clutched at the agent's arm as a bitter wind scurried falling snow into drifts around their feet.

Robert Gilmour shook off his hand contemptuously. 'Shut your face, Wullie Laird, or you'll be joining them. Jamie Soutar kent he'd be evicted if he led another miners' strike. He's brought this on himself!'

'But Kirsty's bairn is due next week,' Wullie pleaded bravely. 'Can they not stay till the New Year? It's no' that long. Och, Rab Gilmour, have a heart.'

Gilmour looked over at the proud figure of Jamie Soutar, arm round his wife Kirsty whose swollen stomach stuck out below a thin woollen shawl. She had thrown the plaid round her shoulders when the mine-owner's factor and his men started hammering on the door.

'Mr Soutar is saying nothing on his own behalf. So why the hell should I listen to you, Wullie Laird?' sneered the factor.

'Aye, and neither will he beg,' Kirsty Soutar burst out. 'My Jamie won't plead with the likes of you, or yer fine master Hamish McClure. And I'm right behind him, come what may.'

'Touching.' Gilmour glowered at the defiant young woman. 'We'll see if you're still behind your man after a night or two in the snow.'

Behind the pair, a sullen shabby crowd had gathered

1

outside the row of miners' cottages in the dark winter evening. Mutters began rising to an angry rumble.

'Right, lads.' The factor called over his dozen men, armed with stout sticks and cudgels. They lined up behind him looking ready and more than willing for a fight.

'Aye, it's as well ye brought over the bully boys from Bargeddie, Gilmour,' shouted an anonymous voice from the back of the crowd. 'You're brave wi' them at yer back. But one day you'll get what's comin to ye, so ye will!'

'Oh, is that a fact?' Rab Gilmour raised himself up to his full height and splayed his short stubby legs, glaring in contempt at the motley, poverty-stricken group. 'Aye, well, I'm telling you now, anyone who takes in Jamie Soutar or his wife will be evicted straight away, day or night, winter or no. We'll see how fine and big-talking you are then without a roof over your heads, nor a job either. Mr McClure leaves the judging of who stays and who goes to me. Understood?'

The rumble quietened to an uneasy murmur again.

'Right, lads.' Gilmour turned to his men. 'You'll stay the night. Divide the shift. Half can wait inside Soutar's while the other half stand guard. You can spell each other off. And make sure nobody thinks of trying anything stupid like taking in that pair.' With that he swung himself on to his horse and rode off into the dark night.

'Och, Jamie, Kirsty, I'm sorry, so I am.' Old Wullie sadly put a hand on the younger man's arm. 'I'd take ye in myself and risk Gilmour, but our Hector and Ellen are staying wi' me till he gets a job labouring. And she's as heavy wi' bairn as Kirsty.'

'What will ye do?' Ellen Laird pushed clumsily through and laid a comforting arm round Kirsty's shoulders.

'Well, they'll no' be comin' back in here whatever they do.' The leader of the agent's men stood in front of the door. 'Ye can get yer stuff in the mornin', ten o'clock sharp, Soutar. Then we're barrin' the door till the new tenants move in next week. Mr McClure told Gilmour to let it right away to the man that's replacing you at the pit.'

'Oh, aye?' Jamie Soutar spoke for the first time. 'I pity the man who gets it ... and his family. The place runs wi'

2

damp. Hamish McClure should put his miners in something more suitable for folk than for animals.'

'Och, and why would he waste good money doin' that?' sniggered the leader, wiping his dripping nose on a grubby sleeve. 'Is that no' what ye are? Keep back!' he yelled in fear as the crowd surged forward, frustration bubbling to boiling point again. 'Put one finger on us and you're out, the lot of ye. Mr Gilmour meant it.'

'Och, don't land in trouble for our sakes,' Kirsty Soutar cried worriedly to their angry neighbours. 'We'll manage.'

'Ye heard her, clear off!' the leader snarled, but still looked uneasy.

'Don't try for Kirkowen the night, Jamie son,' a worn-looking woman advised sadly as the crowd reluctantly dispersed. 'Kirsty will no' make it through the snaw.'

'I ken.' Jamie's voice was anguished.

'Och, don't worry, Jeannie, we'll think of something.' Kirsty struggled to sound reassuring.

'Make a wee shelter in the old byre over the humphy brig',' Wullie whispered urgently. 'That's no' McClure's land.'

'Aye, that's an idea, there's still a roof on the place.' Jamie Soutar glanced towards the river where an ancient bridge led to a field with a disused barn. 'Come on, Kirsty lassie, we'd better get ye out of this.'

'Here's something for the night.' Two men slipped silently after them in the darkness, with an ancient bit of ship's canvas, some blankets and food the neighbours had gladly given, despite their own desperate poverty.

'Och, you're the lads, so ye are. This will do fine for a wee bed.' Jamie set about making a pallet in a corner out of the wind. Carefully he tucked the canvas over some old straw.

'Are ye all right, Kirsty?' one of the men asked anxiously as the young woman huddled, arms round her stomach, by the fire Jamie had lit in the middle of the bare floor.

'Och, not bad, Archie.' She managed a wan smile. 'The fire's just dandy . . . and the draught keeps the smoke from gathering,' she added wryly. 'And at least we've a roof over us, more or less.' She glanced at the small drifts of snow let in through missing slates.

'When ye come back in the mornin' for yer stuff, Hector Laird says he'll take ye into Kirkowen on the coal cart.'

'That's dandy. Now away ye go before the factor's men see ye, or you'll be joinin' us in this fine hostelry.' Jamie Soutar looked grimly round the old barn. 'Och, and thanks to ye all.' He raised his hand in a brief, grateful salute as the men left as silently as they'd come.

'Come on, lass.' Jamie put an arm round his wife. 'We had better eat the bannock and broth and see if we can get some sleep. You're brave so ye are, Kirsty, but I'm sorry I've brought ye to this.' His eyes were dark with sadness.

'Brought me to this nothing, Jamie Soutar!' Kirsty responded with a flash of her usual spirit. 'I've backed ye all the way, through the miners' strikes and everything. And if some of the way is bumpy, well, that's just how it is. Now where's that broth?'

'Comin' up, madam.' Jamie smiled and filled her tin bowl nearly to the brim.

'Jamie, somethin's happening!' Kirsty clutched her husband's back in the small hours of the morning as they lay huddled together, sleeping fitfully in the dank chill of the barn. Outside the wind moaned and gusted, driving snow into the pitch-black ditches.

'Och, Kirsty, not the night!' Jamie Soutar was instantly awake. 'It can't be . . . it's not due till next week.' He sprang up and lit a precious candle from the glowing embers of the fire.

'The pains started hours ago, but I didn't want to tell ye till I was sure. I thought it just might have been the shock, ye ken, and walking through the drifts.' Kirsty spoke through gritted teeth as another contraction shook her.

'I'll get help, Kirsty.'

'Don't leave me, Jamie. Oh, Jamie, stay!' she yelled in fear and pain.

'All right, lassie mine, I won't leave you.' He held her hands for a minute, realising it was too late anyway. A countryman born and bred, Jamie could see the birth was well underway. Instead he began to sort out someplace to deliver and lay the baby that was pushing so determinedly into the freezing, hostile world.

Peggy Soutar was born at five o'clock that dark December morning on the barn floor. She screamed in rage at the undignified entry she made on to some bloody straw. Her father clipped the cord with his bowie knife and wrapped her in a threadbare blanket and bit of musty canvas. Then he ignored the baby's yells as he fought to save his wife. But Kirsty had haemorrhaged to death before her daughter was an hour old and never even heard her protesting cries.

Ayrshire Times Editorial, 20 December 1880

LOCAL WOMAN DIES

The death of Mrs Kirsten Soutar was an unfortunate case, according to the Coroner, but one for which no blame could be directly apportioned. Mr James Soutar, a well-known activist in the trades union movement, had been repeatedly warned that he would lose his job if he continued his activities against the interests of the mine-owner, Mr Hamish McClure. After the last strike, Mr McClure finally told Mr Soutar to go. Soutar was then no longer entitled to live in the tied mine-worker's house.

Some have suggested that the factor, Mr Robert Gilmour, should have allowed a few days' grace before evicting the family, but he was acting quite legally and within the remit of his job. He can hardly be held responsible for the tragic outcome. The child, a female, is reputed to be doing well at the home of a relative of the dead woman in Kirkowen.

'Hamish!' Janet McClure called feebly from the master bedroom of Bargeddie House, as her husband's tall figure passed the door.

'What is it, Janet?' He peered into the heavy dimness, trying not to sound as irritable as he felt. 'I have a meeting of the Borough Council at six and I'm late already, my dear.'

'Please, Hamish.'

5

'Oh, very well.' McClure came and sat by her bedside, lifting the thin hand from the bedcover and touching it lightly with his lips. 'Now what do you want?'

'That poor woman, Soutar ... the one who died last month. I read the inquest in the paper today. Hamish, you didn't tell Gilmour to evict them, did you?' His wife's pale face was drawn and sad.

'Of course not.' His eyes narrowed with annoyance. 'I simply told him to get them out once Soutar had been dismissed, not when to do it.' The answer was studiedly ambiguous. 'That's quite normal, my dear, in a case like this.' He went on quickly, 'Gilmour was perhaps overly zealous, that's all. He's an impulsive man but an excellent factor.'

'Can we not send some money or something? I keep thinking of our baby.' Janet McClure touched her bloated stomach. 'It's due in barely a month. ... och, Hamish, the poor woman. The poor wee motherless bairn.' She began to cry.

'Now, now, Janet!' Hamish McClure shook her frail shoulder firmly. 'Jamie Soutar wouldn't take a bawbee from us if he was dying of hunger, especially not now. Calm yourself, woman, calm yourself, this will do our bairn no good at all.'

'Are you sure you didn't tell Gilmour to evict them?' Janet persisted.

'Of course I'm sure!' He felt his temper rise at her questioning, but with an effort controlled himself. 'And the lass is with relatives, you must have read that too in the *Ayrshire Post*. Folk like the Soutars are as tough as old boots, they can survive anything.'

'But the poor mother didn't,' Janet protested sadly.

'Listen to me, Janet! Soutar is up in Glasgow now. The last I heard, he was hand in glove with his Socialist friends – that trouble-maker Keir Hardie for one. People like that, nobody can help.' Hamish's voice rose. 'I offered Soutar honest toil with a free house into the bargain. But he bit the hand that fed him. He was not a God-fearing man, Janet.' He got up and began pacing the room.

'What do you mean, Hamish?' She half raised herself against the pillows.

'Not a foot has he set in the kirk for years. The man's an Atheist!' McClure thundered righteously. 'An Atheist! The Lord has visited His wrath and just punishment on Soutar, Janet. Rab Gilmour was only His instrument.'

'But the bairn was innocent,' she quavered, knowing she was risking his easily roused fury.

'Now that's enough, Janet!' He stopped and leaned over the end of the bed, his colour mounting. 'Only the chosen, among whom we are thankfully counted, are innocent from conception and therefore saved. You know your Bible, woman. The teachings are clear for all to see.' His purple colour deepened.

'Och, don't be angry, Hamish, please. I'm sorry.' Helpless tears began rolling down her face.

'Don't worry her,' Doctor Logie had warned. 'She could lose the bairn, the state she's in.' Hamish pulled himself together with a great effort and softened his tone. 'Och, it's just your condition that's making you over-sensitive. Soon we'll have a fine son. Our first-born . . . the first of many. And you'll be back to your old self once it's over.'

'Och, Hamish, you're right, I'm worrying about everything.' Gamely she tried to smile. 'But it might be a wee lassie . . .'

'Not a bit of it! Even your mother says it's a lad from the way it's lying. Now I'm away.' He came over and kissed her pale forehead, waved cheerfully and was gone.

Janet McClure shifted her swollen legs restlessly under the heavy beadspread and, leaning over, rang the bell for Libby.

'Yes, madam?' Her personal maid was there at once.

'Bring me a cup of hot chocolate, Libby, then stay and keep me company for a bit.' Janet half closed her eyes.

'Certainly, madam. Then would ye like me to read to ye for a wee while?' The maid was disturbed by her pallor.

'That would be fine,' Janet murmured. 'A wee bit of Miss Austen. Not Mr Dickens . . . not today.' She thought again of Kirsty Soutar and a tear rolled down her cheek.

'Are ye not well again, madam?' Libby was increasingly

7

concerned for her young mistress whose longed-for pregnancy had been a nightmare of ill-health.

'Just tired, Libby.' Janet resolutely pulled herself together. 'I'm just tired.'

Three weeks later, on the first day of February, Elspeth McClure was born after a long and difficult birth. Pacing up and down the corridor, Hamish McClure waited impatiently, wincing at his wife's cries and then worrying over the silence when it seemed to be all over.

'What's happening, Doctor Logie?' He grasped the doctor's arm as he came out of the bedroom, pale with exhaustion after the long night. 'How is the baby?' Anxiously his eyes raked the doctor's face.

'Aye, well, Mrs McClure has had a hard time.' Doctor Logie ignored the question. 'Poor woman. But she'll be fine, if the Lord wills. Listen, Hamish, I'd be careful about any more bairns for a bit, her constitution will not take it.'

'Aye, aye, Logie, but the bairn? Is it a laddie?'

'You've a healthy wee lassie, Mr McClure, and I'm certain her wee problem will not be too much of a handicap in life with all the advantages you can give her,' the doctor replied cryptically.

'What handicap?' McClure was so worried by the doctor's words, he forgot to be disappointed that it was a daughter, not a son. Pushing past, he entered the birthing-room where Janet was propped, tired and grey, on a mountain of pillows.

'Isn't she bonnie, Hamish?' Janet McClure smiled feebly, anxiously glancing towards the sleeping child.

Hamish stood gazing down at his new-born daughter in terrible silence. 'Bonnie is not the word I or anyone else will ever use about her.' The harsh words were ground out.

'Och, maybe it'll get better as she grows,' Janet murmured in a pathetic, conciliatory tone.

In the lavish cradle, the baby stirred and turned, showing even more clearly her little left cheek. A livid port-wine stain covered her face from below the eye to behind her ear and spilled angrily almost to her perfectly formed mouth.

'Not that kind of mark,' Hamish went on bitterly. 'I've

8

seen them before. Let's hope she has attributes other than beauty. She'll need them.' Utter disappointment had put him beyond the release of roaring fury. Face grim and cold he turned on his heel, leaving his wife crying pitiful tears in the big bed.

Chapter 2
A country lad is my degree

Cureeee... cureee... a curlew called incessantly from the dunes just out of sight. Above her bright red head, a seagull wheeled, beady eyes greedily searching the cliff-top for remnants of fish dropped by the carts as they climbed the rocky lane up from the quay. Peggy Soutar rolled over on to her stomach, lying right at the edge of the cliff, and peered down at the sandy beach. Oblivious, a little boy was catching shrimps in a rocky pool.

Beyond them both the sea shone and sparkled in the September sunshine, tossing a million diamonds between her and the Isle of Arran. The dark silhouette of the island lay like a sleeping warrior guarding the Firth of Clyde, helmet tipped back. On misty mornings Peggy was certain he moved. One day he would rise, stretch rocky limbs and walk in three great strides to Ireland, that she knew.

Stealthily she picked up a stone and threw it with deadly accuracy at Tom Laird, bouncing it neatly off his skinny backside.

'Ohya!' he yelped, looking round to see where it had come from.

She ducked down, laughing silently, then waited a few minutes before throwing another, aimed this time at his bare foot.

'Show yer face, ye eejit, whoever ye are!' Tom Laird, realising he was being tormented, hopped up and down in impotent rage. 'I'll do ye, so I will!'

'Ye can't catch me! Ye can't catch me! Me my ma daddie-

10

o, ye can't catch me!' Peggy jumped up and down on the cliff-top in glee at Tom's fury.

'Just you wait, Peggy Soutar. I'll get ye, so I will.'

' "I'll do ye! I'll get ye, Peggy Soutar!" ' she mimicked. Still laughing, Peggy ran home to old Lizzie Weir's, to wait for her father coming in from the pit.

'Can I have a piece, Auntie Lizzie, with blaeberry jam? Go on, just one,' she cajoled the old lady.

'It's just as well yer daddy gives me a decent bawbee to feed ye, Peggy!' The old lady grinned toothlessly. 'Ye eat as much as an Irish navvy off the Stranraer boat! Och, all right, just one.' She gave in and cut a hunk of bread, spreading it thickly with dark, tart blueberry jam.

'Smashin'!' Peggy's cheeky green eyes danced in a jammy face. 'Ye make the best jam in Kirkowen, Auntie Lizzie.'

'Ye could be right,' Lizzie replied immodestly. 'I'm no' bad. Wait a minute, hen, here's Jamie now. That's early! I thought he was on the back-shift.' The old lady peered down the street to where Jamie Soutar's tall figure was striding purposfully towards them.

'How's my lassie?' Jamie hugged Peggy's diminutive body to him for a minute, leaving black marks on her thin cotton pinny.

'Right as rain!' She gazed adoringly up at him.

'That's the stuff! Listen, Lizzie,' he turned to the old woman, 'is there any chance of a cup of tea? I've a couple of things to tell the pair of ye but I need to quench my drouth.'

'Jamie, what's happened?' Lizzie was concerned at once. In Kirkowen unexpected news was rarely good. 'Ye've not lost yer job at Dalgleish's pit?'

'Och, it's not as bad or as simple as that.' Gratefully Jamie drank the thick brew Lizzie thrust at him in a cracked cup. 'Jings, that would put hair on your teeth!' He grinned and shuddered after the first bitter gulp, but went on drinking.

'Aye, well, tea's that dear,' Lizzie replied proudly, 'and I'm no' one for waste. So I just keep the pot topped up wi' water and simmering on the back of the range all day. It draws every bit of taste from the leaves and I can have a right guid cup anytime, morning, noon or nicht, just by

11

adding a wee spoonful of tea and some water now and again.'

'Aye, waste not want not... every mickle makes a muckle,' Jamie agreed cheerfully, finishing it with relish.

'But what's yer news, Daddy?' Mature far beyond her ten and a half years, if pert and naughty at times, Peggy put a hand on his grimy knee and searched his face worriedly. Nobody ever left work in the middle of the day without good reason, especially not from the depths of the mine. 'Why are ye back this early?'

'There was a meeting at the pit-head this afternoon – the Miners' Union, ye ken. Keir Hardie himself was there. The men left the coalface to come up and hear him.'

'Keir Hardie!' Peggy's eyes widened. Jamie was active in the new Independent Labour Party as well as the Ayrshire Miners' Union, so his daughter knew the name well. James Keir Hardie was a local legend and hero to many miners. To the mine-owners he was an arch-enemy.

'Aye, there's a strike brewing again. We'll have to hope it won't be as long or as bitter as the last one. On top of that, Keir Hardie is going to England to stand as an MP, for a place called West Ham in London. You remember, he lost the last election in Mid-Lanark?'

'Aye!' Lizzie and Peggy nodded in unison.

'But that's nothing to do wi' you, is it, Jamie?' Lizzie shrugged and poured another cup for them both.

'Well, it is,' he went on gravely. 'Keir can't carry on with everything he does in Scotland from away down there, so they're going to divide things up. He's asked me to work for the Miners' Union full-time and help edit *The Miner*, ye ken the union paper? But it would mean moving to Glesca.'

'Ye could write the paper no bother. You've taught yerself to be a man of letters, Jamie,' Lizzie broke in stoutly, 'even though ye left school at ten. Ye speak that well, so ye do ... it's as if ye came from Edinburgh!'

'What did you say to Mr Hardie, Daddy?' Peggy asked quietly.

'I said I'd give it consideration and thanked him for the honour, but that I was happy enough here ... and that I'd you to think about. I explained that Lizzie looks after ye

12

when I'm working, but we have our own wee place next door.'

'So you're not going to Glesca?' Peggy tried not to sound as relieved as she felt. Lizzie had been to Glasgow once on the 'Puffing Billy' and told everybody that the noise and smell gave her nightmares for a week.

'Well, I'm coming to that, lass,' her father continued slowly. 'Dalgleish's manager, Ritchie Cleland, saw me talking to Keir Hardie after the rest of the men started heading back to the cage. "Right, Soutar!" he yelled over. "Get to hell down that shaft right now, or ye'll no' have a job to go to." '

'Och, Cleland's a right bad article . . . I wouldn't give him the time of day.' Lizzie had scrubbed floors for his wife long ago and she hated the man.

'Well, I looked at Keir Hardie. He could see what I was thinking and gave me the nod. So I turned and shouted back, "Send the cage down the shaft without me, Cleland, I'm changing my job!" Christ, it was worth it, just to see the bastard's expression. Sorry, lass,' Jamie apologised for swearing, but couldn't keep the grin off his face.

'So ye *are* going? What's goin' to happen to me?' Peggy demanded anxiously.

'You can stay with Lizzie and see out the year till ye finish at Kirkowen Primary . . . if she agrees, of course. Then ye better come to me in Glesca.'

'I don't want to leave Kirkowen!' Peggy's face flushed.

'Now listen, Peggy,' Jamie spoke gravely, 'you can't stay here if I move. Lizzie is flitting to her daughter in Darvel next summer to help with the bairns. Ye ken that.'

'Aye, that's right.' Lizzie sighed. 'I'm right fond of ye, lassie, and you're welcome to stay wi' me till I go. Ye sleep here often enough as it is when Jamie's away on union business. But I've promised to move to our Masie next June. She's expectin' her third and she'll have to work right after in the lace mill. That rotten man of hers spends his pay in the boozers as soon as he gets it, so he does.'

'Och, well.' Peggy shrugged her shoulders, full of the resiliant optimism of youth. 'I suppose if I have to, I have to.

13

At least I've a year left to get the prize at Kirkowen School. And, by jings, I will,' she added determinedly.

'Aye, so you will,' her father replied proudly. 'There's brains in that wee red head of yours, for all it seems full of clitter-clatter at times.'

'Right, class, sit up, eyes front! Tables!'

'Tables!' A sigh of anguish went up from the children.

'Thomas Laird, Dry Measure.' Miss Drummond twitched her thin cane towards the hapless lad cowering at the back of the class. 'On your feet, boy, when I'm talking to you! Begin!'

Fifty pairs of gleeful eyes swivelled round as Tam reluctantly stood up, his face a study in defeated resignation. 'Four gills one pint, two pints one ... er, eh, em ... quart,' he began stumbling. 'Two quarts one ... er, er ...' He dried up altogether. 'Och, I canny remember, Miss ...'

'What?' the teacher screeched, plump face red with righteous rage. 'Thomas Laird, what are two quarts?'

'One, er ... gallon,' he fumbled in confusion.

'Out on the floor!'

Slowly he walked to the front of the class and held out his hands, automatically crossing one on top of the other.

'Thwack! Thwack!' The thonged leather tawse came down on the rough grubby paws with an almighty slap, almost lifting his underfed body in the air. After six slaps, the palm and unprotected wrist above it were burning red. Tam Laird bit his lip but refused to cry.

'Back to your seat, boy! You're a useless lump of humanity!' Anger assuaged, Miss Drummond finally stopped belting and released her victim. 'Margaret Soutar, show that village idiot how it should be done. Continue from where he stopped.' The teacher sat down at her high desk, sweating from exertion and fanning herself with an atlas.

'Two quarts one pottle, two pottles one gallon, two gallons one peck, four pecks one bushel, three bushels one bag, four bushels one coomb, eight bushels one quarter, twelve bags or thirty-six bushels one chaldron, five quarters or forty bushels one wey.'

Without hesitation Peggy rattled off the complicated table

14

with an air of competence which contrasted sadly with the defeated boy in the corner. Tam bowed his head, fighting not to let a single tear drop as the pain throbbed in his burning hands.

' . . . two weys or ten quarters one last,' Peggy finished triumphantly and sat down. The class let out a collective sigh of relief. Miss Drummond was usually mollified after such a fine performance. Today was no exception.

'Exactly, Margaret Soutar. Class, take note, that is how everybody should sound.' She turned like a galleon in full sail. 'Now, Thomas Laird, you will ask Margaret to help you learn the Dry Measure table this evening and I will ask you again first thing tomorrow. Woe betide you, boy, if you make a single mistake. What you got today is only a taste of what is coming! Did you hear that, Laird?'

'Yes, Miss Drummond,' Tam managed to reply without letting his voice tremble.

'Right.' The teacher moved towards the youngest group, who froze in terror. 'On your slates, the letter "l" twenty times. Get the line to cross exactly in the middle. I'll be round to see them in a minute! Middle group finish learning the parable of the Good Samaritan. Now, big group, the main rivers of Europe . . . begin, Elsie Sutherland.'

'I canny learn they tables, Peggy.' Tam Laird's dirty face was a study in despair as they walked the narrow lane that evening, bare feet crunching the falling leaves.

Kirkowen School was strategically placed to serve three villages and was convenient to none of them. Every day Peggy and Tam made the three-mile walk home, barefoot, winter and summer alike, without so much as a thought.

'Och, you can so, Tam, you just don't try.' Clever Peggy couldn't really understand the difficulty. 'Get a rythmn up in your head, like ye were humming a wee song. Two quarts one pottle, two pottles one gallon,' she chirped. 'Come on!'

Slowly joining in, the boy began to sing along, getting them almost right as they reached the cobbled square, where the grey granite 'new' kirk and village hall stood solemnly glowering at one another.

15

'Peggy Soutar!' Mrs Buchanan called from the bakery. 'Come and get your Auntie Lizzie's loaf.'

'Right, Mrs Buchanan. Now, Tam, sing it in your head all night like I showed ye. You'll be fine in the morning.' She gave him a friendly push and ran over to the bakery. 'Och, that smells lovely, Mrs Buchanan.' Her nose twitched at the rich aroma wafting from the shop.

'There ye are, lass.' The baker's wife handed over the bread. 'And here's one of Mr Buchanan's misshapes for yerself.' She gave the girl a malformed drop pancake that had spilled too far across the griddle.

'Thanks, Mrs Buchanan, that's just dandy!' Peggy couldn't wait to get her teeth into the rich yellow dough.

'But listen, Peggy.' Tam Laird was still waiting for her when she came out. 'I canny sing in class, Miss Drummond will hammer me if I sing,' he added anxiously. 'Oh, whit's that?' His eyes fastened on the pancake.

'Och, michty, Tam Laird, you are daft right enough. Just sing to learn it, then talk normal when you say it, but keep the song in yer head to guide ye. Aye, and this is what ye think it is . . . och, here ye are.' She tore off half the pancake and gave it to him. It had gone before her eyes had a chance to focus.

'Thanks, Peggy!' Tam gulped, eyes greedily on her half.

'This bit's mine, Tam Laird! See you in the morning. Remember: four bushels one coomb, eight bushels one quarter . . . keep singing!' Peggy turned into the open doorway, mouth full.

'Tatties wi' buttermilk, great!' She sniffed and peeked into the pot bubbling on the old range as she passed. 'My favourite, Auntie Lizzie.'

'Was that Tam Laird, the poor wee soul?' Lizzie asked idly as she examined the tealeaves clustered at the bottom of the cup. 'Have a look, is that a letter comin', Peggy?'

She peered obediently into the cracked cup. 'No, it's a tree – that's good luck. Aye, it was Tam,' she went on in the same breath. 'Miss Drummond hammered him again the day.' She placed the bread on the rickety sideboard and began laying the table for their simple meal.

'Poor bairn. That's every day this week. Och, has that

16

sour auld maid nothing better to do than to belt wee laddies?' Lizzie pursed her lips. 'I ken what she needs from some big collier... but it's years too late!' she muttered dourly.

'Tam says there's no peace to learn anything at home. With him the eldest of ten and having to milk their wee cow and muck out the byre, he forgets the homework.' Peggy reflected for a moment. 'Och, and Tam's not that clever anyway,' she added with brutal honesty.

'Aye, well, that's not your problem, is it, Peggy Soutar? You're a right wee professor,' Lizzie teased. 'But it's gettin' late. Get on wi' yer own lessons before we eat, or I'll tell Jamie when he comes back this Sunday.'

Lizzie's admonition was unnecessary and unheard. Peggy was already deep in Nelson's *Royal Osborne Reader*.

Jamie Soutar got off the Sunday morning train at Maybole and began the five-mile walk to Kirkowen. Och, it was fine to breathe decent air again after that muck in Glesca. He drank in the pure breeze from the sea, scented with the moors as it blew inland. Pity the lassie can't stay in Ayrshire, but once Lizzie goes, there's nobody else to look after her, he thought ruefully.

Lizzie was just a distant relative of Kirsty's and they were in her debt already for her rough and ready kindness to the motherless girl since she was born. Well, she has a few months left in Kirkowen yet, Jamie consoled himself. And she'll soon be a woman... aye, by jings, so she will! He was shocked at the sudden realisation.

As he turned down the familiar paths, the scent of the sea became stronger. Once he had climbed the rise to the moors and taken a shortcut through the bare, brown fields, the sea came dramatically into sight. Tossing white horses galloped in wild herds towards the horizon. Up here, the wind felt sharper. Jamie shivered, drawing his cap further down on his head and tying the belt tighter round his rough workman's jacket.

November starts next week and soon it's the New Year. A new decade. 1890, eh? What will that bring? Not much for the working man, unless he fights for it!

Resolutely, Jamie bowed his head and covered the last mile or so to Kirkowen as smartly as his steel-plated tackety boots would go.

'Daddy!' Peggy threw herself at him.

'You get bigger every time I see you.' Jamie could see her mother coming through in Peggy's emerging young womanhood. Though he rarely spoke of Kirsty, the thought of her nearly broke his heart even after all these years. 'Och, thanks, Lizzie.' Gratefully he took a cup of broth and settled down by the range to hear their news and to give his own.

'Rab Gilmour has been struck doon in his sinfulness!' Lizzie was dying to get in with the latest local scandal.

'What in the name do ye mean, Lizzie? "Struck down in his sinfulness"? You sound like the Minister when he's preaching hellfire and repentance.' Jamie smiled but was all ears at the mention of his old enemy.

'The auld fornicator was over at "Clooty Kate's", throwing a leg over the burdie like he does every Friday night, the dirty auld rascal!' Lizzie did not modify her words in front of Peggy. Countryfolk called a spade a spade.

'And?' Jamie raised his eyebrows.

'Well, he's wee, fat and bad-tempered,' Lizzie went on, 'and his face is high-coloured, like a big red beetroot . . .'

'I ken, I ken. Get on with it, Lizzie!' Jamie was impatient to know what had happened to the detested factor.

'Aye, it was justice right enough! He was right in the middle of his sinful fornication, when a blood vessel burst in his brain. There he was, wi' his "wee man" stuck fast in Clooty Kate and roaring blue murder that he was in agony and deeing.'

'You're kidding, Lizzie?' Jamie laughed incredulously. 'What the hell happened?'

'I'm not kiddin' at all! Kate finally got him off her and she ran into the street wi' nothin' on but a sheet, yelling for the doctor. Doctor Logie came running the minute he got the word, but Rab Gilmour was in a right bad way. Still is,' she added gleefully. 'The auld swine is paralysed completely. He's in bed being fed like a baby by his guidwife who's as furious as a ferret about the whole of Kirkowen laughin' at his indiscretion and her being left to look after him as well.'

18

'I'd be lying if I said I was sorry,' Jamie said bitterly, remembering Kirsty. 'I hope the old bastard lasts for twenty years and suffers every minute . . . Och, he's no' worth the thought.' Jamie got up. 'I need some exercise, Lizzie. Where's the wood ye said needed chopping?'

'Aye, lad, work it off.' Lizzie understood his feelings and handed him the big axe.

Peggy could hear his rythmic chop, chopping, as he spent some of the old rage and found a modicum of comfort in the hard physical work.

'When are you coming back, Daddy?' Later that evening, Peggy followed her father to the brow of the hill above Kirkowen.

'Not till New Year, Peggy. I haven't the money for trips, you ken that. But I think about you all the time, lassie mine. Folk up in Glesca are fed up hearing about my fine lass with the best brains in Ayrshire.' He put his arm round his beloved daughter's shoulders.

'When I'm big, I'm going to have enough money to travel anywhere I want, so I am.' She held tightly on to his hand, her pretty face serious.

'Aye, well, first you'll have to get a right decent job, Peggy. Working day and night for nothing at all, like the mill-lassies do, breaks the spirit and destroys all your fine ambitions. Learning's the secret. Get as good an education as you can. That's the only way out of poverty for folk like us – barring miracles, of course, and they're scarcer than hen's teeth.'

'Och, I will,' Peggy agreed wholeheartedly. 'School's no problem to me. Not like poor wee Tam Laird!'

'Aye, you're clever right enough, but whatever you do, don't ever forget what you were or where you came from,' her father warned. 'And never do anything to make yourself ashamed of what you've become. Now away back before it gets dark, the gloamin' is setting in already.' Jamie smiled and hugged her tight. For a fond moment, he watched her skipping back through the gathering gloom towards Kirkowen.

Peggy turned at the brow of the hill and waved till his figure disappeared out of sight, then she ran helterskelter down the brae to Lizzie's cottage, singing at the top of her sweet young voice.

'I'll show ye a curlew's nest on the way home,' Tam Laird whispered to Peggy one late-spring morning, as if it was the best secret in the world.

'Oh, aye! Where is it?' Peggy was impressed. Tam knew more about birds and wild animals than all the other children in the school put together.

'On the Heathery cliffs.'

'What are ye showing it to me for, Tam?' Peggy wondered aloud. The boy was notoriously afraid to point out a nest for fear someone would rob it.

'Ye don't herrie the nests and break the eggs. And ye saved me from another belting yesterday.' His reply was as honest as his face.

'Och, I could see you didn't know the first verse of *Jock O' Hazeldean*, so I just stuck up my hand quick when Miss Drummond fastened her wee beady eyes on ye. It's funny that, Tam.' Peggy looked at him ruminatively. 'You can play any tune at all on that wee thing.' Her red head nodded towards the mouth organ stuck eternally in his belt. 'Even if you've just heard it once, ye can do every note. But you can't remember words if you hear them a hundred times. And your writing is like Greek, Miss Drummond says, all backwards and everything.'

'Music is different.' Tam shrugged. 'It dances round and round in my head so I remember it. Words are just a pain – they don't write the way they should. So are figures. Will ye help me with the multiplication again, Peggy?'

'Aye, I suppose so . . . you're rotten at that as well,' she replied with careless condescension.

After school the two headed off towards the cliff-edge.

'Keep yer eyes skint, Peggy, make sure big Archie doesn't see us.' Tam peered behind them to check that the school bully and wrecker of nests was not following.

Save for the plaintive cries of birds from the shoreline and the grating screech of wheeling seagulls, all was quiet in the fresh spring evening. The children ran, laughing and

20

chaffing, till Tam stopped and raised a warning hand. 'Walk soft now, Peggy, we're nearly there.'

'Och, I've been on this cliff many's a time and never seen a curlew's nest, Tam,' she whispered as the boy montioned her to drop down low.

'Aye, maybe that, but they're there all the same.' He grinned and together they crept the last few yards on hands and knees. An innocent-looking dip fell unexpectedly away, forming a sheltered heather-covered outcrop where birds could nest in peace. 'Ye have to ken where to look. See there,' he hissed, pointing to a clump of grass.

'Oh, aye, I see it now!' Peggy suddenly spotted the half-hidden nest.

'The eggs are in there, Peggy. Wheest ... here's the mother!'

Peggy lay on the heather, watching in fascination as the bird looked round uneasily, long curved beak swinging suspiciously to and fro. Then slowly she settled on the clutch. Behind her, in the clear northern light, the sea tossed careless sparkling waves against the grey rocks.

'Arran seems right close the day, Tam,' the girl commented quietly. 'Och, it's lovely here, so it is ... I wish I wasn't flitting to Glesca.' Unbidden tears filled her eyes at the thought.

'Will ye never come back to Kirkowen, Peggy?' Tam turned to look at her, his own face full of sadness.

'Och, it's that dear on the train and such a long way from Glesca, my daddy hasn't the money for trips. And Auntie Lizzie will be living with her daughter in Darvel anyway.' For a moment she felt overwhelmed then drew a deep breath. 'But when I'm big, then we'll see. I'll live where I want and I'll come and see ye then.' She jumped up decisively, causing the curlew to fly off enraged. 'Och, sorry, Tam,' Peggy apologised for her ineptitude.

For once Tam Laird was not annoyed she had disturbed the birds. He leaned over and grasped her arm with a rough brown hand. 'Peggy, I'll miss ye, so I will. Ye make a gowk o' me like the others sometimes, but you're the only one in the school that's ever tried to help me. An' ye never torment wee beasties nor hurt things.' The boy's brown eyes were

21

pools of misery in his thin face. 'When ye go, I'll have nothin' left.'

'Och, fiddlesticks and blethers, Tam Laird!' Peggy was touched, but realised sympathy would only make matters worse. 'You'll be finishing the school anyway. No more Miss Drummond or the belt! Anyway, I told ye, when I'm big I'll be back. Look at this!' She waved towards the Heathery cliffs, the glinting sea and the wheeling, crying birds. 'Just keep me away!'

'What are ye goin' to be when you're big?' Tam asked idly as they covered the miles back to the village.

'I'm going to be rich and famous!' Peggy laughed at his astonished face and skipped on ahead.

'Rich?' he called after her.

'Aye, rich! Why not? Good evenin', Rabbie.' She waved gaily to the ploughman who was following his patient horse back and forth across a rich brown field.

'Evenin', Peggy, evenin', Tam.' The man waved back. 'Och, ye midden, ye've wasted the driel!' he roared as the horse made a wobble in the lovely straight furrow.

'What do ye mean, why not?' Tam repeated in bewilderment. 'Och, Peggy, how can ye get rich and famous?'

'Last at the auld kirk is a tattie-boggle!' And she ran off, ignoring his question, bare feet hardly touching the grass, hair flying like a flame and with skinny Tam in pursuit.

'The J. M. Cochrane prize for General Proficiency, Margaret Soutar.' Mr Hunter, the Minister, shook hands gravely with the red-haired girl, pristine in her Sunday pinny that Auntie Lizzie had bleached and starched till it shone like snow.

'Thank you, Minister.' Peggy bobbed a curtsey as Miss Drummond had taught her. Behind them, scrubbed and combed rows of children at their old wooden desks clapped enthusiastically.

'All right, children, enough is enough. Don't make prize-giving an excuse for rowdiness!' Miss Drummond glowered at them to stop.

'Will ye be going to Maybole High now, Margaret, for a year or two, or starting work right away? Service in one of the big houses maybe? You're a bright lass, you could even train as a lady's maid,' the elderly Minister asked kindly. Though her father was a well-known atheist, Mr Hunter held nothing against Peggy. He was a generous-minded man and a good Christian. Like many in Kirkowen he remembered the tragedy of Kirsty Soutar well. And like many others he laid the blame at the door of Hamish McClure, though he never openly said so.

'Margaret is moving to Glasgow, Mr Hunter,' Miss Drummond broke in with a disapproving sniff. 'Her father works there now.'

'Oh, dearie me, is that a fact?' The Minister was instantly concerned. 'Aye, well, you take care. Without a mother, Margaret, Glasgow can be a dangerous place for a wee lassie. Guard yerself against the temptations of Satan and his agents who hide behind gaudy as well as ugly guises.' Mr Hunter's long nose wriggled sorrowfully. 'Glasgow is nothing but a sink of iniquity. A sink! Is that not so, Miss Drummond?'

'Indeed, Minister!' The teacher pursed her lips and her ample bosom swelled.

'Och, well, Margaret, Miss Drummond has given you a fine start on the straight path to the Kingdom of Righteousness. Make sure nobody leads you up the winding Road of Perdition instead. Broad and fine that road may appear to the unenlightened, Margaret, but hellfire and brimstone is waiting at the end! Will you remember to avoid glittering Dens of Sinful Pleasure, lass?'

'Oh, I will, Minister,' Peggy replied solemnly, but her green eyes danced at the very idea of some brightly clad devil waiting up a Glasgow close to catch her by the heels. Jamie Soutar had told her many a time that heaven and hell, devils and the like, were no more real than Lizzie's tales of boggles and ghaisties! 'They're just invented by the Kirk, the landlords and the politicians to keep ordinary folk from improving their minds,' he assured her. Peggy Soutar had no fear of Old Nick.

Bessie Mauchline, knitting and sewing prize; Jessie Buchan, cookery; Houston Brown prize for woodwork ...

Prize-giving over, soon they were out and away for ever

23

from the bare yard and dark granite walls which had dominated their childhood.

'Have you got a job right enough, Tam?' Peggy asked on
their last walk back to Kirkowen.

'Aye, I'm starting work in the mornin' at Ballochyaird
Farm. Thamson's, ye ken that fine.' He half scowled.

'Well, you've been working every hour the schoolboard
let you for the man since the day you turned ten. He owes
you a job. What will ye get?'

'Five pounds for the summer half and three for the winter.'

'Wi' meat and keep?'

'Aye . . . and a sack of oats every quarter,' Tam added with
a touch of pride.

'It's not much, but your mither will be glad of it,' Peggy
said philosophically.

'My fee will go up a bit when I'm fourteen and there's
one less for her to feed as well.' Tam shrugged. 'Och, what
else is there here for me, Peggy? Wi' no book-learnin' and
jobs like hen's teeth in Kirkowen, I'm lucky Thamson will
have me. When are ye goin'?' Tam looked down at his bare
feet.

'In the morning.' Peggy shrugged. 'Daddy is over at
Auntie Lizzie's the now, helping her pack for Darvel.'

'I wish ye were stayin'.' Tam took out his worn mouth
organ and began playing his favourite *Jock O' Hazeldean*
plaintively. Each beautiful note swelled for a second in solitary glory then disappeared on the breeze, as they covered
the last mile companionably together.

'Right, up you go, Peggy.' Jamie Soutar helped his daughter
up the iron stairs into the third-class carriage as the 'Puffing
Billy' stood belching impatiently at Maybole Station next
morning.

'Where's my bag, Daddy?' Panic gripped her momentarily.
Her few personal belongings had fitted with plenty of room
to spare into an ancient carpetbag.

'In the guard's van with the rest of my books.'

'Right, all aboard!' With a roar and howl the train threw
a parting blast of cindery smoke into the pure air. Clanking

and whistling, it charged busily off northwards in the direction of Glasgow.

Down in Thamson's farm a skinny boy opened the barn door and began leading the cows out to pasture. It was the first day of a lifetime's work. Across the valley he heard the howl of the 'Puffing Billy'. Tam knew which train it was and who was on it. Leaning against the soft, warm flank of Bessie, Thamson's best milker, he wept forlorn tears till he could weep no more.

Chapter 3
Curlews are calling . . .
she's gone for ever

At every small country station on the way, the Glasgow train disgorged bewildered folk, hens, dogs, oat-sacks, baggage and crates of cabbages. Then, with a heave and a gulp, it slurked in more of the same, before continuing its smoking, screeching journey to the city.

Peggy watched the passing countryside in fascination and hung out of the window each time they stopped. She caught tantalising glimpses of solid tradesmen and shopkeepers piling into the second-class carriages and the occasional billowing skirt and beribboned bonnet disappearing elegantly into the first.

'Glasgow St Enoch's Terminus! All change!'

The huge glass-and-iron station was full of vendors selling papers, sweets, fruit and flowers to milling passengers. Tearooms and buffets were full to bursting. Beggars sat at the entrances. Old men, dirty women with gluey-eyed babies wrapped in filthy shawls, and ex-soldiers with crutches, cried out their laments. Young lads made music or danced a hornpipe for a few coppers. Peggy's eyes were everywhere.

'Welcome to Glesca, Peggy. The great beating commercial Heart of Scotland!' Jamie smiled grimly at his daughter's horror-stricken expression when they came out into the clatter and racket of the traffic.

'Michty me, you take a chance here!' Clinging to his arm, she peered around.

'We'll take a tram.' Jamie held her close to his side as they crossed the busy street. Peggy expected to be mown

26

down any minute by the horses, carts and carriages passing on either side of the central tram-lines.

'You'll soon get used to it, lass,' Jamie replied heartily. 'Come on, here's a seat.'

'Jings!' Peggy tumbled on to the wooden bench as the dark, bizarre 'car' clanked and rattled off on iron rails, pulled by the sure-footed horse. 'Where are we staying, Daddy?' she ventured after a few minutes.

'Cowcaddens, it's quite handy for the centre. And it's not as bad as the Gorbals where I've been in digs up to now,' he explained. 'We're going there first to get my stuff. A pal of mine is a coalmerchant's carter. He's got all our bits and pieces ready and waiting on his wagon.'

'Right ye are.' Peggy tried to sound wordly wise and at ease, but failed.

'Och, you'll be a wee bittie upset after Kirkowen, Peggy. Glesca isn't Ayrshire, neither it is. But you'll get used to it.' Jamie put a reassuring arm round her shoulders.

'Och, aye, I'll get used to it.' Peggy peered doubtfully out of the tram at the high grimy buildings on either side and the shops of every sort which went on and on in endless rows. In Kirkowen the baker, butcher, fishmonger, haberdasher, chemist and the new co-op store were neatly spread round the old square. This place had no order, no soul.

For a minute she wondered how so many shops could survive. Then she glanced round at the endless mass of humanity in the streets, the crowded carriages, carts, trams and cabs, and wondered no longer.

'Right, here we are.' Jamie led the way off the tram, carrying Peggy's bag, and she hopped down and scurried anxiously behind him. Almost immediately he turned down a narrow alleyway where a big man, face and hands as black as the coal he worked with, was stacking bulging sacks in the back courtyard of a filthy close.

'Right, Billy?' Jamie greeted him.

'Aye, right as I'll ever be, Jamie. That's your lassie then?' The carter nodded towards Peggy, standing bright-eyed, taking everything in.

'Aye.'

'Bonnie wee thing, so she is . . . Up ye go, hen.' Conversation over, he nodded towards the empty places on the dusty wooden seat beside him. 'I've cleaned it a bit.'

'Thanks, it's fine, mister.' Peggy smiled graciously and climbed on to the coal-cart like a duchess going to a ball.

Their sticks of furniture and bundles of belongings shuddered and swayed behind them on the jolting journey. Through the Glasgow backstreets they rattled for half an hour. Peggy sat in silence as the noise and sheer size of the city overawed her.

'This is Cowcaddens now,' Jamie pointed out as the cart at last turned down a long, cobbled road and Billy the carter began yelling insults at his horse.

'Woah, Neddy!' Plodding steadily on, the big animal ignored his master's voice, great hooves clopping rhythmically. Billy pulled sharply on the reins. 'Woah! Woah, ye glaikit beast! Stop or yer for the knacker's!' he bawled.

'Is this us, Daddy? Owya!' Peggy was jerked so hard as the cart finally stopped, she nearly fell headlong on to Neddy's steaming rump.

'Aye, this is us, lass.' Jamie lifted her down. 'Just remember, get off at the second stop on Dobbies Loan, Peggy, if ye have to come back in a tram by yourself,' he instructed. 'The blue-tram comes out this way right up to Clancy's Lane. That's our close, we're at number 15.' He pointed to a grimy entrance in a high tenement building. It looked like every other Peggy had seen so far.

Dirty-faced, ragged children played peerie and booles on the road in the sultry summer evening. Ill-clad huddles of men and women gossiped in segregated groups and turned to stare as the cart stopped.

'Good day, Mrs Naughton, Mrs Macpherson. Aye, Jock! Aye, Alec! Fine evening, Wullie.' Jamie nodded his greetings and went in, Peggy close on his heels.

'How do you ken the folk, Daddy?' Her voice echoed back at her in the dim close mouth.

'I've been round here a lot, Peggy. A lad from the union had this single-end before me. I stayed here sometimes when he was away, taking care of the pamphlets, sorting stuff for the paper, things like that. That's how I got the place when he left for Dundee. I told everybody on our landing that we were moving in the day, just as soon as I got back from Kirkowen.' Jamie tossed the information over his shoulder. 'Folk are decent in this close, they'll keep an eye on you when I'm not here.'

Hot on his heels, Peggy said nothing. She felt as if she was being swallowed alive by this dark, dingy tenement. As they climbed two flights of steep stone stairs, bevelled with the passage of many feet, she could see they were still damp from the weekly wash.

'Cludgies!' She sniffed the dank air. The toilets on the landings stank like cludgies everywhere, but the foetid smell was far more oppressive here in the confined close than it had been in Kirkowen's outside toilets. Peggy sighed and expected she would get used to that too.

Windows with cracked and missing panes let dusty summer light into the landings, unkindly picking out places where wall tiles had fallen off or were smashed. She stood on tiptoe and peered out as they passed each landing. In the cobbled courtyard below, row upon row of ragged washing hung on sagging lines held up by long poles.

Somewhere a baby wailed, trailing off at the end of each cry on a penetrating high note. On a floor far above, a man and woman were arguing loudly in language so raw the girl wondered they weren't ashamed to be heard. She glanced at her father, expecting some reaction to the foul-mouthed pair. He seemed totally oblivious. Jamie Soutar had been too long in the city for such things to register any more.

'Right, we better go down and help Billy up with the stuff. I'll just dump this lot.' He turned the key, swung open the door and slung in her bag. 'Aye, it's lucky I managed to get a corner single-end. They're a wee bit bigger. Look, Peggy.' Jamie pointed into the depths of the gloomy room to a wall bed. 'It's got an inshot that'll do you fine. We can put up a wee curtain and it'll be right private, lass. I'll put my bed-chair over there in the other corner. Well, what do ye think?' He tossed his cap on to a peg behind the door and looked questioningly at his daughter.

'Aye, it's fine, Daddy, so it is,' Peggy replied brightly, trying not to let her utter disappointment show at the barren

29

shabbiness of the place. She had not expected much, but this was even less than she had imagined.

'Come on then.' Her father led the way back down to the street where Billy was patiently waiting, leaning against the cart and smoking a clay pipe.

'They're startin' the flittin'!' Within seconds of Billy untying the ropes on the cart, hordes of Clancy's Lane's scruffy children left off playing in the gutters. In seconds they were swarming round like midges, scuffling and giggling, hoping for entertainment. A dirty-faced boy in a pair of baggy, cut-down trousers and filthy man's shirt, poked the bundles with a nosy finger.

'Clear off, you!' Billy roared.

'Owya!' the lad yelled and fled to a safe distance as the carter's tackety working boot caught him hard on his ragged backside.

'Och, evictions is better.' The barefoot children sat on the kerbs, quickly bored and unimpressed by the Soutars' few unpretentious possessions.

'Aye, I like when the bailiff's men sell the stuff in the street and the missus starts screaming and carrying on. That's rerr!' A curly-haired urchin scratched his head, picking out a louse and examining it thoughtfully.

'An' it's great when the man comes up from the pub roarin' drunk and challenges the bailiff to fight and the polis come and take him to jail.'

'Aye, right enough! Then his missus and the bairns howl and greet and carry on again!' His friend's lousy curls bobbed agreement. 'Rerr!'

'Shift!' Billy's big feet scattered them like flies as he pushed past with a box of Jamie's books.

'Aye, you'll be fine here, Peggy, when I have to be away for the union.' Jamie looked approvingly down the street as they waved Billy off.

Women, plaid shawls round their shoulders, leaned out of windows or stood at the close-mouths gossiping. Groups of men gathered at the corners. Some stood, some crouched on their haunches, bare arms sticking out of worn shirt-sleeves, tied above the elbow with string or cord, and flat caps pulled well down despite the summer warmth.

30

Jamie stoped for a minute beside one of the men and muttered in a low conspiratorial tone: 'Listen, Hamish, I heard they might want hands at the Govan boatyards on Monday. The foreman telt Rab Duncan and he telt me in the tram to Billy's. There's a navy contract due in.'

'Is that a fact? I'll be round there first thing. Thanks, Jamie, I owe ye one, so I do,' the man stuttered in gratitude.

'Ye owe me nothin'! But take a blanket and get there the night. Rab says the word will have got as far as Greenock by the mornin'.'

'Cheerio then, I'll away!' Tipping his cap, Hamish shuffled off, fired by hope.

Peggy looked around proprietorially at her new home as they went back into the close-mouth. Voices from the windows joined those from the street and echoed eerily up and down the passageway, spilling into the courtyards rattling among the overfull bins. Privacy did not exist in these smelly, noisy closes, but the nearness of people was comforting in a way. She knew there was no going back to Kirkowen and if others could survive here, Peggy decided she could too.

'Och, you've done the place a treat!' Jamie looked round in pleasure after she had finished fussing and moving their sparse furniture here and there.

'Aye.' She nodded doubtfully. Jamie had bought an old table, a couple of chairs, two ancient bookcases and a rickety sideboard. But he had not thought of curtains, or tried to whitewash the grey walls, zig-zagged with fretted cracks from years of damp and shoddy workmanship.

'I'll make us a wee cup of tea then, lassie dear, and show you how to work the range.' He rattled the front of the coal cooker. 'It's a bit like Auntie Lizzie's so you'll soon learn . . . Och, brighten the place up a bit if ye like, Peggy.' He had noticed the despondent expression, despite her brave efforts. 'Men are not as smart as women with that sort of thing.' Smiling, he hugged her. 'Tell ye what, we can do it together. You come up with the ideas and I'll be the muscle! But don't expect silks and satins, lass!'

'Right enough!' The girl was instantly cheered by his

31

understanding and watched intently as he put an old iron kettle on the range.

'Maggie Naughton lit it this morning to air the place . . . salt of the earth, so she is,' Jamie commented. He blew, stirring the ash into a glow, then carefully put on some small coal to get the fire re-started and the heat up.

I'll be able to fix that myself by the morning, Peggy thought resolutely.

Jamie ran a finger down a long jagged crack by the door. 'I'll put a wee bittie whitewash on, if you like? It won't mend these cracks, but it'll hide the worst.'

'Och, would you, Daddy?' Her spirits lifted once more.

Within days Peggy had done what she could with the small apartment. Under the window, the deep chipped porcelain sink and the ancient cooking range stood side by side, separated by a cracked draining board. In front, the shaky wooden table was carefully covered with cheap yellow and pink flowered oilcloth. A dull brown drape screened off Peggy's recess bed and made the room cosier.

Jamie had taken her to the 'Barras', the street market that sprawled over half Gallowgate. For coppers they had found three worn wicker-seated chairs. One was placed at each end of the table and another waited expectantly for visitors against the wall behind it. A few dark pictures of highland cattle at a farthing each, a Pears soap calendar free from the Co-op, and a union poster, broke the monotony of bare white walls.

'Move the oil-lamp, Daddy, and pull over the chair, I've just made a cup of tea.' Peggy was all housewifely bossiness. Fondly, her father hid a smile.

'Would you like a tattie scone – though they're no' as good as Anutie Lizzie's? I haven't got the hang of the griddle yet?' Shyly she offered a plate of frazzled-looking potato cakes.

'Och, you're a marvel, Peggy, so ye are!' Jamie praised her lavishly, understanding the great effort she was making.

'Wait a minute, I'll close the window. They bairns have been at that all afternoon.' Peggy bustled off tut-tutting as if she was middle-aged instead of only eleven. 'If they don't pack it in, some man on the night-shift will give them a doing! I just opened it a wee bit to let the smell of the whitewash out. Listen to that!' A chant drifted up from three stories below.

> *'Old Mother Riley at the pawn-shop door,*
> *Baby in her arms and a bundle on the floor,*
> *She asked for ten bob, she only got four,*
> *And she nearly took the hinges off the pawn-shop door.'*

Crash! Rumble! Crash! The children clattered bits of metal on to tin sheeting in an incredible cacophony, then began the chant all over again.

'Aye, that's better.' Jamie nodded as the horrible din faded a little. He took a scone and eyed it thoughtfully. 'Lassie mine, we have to decide what you're going to do.'

'Aye?' She sat down, instantly attentive.

'You don't have to go school here if you don't want. You're old enough to leave altogether. Given your proficiency, you can stop at eleven and get a wee job.'

'I don't want to leave.' Peggy looked anxious.

'Good, I'd like you to get a bit more learning, so you can get something decent later.' Jamie was pleased by her response. 'Though I criticise Scotland and its injustices, I'll say this much – there's far less "class" nonsense here than in England.'

'What do ye mean?' Peggy regarded Jamie with puzzled green eyes.

'I mean, with a decent education and a wee bit of luck, even the children of working folk can aspire to better themselves and not have a finger pointed at their origins. Look at rotten McClure strutting around like a cock on a midden-heap. His folk were nothing but smugglers on the Ayrshire coast a hundred years ago. The old house at Bargeddie, before the one that's there now, was paid for in kegs of French brandy! Och, mind you, McClure's not much better than a bandit now either, come to think of it. . . . bad blood through and through!'

'And Rabbie Burns, Daddy.' Peggy was off on her own track of dreams. 'He was just the son of a poor tenant farmer to begin with and pushed a plough, then he became a poet.'

'Aye, mind you, the man was a genius . . . that helps.' Jamie gave a wry smile. 'Anyway, I was thinking that you could get a job in the Co-op office or something like that when ye finally leave . . . I could put in a wee word through the union. You're a clever lassie, winning the Kirkowen School prize.'

'Och, there wasn't much competition in Kirkowen,' Peggy replied honestly. 'But I'm not sure I want to work in an office.'

'Well, we can argue about that when the time comes.' His expression was indulgent. 'Right then, I can promise to keep you at school till you're fourteen, like the Education Act covers you for, Peggy, but there's no guarantee I can go on after that,' he warned. 'The union is struggling to pay me as it is, and there's talk that I might have to find another job if the amalgamation comes off.'

'Two years is two years.' Peggy, full of short-term optimism, took a satisfied bite of burnt scone.

'It'll be your turn to clean the cludgie and the stairs after Kirsty Frielan, hen.' Big Jinty McPherson fetched Peggy on Friday morning.

'Oh, aye, that's fine, Mrs McPherson.' Peggy knew the score. Auntie Lizzie's cousin in Glasgow had visited Kirkowen and warned her well. 'I ken everybody does a turn scrubbing out the cludgies and then doing the stairs.'

'Well, imagine that!' Big Jinty said in admiration. 'I thought I'd have to tell ye, so I did . . . Here's Kirsty comin' up the stairs. Haw, Kirsty!' Jinty bawled down the close, like a foghorn. 'Kirsty, can ye hear me? C'mere and shake hands wi' wee Peggy Soutar. She's no' as daft as she looks, neither she is!'

'Pleased to meet ye, hen.' Kirsty puffed up the last flight and placed a threadbare shopping bag at her feet, gasping for breath.

'I'm showin' wee Peggy Soutar the stairs and the cludgies,' Big Jinty explained.

'Are ye up to it, hen?' Kirsty eyed Peggy doubtfully. 'Och, I think she's a bit too wee yet, Jinty.' The women on the landing had hoped Peggy would be older and could share the burdens of communal life.

'I'm not too wee at all, I can do my turn, Mrs Frielan!' Peggy's determined chin went up. 'But you'll have to show me how to make they nice patterns with the pipe-clay.' She pointed to the ends of each stair which were edged with whorls and loops in chalky white.

'That's the way, hen! Och, ye look a strong wee thing, whit age are ye? Eleven . . . och, you'll do. I'm Maggie Naughton.' A skinny woman, almost eclipsed by Jinty McPherson's huge form, came forward and held out a worn hand. 'I've to keep an eye on ye when yer daddy's away. I'm next door. Our Hughie's a wee bit older than you, he can keep his eye on ye in the street.'

Peggy nodded gravely. 'Thanks, Mrs Naughton, but I'm sure I'll be fine.'

'Are ye comin' then, hen?' Jinty rolled up her sleeves over massive forearms.

Kirsty drew her shawl round bony shoulders and picked up the shopping bag. 'Ye'll be all right, hen,' she called over her shoulder. 'None of the men on this landin' drinks themselves stupid, then boaks up their supper over the cludgie . . . well, no' every Saturday night anyway.'

'Great.' Peggy nodded in relief. Auntie Lizzie had told her that vomiting drunks were the curse of tenement life.

'Right then, let's see the stuff Ayrshire lassies are made of!' Jinty folded a voluminous apron over her generous middle, tying the strings firmly in a precise bow.

'Comin', Mrs McPherson.' Peggy put on her own apron and followed obediently. By an act of will, she banished pictures of heathery cliffs and wheeling, calling sea-birds from her head and began scrubbing out the foul toilet. Nobody could say Peggy Soutar was afraid of doing her stint. Glasgow wouldn't beat her, neither it would!

Chapter 4
Hope and Fear's alternate billow

'What a shame! That sort of thing is worse for a lassie than a laddie.' Whispers greeted Elspeth McClure's entry anywhere she was not well known. Automatically she lifted her chin a little in defiance of their pity and stood, showing no emotion, as her governess fussed and fumbled in her bag.

'Elspeth, did you see where I put the list your mother gave me with all your things for school? Oh, dear me, I know I have it somewhere.' The middle-aged woman clutched her ample chest in distress. 'Can you find it, dear? Oh, this is giving me the vapours!' She produced a small phial of smelling salts and waved it under her nose.

'Give the bag here, Dallie.' After a moment Elspeth produced the missing paper.

'Wonderful! Right, we'll start with your bonnet. Something for Sundays, Mistress McClure said. She told me she'd like you to pick one a wee bit brighter than the last time.'

'Oh, fiddle!' Elspeth retorted, her face a study in stubborn boredom.

'Now don't look like that, Elspeth!' the governess twittered in anxiety. 'Your mama said so. Maybe blue would be nice this time. It would so suit your pretty colouring. Blue is dainty with light brown hair ... and we could pick one with a decent brim round the edge ...'

'I like grey and I like brown, Dallie, I'm not having blue.' Elspeth's reply was uncompromising.

'Those are not colours for a girl of fourteen, Elspeth, they're for a much older person. You know that fine.'

'They suit me.' She dug in her heels. 'You and my mother

36

are forever trying to make me what I'm not, and that's a beauty.' Her bright smile was in bizarre contrast to the hard words. 'And a brim the size of a horse-collar won't hide the mark on my face, Dallie, whatever you and Mama mistakenly think.'

'Elspeth!' The woman was shocked. 'Don't talk like that, your mother is only concerned that you make the best of what you have. And you're not a bad-looking girl . . . er . . . otherwise. Och, it's only a birthmark, it's not that bad . . .' she trailed off, unable to lie about the disfigurement. Victorian ideals of beauty were firmly set.

'It's bad enough to keep the Ayrshire gallants away. Nobody will want to marry me for either looks or temper,' Elspeth responded with characteristic bluntness, unnerving in one so young. 'Mamas want a pretty vacant face and simpering smile in a daughter-in-law, not somebody with a sharp tongue and a big red mark on their cheek. And I don't care a fig either! Most of the lads I know are stupid, clumsy clodhoppers. If some man wants to marry me, it'll be for my father's money not for my bonnie face,' she concluded forthrightly. 'So that means I'll not be getting wed. I'd let no man take me for either money or pity.'

'Oh, Elspeth, that's no way for a young lass to think.' Miss Dalrymple shook her head.

'Come on, Dallie, let's look at brown and grey bonnets.' She linked her arm in that of her companion. 'And don't look so upset, you've done your best.' Elspeth felt sorry for the position the poor woman was in. 'I'll tell Mama it was I who insisted. She knows what I'm like, she'll not scold.'

'You can be a right wee madam at times, Elspeth McClure.' Miss Dalrymple smiled ruefully. 'It's as well I know you've got a good heart beneath all that prickly manner. Just wait till you go to Miss Lovat's Academy in August, we'll see what she makes of you and your independent ways!'

'Oh, Dallie, I can't wait!' Elspeth's eyes glowed.

'. . . but I must say, I'm surprised your father agreed to let you go there,' Miss Dalrymple rambled on, happily contradicting her earlier pronouncement. 'Miss Lovat's is considered to be very advanced . . . the most progressive academy for young ladies in Scotland, I believe.' The governess almost whispered the words. 'I was a bit shocked when my cousin told me what she had heard. You know who I mean, Florence Dalrymple in Mussleburgh that's a martyr to swollen feet ... Wait a minute, Elspeth!' She broke into a trot to keep up with her charge's long stride as they made their way through the House of Eccleston's exclusive Glasgow store towards the bonnet department.

'I was surprised myself when Mama handed me the prospectus without so much as glancing through it. It seems such a wonderful school,' Elspeth agreed as the governess caught up puffing and panting.

'How did she choose it?' Miss Dalrymple hadn't dared ask Elspeth's mother outright herself.

'By wonderful accident! An old friend of Mama's in Edinburgh sent her three girls there.' Elspeth gave a satisfied smile. 'Father insists I have to go away to school and poor Mama was so pleased at having the problem solved without any effort on her part, I don't think she gave two thoughts to curriculum or school activities. Do you know, Dallie, it said in the prospectus that some of her girls have even gone into business.' Elspeth breathed in pleased awe.

'Michty me!' Miss Dalrymple forgot her usual polite accent. 'Businesswomen ... whatever next!'

'Let's just hope they don't find out till it's too late,' Elspeth chortled with real amusement, then her face became grave. 'Not that they will. Poor Mama is so sick these days, I don't think she would do much even if she did know, and Father doesn't care what I do so long as I keep out of his sight,' she added coldly.

'Och, Elspeth!' Miss Dalrymple was flustered all over again, but could hardly contradict the girl. It was no secret that Hamish McClure rarely spoke to his only child, the daughter who had been born instead of the son he had longed for and who was so disfigured, in his eyes, he was certain no man would want to wed her unless bribed with his precious cash.

'Now listen!' Elspeth turned on her governess, with a vehemence that made the older woman shrink back. 'If you breathe a word of what I've just told you, Dallie, or if my

38

parents hear a whisper from you about Miss Lovat's being progressive, then your remaining time at Bargeddie will be made an utter misery . . . by me!'

'Och, I won't say anything, Elspeth, you know that,' the governess promised hastily. Despite the girl's lonely, loveless upbringing and the scar that encouraged her defensive, prickly exterior, Elspeth was never vindictive or cruel. But neither did she make idle threats.

'I'd like to look at some bonnets, please. Grey or brown, and rather small brimmed.' Elspeth began speaking to the assistant, hovering at the counter.

'Er, yes, miss.' The shop-girl tried awkwardly not to stare at the livid mark spread across the left-hand side of the girl's face. So confused was she, it hardly registered as unusual that the young lass herself gave the order, not the middle-aged lady accompanying her.

'Mama, are you awake?' Elspeth knocked gently on her mother's bedroom door when they got back to Bargeddie.

'Is that you, Elspeth? Come in, my love,' Janet McClure replied feebly.

'I got all my school things, aprons, paints, napkins . . . oh, and a Sunday bonnet. It's grey. I insisted on that, so don't blame poor old Dallie,' Elspeth said firmly before her mother could complain. 'Poor Mama, have you one of your megrims?'

'Terrible, Elspeth. They're getting worse. And those drops Doctor Logie prescribe me make me so sleepy. Oh, but they give me such happy dreams.' A soft smile played about her weary mouth. 'They're very good, Elspeth, very.' Lovingly she patted the dark blue bottle of Laudanum on the mahogany cabinet by the bedside.

'Hmm . . .' Clever Elspeth understood exactly what the opiate Laudanum did.

'Oh, but couldn't you have got something brighter than grey, Elspeth?' Janet continued fretfully. 'Grey's no colour for a fourteen year old.'

'It is for me. I know what I look like, Mama. You can't make a silk purse out of a sow's ear.' Elspeth had long

39

developed an unnerving directness that acted both as a weapon and a shield.

'Well, I'm not going through that argument again with you, Elspeth.' Janet McClure shifted restlessly. 'In my eyes you're bonnie, I've always told you that. That mark is not nearly as bad as you make it out to be . . . a wee bit of paste would dull it nicely. But you just go your own way whatever I or anybody else says. Strubborn as a mule!'

'Is Father home yet?' Elspeth changed the subject before her mother worked herself up into a fit of vapours.

'I don't think he'll be back from Glasgow till Friday . . . you'll be gone by then. Did you want him for anything in particular?' Surprised, Janet struggled to raise herself higher.

'No, but I prefer being alone with you for the last few days before school starts, Mama. It's more comfortable when there's just the two of us and Libby. We're all happier without him. Father is never glad when he's here.' Elspeth sat on the edge of the bed and took her mother's thin hand in hers. 'He doesn't want either of us, does he, Mama?'

'Don't say that, my love,' Janet protested feebly, though in her heart she agreed.

Why an invalid wife and scarred daughter had been visited on him, was something Hamish McClure could not understand. The Lord had not repaid His servant as He should have. It took a plump young woman, set up in a comfortable flat in Ayr, to soften the oversight of the Almighty. And a few others, somewhat less expensive, in Kilmarnock and Glasgow to take the edge off his troubles and cool his temper.

'Why don't you divorce him, Mama?' Elspeth asked abruptly. 'People do divorce these days. You've got your own money. Grandfather McKelvie tied up a decent sum for you when you married. Father can't touch it.'

'I was brought up to believe that a wife stays with her husband, Elspeth, whatever the circumstances,' Janet replied with a weary wave of her thin hand. 'For all your father gets angry, he's never laid a finger on me. And he's . . . er . . . considerate. He . . . er, doesn't bother me any more. Och, you're too young to understand.' She glossed over the intimate details. 'Anyway, it's too late, I'm too tired.' She sank back on her pillows. 'Too tired . . .' Her head flopped and she muttered, 'Elspeth, call Libby'

'Sorry I asked about him, Mama.' The girl was distressed at her mother's discomfort and weariness. Elspeth felt at times like these that Janet had really died and left this pathetic shell lingering like a wraith in some sort of limbo. 'Don't worry, I'll get Libby. You have a wee sleep.' Softly she went out and closed the door.

The door opened instantly as the carriage drew up at the stately entrance to a fine Georgian house in a fashionable Edinburgh crescent. 'Welcome to Miss Lovat's Academy, Elspeth McClure.'

'Er . . . thank you.' Elspeth was surprised to be so obviously expected.

A bright-faced young woman in her late-twenties held out her hand. 'I'm Jessica Lamont, your personal tutor. "Guides" we call ourselves. At other times I teach English Literature and French.'

'How do you do, Miss Lamont?' Elspeth bobbed a curtsey, relieved at the warm welcome but still braced for the worst. As she took off her coat, she peered curiously down the bright, broad hall stretching behind her mentor. Girls of her own age and older came and went in small groups up and down a staircase at the far end.

'That's your peg, third from the end, second row.' Miss Lamont pointed to rows of personalised coat hooks.

'How did you know it was me when I arrived at the door?' Elspeth asked, hanging up her coat and hat.

'Oh, almost all the other new girls came last night. We know the old hands, of course . . . anyway, your distinctive appearance was noted on the health and character folio we asked your family doctor to send.' Jessica Lamont made a light dismissive gesture towards her cheek. Her gaze met Elspeth's fair and square.

'Fine.' A brilliant smile lit up Elspeth's scarred face and lovely eyes. It was the first time in her life she had been greeted so openly and her birth mark referred to directly without embarrassment. A bubble of unexpected happiness

41

burbled up inside. Hope began to creep into her watchful, vulnerable heart.

'There's a talk tonight in the assembly room, "Women as a Force in History". It's being given by Miss Baxter, our historian, she's an excellent speaker,' Miss Lamont continued as she led the girl up the passage. 'If you're too tired from the journey, don't bother to come, it's a long way from Ayrshire to Edinburgh ... but it should be very interesting.'

Elspeth thought of her father's expression if he knew she was going to such a lecture ... and in school of all places! 'Oh, I'm fine. Not tired at all. I'd like to come,' she replied joyfully.

'Good.'

She followed the tutor upstairs, into a long bright corridor with rooms off either side and flowers at the end.

'The girls share four to a room, one from each year group. This is yours. You're the "baby", of course. None of our girls is younger than fourteen.' She threw open the door to reveal a simple, sunny dormitory with four beds, four narrow wardrobes, four individual bookcases and desks. 'Naturally you've been left the worst bed.' Miss Lamont gave a tinkling laugh and pointed to the only place unadorned by personal nick-nacks. 'Nobody ever wants the one by the door, they get disturbed first each morning. First come, first served, and you're the youngest, poor thing. Next year you can move up a notch!'

'Oh, I don't mind.' Elspeth looked curiously around her. The simple room was in stark contrast to the luxury of Bargeddie. She peered at a bookshelf standing primly by the door and stopped in astonishment. *Explorations in Egypt*, *Studies in Eastern Religion*, *Women Who Changed the World* ... Elspeth's eyes widened at the liberal titles. She began to think she was dreaming, or had died and gone to heaven.

'Yes, we believe in developing our girls' minds, not putting them in straightjackets.' Miss Lamont read her thoughts uncannily. 'Unpack, Elspeth, put on your uniform dress and pinafore, then come down to the refectory. It's the first door on the right at the bottom of the stairs. High tea in half an hour. We all meet for a chat first.' She closed the door, leaving Elspeth alone in the quiet dorm. Laughter and chatter floated up the stairwell, danced along the corridor and slipped under the door. Somewhere a piano played a sedate Sarabande which transformed itself suddenly into the tinkling notes of a popular piece.

Long ago Elspeth had accepted she was destined to be solitary. Tears were shed alone and joys were protected secretively. But now within a short half-hour, hope was battering louder and louder at the walls of isolation she had been forced to hide behind for far too long. She gave a little skip, heavy travelling skirts, swishing. 'I'm going to like it here!' With hands that shook slightly from apprehension and expectation, she changed into the school apron and, head held high, Elspeth McClure went down to meet her world for the next four years.

Chapter 5
Forward I cannot see

'Aren't you finished that Latin yet, Peggy? It's nearly ten o'clock,' Jamie Soutar chided her in concern. 'You're at it every night, lass.'

'I must get these declensions off by heart, Daddy. There's a test at the end of the week.' Wearily she rubbed her eyes. 'Och, I suppose you're right, I won't learn any more when I'm this tired.' She gathered her books together on the table and piled them into a well-worn satchel.

'How about a cup of tea before you go to bed?' Jamie filled the kettle and set it on the range. 'I need to have a wee word with you anyway.'

'What about?' Peggy felt her stomach contract with foreboding.

'School, lass.' Jamie fiddled with the kettle lid.

'Can't I go on?' She held her breath.

'Well, you're sixteen,' he replied. 'I promised I'd keep you till you were fourteen and I've managed two extra years on top of that. But it's hard, Peggy, especially now I've had to take a cut in wages. The Miners' Union is having a rough time. They really can't afford me at all, but they don't want to lay me off. Anyway, there's no money in working for the Labour Movement. That's not the idea. We do it for love . . . for principles . . . not reward.'

'Och, I know.' Peggy sighed, heart in her worn boots. 'And you've done more than most fathers would, keeping a lassie at school this long. I know it's not the done thing . . . especially in Clancy's Lane.' There was a touch of bitterness in her voice.

'Och, Peggy, that's not how I see it at all,' Jamie protested. 'I've never treated you any different from I would a laddie. We talk about everything. I ask your advice on articles for the paper ... you've a great brain, Peggy, and I'm sorry I can't help any more.' Jamie ran his fingers through greying hair in a gesture of distress. 'I can just about do without you earning a full wage, but I can't pay for the extra fees, uniforms and books. If it wasn't for the wee bit you earn at Miss Cranston's Tearooms on Saturdays, I'd have had to go to a money lender before now.'

'Never! They're rotten swines!' Peggy spat out the words. 'Look what they did to poor Jinty and her man, taking every stick they had! Once they get their hands on you, that's that. But do you mean what you say, Daddy?' Her green eyes sharpened. 'Could you manage the rent and to feed us, if I find the money for the other things?'

'Just about, though there wouldn't be much jam on the bread.'

'Och, who needs jam?' There was a poignant touch of the old carefree Peggy in her reply.

Jamie realised with a shock how withdrawn and self-contained she had become over the years. Living in this place has knocked the joy out of the lass, he realised. The thought was depressing. Over the years he had seen Peggy retreat more and more into the world of books. Jamie was certain she used them as an escape from the grim reality around her. 'What are you thinking of doing with all this learning, lass?'

Peggy ignored the question and rushed on, 'Miss Cranston asked me last week if I could work evenings as well as Saturdays, and help with the baking on a Sunday night.'

'No. You're tired enough as it is, Peggy.' Jamie shook his head decisively. 'You couldn't manage school and all the extra work too?'

'If you want to do something badly enough, you can. You've told me that yourself.' The determined red head bobbed. 'I could ask the teachers what we're going to cover in the coming week and work at it any chance I get.'

'Would they agree to that, lass?' Jamie thought doubtfully

of the formidable bunch of old maids that ran Cowcaddens Girls' High School.

'Daddy, nobody else in the class gets marks like me. They'll agree if I put it to them in the right way,' Peggy spoke with the self-confidence of a natural academic. 'And I've inherited the stubbornness of the devil from you . . . and Mammy from what I've heard. Oh, they'll agree all right.'

'What a lassie! Och, you're more like my poor Kirsty every day, so ye are.' Jamie couldn't hide his pride or admiration. 'But why, lass? What on earth do you need a Leaving Certificate for? Here, take this before I spill it.' He handed over a cup of dark brown tea.

'I want to be a doctor.'

'A what?' Jamie froze, cup in hand, his face a picture of incredulity.

'A doctor.'

'Och, Peggy!' he protested. 'This is just daft! I know a lot of working-class folk with aspirations, the Labour Movement is full of them. . . . I had one or two myself till life took its toll! But I've never met a laddie among them that became a doctor, let alone a lassie. Even tradesmen can't afford the fees. It's a middle-class profession, so it is . . . the aristocracy don't like dirtying their hands.'

'I know all that.' She crossed to the window and gazed into the blackness outside. 'But that's the point. I've seen it all here in this rotten old building: births, deaths and every kind of sickness. You know what it's like, we help each other as much as we can, but when a doctor is needed, we scrape together our bawbees, then some pompous body comes reluctantly up the close and looks down his nose as if we stink!' A flush rose to her pale cheeks. 'It's not fair! Ordinary folk deserve to be treated by doctors that respect them. Anyway, it's what I want to be,' she said firmly. 'Maybe I'll never make it, but I can try.'

'All you're likely to meet is disappointment and sorrow,' her father cautioned. 'Why didn't you tell me before?'

'You never asked . . . and I want to be a doctor,' Peggy repeated stubbornly.

'Och, set your sights a wee bittie lower, Peggy,' he pleaded.

46

'I suppose you could be a nurse if you want to help sick folk, though it's no profession for a decent lassie.'

'Blethers!' she riposted. 'Miss Nightingale showed how the job should be done in the Crimea. And since then the new training schools have made a big difference. Nursing is far better regarded than it used to be, Daddy.'

'Hmmm . . . well, why not then?'

'I want to be a doctor, to make decisions, not just carry out orders.' Her face blazed with courage and the kind of inspiration he had once had himself. . . . and she was so heartbreakingly like her mother. Jamie weakened.

'I still think doctoring is daft, but all right, we'll try for the certificate. . . .' The rest of his sentence was buried deep in Peggy's embrace.

'Wait for me, Peggy, I've been looking for ye all week! Have ye changed yer tram or have ye started workin' right enough?' Hughie Naughton, Maggie's eldest son, caught up with her as she walked home to Clancy's Lane next day.

'Yes and no, Hughie.' She grinned at his perplexed expression. 'Yes, I changed my tram. And see.' She held up her bag.

'Och, yer no' still at the books?' Hughie's face fell. 'I thought ye'd chuck the school for good this year. I don't understand, Peggy, neither I do! All the other lassies are workin' or married at sixteen, so they are.' The young man took the bag automatically, as he had done for years. 'Why don't ye give the school a bye, eh? Take a hale-time job and have a wee bit fun. We could start winchin' . . . save to get hitched, eh? Couldn't we, Peggy?' Hughie was off on his familiar theme.

'Och, Hughie!' she protested, but he continued doggedly, 'I've only a couple of years left of my time at the shipyards. I'm no' stayin' in Clancy's Lane all my life, Peggy, I'll do better for my wife and weans, so I will. Come on, how about it?' His cocky grin was disarming.

'I don't want to go out with you, Hughie . . . or anybody,' she said patiently as they climbed the stairs, side by side. It never occurred to her to tell him of her real ambition, she knew he would just be more bewildered than ever.

47

'But ye like me, don't ye, Peggy?' Hughie's good-looking face was hopeful. 'Mammy says I'm right sharp when I'm no' in my workin' togs! And there's no many wi' a good apprenticeship at the docks . . .'

'I'm not going to get married, Hughie, I've told you that till I'm blue in the face.' Peggy insisted good-humouredly.

'Och, it's a rotten waste, so it is!' Hughie shook his head. 'I don't mind that ye talk nice and that, Peggy,' he added magnanimously. Hughie had adored her for years and wasn't ready to give up yet.

'Well, isn't that lucky?' She grinned. 'Thanks for carrying the books, Hughie, I'm off to Miss Cranston's in five minutes.'

'Mammy says all that book learnin' isn't good for anybody, Peggy, 'specially no' a lassie.' Hughie handed her the heavy bag.

'And your mammy should know,' Peggy commented with a wry smile that left him staring after her in puzzlement.

'Och, it's a right waste of a bonnie lassie, so it is!' Hughie sighed, and went in for his tea.

'Are ye after Peggy again, Hughie?' His mother shook her head as she heard the Soutars' door close and read her son's face. 'Ye'll never learn, neither ye will.'

'Aye, neither I will.' He took off his working clothes and scrubbed himself at the basin by the door.

'Yer wasting yer time,' Maggie Naughton cautioned, leaning against the wall as he washed. 'She'll break yer heart, son. Peggy's no' like the other folk in this close. Och, it's no' that the lassie has airs and graces, but she doesn't think the same as us. Here.' Maggie handed him a rough towel.

'I ken that.' Hughie shrugged and rubbed his face and body dry. 'But that's whit makes her special. Whit's for tea, Mammy? I could eat a cat wi' fleas!'

Each evening Peggy worked at Miss Cranston's Tearooms from five o'clock till nine and then did her homework. It was a punishing schedule for a young girl. Sometimes, as she ran up and down with trays of tea and plates of scones, she thought she would die of weariness. But her young legs carried her through and her strong spirit drove her on, holding her awake by the light of the oil-lamp, till the Latin was learned, Maths done and the essays written.

'Och, lassie, you should try to get a wee bit pleasure. All you do is work.' Sometimes Jamie would look at her pale face and feel obliged to intervene. 'How about going out for a wee walk on Glesca Green on Sunday with young Hughie? He'd dye his hair pink for you, so he would.' Peggy was silent, so Jamie went on: 'You could do worse, lass, than Hughie. Once he gets out of his time he'll have a good wage and steady work. There's nothing wrong with honest toil, or the man who does it. And he's not a drinker either, from what I've heard.'

'I find pleasure enough in my books, Daddy.' Peggy knew she sounded hoplessly prim. 'Och, if you like I'll come for a wee walk with you, but I haven't time for Hughie.'

'Please yourself, ye usually do.' Jamie sighed and gave up.

Just before New Year 1897, seventeen-year-old Peggy began finding out about medical training for women.

'We do not take female students.' Most replies were curt to the point of rudeness. 'Apply to Dublin or London,' one bursar suggested, 'they are reputed to take female students. We do not.'

'Dublin, London? I might as well be told to apply to the moon, Daddy,' she moaned.

'Och, listen, lass, think of something else, forget this daft doctor business.' Jamie looked anxiously at the dark circles under her eyes and the disappointment in her face. 'Librarian, how about that?' he suggested with a mixture of hope and despair in his voice. 'That's a real high-class job for a working lassie, though the pay isn't up to much. You love books. Aye, librarian ... that's just dandy, isn't it?' Jamie was worried she would end up warped and bitter.

'I'm not ready to run up the white flag yet. The fight's just begun!' Peggy's mouth set grimly. She wrote to the new medical licensing body in Scotland, the Scottish Cojoint Colleges, which had just opened their doors to women. After an anxious month she got an ambiguous reply.

'Women may now enter for the qualification of Licentiate.

49

This allows the holder to practise medicine, though is a lesser qualification than a university medical degree. However, most of the non-university medical colleges which are permitted to grant the Licentiate do not feel they have the facilities needed to cater for women students.'

'Facilities! Under all that official blethers, they just mean no, get lost ... hard luck. Oh, damn! Damn! Damn!' She slammed the paper down in frustration and picked up another letter which had come in the same fateful post. 'Daddy, I think they've sent me the fees list at last!' Anxiously she peered at the SCC crest and sliced open the envelope. 'Oh, God!' Peggy gasped, handing the letter to Jamie. 'It's far more than I thought. They say Glasgow fees are the cheapest in Britain, but even so it will cost a minimum of £400 for the five-year course ... and they want the first year's fees guaranteed through the bank of a responsible male before they will consider my application.'

'Peggy, how can we raise that kind of money?' Jamie shook his head. 'It's more than most men earn in ten years. No, lassie, it's impossible.'

'If I work for a couple of years after I leave school,' Peggy went on, 'I can put every penny towards the first year's fees at least. Maybe something will turn up then.'

'Och, lassie, lassie!' Her optimism cut him to the quick. Jamie knew it was only a pipe-dream. 'Peggy, you would have to work three years at Miss Cranston's to save enough for one year's fees ... and they want the whole course guaranteed.' He looked helplessly at the information the SCC had sent, then picked up the other letter again. 'And medical schools aren't exactly welcoming women with open arms, are they?'

'No. But I'm not bothered about that,' Peggy said proudly. 'I can do without a red carpet and the band playing, so long as I get in somewhere. Och, let's not talk about it any more.' She tossed her bright head and blinked away the tears that threatened to spill. 'First I have to get a good Leaving Certificate. I'll worry about the rest when the time comes.'

'Good idea! Get your exams behind you, them we'll see.' Jamie hoped she would forget the idea of becoming a doctor by then. Maybe once she starts working, she'll see that being a doctor is way beyond our means. Lassies of that age change their minds all the time, he consoled himself.

As expected, Peggy Soutar cleaned the board with her exam marks and left school in a blaze of glory. Grateful that she had a job to go to, for the time being she began working full-time under Miss Cranston's watchful, speculative eye. After a week, she found herself helping more and more with working the till, doing the day's accounts, and serving less and less at table.

Hughie turned up at closing time to escort her home most nights. Making an absolute out of a half-truth, Peggy told him Miss Cranston didn't approve of her girls keeping company. 'Well, I'll wait at the corner for ye when I'm no' workin' the back-shift,' he insisted, 'the auld witch doesn't have to ken. Yer no' at the school any more, Peggy, just give the word and we'll be winchin' proper.' Hughie smoothed back his glossy dark hair with a determined hand, then crooked his arm for her to take.

'You'll be waiting a long time before I start winching, Hughie,' Peggy said warningly, but slipped her arm in his.

'It's my time, and I'll do what I like with it, long or not.' Hughie squeezed her arm meaningfully against his side. 'Ye will walk home wi' me if I wait?' His expression was anxious.

'Och, I suppose so. I'm doing it now, am I not?' Touched, she couldn't bring herself to refuse. 'But just remember what I said, Hughie!'

Jamie, Maggie Naughton and the neighbours all said it was fine to see the young pair getting together nice and proper at last. The close had been expecting it for years.

But though she knew what everybody was thinking about her and Hughie, Peggy hadn't given up her dream. Quietly she devoured books on anatomy, physiology and pyschology, haunting the science sections of the big Glasgow libraries, to the disgust of the librarians who thought she was depraved.

'Haven't you borrowed enough? Young women should not be allowed to read such immoral and corrupting material!' After a week of disapproving sniffs, the librarian finally spoke her mind, ice in every word.

'No, I haven't borrowed everything I'm going to either!'

51

Peggy smiled enigmatically and consulted her list. 'Please order *The Illustrated Human Anatomy.*'

'Och, there's no morals in some folk!' The librarian reluctantly wrote out the chit.

Each week she saved every penny she could ·from the tearooms, but the dent in the £400 she needed was tiny. Peggy's optimism began to seem crazy to her too, and in honest moments she had to admit that she found comfort in Hughie's total adoration.

'I'd let ye work. Ye can do anything ye like. Even if Miss Cranston made ye the boss, I wouldn't say a word, neither I would. Come on, Peggy, I dote on ye, so I do.'

'Och, I need more time, Hughie.' As always she made her excuses.

'Aye,' he sighed and went on turning up to meet her each evening when the tea rooms closed.

But the final blow to her ambitions was nothing to do with Hughie Naughton, fees or places for women. Instead it was brutal and heart-breaking.

'Are you going to the ILP meeting in this snow, Daddy?' Peggy fussed worriedly round her father. 'You've still got a rotten cough. Go on like this and you'll end up with TB.'

'Keir Hardie needs me to back him, lass. The election is likely to be called this year. I promised.'

'Keir Hardie will kill you and himself too! Skin and bone! He drives himself like a madman and never even eats properly. Lives on porridge and scones. I've never seen him take a decent meal.'

'Och, well, I'll just go this once.' Jamie Soutar sounded as weary as he looked. 'I promise, Peggy, just this once.'

'I've heard that before,' she rapped back sternly. 'Och, at least take your scarf.' Like a mother she tucked a muffler round Jamie's thin neck and pulled his flat cap down more securely on his greying hair.

'You're a good lassie, Peggy.' He smiled gently. 'What would I have done without you all these years? I just wish I had the money to make your wishes come true.'

'Och, you're the best father in Scotland, so you are. It's not your fault'. She hugged him. 'The old goats of professors should be delighted to have a promising student like me applying, not go on about whether I'm a woman or not. And as for the money... well, something might turn up. I'm still young enough to believe in miracles. No, Daddy.' The green eyes hardened. 'I'm not giving up yet!'

'Stubborn as a mule!' Her father shook his head. 'See you about ten, lass.' Jamie lifted up the worn collar of his thin coat and headed out into the raw January night.

Jamie Soutar never recovered from the chill he got at the meeting. First it went into his lungs as bronchitis, exacerbated by the filthy, smoggy city air, then pneumonia set in. Peggy nursed him as skilfully as anyone could, with hot goose-grease poltices and tonics from the chemists. Antibiotics would have done the job, but it would be fifty years before those would be available. So, Jamie coughed and wheezed till his lungs bled and he lay gasping agonisingly for breath.

'Peggy!' The sound was barely a whisper, but she was instantly awake.

'I'm here, Daddy.' In a second she was across the room and kneeling at his bed side. 'Can I get you something? I thought you were sleeping that well tonight, I'd not bother you with tea before I went to bed.'

'Listen, lassie dear.' Jamie's voice was drowned in a terrible gasp which went on for agonising minutes before he managed to talk again. 'I was dreaming of Kirsty. She's that glad I'm coming to her, so she is... I think it's the end for me, Peggy.'

'No!' Peggy took his hand. 'Ye've not to leave me, Daddy, ye've no' to go!' The accent of her childhood overrode the years of education between.

'There's not much I can do about it.' Jamie managed a wry smile. 'When the time comes, there's no choice for anybody, Peggy.' Again he was shaken by a terrible gasp as he fought to breathe. 'You'll manage, you're a brave lassie,' he eventually whispered hoarsely. 'I'm sorry you'll never make a doctor, for you'd have been a right fine one. Och, but don't let it eat your heart out, you'll do well at other things instead. And don't ignore that lad next door, you could do worse.'

53

'I don't want Hughie or anybody, I'm happy the way we are, Daddy. I don't need anything more than you and my books . . .' A sob broke, despite her attempts to control it.

'Aye, I know that, but you'll be on your own from now on, Peggy.' With an effort he raised himself on to one elbow. 'Listen to me, lass. If the hand of true friendship is extended, don't ever turn away. Independence is fine. Good friends . . . and a good man, respect that, they don't take it from you. Promise me,' his voice grew stronger, 'promise that you'll judge folk for what they are themselves, not where they come from? Och, what am I saying? Of course you will, you're a great lassie . . . a fine young woman. Kirsty would be proud of you. I just hope I've done all right by you, lass, I've tried the best I could . . .'

'Daddy.' Tears ran down Peggy's face and dripped unfelt on to her arms. 'Nobody could ever have had a better father than you. Nobody.'

'What's that, Kirsty?' Jamie, oblivious of his daughter now, was smiling happily into the corner of the shabby room, sounding jaunty, like the youth he had once been. 'Aye, bonnie lass, I'm coming. We'll go up the Heathery cliffs and watch the sea-birds fly, Kirsty. Tell yer mammy not to worry, I'll have ye back before the gloamin' . . .' A violent fit of coughing broke into his voice, but was sharply cut off in a dry rattle. Jamie Soutar sank back on to the pillow and spoke no more.

Peggy sat holding his limp hand, weeping in great tearing sobs. There was no one now to share her impossible dreams, no place left for crazy ambition. After an hour she got up and wrapped a coat round her shoulders. Bravely she dried her eyes and went out on to the dark landing. Maggie Naughton wouldn't mind being wakened, she always laid out the bodies in Clancy's Lane. Hughie could go over tomorrow and tell the union. It was good to have folk to turn to at a time like this.

Peggy took off her hat and coat in the empty single-end after the simple ceremony in the municipal cemetery. At least there were no bills to pay; Jamie had taken out funeral insurance with the union years before. There had been a fine gathering at the graveside. His ILP friends, even the great Keir Hardie himself, turned out in force to pay their last respects. Peggy managed it all with dignity and courage. Hughie had stood sad but hopeful at her side in his best jacket, flat cap and string cravat.

'No, thanks, Maggie, Hughie, Mr Naughton, I'd like to be on my own,' Peggy gently refused their offer to come in for a while when they came back to Clancy's Lane.

'Aye, well, we're here if ye need us.' Maggie laid a comforting hand on her arm.

'I know that,' she replied gravely. 'My daddy always said you're the salt of the earth.' Feeling utterly bereft and weary, she went in and lifted her father's worn jacket from the back of the door. She placed it in a box with his other few bits and pieces. Peggy thought her heart would break in two.

Just as she began sadly filling the kettle, someone knocked. Putting it down on the stove, she opened the door, expecting to see one of the neighbours offering a word of comfort. Instead it was Mauchline the house factor, looking more furtive and ill at ease than usual.

'Come in, Mr Mauchline.' She stood aside. 'I've just got back from the funeral. You know about my father?'

'Aye, I ken, Peggy. I heard about Mr Soutar, that's why I'm here. Bad that, so it was... he wasn't an old man, neither he was. Aye, ye never ken the hour nor the minute...' Uneasily he shuffled over the threshold and stood staring for a moment before blurting out, 'Sorry, Peggy, but ye've to get out of the single-end, it was in yer faither's name.'

'Why? I can take it over.' The blood drained from her face.

The house factor shrugged his shoulders. 'Mr Brownlee doesn't let to lassies.'

'Oh, doesn't he, Mr Mauchline? Why not?' Peggy was shocked out of her numbing misery.

'Don't ask me. Och, it's not just him, hen, nobody does, do they? Anyway, that's what he said, it's no' my fault.'

'I want to speak to him myself.'

'What?'

'You heard, man. Tell him that.' Her green eyes narrowed.

55

'Aye, well, if ye insist I'll tell him, but it'll do no good, he'll no' see ye.' The factor shrugged and left.

Defiance spent, Peggy sat by the table gazing into space. What the hell am I going to do if I lose this place on top of everything else? Panicky thoughts swirled hopelessly round and round in her aching head. But whatever happens, I'm not marrying Hughie Naughton to put a roof over my head. I've too much respect for the lad than that! I don't love him and I never will. Och, he deserves better!

'Have you found anywhere yet, Miss Soutar?' Miss Cranston asked kindly the following Monday morning as, sad-eyed but composed, Peggy opened the till and signed for the float.

'No.' A deep sigh shook her slim body. 'I've asked to speak to the landlord, but I've heard nothing. The factor told me I've just got the week to find somewhere. He thinks that's generous, Miss Cranston.' Peggy's drawn face was bitterly sardonic. 'The new tenants are due in on Saturday. I've walked the feet off myself all weekend trying to find somewhere. All the landlords want a man's signature on the rent-book, and they say I'm just a lassie, not even a woman.' Peggy's eyes flashed with irritation. 'It's daft considering that there's loads of men out of work in Glasgow and I've held down this job with you for ages, even before I left school!'

'Yes, you've done well here. And of course I'll give you a prime reference if you think it will help?' Kate Cranston replied with her customary magnanimity.

'Thank you, Miss Cranston.' Peggy smiled her gratitude. 'But whatever happens, I have to find something soon.'

'Why not go into lodgings? Most young ladies would consider that a respectable option, Miss Soutar.'

'I'd prefer a place of my own.' Peggy's face set stubbornly. 'And with respect, Miss Cranston, you're probably thinking about lodgings in a nice district like Woodside, or Anniesland, or out at Barrhead where you live. I haven't the money for those. It would have to be the Gorbals, Bridgeton or Cowcaddens. Decent digs are hard to find in places like that. And it would mean sharing a room. I'd have no peace to study at all.'

'Well, you know your own mind.' The older woman nodded kindly. 'And I'm a great one for a woman making her own way in life. After all, my tearooms are well-known in Glasgow. Miss Cranston's is a name to be reckoned with.' She drew herself up proudly, black silk gown crackling. 'You could go on working for me. There's the possibility of advancement here. Why bury yourself in books now you have your Leaving Certificate?'

'I admire you, Miss Cranston,' Peggy answered without obsequiousness. 'You're a model for women, so you are. But I want to become a doctor.'

'A doctor! Good lord, child, that's impossible for a young woman in your position.' Kate Cranston looked stunned at Peggy's audacity in even considering such a thing. 'Don't you think your ambitions are a bit high for a lass with no capital and no one to back her? I inherited the means to do what I've done here from my father. And my dear husband, John Cochrane, has been a great encouragement to me too even respecting that I use my maiden name in a professional capacity. I'm not ashamed to admit it would have been practically impossible any other way. A doctor? Och, no, Miss Soutar . . . Peggy lass, it's not realistic.' Jet earrings flashed black fire as she shook her head.

Peggy looked at her with absolute determination. 'Miss Cranston, my mother died for lack of medical care and because of man's inhumanity to man. Now my father's joined her for more or less the same reason. All my life I've been surrounded by poverty and folk being treated as less than human because they can't pay for proper medical treatment. I want to do something about it. I have to try for this, though God knows how now Daddy's dead.' She bit her lip sharply to stop it trembling.

'I respect your feelings, but the idea is absurd. Och, Peggy.' Miss Cranston laid a kindly hand on her arm, 'Listen, lass, when you finally give up these daft dreams and start looking for a decent career, let me know. My dear husband and I have no children . . . me being beyond the age when such things are possible by the time we wed.' She coughed decorously. 'I can maybe see a sound manager in you, perhaps

57

more than that, given time and maturity. I have a lot of tearooms, Peggy, and they are very profitable. Very.'

'Thanks for your faith in me, I really appreciate it,' she said sincerely. 'And I'll certainly remember what you said, but my first concern right now is to get somewhere to live.'

By Sunday morning, Peggy was thoroughly worried about even getting reasonable digs. The only place she had managed to find was sharing a room with three girls from the tobacco factory, in a seedy tenement near Bridgeton Cross. There was one day left. Reluctantly she began packing.

'We wid take ye in, hen, ye ken that.' Maggie Naughton's honest face was anxious. 'Our place is a bit bigger than here, but we've still jist the one room and kitchen. It wouldn't be right wi' you and Hughie and that. Do ye ken he's threatenin' to chuck his apprenticeship so he can take a man's job and keep the pair of ye?'

'Och, no, that would be terrible!' Peggy was horrified. 'Tell him from me, I won't hear of it.'

'I did.' Hughie's mother looked sheepish. 'I kenned what ye would say.'

'Good.' Peggy breathed out.

'That's the door, hen. Och, it's that rat-faced Mauchline. I'm away.' Maggie left, letting in an unusually diffident factor.

'Mr Brownlee will see you tonight, Peggy,' Mauchline spoke through a deep flush of embarrassment.

'What made him change his mind, Mr Mauchline?' Peggy's voice was sharp with astonishment. 'You told me two days ago he refused.'

'Aye, well, it's a wee bit complicated.' The factor sat down heavily at the table.

'What do you mean?' Peggy wondered what was coming.

'Ye ken we have tenants lined up for here?' He blew a great puff of pipe-smoke to punctuate every word.

'I know that.'

'Well, I was talking to him last night and he was kicking up a right fuss about folk that don't pay their rent. We just managed to evict a family from a single-end in Brannock Street. They were five months in arrears! We had to call the bailiffs in. Would you believe the dishonesty of some folk?' Mauchline sounded shocked.

'Aye, life is hard,' Peggy answered ambiguously.

'Well, we'd had a wee glass or two of whisky. Er, ye ken Mrs Brownlee and her sister are visiting their mother in Edinburgh with all the bairns? Aye, well,' he went on, shuffling uneasily, 'Mrs Brownlee doesn't hold with alcohol, ye ken, she's in the Temperance Society.' He squinted down at his shoes as if they were biting his feet.

'Oh, I know all about Mrs Brownlee.' Peggy's sad face lit up in amusement at the man's discomfiture. 'She and Miss Cranston are thick as thieves. I've read the letters she sends to the *Glasgow Herald* and heard her speak once at a Temperance rally in Glasgow Green. Mrs Brownlee is not a lady to mince her words.'

'No, neither she is.' Mauchline visibly shuddered. The landlord's formidable wife clearly terrified him. 'Och, anyway, it was a driech night, cold and miserable . . . and we were a wee bit, er, unco' happy, ye ken?' His heavy-lidded eyes rose and fixed over her head on a blue-bottle buzzing against the cracked window.

'You're entitled to your wee pleasures, Mr Mauchline,' she said politely. 'But what's this got to do with my problem?' Despite her grief and anxiety, Peggy smothered a grin. Everybody knew Mauchline tippled liberally when he got the chance and it sounded as if he had a soul-mate in his boss . . . at least when Mistress Brownlee was out of the way.

'Well, it's like this.' His face reddened and he rubbed the toe of one black patent shoe against a stripped trouser leg. 'After a few glasses, Mr Brownleee said that he was scunnered with feckless folk that didn't pay on time and a lassie would make a better tenant. So I said he wouldn't dare to give a lassie a rent-book.'

'And what did he say to that?' Peggy was alert at once.

'He had another glass or two and then said he would give a rent-book to Auld Nick himself if he paid on time, let alone a lassie. I said he wouldn't. He said he would. So the long and short of it is we agreed that you should go round

59

the night at six and discuss the matter. But I warn ye, Peggy, he might be of another opinion in the cold light of day.'

'Och, I'll be there, Mr Mauchline, just give me the address.' Peggy hardly dared hope. The long afternoon passed agonisingly slowly and she packed just in case.

A few minutes before six o'clock, she left the bus at the bottom of Great Western Road and walked down a fine tree-lined avenue to Mr Brownlee's house. Taking a deep breath, she pushed open the iron gate and climbed five spotless polished-granite stairs. Courage in both hands, she rapped firmly with the shining brass door-knocker.

'Ye've come to the wrong entrance!' A maid opened at her ring. 'Roun' the back and rap at the basement door.'

'I've an appointment to see Mr Brownlee. My name is Peggy Soutar.' She was not going to be intimidated by an uppity maid.

'Is that a fact?' The girl looked Peggy up and down from her shabby polished boots and threadbare coat to the well-worn felt hat. 'Wait there.' She closed the door in her face, leaving her shivering on the dark, windy doorstep.

'Put a beggar on horseback and she'll ride to hell!' Peggy gritted her teeth and turned up her collar.

After a few minutes the girl was back, rude as ever. 'Mr Brownlee has important business the now. Ye'll have to wait till he's free.'

'Where do you want me to wait?' Peggy looked beyond her at the closed doors lining the long corridor. 'You don't expect me to stand on the doorstep, do you? I might make the neighbourhood look untidy!'

'Ye can wait in the hall. Just don't touch anything,' the girl replied insolently.

'Wee scunner!' Peggy muttered as the maid flounced off, white starched apron strings bobbing against her long black skirt. 'I bet she doesn't get more than a pittance a year and skivvies from morning to night for it as well.'

Almost half an hour later, James Brownlee beckoned her into the library, eyes flicking over her glowing hair and neat figure. 'Ah, so you're the young lady my factor was talking about.' Unlike Mauchline, who was thin and deathly pale, James Brownlee's florid face was round and puffy above a stiff white collar. A well-tailored jacket gallantly contained his substantial bulk and a gold watch chain helped the silk waistcoat hold in his generous paunch.

Peggy followed obediently, noting the heavy mahogany opulence and appreciating the warmth of the room.

'Sit down, Miss Soutar.' He waved a podgy hand.

'Thank you.' She perched on the edge of a deep leather armchair placed in front of a huge coal fire.

Comfort for some. She thought of Clancy's Lane. Momentarily a surge of resentment nearly choked her, but was quickly smothered. Antagonism towards the man would get her nowhere.

'Well, it's not the done thing to let a lassie have a rent-book, Peggy, if I may call you that?' James Brownlee sounded avuncular but doubtful. 'But Mauchline says you're steady and reliable,' he went on slowly, 'and that's an important consideration. Och, we've been scunnered trying to get the rent out of some tenants, bawbee by bawbee.'

'I'd never miss a turn with the rent, Mr Brownlee,' Peggy broke in earnestly. 'I can promise that. I've even brought a reference from my employer, Miss Cranston.'

'Ah, Kate Cranston – er, yes, an excellent lady. Married John Cochrane a couple of years ago.' He pursed his lips.

'Just give me a chance to prove myself,' Peggy went on. 'You can always throw me out if I don't pay.' She rustled up a charming smile. 'As you say, I'm only a lassie.'

'Och, all right, we'll give it a try!' Brownlee gave way, persuaded by the daft position he had got himself into with his factor and the bonnie, eager face of this strange lass with the polite voice, coaxing him into agreement. He eyed her speculatively. 'You can keep the single-end for the time being. Mauchline can find somewhere else for the other tenants ... I've plenty of tenements.' His heavy gold ring flashed dully in the firelight.

'You'll not be sorry, Mr Brownlee!' Peggy's green eyes shone.

'Come to the office for the rent-book in the morning. My clerk, Alec Murchison, will fix it tonight. He's coming over shortly, we've a wee bit business to attend to, Sabbath or no. Och, it's not easy running a business these days ...

61

nothing but worry!' Brownlee puffed on a cigar. 'I'll tell him then. Do you know where the factor's office is?'

'120 Bothwell Road.' Peggy had made it her business to find out from Mauchline.

'Smart lass!' Brownlee was even more intrigued. 'And all alone in the world, Mauchline tells me. Maybe I'll call in myself one of these days and see how you're getting along.' For a moment his puffy eyes devoured her, then he leaned over and fondled her knee. 'There might be a better place for a bonnie wee lass . . . a clever wee lass . . . than Clancy's Lane.'

'It's very kind of you to think about my welfare like that, Mr Brownlee.' Peggy neither looked down at his hand, nor flinched from his greedy gaze. 'Och, but there's that many bad-minded folk these days.' The red head shook sorrowfully. 'It would be an awful shame if one of them said something to Mrs Brownlee. I've heard her speak often at Temperance meetings. What an interesting lady! And such a good friend of Miss Cranston's too. Och, I would be that worried I might let drop a careless word at work. It would be terrible if she was persuaded that you were compromising yourself by visiting me . . . even though we both know it would be just an act of Christian kindness.' Peggy looked demurely into his horrified face. 'False rumours travel fast right enough, don't they, Mr Brownlee?'

'Aye, you could be right!' His hand shot away as if it were burned. 'There's too many folk reading what's not intended into everything these days! Well then, that's that! I'll see you out.' With no more ado, he hustled her into the wintry evening himself without ringing for the maid. 'Good night to you then, Miss Soutar.'

'Good night to you, Mr Brownlee, and thank you very much.'

James Brownlee grunted in reply and closed the door. 'Aye, the world's full of nosy parkers!' he murmured. He wandered back into the warm comfort of the library and poured a stiff whisky. Like the one that mentioned to Helen about the wee incident in the still room with the last maid. Bonnie wee thing, I wonder what happened to her? he thought idly. I'm sure she wasn't with bairn, whatever she said. Och, I expect she got a job somewhere else. Though I'm not sure Helen gave her a reference, she was that mad . . . He sat in the big armchair, picked up the *Herald* and forgot both Peggy and the sacked maid.

'I can stay!' Peggy's feet in her worn button-boots, hardly touched the wintry cobbled streets as she went back to Clancy's Lane. With a lighter heart she unpacked the few things she possessed. For the first time since her father had died, she saw a glimmer of light, a pin-prick at the end of the pitch-black tunnel.

'Aye, it's waiting!' Next morning Alec Murchison, cadaverous and fifty-past, coughed and spluttered, nodding at the coveted rent-book lying in front of him. She could see 'Margaret Soutar' printed neatly on the cover.

'Thanks, Mr Murchison.'

'Och, I've never heard the likes of it,' Murchison muttered. 'A slip of a lassie wi' a rent-book! What's Mr Brownlee thinking about?' Out of the corner of his eyes, he shot an assessing, lascivious glance at the young woman.

'It was on personal recommendation, Mr Murchison. Mrs Brownlee is a fine woman,' Peggy replied primly and ambiguously, knocking the suggestion of payment in kind on the head at once.

'Oh, aye, Mrs Brownlee, is that the way? In that case I can believe it! Lassies wi' rent-books!' The clerk rolled a tiny cigarette and lit it from the gas light on the wall. 'But I don't hold wi' it anyway.' He threw the little black book across the table at her. It landed with a clatter, making Peggy jump.

'Thanks.' She picked it up.

'Ye'll be wantin' the vote next! Eh, eh, eh?' Hairs from a wart on his nose twitched angrily. 'Yer no one of they suferyejits, are ye? Like that auld witch Pankhurst. Eh? Eh? Ye sound awful high-falutin' for a working lassie.' Taking a long drag, he broke into a paroxysm of coughing, slapping his chest till it subsided.

'Suffragettes?' Peggy smiled as she checked the details on the cover of her rent-book. 'No, I'm not, but they could be right enough, Mr Murchison. Why not votes for women?

The ones I know have more sense than their men: And I'm not high-falutin' ... just the product of a decent, Scottish school higher education! You must be glad your taxes are being put to good use?'

'Whit?'

'Cheerio, thanks for the rent-book.' Peggy grinned cheekily and bade him good day, carefully placing the precious thing in her bag. Not yet twenty, Peggy Soutar was in charge of her own life, for better or for worse. But with rent to pay on top of everything else, her real ambition seemed further away than ever. In the lonely darkness of night-time reality she knew it was hopeless.

Chapter 6

Real friends I believe are few

'Who have you asked to the final prize-giving in June?' Ellie Buchanan asked casually as she and Elspeth prepared posters for Mrs Emmeline Pankhurst's talk next day. A roaring log fire blazed in the grate, dispelling the January gloom and reflecting gaily off the brass fender.

'No one, Ellie. Mama can't, of course, and my father has no interest in my welfare.' Elspeth gave a careless toss of her dark head.

'Do you mean that?' Eleanor Buchanan stopped painting in surprise.

'Of course I do,' Elspeth went on softly. 'In fact, if he knew what we got up to here with suffrage meetings and discussions about Theosophy, he'd move me instantly.' A smile of secretive pleasure lit up her face. 'But since he barely acknowledges my existence, I've had three and a half glorious years here.' She put down her pen and stared thoughfully into the glowing coals. 'Till the day I die, I'll look back on my years at Miss Lovat's Academy as the happiest and most carefree time of my life.' Elspeth's even tone did nothing to hide the emotion of her words. 'Before I came, I thought the world held nothing for me . . . nothing. Then the miracle happened. Here I found true friendship and the real value of women as more than breeders of children. And learned something of my own worth.'

'Miss Lovat says we have to respect ourselves for what we are . . . to know no artificial boundaries of gender!' Ellie repeated the oft-quoted school adage. 'But, Elspeth,' she persisted with a puzzled look, 'why did you think life was so bad? Oh, I can't believe your father doesn't care for you!'

'Well, he doesn't!' Elspeth waved one graceful hand in a dismissive gesture and her shoulders rose in resignation.

'Well, your mother then. Surely she . . .'

'Oh, poor Mama barely knows who I am these days.'

'Surely not!'

'Surely, surely, Ellie dear,' Elspeth replied wryly. 'But anyway, Mama pays my fees . . . or at least Mr Sinclair, her lawyer, does from the Trust my grandfather set up on Mama's behalf when she married.' Firelight glowed on Elspeth's glossy dark head as she bent over the paper and began tracing again. 'It's fortunate that Sinclair sends Miss Lovat the quarterly cheque, otherwise Mama would certainly forget.' The comment was damning in its practicality.

'Is your poor mama very ill?' Eleanor touched her friend's arm sympathetically. Like most people at the school, she understood Elspeth's mother to be an invalid and imagined her father was often abroad. Elspeth never had relatives visit the school, and though she was friendly and very popular, until now she had avoided talking about her background. No one tried to intrude, not even Ellie; that wasn't the way at Miss Lovat's.

'Oh, no more than before . . . it's the Laudanum.' Elspeth carried on writing, talking more to herself than her friend. 'For years she has been slowly dying of my father's dislike and his very obvious disappointment that she didn't produce sons. Or at least a more marketable daughter! I suppose it grieves her that he cannot stand my presence in the same house, let alone in the same room.'

'Oh, come on, Elspeth, you can't mean that!' Ellie was shocked, thinking of her own warm, easy-going father.

Now Elspeth had started talking, the bitterness flooded out. She looked up, eyes dark with pain and blazing anger. 'Of course I mean it. Mostly he doesn't look at me, but when he does, he sees only this.' Her hand flicked against the livid port-wine stain that had not improved with the years. 'Sometimes he visibly shudders.'

'Oh, how cruel!' Ellie gasped. 'I hardly notice it at all

now. It's just you, Elspeth. Anyway, at Miss Lovat's nobody would dream of remarking on something so personal.'

'That's one reason why I adore this place.' The anger died and Elspeth continued with heart-felt fervour, 'From the moment I came here, I felt accepted for the person I am, not judged by a stupid mark on my face. For the first time in my whole life, I was made truly welcome and liked, appreciated, just as I am. Oh, Ellie, it made such a difference to my life . . .' She broke off and gazed into the fire.

'But why does he react so badly . . . your father, I mean?' Ellie still looked bewildered.

Elspeth thought for a long moment before replying. 'My father was an only child. His parents died when he was young. Father was heir to the McClure Estates, but till he reached majority, was at school in Kilmarnock. Mama told me long ago that he was bullied endlessly . . . she said it warped his nature and he isn't entirely to blame for the man he has become.' Her face hardened. 'Mama is too soft. I can't agree . . . we are all responsible for what we are, including Father. Miss Lovat says that however badly life treats us, we have the free will to chose how it affects our spirit and how we treat others. I cannot forgive my father for what he has done to Mama and me, Ellie, and I never will.'

'Oh, no, Elspeth!' Ellie protested.

Elspeth ignored her. 'Poor man,' her young voice dripped bitter sarcasm, 'Hamish McClure, Ayrshire's richest mine-owner with power over hundreds of wretches who work for him. Money, position, wealth – and no one to hand it on to.'

'He does have you . . . even if you have . . . er . . . that wee thing,' Ellie ventured hesitantly.

'Yes, he has me, an ugly girl.' Elspeth smiled grimly. 'Oh, how he hates the idea of my inheriting anything! He's always had a terrible temper, in private at least, Ellie, and that particular thought makes it no better. If only Mama had the decency to die, he could marry again and rectify the situation,' she added bitterly. 'But, no, she drags on miserably, year after year, lying in that room and dosing herself into a stupor with Laudanum.'

'Oh dear, that's terrible,' Ellie whispered, aghast.

67

'Mama knows full well he wants her to die. Once she even imagined he was trying to poison her. Since then her maid Libby buys and prepares the little food she eats.'

'And was he poisoning her?' Ellie's eyes were like saucers. She sat, brush frozen in the air, listening in horrified fascination to Elspeth's unexpectedly shocking revelations.

'Oh, I shouldn't think so . . . he's no murderer, for all his faults.' Elspeth shook her head. 'Perhaps he could kill in rage, but never premeditated. It's true she was ill with a strange stomach complaint for a time and Doctor Logie could find no cause. But I expect it was some of those dreadful medicines she doses herself with.'

'Do you ever talk to your mother about it?' Eleanor was completely bemused. Her own wealthy parents lived in Italy most of the year and were kindly, indulgent and rather bohemian. Harry Buchanan enjoyed wine, food and sunshine, while Ellie's mother, Daisy, wrote poetry and entertained kindred spirits on the sunny terraces of Tuscany.

'No one can talk to Mama any more, Ellie. Well, maybe Libby can,' Elspeth corrected the statement with characteristic objectivity. 'Last time I saw her, she was too doped to do more than greet me . . . Oh, it was different when I was little. She was loving and affectionate then. In those days she and Libby took me for lovely walks along the cliff-tops and even trips to Ayr in the carriage . . . and then for a while there was poor Miss Dalrymple. How I teased her. But she was kind. Now . . . nothing . . . no one. At Bargeddie, I walk the moors alone or read in my room.'

'But, Elspeth, you should have told me this before . . . we're best friends,' Ellie protested. 'You know what they say. A burden shared . . .'

'I don't like talking about it,' she said bluntly. 'In fact, I never think of my past, my parents, or Bargeddie when I'm here. It was just the sudden realisation that the time left at Miss Lovat's is so short. Soon I have to face it all again.' Her grey eyes became bleak and sad. Then she shook herself like a cat and went on crisply. 'Anyway, no more of my parents. I have still six months at Miss Lovat's and I want to make the best of them. Not a word to anyone about what

I've told you, eh, Ellie, promise?' She took her friend's hands.

'Of course not,' Ellie reassured her. 'But what then?'

Elspeth sighed. 'Finishing school, I expect, for two years. Lucky old you, going straight to Italy.'

'Come with me?' Ellie invited. 'Mama and Papa would welcome you . . . we keep open house.'

'Thank you, my dear, but I wouldn't be allowed.' Elspeth looked down at her hands. 'Probably I'll end up in France or Switzerland. Oh, how I wish I could stay here for ever!' She grimaced. 'Can you just see me with all those prissy little ladies, bored to death in some genteel alpine establishment where they teach manners and how to titter coyly at potential husbands? Well, they'll be wasting their time with *me*! Ugh! Horrible!'

'Why don't you just say you're not going?' Ellie demanded.

'Mama insists and I don't want to upset her.' Elspeth shrugged. 'But after that I shall do something useful with my life.'

'Such as? Here, have one of these.' Ellie offered a plate of biscuits.

'Well, I know I'll never marry,' Elspeth commented in a matter-of-fact tone as she selected a chocolate Vienna, 'so I'd better find some interesting way to pass the time till I die!' A sardonic smile lit up her flawed face and twinkled deep in the fine grey eyes.

'You can't be sure of that,' Ellie protested, through a mouthful of Rich Tea. 'You think men only see your birthmark. It's not true or fair. I know plenty who look beyond that sort of thing.'

'Oh, yes, at my father's bank-balance and my future inheritance.' Elspeth was unconvinced. 'I don't need or want a man to be fulfilled in life! Anyway, Ellie, you know how I enjoy studying and going to lectures. I would be bored stiff sitting around doing petit-point!'

'Oh, you've got brains, Elspeth, far more than me. But you're not thinking of going to, er, university, are you?' Ellie almost whispered the question, even though Miss Lovat's was one of the few girls' schools which prepared students for such an option.

'Why not? In fact, I'm thinking of taking up medicine.' Elspeth enjoyed shocking Ellie. 'Becoming a doctor might be rather amusing ... different from the usual dull occupations reserved for young ladies.'

'Now I know you are joking.' Ellie laughed in relief. 'Your father would never permit such a daring thing.'

'We'll see, my dear Ellie.' Elspeth picked up the completed posters and looked at them speculatively. 'We'll see.'

Elspeth McClure celebrated the new century at Châtillon Finishing School for Young Ladies. She was the only student who did not go back to Britain for the fireworks displays and parties being held in every village and town. Instead she watched alone from the dormitory window as bonfires glowed from mountain tops in the surrounding Alps.

The school was as bad as she had feared. Stoically she counted the days till her two-year 'sentence' ended. Only fear for her mother's increasingly delicate health, made her grit her teeth at the daily torture of dancing classes, embroidery, etiquette, piano practice and endless attempts to make her disguise her 'disfigurement'.

> Châtillon, 2 January
> The Dawn of a New Era

Dear Ellie,

How I love your letters, so full of the sun and flowers of Italy ... well, most of the year ... and how I envy you! Did you celebrate the new century in style on the hilltops of Tuscany? I was invited to join the teachers at their little party, but declined with my usual diplomacy! Still the fires on every mountain top casting light on gleaming snow and great glaciers gave even my cynical heart some hope for the future when this torture is over.

Here is much the same as always. I think the other pupils regard me as harmless enough these days. I'm neatly slotted in as an ugly blue-stocking eccentric, who is no rival for the few men they meet. I am left well alone.

One or two who still try to tease me have to be reminded now and then that my sharp tongue is my best weapon!

You asked if I had made friends yet? I'm afraid not, my dear, this is not Miss Lovat's. There is not a single girl I feel any affinity with. In dark moments, I lean on the memories of those happy days and friendships. Do keep writing, Ellie, you and my other dear friends from 'Paradise Lost' are my line to sanity. May the Twentieth Century bring us all we desire.

Your dearest friend,
Elspeth.

Elspeth tried not to think about what would happen at the end of her time at Châtillon. That was another abyss to be crossed and as yet there seemed no bridge, however flimsy, to help her. Occasionally, as she walked by the lake alone, she thought how deep and peaceful it seemed.

She had been to Bargeddie only once since she began finishing school, at the end of the first year. Hamish had avoided her as usual and her mother was incapable of more than the briefest greeting. Libby felt deeply concerned for the young woman, but had no time to spare. Her life was spent caring for Janet like the demanding, dependent baby she had become. Elspeth passed the four weeks riding alone across the moors, or reading and writing in her study. Sometimes, with a feeling of despair, she wondered how it would all end. From then on she spent vacations in Châtillon. When it was empty, school was preferable to the problems simmering at home. But the return of her companions after each holiday, giggling and talking endlessly about beaux and marriage, destroyed the alpine peace.

Shortly after the first term of 1900 began, four weeks before Elspeth's twentieth birthday in February, her mother died in her sleep.

Doctor Logie looked at the empty bottle of Laudanum, opened the bedside cabinet where Janet kept her medicines, and removed three more. Sorrowfully he shook his head.

'I'm sorry, Hamish.' The old doctor looked down at the

71

skeletal frame of Janet McClure. 'There was nothing I could do. Och, well, poor woman, she's found peace at last.'

'What do you mean by that remark, Logie?' Hamish McClure snapped.

'Your wife was an unhappy woman, Hamish.' The old doctor was near retirement and had looked after the family too long to fear the mine-owner's wrath. 'She was drinking far too much of this stuff. Och, you know that fine yourself, man. I imagine she got Libby to send a boy up to Ayr for extra supplies. I only let her have one bottle a week . . . and that should have been more than enough. Poor soul, I suppose the opium in it made the world seem a little kinder.' He closed his big black bag with a snap. 'I'm just surprised she lasted so long at the rate she was swallowing the stuff.'

'Janet had everything a woman could ask for,' Hamish McClure blustered, face red with anger at the doctor's comments. 'Now if you'll excuse me, I have the funeral arrangements to attend to.' Brusquely he ushered Logie out and closed the door firmly on his wife's remains.

Libby slipped in as they left and sat mourning by her dead mistress, head bowed. It was she who had found Janet that morning and she was still in a state of incredulous shock. Janet McClure had been Libby's life and work since she began at twelve as a young maid in the McKelvie family home, more than thirty years before.

'Och, my poor wee mistress.' She leaned over and touched the motionless figure on the bed. 'What am I going to do now? Where will I go? The master will not have me here.'

The maid knew the corpse would be barely buried before she would be given notice. Hamish McClure was unforgiving to those who were not clearly on his side. Libby had detested the man ever since Janet married him, and he knew it.

Libby's tears fell on to the coverlet. 'And there was that wee business over the food. I ken he was trying to do away with ye, madam, whatever anyone else thinks,' she told the still figure earnestly. 'Aye, I ken he was and he knows I ken! Och, madam, I'm well over forty. Getting a new place won't be easy, especially without a decent reference. What am I going to do?' And she wept heartbrokenly in the darkness.

*

72

'Bargeddie!' Elspeth shuddered involuntarily when the great house loomed out of the darkness as she finally arrived, travel-stained and weary, from France.

'Sad homecoming, Miss Elspeth, so it is!' the groom said sympathetically, helping her down from the carriage.

'It is, Robertson.' Elspeth nodded and mounted the massive granite stairs, her stomach a knot of tension. 'Is my father waiting for me in the study, Mrs Price?' she asked the red-eyed housekeeper, who stood at the open door and wordlessly took her cloak.

'No, he's gone to Ayr the night, Miss Elspeth.' The woman couldn't meet her eyes. 'But he'll be back the day after tomorrow in good time for . . . och, ye ken . . .' she trailed off.

'Where is my mother's body?' Elspeth didn't waste any more breath on the subject of her father.

'Libby's with her. She won't leave. The poor mistress is in the blue drawing room. Do you want me with you?' Mrs Price offered kindly.

'No, I'll go myself.' Slowly Elspeth walked up the sweeping staircase, heels rapping a sharp tattoo on the marble. She slipped into the dim room, lit by flickering candles and smelling of lillies and death.

Janet lay on a bier in the middle, with Libby keeping vigil by her side. Elspeth stood for a sad moment looking at the still face of her mother, unlined as a girl's and with no trace of the sorrows she had suffered in her life. Feeling too detached to mourn, Elspeth laid a comforting hand on Libby's shoulder and left her to grieve alone.

People Elspeth had never seen in her life before flocked to the graveside in Kirkowen kirkyard. Janet McClure may have been an unhappy recluse those last years of her life, but she had been a significant personage in the district. As daughter of the wealthy McKelvies of Paisley and the wife of a leading Ayrshire mine-owner, she was entitled to the last respects of her peers.

First the regiments of prosperous strangers went to Hamish to offer their condolences. He received them with the dignity and condescension he habitually reserved for public life. For the sake of politeness they then sought out Elspeth where she stood apart from the crowd. Head high with hard-won self-discipline, she did not flinch as those who did not know her started as they saw her face, then tried not to stare.

'I'm sorry about your mother, Miss McClure.' Voices came and went.

'Thank you.' Her bow was distant and did not encourage further conversation.

There must be well over a hundred here, Elspeth thought, looking round the windswept graveyard. Pity some of them couldn't have spared Mama a kind word, or a visit when she was alive. Bitterness flooded through her tall, slender frame. Poor sad Mama. But only Libby will truly miss her. Elspeth was brutally honest with herself. For years she had been cut out from her mother's wasted life, though in her heart she wished she could have loved the sad woman more. Fear and loneliness came in waves as the empty future loomed, dominated by a despotic Hamish. I must do something or I'll be buried alive here till I join Mama! The open tomb gaped a warning. Elspeth McClure had learned courage over the years and she knew she was going to need it.

Motionless, she watched as the ornamented oak coffin was carried out of the draped funeral carriage drawn by six black horses, great plumes dancing in incongruous gaiety above their heads. Only the drone of the minister's voice, the staccato clatter of hoofs on the icy gravel and the horses' occasional snorts, broke the solemn silence.

Janet McKelvie's remains were slowly lowered into the McClure family vault. Once the huge stone doors were closed, frozen mourners turned gratefully towards Bargeddie and the generous refreshments provided by the widower.

Chapter 7

Give me a spark of nature's fire

Elspeth decided to tackle her father as soon as the last of the visitors had left and they were alone. She knew there might be few other opportunities to talk. 'What did you say?' Hamish glared at her, not bothering to modify his habitual distaste. The antipathy between them was palpable as always.

'I said, there's no point in going back to Châtillon. It's a waste of time and money.'

'Please yourself. They'll never make anything of you anyway.' Hamish McClure topped up his tumbler. 'It was your mother's misconceived idea to send you there. Finishing school! What's there to finish?' His glance said far more than the words. 'But what do you intend doing if you don't go back, eh?' Irritably he walked up and down the room. Elspeth noticed that the signs of over-indulgence and age had begun to ravage his once handsome face.

'I'd like to study. Perhaps I should take a town house in Glasgow for a time, Father.' Deliberately she kept her voice low and steady.

'A town house in Glasgow? Don't be ridiculous!' Hamish swung round in surprise.

'What do you want me to do instead then?' Elspeth knew she mustn't give way or everything would be lost. 'Shall I stay here at Kirkowen and keep house for you?' Despite her efforts, her expression became sardonic. 'In a year I'll be twenty-one. I could be the lady of Bargeddie, Father. It's such a long time since Mama was able to stand by your side, perhaps its time for me to entertain your guests. You could introduce me to the best of Ayrshire society, couldn't you, Father? Take me to the Hunt Ball, the annual Burns Supper, to meet your friends in Ayr . . .'

'Well . . .' Hamish could not meet her eyes. 'Och, I suppose a town house might be possible,' he muttered. 'But studying . . . what?'

Elspeth took a deep breath. 'Medicine.'

'Medicine?' Hamish glared in astonishment. 'You must be mad, girl! That's no subject for a well-bred woman.' His face was sufused with angry colour. 'I'll never agree to that sort of nonsense. And I certainly won't pay for it. Find something more appropriate! Do good works for the Kirk. They always need old maids to run sales of work and organise blankets for the African missions. Now I have things to do, your mother's lawyer is coming tomorrow afternoon!' He stormed out.

'First round, one each. At any rate, I might get my own house, even if it's just to get rid of me.' Elspeth's thudding heart steadied and her young face hardened. 'But he won't stop me becoming a doctor.' The fact that Hamish had disapproved of her choice made her even more determined to go ahead. 'The minute I get a chance, I'll get the books I need for the entrance exams and study in secret. Still, there's plenty of time. I just hope I can somehow press the money out of father for the fees. Perhaps I can sell some of Mama's jewellery if it's left to me . . .'

'Make this quick, man,' Hamish instructed the lawyer. 'I'm leaving for Kilmarnock on, er, business, as soon as this is done. The carriage is waiting below!'

'Aye, I saw it as I came in, Mr McClure. I'll be as brief as the occasion allows,' the lawyer added dryly, and took out the slim file from his case. 'As is normal within the law governing the property of a married woman, the bulk of Mrs McClure's estate goes to you, Mr McClure.' Sinclair looked at Hamish and Elspeth, then hesitated. 'But there are a couple of unusual wee provisions. They were made some time ago, before Mrs McClure became a little less . . . er . . . when she found it easier to concentrate.' Respect for the dead made him reluctant to spell out that it was the poor woman's dependency on the opium-based sedatives that had finally killed her.

'Oh? Small bequests and so on? Aye, that's normal.' Hamish nodded confidently. 'Sit there, man.'

'Aye, thank you.' Sinclair sat down behind the big desk. 'Yes, bequests, that sort of thing, you might say. Mistress Purdie – that's Libby, of course – gets the annual income from an investment of £2000 for life,' he began. 'Of course, she's not able to touch the capital. On her death that will revert to the estate.'

'Preposterous sum!' Hamish snapped, but let the matter go. 'Right then, man, what else?'

'There is one legacy concerning your daughter and another I'll come to in a minute.' The lawyer shuffled the papers uneasily in his hands.

Aha, what was this? Elspeth sat bolt upright. She had known very little about her mother's affairs other than the existence of the Trust which had kept her at Miss Lovat's.

' "To my dearest daughter, Elspeth Janet McClure," ' Sinclair read solemnly, ' "I leave the McKelvie jewellery brought with me as a bride. As I am within my rights to do, I also pass on the Trust set up for me by my father. If the provisions of this Trust are examined, it will be noted that it can only go to my children, or, failing that, to a charity. In the event of Elspeth's dying before me, I would like the Paisley Presbyterian Charity for Destitute Gentlewomen to receive the money. Assuming Elspeth outlives me, she cannot touch the capital at any time. I wish the present board, under the chairmanship of my lawyer, J. S. Sinclair, to administer the Trust on her behalf. The income is to be Elspeth's totally. Through Mr Sinclair's careful stewardship, I believe there is now a substantial annual sum available." ' '

Now stop me doing what I want, Father! In her astonished relief, Elspeth couldn't help but shoot a look of pure triumph at Hamish whose face had gone an ugly puce.

'The final bequest is complicated.' Mr Sinclair peered anxiously over his round horn-rimmed spectacles at the storm gathering on McClure's face, and knew he was going to make things very much worse. 'It relates to someone whose whereabouts are totally unknown at present.'

77

'In the name of God, Sinclair, what nonsense is this now?' Hamish got up and paced the room. Damn Janet! he thought angrily. Not only had she hung on to the last miserable minute, while depriving him of a chance of remarriage and children, but in death she was trying to exert an influence she would never have dared to in life.

' "A matter has weighed heavily on my conscience for many years," ' Sinclair continued, and shifted nervously in his chair. ' "It concerns the death of a poor woman in childbirth, brought on prematurely by her eviction from a tied cottage belonging to my husband." '

'Soutar!' Hamish hissed the detested name.

' "I wish the child, whom I believe to be called Margaret Kirsten Soutar, to be traced," ' the lawyer continued. ' "In order that she may be trained in a useful occupation, I have instructed Mr Sinclair to pay an apprenticeship fee of up to £100 per annum, for a period not exceeding four years. The money will be drawn from a discretionary portion of the Trust's income. After the allotted period, the income from this portion will revert to my daughter, Elspeth McClure. If Margaret Kirsten Soutar is dead, the money will pass immediately to Elspeth." '

'Soutar's daughter! Over my dead body she'll get a penny!' Hamish McClure bellowed, rage exploding like a volcano. 'Let me see that Will!' He lunged at the hapless lawyer.

'Calm yourself, Mr McClure!' Sinclair dodged with amazing dexterity for such a stick of a man. 'There's no changing a Will, it's a grave offence to interfere with the law, sir.' He nipped round the other side of the table as Hamish lumbered after him. 'There's another copy in my office.'

'Oh, for heaven's sake, Father,' Elspeth broke in dryly. 'Must we have these histrionics? I don't know who this Soutar girl is, but she might well be dead or else never found, even if she is alive.'

'You! Get out!' Hamish turned on her in fury. 'You and your mother have planned this well. Don't tell me you didn't know all about it! Well, it's not finished yet, Elspeth McClure. I'll contest this in court and see you in the poor-house. Now take your ugly face out of this house. I never want it here again!'

Elspeth got up and smoothed down the skirt of her mourning dress, outwardly calm and composed. 'Well, Father, at least now we know where we stand,' she said. 'I'll leave right away, with pleasure.'

'Oh dear, oh dear! Er ... Miss Elspeth.' The lawyer coughed apologetically and caught up with her as she was leaving the room. 'Och, this is a bad business! I'm sure he doesn't mean it.'

'I hope he does,' she replied with an enigmatic smile. 'Anyway I'm taking him at his word ... with you as witness.'

'Oh, dearie me! Well, if you do go, come to my office in Ayr around four o'clock.' The lawyer glanced uneasily over his shoulder. 'It's not right for a young woman to be thrown out ... or to leave. Oh, michty!'

'I'm going,' Elspeth said with a look that silenced the protest on his lips.

'Well, maybe we can sort out ... er ... um ... some practicalities till you and your father are on better terms,' Sinclair whispered. 'I have your mother's jewellery and a wee bit cash in my safe. She had Libby bring it up some time ago.'

'Don't worry, Mr Sinclair, I'll be there ... and I don't think we'll ever be on "better terms".' Elspeth cast a last defiant glance at her father who, having vented his spleen for the moment, stood glowering out of the window at the snow drifting over the moor.

'Soutar! Damn the Soutars to hell! He was a thorn in my flesh for years. It was nothing to do with me that his wife died! Nothing, whatever folk whispered behind my back! Sinclair, do something, man! By the time I get back from Kilmarnock, you had better have proved my wife was incompetent. That shouldn't be hard, she was opium-sodden for years!' From the landing, Elspeth could hear Hamish McClure berating the hapless lawyer as the two men went their separate ways. The great door shuddered violently as it slammed shut. It was not in McClure's nature to show restraint when his blood was up.

Despite the brave words to the lawyer, Elspeth was in a turmoil. I must get out before he gets back from Kilmarnock and changes his mind! Excitement, fear, apprehension, fought each other crazily in her head, but underneath a seed of hope that she might be free from her father began to grow. She smiled grimly as she opened the bedroom door. *It would be ironic if I was liberated by a combination of poor Mama's legacy and Father's foul temper . . . so long as he does not take me to court and win. No! That idea was terrifying.* Elspeth refused to linger on it.

'Get our clothes ready, Libby,' she called to the maid at once. 'We're leaving for Ayr as soon as we can.'

'Today, Miss Elspeth? Are ye all right?' Libby took in her flushed face and excited manner.

'Today. And, yes, I'm fine! We're going the minute we're packed, in fact. My father has thrown me out, Libby! I want to leave before his temper cools and he realises what a bad impression that might make on his fine friends.' Elspeth stated the bald facts, then added, 'Mama has left you a wee legacy, Libby. It's enough to keep you in comfort if not luxury. Are you sure you still want to come with me?'

'Of course I'm sure,' the older woman said without hesitation. 'It wasn't just fear for myself that made me ask ye. I need to keep busy, so I do.' Libby had pleaded the night before, knowing full well the young woman would try to break away from her father in some way if she could: 'Can ye not find a corner for me if you leave Bargeddie, Miss Elspeth? My meaning in life died wi' your poor mama.'

'Oh, why not? We may as well stick together if I do get Father to agree to a town house, Libby,' Elspeth had replied, having neither the heart nor the inclination to refuse the poor woman. Her mother would have wanted it and, anyway, she would need to hire a housekeeper if all went well; Hamish would never check who she engaged, of that she was convinced. Libby was faithful, devoted and competent. Why not indeed?

'Well then,' Eslpeth said now, 'tell the grooms we need a carriage for ourselves and a covered cart for a few special pieces of Mama's furniture. Lucky I told you yesterday which things I might want. And later you can tell me who Soutar is or was,' she added casually.

'Soutar! Who mentioned Soutar to ye, Miss Elspeth?' Libby's mouth hung open in astonishment.

'Oh, never mind Soutar now, Libby, I shouldn't have brought up the subject yet.' Elspeth realised the lawyer had opened a Pandora's box. 'We can talk in the carriage. Come on, woman, hurry. I won't feel safe till I'm out of here.'

'I'll see to it.' Libby asked no further questions. Black skirts billowing behind her, she scurried off to arrange the packing and transport. The maid was not surprised that Elspeth was leaving Bargeddie, but was astonished they were going so soon.

'Have you an address for the carter, Miss Elspeth?' Libby was back quickly, red-faced and puffing with exertion.

Elspeth looked up from the trunk of books she was carefully packing. 'Tell him to come up for these, then head straight for the lawyer's office. Sinclair's clerk will arrange storage for the time being. We can stay in a hotel in Ayr until Mr Sinclair helps me sort out Mama's jewellery and the Trust.'

Within a couple of hours, without a backward glance, Elspeth McClure left Bargeddie and sat contentedly as the carriage put mile after mile of sea and moor between her and her father's domain.

'I'm sorry, Miss Elspeth.' Sinclair sent for her a second time later that week. 'I've just been served papers on your behalf.' Elspeth paled as he went on, expression grave: 'Your father insists on contesting the Will and wants you to return to Bargeddie.'

'On what grounds is he contesting?' But Elspeth suspected the answer already.

'That your mother's dependence on Laudanum made her incapable of competent judgement as defined by the law.'

'Will he win?'

'Aye, well, that's a good question. Your mother really only echoed what her own father had intended with regard to the Trust. But your father is your father and that means a lot under the law. He could well get charge of you till you reach majority, and he'll certainly make sure the clause on

81

the Soutar girl is overturned . . . it's an obsession with the man, so it is.'

'Majority? Twenty-one? That's more than nine months away.' Elspeth shuddered involuntarily.

'Well, I'm afraid it could be worse even than that. The court might make majority much later, if they believed it was in your best interests.' The laywer felt he owed her an honest answer. 'On the other hand, your father did throw you out – with me as witness – even though he says he didn't mean it and now insists you come back. But courts generally don't back a lass against her own father, you have to know that, Miss Elspeth.'

'Can I use any of the Trust income in the meantime?' She refused to countenance defeat.

'I'm afraid not, till the case has gone to court.'

'Then I'll sell some of Mama's jewellery, if I can. I've no great sentiment over McKelvie heirlooms.' Elspeth's brisk tone hid her terrible anxiety. 'As I understand it, they were bought for Mama as bridal gifts. I presume he can't touch those?'

'Well, Mr McClure could claim they were dowry and therefore his, but since it is normal that a daughter inherits such things, I don't imagine he will. It wouldn't look good.' Sinclair spoke more positively than he felt. 'And we both know that despite his outbursts when he's roused, Hamish McClure doesn't like to be thought ill of by his peers.' The lawyer gave a dry smile. 'Anyway, the documents his lawyer sent are very specific and they don't mention the jewels at all. Och, no,' Sinclair nodded confidently, 'I think you're safe enough selling a wee piece or two. And one bit of good news.' The smile reached his eyes this time. 'I've to tell you he's decided not to force you home physically till the court rules. Mr McClure is very sure of the outcome, you see.' The lawyer's expression became serious again. 'There's no point in an unnecessary scene.'

'And you agree with his opinion, don't you?' Elspeth asked, white-faced.

'Aye, I'm afraid he has every right to be confident.' The lawyer sounded rueful. 'Still, there's another thing. He's not bothering to contest Libby's bequest. It's such normal

82

practice for a personal maid to be looked after in that way, folk would talk if he tried. So she'll be all right at any rate, though it will take a wee while to come through, because the rest of the Will is challenged. It won't be any help to the pair of you right now.' Sinclair hesitated in embarassment. 'Er, do you need a wee advance? I've still got your mother's cash, though it's not that much . . . twenty, thirty pounds or so.'

Elspeth smiled gratefully. 'Yes, please, I've used up the money I brought back from France. I need just enough to pay for accommodation for Libby and myself. We can move into a rented place straight away, that will save hotel bills.'

'Och, my clerk can sort that side out for you,' Sinclair said reassuringly.

'Why are you helping me, Mr Sinclair?' Elspeth asked suddenly with characteristic candour. 'Most lawyers wouldn't touch a case like this for love or money.'

The lawyer stood up and gazed out of the window to the cobbled streets of Ayr below. 'Aye, I suppose you're right about that. In fact I've told your father he can take his own affairs elsewhere. I've had enough of the man! Och, the McClure portfolio has never been wholly ours in any case,' he added with a shrug. 'I mostly looked after your mother's interests . . . the McKelvie Trust fund and so on. Mr McClure has always had his fine Glasgow lawyers to take care of the business end of things. I suppose we're too provincial for him.' Sinclair sniffed then turned back to Elspeth. 'Och, but it's not that at all.' His voice softened. 'I was fond of your mother, Miss Elspeth. She was such a bonnie, bright lass when she came to marry McClure. Her father brought her to us to draw up the Trust and she visited many times over the years . . . before . . .' He trailed off for a moment. 'I was a young solicitor in those days and it was always my special duty to look after her when she came. Och, it was a pleasure not a duty. The sun shone when she smiled, she was that kind and gentle. We always had a lovely cup of Darjeeling together and a wee slice of Dundee cake – she loved that, so she did. It saddened me to see her decline, year after year.'

Elspeth was surprised and touched, but rose to her feet

and said crisply, 'Good, then you can act for me. Of course, I'll have to win to pay you properly.' A brilliant smile lit up her face and for the first time Sinclair could see her mother in her.

'I had already decided to act for you, if you want me to, Miss Elspeth,' he replied without hesitation. 'Your father has not endeared himself to me, neither he has.'

'He endears himself to very few, Mr Sinclair,' she replied dryly.

The case looked grim for Elspeth. The judge said in the opening statements that he had little sympathy for lasses who defied family authority. Elspeth knew she would have a hard job persuading him that she should not return to Bargeddie at once, or that her father should not hold the purse strings.

Sinclair's heart had sunk steadily as he prepared Elspeth's arguments in favour of the Will being unchanged.

Evidence in defence of Janet McClure's legal competence was hard to amass. Even Doctor Logie was forced to admit under cross-questioning that she had taken opiates over a very long period of time.

'Do you think it affected her judgement, Doctor?' the judge asked during the first day's hearing in Ayr.

'Personally I don't, Your Honour. Mistress McClure always seemed lucid enough when I talked to her . . . tired maybe but lucid.' Poor Logie did his best.

'But you can't be sure?'

'Not absolutely, of course.'

'Mr Sinclair.' The judge turned to the lawyer. 'Bearing in mind that you are acting for Miss McClure and therefore can be considered biased, in your sworn affidavit you say that Mrs Janet McClure was perfectly capable of making proper decisions till she died. Is this still your opinion?'

'Yes, Your Honour, because . . .'

'That's fine.' Sinclair was cut off in mid-stream. 'Call Mr McClure.'

Hamish McClure took the stand, confident and triumphant, the picture of a prosperous and solid citizen, pillar of Kirk, Commerce and Country. Like everyone else in the courtroom, he could see where the judge's sympathy lay.

'Why do you wish to administer the Trust on your daughter's behalf, Mr McClure?'

'Elspeth is impulsive and immature. You can see that by her actions now, bringing shame on the good name of McClure in public. In any case, a young woman should be guided by her father, Your Honour.' Hamish spoke with appropriate solemnity.

'In the evidence presented earlier by Mr Sinclair,' the judge said sternly, 'he claims you had already washed your hands of the girl . . . thrown her out of the parental home.'

'Not at all!' Hamish was all paternal sadness. 'It was just a few hasty words in the heat of the moment, Your Honour, after a sad bereavement. What man among you has not felt the same at times when a beloved child behaves in such an ungrateful way?' Around him, the court nodded in sympathetic unison. 'Elspeth deliberately chose to misunderstand my fatherly chiding and left the house immediately without even saying where she was going. Imagine my distress, Your Honour, when I got back from business in Kilmarnock to find she had gone!'

'And why do you think she took such action, Mr McClure?' the judge asked.

'My daughter has plans to ruin her life with unsuitable activities,' he replied. 'She knew if she remained under my roof, I would try to curb her excesses. That is why she fled on the flimsiest of excuses. A father must rule with a firm rod at times, standing as he does in place of the Almighty as head of the family.' Hamish bowed.

'Och, indeed he must, Mr McClure, indeed,' the judge agreed wholeheartedly. 'And may the court hear what activities?'

'The girl wants to become a doctor.' Hamish's damning words rang round the courtroom. A gratifyingly shocked buzz broke out.

'A doctor?' The judge swung round and glared at Elspeth, incredulity in every syllable. 'Can this be correct, Miss McClure?'

'Yes, Your Honour,' Elspeth replied, head held high but

sick to the heart, well aware she was about to lose everything.

'That's no work for a gently bred woman, or any woman at all for that matter,' the judge pronounced sternly. 'You would do well to heed your father, young lady, and be guided by his wisdom and paternal love. This court orders you to return to your home and behave as a well-bred young woman should, instead of making a public spectacle of yourself. It is entirely appropriate that your father administer the Trust on your behalf at least until you reach twenty-five or even thirty. A doctor? Och, dearie me!'

Hamish sat smiling in triumph. Elspeth had lost. It only remained for the judge to decide on the exact period and details. At best she would be placed totally under his control, at worst she would have to come cap in hand for every bawbee – if he didn't just have her committed to some institution for the insane. People were sent away for less, he thought happily. The money from Janet's precious McKelvie baubles would be eaten up in costs. This daughter would find herself destitute by the end of the day.

'May I say a few words, Your Honour?' Elspeth asked so gently and politely she could hardly be refused.

'Er, yes, Miss McClure.' The judge looked at his fob-watch. 'But you'll have to be quick, young lady, I consider you've wasted enough of the court's time.'

Desperate but outwardly calm, she took one last great gamble. 'I ask to be made a ward of court instead, until the age of twenty-one, or later if you insist.'

'On what grounds?' The judge was astonished.

'On the grounds that I fear physical harm from my father because of his ungovernable temper.'

'What!' Hamish started to his feet, then realising the stupidity of showing anger in court, sat down again.

'I hope this is not just more nonsense on your part, Miss McClure.' The judge eyed her sternly.

'Not at all.' Elspeth lowered her eyes demurely and tried to keep her hands from shaking. 'I will explain further in a moment, but first I wish to plead for the court to retain a clause in the Will which has also been contested and is in danger of being lost by default?'

86

'Well, it is a most unusual request, but go on.' Despite himself the judge's curiosity was aroused.

'Irrespective of what you decide about me, I beg you to uphold that part of my mother's Will concerning a small bequest to a woman called Margaret Kirsten Soutar. Please may I ask my father some questions about this?' A fresh buzz broke out at the mention of the Soutar name. Memories were long in Ayr.

'Oh, yes, we've still to deal with that matter.' The judge sighed resignedly, leafing through the papers. 'Well, I suppose you have no objections to questions, Mr McClure?'

Hamish, in the role of caring parent, flushed deep red but could hardly refuse. 'Er, no, Your Honour.'

Elspeth looked gravely across the silent court. 'Father, you have contested the clause relating to the bequest for Margaret Soutar. This has been overshadowed by our own dispute, but if I lose this case that is also lost, since Mama's competence affects both cases equally.'

'Of course it will be lost. It's unacceptable.' His eyes were wary.

'Unacceptable? You let Libby's bequest stand, yet the sum involved in the Soutar bequest is even smaller in terms of your total wealth. Why do you chose to contest it?'

'I refuse to answer,' Hamish said curtly, and sat down.

'Mr McClure, you agreed to cooperate,' the judge insisted.

'My wife had an obsessive fixation about the family,' he snapped.

'A fixation? Why?'

'Some ancient history about an eviction.'

'Eviction? Please explain further, Mr McClure.' The judge was not an Ayrshire man and leaned back, intrigued by the tangible increase in tension and interest throughout the court room since the Soutar name was mentioned.

'The Soutar woman was evicted from her home along with her husband. He was a trades union agitator.'

'Well, so far this sounds reasonable.' The judge was puzzled. 'You were no doubt within your rights.'

'It was reasonable.' Hamish McClure's face purpled despite his attempts at self-control.

'The woman gave birth that winter night in a barn, Your

Honour,' Elspeth broke in desperately. 'She died. My mother, who was expecting me, heard what had happened. She felt great sympathy for the tragic mother and the infant left behind.'

'A worthy Christian sentiment.' The judge nodded.

'That is why she wanted to leave money for the child,' Elspeth rushed on. 'Mistress Purdie, her maid, told me she had always said she would do this, long before there was any question of dependence on Laudanum. You can call her to the witness stand if you wish, she's in court.' Elspeth nodded towards the respectable black-clad figure sitting primly at the back of the room. 'Please respect Mama's wishes in this respect, Your Honour, it meant a great deal to her.' Elspeth's clear voice carried well. The packed gallery hung on every word. 'I have no more questions for my father.'

'I don't see the point of the ones you asked already, young woman.' The judge shifted irritably in the high chair. 'But, yes, yes, I agree that the clause concerning the Soutar bequest should stand. Mr Sinclair, you may proceed immediately with attempts to find the recipient.'

'No!' Hamish McClure was on his feet. 'Never! Never! Never! Damn the Soutars. They're not getting a penny. Your Honour, she's tricked you.' He pointed a shaking finger at Elspeth. 'I'll not stand for it!' His voice roared round the court.

'Let Margaret Soutar have the money, Father, she deserves it after what you did.' Elspeth added fuel to his rage.

'Soutar was a thorn in my flesh ... he led strikes ... folk blamed me for the death, despite what they said to my face.' Hamish lost control altogether. 'For years I put up with whispers behind my back. Look at them!' He glared at the shocked gallery. 'They're doing it now! No, I'll not allow it! Soutar's brat can starve in the poor-house!'

'Mr McClure, please!' His own lawyer tried to quieten him.

Across the room Elpseth said no more, but smiled scornfully straight at him, knowing what effect that would have.

'Get off!' Temper up, Hamish McClure was beyond

reason. Brushing away his lawyer's restraining hand, he crossed the court in a furious stride. 'Sitting there smirking all over your ugly face, you scheming madam!' he shouted at Elspeth as if they were alone. 'This is all your doing. I'll Soutar you!'

Hamish lifted his hand and struck her across the port-wine stain so hard, her nose spurted blood over the polished mahogany bench.

Chapter 8

To whom has much shall yet be given

The court dissolved in chaos and Libby rushed forward with a huge white handkerchief to stem the flow of blood gushing from Elspeth's face. Next day to a packed court-house, the judge revised his earlier pronouncements. Hamish McClure lost the case in his conspicuous absence.

Sinclair and the original trustees were to continue administering the Trust, but the judge was wary of Elspeth's competence to manage her own affairs, even when she reached twenty-one. He put her under 'the guardianship of the Trustees, primarily Mr Sinclair, who has indicated his willingness to take on the task'. He ruled that she was not to have full control over her income until she was twenty-five. 'To additionally protect her from rash and impetuous decisions, neither will she be allowed to pursue any career until she has reached the age of twenty-five.' The judge turned to Elspeth, 'Do you understand all this Miss McClure?' he asked sternly as she sat in court next day.

'Yes, Your Honour,' she replied, eyes downcast to hide the excitement that had kept her awake most of the night.

'And you will abide by the rulings?'

'Oh, yes, Your Honour.' Elspeth nodded, but incorrigible as ever, muttered under her breath, 'At least my own interpretation of them.'

'And I hope you'll forget this nonsense about employment.' He sounded as if she was going to sell herself on the street. 'It's not fitting for a woman of your station, as I'm sure you know. But if you are still determined to enter a profession, for goodness' sake, young lady, choose something

more suitable than medicine . . . though I can't think what!'
he rumbled. 'As primary Trustee, Mr Sinclair will decide
whether your choice is appropriate. It is his sworn duty to
bring it back to court if there is dissension between you.'

'Yes, Your Honour.' Elspeth's features were composed
and calm, but inside her heart was singing 'Freedom!
Freedom!' so loud she thought everyone must hear it. Sinclair was far easier to manipulate than Hamish ever would
have been. At last her luck seemed to have turned and done
so with a generous flourish.

Within a few months Elspeth was installed in a fine eight-
roomed sandstone house near Glasgow's Great Western
Road. As well as a kitchen, down in the basement there
were quarters for the cook, scullery-maid and 'tweeny' to
do the skivvying. With respectable, indomitable Libby
installed as housekeeper, Elspeth used guiles she didn't
know she possessed to persuade Sinclair that her mother's
former maid was chaperone enough.

The lawyer explained the arrangements before they
moved in. 'The house purchase was easily met from the
accumulated Trust's yield of previous years. Your mother
had us place it in a separate account and used virtually
nothing herself.'

'And my own income?' Elspeth tried to keep her feet on
the ground and be practical, but it was hard when she really
wanted to dance and sing.

'You'll have a private income of just over £300 per annum,
but for the next five years or so, I have to give you what
you need for personal expenses and in return must have full
accounts to show the other Trustees. If you don't want to
be bothered, I can appoint an advisor to submit them on
your behalf. Just hand him the receipts.'

'Oh, I can manage that myself,' Elspeth smiled. 'After all,
I'm over twenty now . . . nearly competent. That's the right
term, isn't it?' Her eyes twinkled.

'Aye, well, all right, but ask for help if you need it.' Sinclair
looked doubtful. Crossing his fingers he went on, 'Libby will
be keeping the household books as she has been taught to
do. I've no worries on that score.' The lawyer sighed with

relief that something in this odd case was working out as it should. 'In fact she's a natural, according to my clerk. And with luck and sound placement of the capital, I should be able to improve on your income, year by year. By the time you are twenty-five and free to spend as you please, it should be a nice wee sum.'

'Wonderful,' Elspeth breathed.

'Aye, in anyone's opinion, Miss Elspeth, you're a moderately wealthy young woman,' Sinclair concluded. And a terrifyingly independent one, he thought to himself as he finalised the papers. She didn't get that from bonnie, wee Janet Mckelvie.

'Landsdowne Crescent is an excellent address, isn't it, Libby?' Proudly Elspeth admired the elegant building with its fine private garden at the back and bow windows overlooking a leafy park in front.

'Aye, it is that, Miss Elspeth.' After all the sadness and fear, Libby could hardly believe how the fates had gone their way. 'Och, that Mr Sinclair has done ye proud.'

Elspeth opened the polished mahogany door of her new house. 'Indeed he has.'

Elspeth wrote with glee to her friend Ellie in Italy:

Now to lead my life as I want it! I'm going to meet *all* my old suffrage friends from Miss Lovat's and I'm starting to write for the broadsheets again . . . though it might be wise to go on using a pen-name till I reach my majority. Oh, Ellie, I am so *very, very* happy! Poor Mama's death and Father's beastliness have kept me well and truly out of the struggle, but no longer! *Votes for Women!!*

Christabel Pankhurst is coming up next week and she's bringing her younger sister with her. I've never met Sylvia, but I do know she is a sensitive soul and an accomplished artist. Oh, it's all too exciting. Sometimes I have to pinch myself to believe it is all really happening! Do tell me the *very minute* you are coming to Britain again and we *must* meet. Wouldn't that be marvellous?

*

'May I lie down for a few minutes?' Sylvia Pankhurst leaned weakly against the banister. 'I am such a martyr to these dreadful headaches.' Her large, luminous eyes were tragic in her pretty, childlike face.

'Of course. I'll call Libby.' Elspeth could barely hide her surprise. 'Is she all right, Christabel?' she asked once the younger girl had gone. 'The poor thing looks so sad and pale, she's not at all what I expected. I thought she would be . . . er, energetic, like you!'

'Oh, Sylvia has been having fits of the vapours ever since dear Father died.' Christabel rolled her eyes to heaven in exasperation. 'I suppose it was being alone with him when he passed on. Maybe if Mama or I had been with her . . . but I was still in Switzerland then as you know. Oh, well,' she shrugged, 'we can't be everywhere at once. Still, Sylvia should pull herself together.' She grimaced. 'It's almost two years now, Elspeth! The girl is eighteen after all!'

'Give her time, she does look peaky.' Elspeth thought again of the great haunted eyes.

'Oh, don't you start! I think she gets far too much sympathy as it is,' Christabel snapped. 'Everyone fussing just encourages her. Sylvia is far too emotional for her own good. Completely lacks discipline. All the way up in the train she's been driving me crazy, wittering on about one outrageous scheme after another. Suffragettes should be passionate in the cause, Elspeth, but logical and cool-headed too,' Christabel insisted. 'Sylvia doesn't seem to realise that.'

'Stop worrying, my dear.' Elspeth knew Christabel well of old and guessed the real root of her friend's irritation. She played the peacemaker. 'The movement looks to you and your mother as its leaders. Let Sylvia have her little fantasies, you don't have to follow them through.'

'Perhaps,' Christabel sniffed but, modified, followed Elspeth into the cosy sitting room. 'In fact I'm not happy with our present arrangements myself,' she said. 'I told Mother last week that we need to be far better organised than we are just now if we are to get the vote at all.' Christabel threw herself into an armchair and drummed impatient fingers on the armrest.

'Did she agree?' Elspeth knew that although Christabel

and Emmeline Pankhurst were close, they were spirited, highly intelligent women who often argued.

'Oh, yes. Mother and I usually see eye to eye.' Christabel waved an elegant arm, then gave the lie to her claim at once. 'Though she is too old-fashioned.'

'Mrs Pankhurst, old-fashioned? Surely not! What on earth do you mean?' Elspeth demanded.

'I asked her outright how long women had been trying to get the vote,' Christabel replied defensively. 'Too long,' she said, 'and we're no nearer.'

'Well, that's true enough,' Elspeth replied. 'You'd have said the same yourself. What other reply is possible?'

'Exactly! "Well, for my part I mean to get it!" I told her. "We're in the Twentieth Century, for goodness' sake! Our time has come!" ' Christabel leaned back on the cushions in satisfaction.

'And?' Elspeth felt confused.

'And,' she said with a smile of triumph, 'after quite a to-do, I finally persuaded her that she and I should set up a new suffrage organisation which will concentrate on far more militant action.'

Elspeth raised a questioning eyebrow. 'What do you mean, "militant"?'

'The struggle has been too passive, Elspeth, nobody really takes us seriously. We need to make Parliament take note . . . that's what I mean! Our protests need to be noticed!'

'I see. At least, I think I do.' Elspeth nodded slowly. 'Have you decided what to call it?'

'Yes. We want to emphasise both the political and social aspects of our demands, so I suggested the Women's Social and Political Union, or WSPU. And Keir Hardie approves.'

'So do I.' Despite her earlier doubts, as always Elspeth was fired by Christabel's charisma and enthusiasm.

'It will be open to all suffrage workers, old and new.' Christabel grasped her old friend by the arm. 'Are you with us, Elspeth, heart and soul?'

'Of course I am, Christabel,' she replied at once, face glowing. 'Just try to keep me out! When do you start?'

'As soon as possible, but we want to do things properly.

94

There have been too many uncoordinated suffrage groups in the past. This time we're going to get things right.'

Sylvia came back and stood rubbing her eyes, but looking less pallid and wan. 'Your housekeeper gave me a draught, Elspeth, and I'm much better. Has Christabel told you about our plans for a WSPU?'

'My plan,' Christabel said huffily.

'Yes, it all sounds wonderful,' Elspeth broke in, realising the sisters were about to start bickering.

'Oh, it is!' Sylvia clasped her hands and sank gracefully into a chair. 'And in the meantime we shall continue with outdoor meetings and producing leaflets. Everyone must know what our demands really are. There is so much to be done in bringing information to those who need it most. Working-class women, for instance, really need our encouragement to break the bonds of poverty and man-made slavery . . .'

'Yes, yes, Sylvia,' Christabel interrupted. 'Working-class women . . . yes . . . naturally.'

'If you are producing a new leaflet soon,' Elspeth said eagerly, 'I'll be happy to write for it, of course.'

'I'd love to take the chance of working with you while we're here,' Christabel sighed. 'You were always so full of excellent ideas at dear Elizabeth Lovat's . . . and you wrote such wonderfully radical articles, Elspeth. The public loved them. The press always quoted bits and pieces, even if only to lampoon us.'

'Sticks and stones may break my bones, but scorn doesn't worry me so long as we get the public's attention,' Elspeth parodied, with a broad smile. 'I'll do it again, even if I have to hide behind a pen-name for a while longer. Oh, roll on the day when I can come totally out into the open. Father will loathe hearing about provocative articles calling for Votes for Women written by one Elspeth McClure!'

'Hah! We'll have the vote already by the time you're twenty-five, Elspeth,' Christabel replied stoutly. 'But, anyway, we can't do it this time.

'Why not?'

'There's just no money this month for printing,' Sylvia said with a sigh. 'We're broke as always.'

'Don't worry, I'll fund this one in celebration of my freedom.' Elspeth put an arm round each of them. 'Sinclair gave me some pocket money – "for clothes and fripperies", he said. I'll use it far more wisely, though I'd better call it something different in my accounts!'

'Wonderful!' Christabel cheered.

'Votes for Women!' Elspeth laughed, raising both arms in the air, then turned to practical matters. 'Lauchlan's at Anniesland Cross did my visiting cards. If we do the pamphlet now, he could have the copies ready for distribution tomorrow. You can take some back with you.'

'Will he do it?' Christabel asked from long experience. 'Many printers won't handle suffragette material, Elspeth.'

'Libby told me Lauchlan doesn't care what he prints,' Elspeth reassured her, 'so long as he gets paid.'

'Then let's get started.' Christabel took off her jacket.

'I'll get Libby to send round for Helen Fraser and Miriam Gilchrist,' Elspeth suggested. 'Do you remember them?'

'Of course, I've met them many times at rallies. They're wonderful girls!' Christabel was delighted.

'If they're home, they'll want to help.' Elspeth bustled off and was soon back, ready for action. 'Now while we're waiting, update me on the last Private Members Bill and we can start making the broadsheet outline. Will you illustrate, Sylvia?'

'Naturally.' She picked up her pen and began drawing a fine black and white ornamental outline for the front of the page.

'Well, come on then, Christabel, how about two articles on the new Bill just here?' Elspeth reached for a sheaf of paper and they began planning.

'I've brought some tea and a wee plate of scones, Miss Elspeth.' Libby interrupted the five young women later that day as they sat, heads down, working tirelessly on the suffrage leaflet.

'Thanks, Libby, put the tray over there.' Elspeth waved vaguely with her pen.

'Och, have you lot been at this solid since Miss Helen and

Miss Miriam joined ye? Ye'll all end up with the megrims, so ye will!' The housekeeper shook her head in disgust.

'Nonsense, Libby.' Elspeth smiled. 'It's all in a good cause.'

'Good cause, my granny!' she sniffed.

'That's a splendid article, Helen! Christabel, Elspeth, come and read this!' Miriam held up the page.

'The tea is getting cold,' Libby interrupted huffily, pointing towards the neglected tray.

'Quite right. Sorry, Libby. Come on, let's have a break.' Elspeth poured China tea, while Libby handed round warm scones spread lavishly with butter and strawberry jam.

'Have you seen Keir Hardie lately, Christabel?' Miriam Gilchrist asked as they ate.

'Not for a month or so ... Oh, delicious, Libby! Mmm, like a feather!' Christabel bit into a floury scone with relish. 'Some people in the ILP ... far too many ... oppose votes for women. Keir is greatly handicapped in what he can do.'

'Oh, well,' Elspeth shrugged, 'at least we have a politician on our side ... albeit one without a seat in Parliament!'

'Oh, that's only a matter of time.' Sylvia's great eyes glowed. 'Keir is bound to get elected next time. He's such a wonderful man.'

'*You* certainly think so,' Christabel commented spitefully. 'Though I have my doubts sometimes about his commitment to the cause.'

'Christabel, you are unjust!' Sylvia flushed.

'Er ... look at the time! Back to work!' Elspeth intervened before a row erupted.

'Votes for Women! Pamphlet, sir?' Next afternoon the five of them enthusiastically distributed their first batch of leaflets in the centre of Glasgow.

'Get back home where you belong! What on earth are your parents thinking about?' A well-dressed man looked affronted at being approached.

'Votes for Women!'

'Stick it up yer arse, ye wee slut!' Red-faced, a carter brusquely pushed away the sheet Helen Fraser proffered.

'Votes for Women!'

'Whit? Oh, aye. Thanks, hen.' A bewildered woman,

97

carrying a child in a shawl, took the leaflet politely and then stuffed it down the nearest pavement grating.

'Votes for Women!'

'Good luck to your cause, ladies.' One elderly gent stopped and shook hands. 'I believe women should have their say.'

'Thank you, sir!' They beamed in pleasure.

'Votes for Women!'

'Strumpets!' A clergyman shook his fist as he hurried past. 'Godless creatures! The Lord will be avenged!'

'No convert there.' Elspeth grinned. 'Come on, comrades!' Stolidly they worked on, handing out the broadsheet. Soon they were almost finished. The blowy, chill November day made even ardent suffragettes disinclined to linger.

'Gracious! It's time to go to the station.' Elspeth looked at the watch pinned under the lapel of her coat. 'Look, we've almost finished this batch. If you two don't go, you'll miss your train. Helen, could you and Miriam hand out the rest while I run to the station with Sylvia and Christabel?'

'Of course.' Helen Fraser nodded at once. 'Oh, Elspeth, will you be at the meeting tomorrow in Kelvingrove Park?'

'I'll have to be. I'm speaking.' Elspeth smiled.

'Good luck, Christabel. 'Bye, Sylvia.' Helen and Miriam took the remaining loose pamphlets and walked off crying, 'Votes for Women!'

'Come on, this way, it's shorter!' The three women held their hats and sprinted from Buchanan Street down Hope Street to Central Station. Panting, Christabel and Sylvia collected their carpetbags and a box full of pamphlets from left-luggage.

'These will open a few eyes in Manchester!' Christabel clutched the precious load.

'I hope so. Now come on!' Elspeth led the way through the crowds to the platform. The two women threw themselves on to the train and then leaned out of the window.

'What a fine job we did in such a short time,' Christabel shouted. 'More sessions like this and we'll win! Votes for Women!' she yelled as the train pulled out.

'Votes for Women!' Elspeth called back, ignoring the tut-tutting and stares from others on the platform.

'Good God, I'm certain that's the McClure girl. There can't be two birthmarks like that. I wondered where she'd gone to earth after that court case.' A stout gentleman waving off his wife's sister peered over. 'Wait till I tell Burness at the bank in Ayr what she's up to . . . I'm sure I read in the *Post* that he was one of her Trustees. Votes for Women, indeed!'

Pulling up her collar against the chill wind, Elspeth cheerfully left the crowded station and beckoned a cab.

This WSPU is just what we need, she decided. As the carriage clattered back to Lansdowne Crescent, Elspeth thought with glee about the militant new organisation. And I'll be a founder member! Maybe we can start a separate Scottish branch too. Why not? I'll suggest it at the next meeting of the Glasgow Suffragettes.

'Is that you miss Elspeth?' Libby was waiting as she came in. 'Now warm up a bit before you do anything else, I've just got a fire blazing in the sitting-room. How about a wee cup of hot chocolate? Och, look at ye, your hands are frozen stiff.'

'I can only spare a minute, Libby.' Elspeth swallowed her irritation at the housekeeper's eternal fussing. 'I have to get on with my other work.'

'Och, ye'll kill yerself!' Libby shook her head, but seeing the warning look in Elspeth's eyes, satisfied herself with that and disappeared back into the kitchen.

'Now, where was I?' Once her chilled fingers had thawed out, Elspeth picked up her medical books and singlemindedly buried her head in them.

The court might have ruled she couldn't start a career till she was twenty-five, but they hadn't said she couldn't study. Anyway, tutors at the medical preparatory college told her it would take two years before she would be ready to sit even the entrance exams, since she had no prior training in the subjects. And then there was the medical studies to do after that. Elspeth had doggedly studied for over a year already. Her goal was firmly in sight, though there was no great hurry. There were still votes for women to win as well. She revelled in this new era of fulfilment. Yes, there was time for it all.

99

Elspeth never wondered why she was fighting for women's suffrage; that conviction was spontaneous, deep and sincere. She confided her feelings to Ellie in one of many letters:

How I wish you were here to share our WSPU activities, as you were at Miss Lovat's. Oh, Ellie, why do people not realise that women should have the right to chose their government . . . their *destiny*? After all, we are at least as intelligent as men. I will never, in the whole of my life, accept being dominated by a man. Never.

You ask me yet again about my choice of medicine. Well, that's a hard question to answer, my dear. At first I think it was partly to annoy Father, since I knew he would never approve. But now, Ellie, now I've begun really studying, I feel differently. To understand the form and functions of this marvellous machine, the Human Body, and eventually to be able to influence how it works, has become a true fascination for me.

Life was full of intellectual satisfaction, sisterhood and purpose. Cushioned by her income and driven by a powerful personality, Elspeth McClure was content as she steadily pursued her many ambitions.

'Och, why don't you powder over that wee mark, now you're a grown woman and well over twenty-one?' Libby asked one morning as she watched Elspeth switch her dark brown hair into its usual severe bun.

'Nothing hides port-wine stains,' she replied without rancour. 'If I cake it in paste I just look ridiculous, like some raddled music-hall singer! Anyway, I'm used to people gawking at me, Libby. It doesn't worry me a bit. This mark is just part of me. Others have big noses or flat feet to put up with, I have this!' Smilingly she touched her face, moving her head to one side so the full extent of the stain was reflected in the mirror.

'Och, but maybe some young man . . .'

'Libby, I gave up the idea of anybody marrying me years ago, you know that.' Elspeth turned to the housekeeper and put her hands on her shoulders. 'There are plenty of pretty faces around for gallant lads to chase. Oh, somebody might want me for my money, but I'd be black affronted to accept in that case. Especially as they would probably want to keep a couple of comely mistresses in comfort, on my bawbees, as consolation for having such an ugly wife!'

'Miss Elspeth, you're not a bit ugly! Och, I wish ye wouldn't say things like that.' As always in such encounters, Libby ended up shocked and upset.

'Serves you right for asking.' Elspeth grinned wickedly at her outrage. 'No, I'm happy as I am,' she said firmly, 'so now, no more please.' Elspeth knew that Libby meant well and spoke from misplaced love and loyalty. Much of the absolute devotion once given to Janet had been switched to Elspeth. Libby was deeply concerned for her happiness. Rather too concerned for Elspeth's free spirit to tolerate at times.

'If ye insist.' Libby gave up for the moment. 'Are you going to that medical college place again today, Miss Elspeth?' she asked in the slightly bemused tone she used for all her young mistress's ploys.

'No, not today, Libby.'

'Och, it's not one of they suffrage meetings again, is it?' Libby sighed. 'There was spittle on your coat-sleeves after the last one. Imagine the dirty articles that spit on women!' she fretted. 'What do ye do it for?'

Eyes twinkling, Elspeth put her head to one side and studied the affronted housekeeper. 'Though you won't believe it, Libby, I do it for you and folk like you . . . as well as for myself, of course. But, no, today I have a meeting with Mr Sinclair in Ayr.' She picked up her fur-trimmed coat and swung it lightly over her slender shoulders. 'Send Tweeny down to Great Western Road to fetch a cab please, Libby. I have to get to St Enoch's Station by one o'clock.'

'But . . .'

'Now don't start mithering.' Elspeth held up a hand and forestalled the next query. 'I promise I'll eat in the Ayr Station Hotel when I get there.'

'Och, I'll believe that when it happens!' With a martyred look on her face, Libby left.

Later that afternoon Elspeth arrived at the discreet, prosperous offices of her lawyer in Ayr. 'Come in, come in, Miss Elspeth.' Sinclair shook her hand warmly. 'I trust you had an agreeable journey?'

'Travel by train is very comfortable indeed these days, Mr Sinclair.' Elspeth smiled. 'Think what the journey from Glasgow to Ayr must have been like in a carriage!'

'Terrible, .terrible. I remember it well as a child. It took hours.' The elderly lawyer shuddered.

'What did you want to see me for? The usual papers?' Elspeth had already pulled off her right glove in readiness to sign.

'Two main reasons and some wee ones,' the lawyer began. 'The first is about your, er, activities with the sufragettes.' He decided to tackle the most sensitive issue first. 'Word has come to one of the Trustees that you've been taking part in public displays of support, even talking at meetings in Kelvingrove Park.' Burness had thoroughly checked the authenticity of his tip-off before complaining to the others.

'Yes, that's true enough.' Elspeth gazed steadily back.

'Well, the Trustees don't like it, Miss Elspeth.' His face was grave. 'They threaten to restrict your income if you continue and have asked me to excercise more control.'

'Mr Sinclair,' Elspeth's voice was icy, 'tell the Trustees that they have no legal right to do so.'

'Well, that's not exactly so,' he cautioned. 'Until you reach full majority at twenty-five, they can take action if they think your behaviour is detrimental to your well-being.'

'And do you agree with them?' She raised a quizzical eyebrow.

'Well,' he replied, face the picture of embarrassment, 'I've come to know you a lot better since your dear mama died, and believe it or not, for a fusty old solicitor, I don't regard you as a simpleton just because you're a lass. In fact, I greatly respect your intelligence, though some of your ideas maybe less.' A dry smile lit up his face.

'I'm pleased to hear that at least.' Elspeth grimaced.

'Och, can you not compromise a wee bittie, Miss Elspeth?' the lawyer pleaded. 'Your father isn't finished yet, you know. There's rumours of an appeal. It would be sensible to lie low for a while and not antagonise the Trustees.'

102

'Thanks for your advice, Mr Sinclair,' Elspeth said more gently, recognising his genuine distress and concern. 'But women's suffrage is something I believe in too strongly to ignore, or put on the shelf for fear of my father.'

'Och, that's what I expected you to say.' Sinclair shook his head in resignation. 'Oh, well, I'll do my best to talk round the other Trustees for the time being. But you will try to be more discreet at least, lass, won't you?'

'Probably,' Elspeth replied enigmatically. 'Now what's the other matter you wanted to discuss?'

'Aye, the other matter.' The lawyer rummaged through the papers on his desk. 'We may have located Miss Margaret Soutar.' He drew forward a stout portfolio. 'I might as well update you and spare you another journey down to Ayr . . . Er, you've never been back to Bargeddie since the business in court have you?' he asked tentatively.

'No.' Elspeth's expression became remote and unreadable. 'You didn't really think I could go back?'

'No, no, I didn't. But I just wanted to make sure. I don't keep tabs on you, you know . . . though some think I should.'

'I know you don't and I'm grateful for it.' Elspeth rewarded him with her lovely smile then went on softly, 'When Father remarried barely three months after Mama's death, any chance of a change of heat on either side went from extremely improbable to utterly impossible. The court-case just formalised things.' Her smile became wry. 'I've nothing against Flora, Mr Sinclair. The one occasion we saw each other . . . you remember I told you we met in the ladies' withdrawing room at the Ayr Court the day the papers were to be signed? . . . she seemed pleasant enough, but so young and innocent.' Elspeth could not keep the pity out of her voice. 'She was terribly embarrassed to meet me. Poor, poor girl.'

'Aye, it was a little soon for your father to wed again perhaps, but I believe he's anxious to have more heirs. A son. Och, it's understandable that a man in his position would want a laddie to follow in his footsteps, and he's getting no younger.' For all he heartily disliked the man, Sinclair tried to be fair.

'I admit that's the way the masculine world looks at things,

Mr Sinclair.' Elspeth's grey eyes fixed him coolly. 'And since Flora, my new step-mother, is exactly a year younger than me, they should have a good chance of fulfilling his wishes . . . if she's a good breeder.'

The lawyer winced at her bluntness. 'Hmm, age differences are not considered such a barrier when the man is older than the woman. The other way round is rarer.'

'Benjamin Disraeli, the Earl of Beaconsfield, had a very happy marriage and his wife was many years older.'

'Yes, hmm, but he obviously wasn't thinking of, er, heirs. Hmm, aye . . .' Sinclair felt this was hardly a subject to be discussing with a young lady, but Elspeth McClure was unusual by anybody's standards.

'So, back to business, Mr Sinclair!' His discomfort amused her. 'You've found the elusive Miss Soutar at last. Is she still Miss Soutar or has she married? I believe she's the same age as me, isn't she? Or a couple of months older, according to what I could drag out of Libby.'

'No, surprisingly not, though most women are usually wed by then, whatever their class.' The lawyer suddenly realised his faux pas. 'Er, if they choose to be, of course. The state of matrimony is not to everybody's liking!' He looked down at the document instead of at Elspeth's sardonic grin. 'Aye, if this is the right person, she appears to be still unmarried. But that's all we know at present.'

'How did you trace her?' Elspeth was intrigued. 'Where does one begin such a search?'

'Och, a private investigator was dispatched to find her in the end. All our adverts failed. Amazingly, he seems to have succeeded.' Sinclair's sniff relegated private detectives to the same class as bookies' runners or spivs.

'Where did you advertise?'

'The cheaper broadsheets. Normally we would have used the *Glasgow Herald* and *The Times*, but it was inappropriate in this case.' Sinclair gave a thin smile. 'Newspapers of that calibre are hardly reading material for working women. Maybe we should have advertised in some of the "penny dreadfuls" as well. But in any case,' he shrugged, 'it would seem she is living in Glasgow. The Cowcaddens district. Not the most salubrious of areas. What she'll be like, I can't begin to guess. Och, well, it's part of the job.' His expression was tinged with martyrdom bravely borne. 'I'm meeting her here next week.'

'She's coming to your office?' Elspeth raised a finely arched brow.

'Necessary, I'm afraid.' Sinclair tapped the desk with his pen. 'There are certain things to establish, papers to sign, questions as yet unanswered and so on. Otherwise we would try to see her in Glasgow and save her the journey.'

'That might have been kinder. Ayr is a fair distance if one is not used to travel.' Elspeth thought of the times she had handed out pamphlets in the Glasgow slums and how small horizons seemed to be there.

'Yes, poor woman, she'll probably be scared to death, coming all the way from Glasgow in a train. And, of all things, to a lawyer's office.' Sinclair had a sound notion of his profession's importance.

'Indeed.' Elspeth hid a smile.

'We sent her a third-class ticket from Glasgow and a very simple map of how to find the office from Ayr station. The messenger told her to show someone the address if she can't find us. Though everything is printed out neatly in clear big letters for the poor soul.'

'Very thorough,' Elspeth murmured dryly, wondering if he would have treated a man as such an idiot, working-class or not.

'Oh, I try to be, Miss Elspeth.' The lawyer accepted the comment as a compliment. 'And in the meantime, we are checking out her credentials as far as is possible, so we can be sure we've got the right person.'

'I do hope you have.' She laughed. 'Libby says the name Soutar has always been a *bête-noire* for father. I think he feels horribly guilty, however much he denies it. And so he should! But this poor woman . . . will she accept anything from a McClure, do you think?'

'Och, good lord, I expect so.' The lawyer raised his shaggy brows expressively. 'Yes, yes, no doubt about it. She would be an utter fool to refuse. Apparently her father has been dead for almost two years. What working woman totally alone in the world, living in a terrible place like Cowcaddens, could be stupid enough to turn down the means of getting a decent trade? If she is capable of learning one, that is.' His face clouded. 'That's one of the things we have to establish.'

'What if she can't?' Elspeth asked.

'Then I might suggest training for some simple occupation – laundry-maid perhaps. But if she is capable, the terms of your mother's Will are more than enough for a top-class apprenticeship. Perhaps she could become a milliner or seamstress, even a florist! Then she could set up a wee shop of her own if she had the notion to be independent. We could be generous with any capital left over.'

'And I could buy flowers from her. Or bonnets.' Elspeth smiled. 'As long as they were grey or brown!'

Chapter 9

We are na' to be bought and sold

I must be the only tea-shop assistant in Scotland with a qualification in anatomy and physiology, Peggy thought wryly to herself as she checked the till and closed the busy Argyle Street branch of Miss Cranston's for the night. But where has it got me? Precisely nowhere! Sighing, she drew out a letter received that morning.

'February 10, 1901, Dear Miss Soutar, We are pleased to inform you . . .'

The results of her exams were excellent, painfully studied for by lamplight late in the evenings and paid for out of hard-earned money. She would need all of them for entry to any medical school. But passing, and with such brilliant marks, was bitter-sweet. Peggy felt more confused now she had achieved this goal than before.

I'd love to go to Queen Margaret's College, she mused longingly. Nine years earlier, the women's college of Glasgow University had opened a proper medical school. They say QMC offers the best medical education for women in Scotland. But I'll never afford it. She fought off a wave of increasingly familiar despair.

Two years of working her heart out, even after promotion at Miss Cranston's, saving and scrimping every farthing, still left her with a pitifully small bank balance. The tiny single-end had to be paid for and she had to buy her work uniform. At least she ate free. Even faithful Hughie Naughton was beginning to falter. 'Will ye no' give up whatever it is yer after, Peggy? I want us to get hitched the minute I come out of my time. Can I have yer word on it at least?' he had

107

asked the Sunday before as they had walked in Kelvingrove Park.

'Hughie, I'm still of the same mind, I don't want to wed,' Peggy insisted. 'I'm really fond of you, you know that. Och, it's just I'm not the marrying kind.' She tried to soften the disappointment that always clouded his face when the subject was brought up. 'It would be better if you courted another lassie, somebody more worthy of you.'

'I'm beginning to think ye mean it.' Hughie looked down at his best shoes, shining with blackening. 'Look, Peggy,' he said after a few silent minutes, 'I'll no' ask ye again till September when I come out of my time. If ye say no then, I'll look elsewhere.' A pretty picture of the new lass at the Co-op cake-shop drifted unbidden in front of his eyes, but years of devotion to Peggy made him quickly squash the momentary unfaithfulness.

'It's a deal.' She grinned and the two of them walked on, happier for the clearer air between them.

Peggy pulled her worn felt hat further down as she left Miss Cranston's later the same week. God, it was cold! The chilly night air cut through the thin fabric of her coat, making her shiver. Hughie was on night-shift all week and couldn't meet her. Cold or not, Peggy was glad of the chance to think in peace. I'm getting nowhere. I'll just have to forget the whole idea of medicine and take the chance of a career when I have it, she admitted reluctantly. Miss Cranston has been kind to me, but if I'm going to train as a proper manageress, I had better let her know soon. My God, most women would give their eye-teeth for the chance she's offering me. Maybe I should just give up now and take the job before she finds someone else. Thoughts spun round and round in her head as she walked the long miles home through the smoggy city.

'Yer late the night, hen!' A prostitute, shivering on the corner, greeted her cheerfully.

'Aye, we stayed open for a bit longer,' Peggy called back. Years of penny-pinching meant she knew every step of the way, every pub, every alley. Most of the girls she passed, frozen stiff as they waited for customers, worked the same patch every evening. She was as familiar to them as they

108

were to her. Peggy felt no fear. Glasgow was a rough and ready place, but there were rarely attacks on women.

Finally she turned into Clancy's Lane. You're twenty-one past now, Peggy Soutar, she told herself sternly. It's February 1901, the New Era has arrived. Get your life in order!

'I dinna ken what Hughie Naughton sees in that one!' a voice carried spitefully as Peggy passed a little huddle of women coming in from the tobacco factory back-shift. 'She talks as if she has a bool in her mooth! Och, she's no' bad-lookin', but the laddie's no' bad himself, he could have his pick of Clancy's Lane.'

'That's no' fair, Aggie,' Kirsty Frielan defended her stoutly in a loud whisper. 'Peggy's a kind lassie. When my wee laddie nearly died of the meningitis last year, she nursed him day and night and pulled him through when the doctor gied up.'

'And she sat wi' me when I had my seventh.' A woman from the landing below Peggy's added her voice. 'Leave the lassie be. She's just a wee bittie funny in the heid.' She tapped her straggly hair. 'It's all that learnin', it addles yer brains, so it does.'

Peggy knew what was being said, but she bade them a polite goodnight and went her way wearily up the familiar cracked stairs. At the door she fumbled in the darkness, trying to put her key in the lock. 'In the name of the wee man! What the hell are you doing jumping out at folk in the dark?' Peggy gasped, shock making her tongue sharp as a figure stepped out of the shadows.

'I've been waiting here off and on for nearly five hours,' the stranger replied brusquely. 'Your neighbours are a right nosy lot! Are you Margaret Soutar?'

'Yes,' Peggy replied cautiously, frantically trying to think if she had broken any law or not paid her rent. He smacked of that kind of trouble.

'Did you come from Ayrshire?'

'Yes.' Her green eyes narrowed.

'Kirkowen?'

'Yes.'

'What's your full name?'

'Margaret Kirsten Soutar. But I can't imagine what it has to do with you!'

'Your father's name?'

'James Robert Soutar. Look, what is this all about?' Peggy was thoroughly worried.

'Then can I come in and talk to you, please, Miss Soutar?'

'I don't let strangers in. Talk to me out here.' She hoped somebody was in the Naughtons' and would come running if she screamed.

'No, I don't think you'll want that, when you see who I come from.' With a flourish, he showed her Sinclair's card, lit by the flickering light of a match. 'He's put a word or two on the back. Can ye read?'

'Of course I can.' Peggy peered at the graceful type then turned the card over. Reluctantly she held open the door.

'Miss Soutar is here, Mr Sinclair,' the lawyer's clerk announced in a hoarse, graveyard voice.

Despite the terrible map, Peggy arrived punctually at the office the following Tuesday afternoon, her half-day off from the tearoom.

'Show her in, McCurdy.' Sinclair got up, ready to be as reassuring as he could. 'The poor woman must be terrified, or at best totally overawed,' he hissed to the clerk.

'Aye, well, Mr Sinclair, I'm no' sure . . .' McCurdy began.

'Och, don't fuss, man,' the lawyer interrupted. 'I'll try not to make matters worse for her.' Carefully he formed his face into an unctuous smile and went to the office door.

'Ah, Miss Soutar, welcome to Ayr. I hope the journey wasn't too terrible . . .' The lawyer came forward busily then stopped short. This was no nervous working-class woman, but a person very much in control of herself and apparently totally at ease.

'How do you do, Mr Sinclair?' Peggy held out her hand with a confidence completely belying the shabby coat, ancient felt hat and well-worn boots.

'Er, do sit down, Miss Soutar.' He quickly regained his aplomb. 'I'm sorry to drag you all this way, but it is in your very best interest, I assure you of that, my dear Miss Soutar.'

'Indeed?' Peggy looked quizzical. 'I can't imagine why,

Mr Sinclair. The detective told me absolutely nothing. He seemed more interested in my father and my childhood than in explanations. Perhaps you instructed so?'

Good Lord! She's an educated woman and a bonnie one! Sinclair realised, becoming more bemused by the minute. Och, yes! A comforting solution came to mind. Her father was involved in the Miners' Union and then that dreadful Labour Party after the mother died. They're great ones for self-education and that sort of thing. Maybe she went to those godless Socialist Sunday Schools, or whatever they call the heathen things!

'I'm curious to know why you sought me out, Mr Sinclair,' Peggy said politely as he sought for an answer. With a calm movement, she folded her hands in her lap and waited expectantly.

'Naturally, naturally. I'll do my best to explain the situation,' he said briskly. 'Though it is unusual.'

'Thank you.' Peggy sat back in the chair as he began long-windedly to clarify the terms of Janet McClure's Will.

' . . . And so, Miss Soutar, Mrs McClure generously left a sum of money for you to serve an apprenticeship. You can chose any trade – within reason, of course,' the lawyer concluded pompously.

Peggy had listened expressionlessly as he spoke. When he finished she sat motionless for such a long time that Sinclair finally broke the silence himself.

'Oh, I know you must be overwhelmed by all this, Miss Soutar.' Nervously he rubbed his forehead. 'One hundred pounds per apprenticeship year for four years is a very generous bequest. But don't worry, you don't have to decide which trade now. You can come back next week. Or maybe you don't understand? It's a wee bittie complicated. Shall I go through it all again?'

'Oh, I understand all right, but I won't be coming back next or any week, Mr Sinclair,' Peggy said quietly. 'McClure money is tainted so far as I am concerned. I won't be bought like that. My mother bled to death in a snowy barn . . . like an animal . . . because of that family. So far as I am concerned, they can rot in hell, every one of them, together with their money. Restitution for Kirsty Soutar's stolen life

111

and Jamie Soutar's grief cannot be bought for four hundred pounds . . . or four thousand for that matter.' Deep colour flared in her pale cheeks, making her pretty face startlingly beautiful.

'But, Miss Soutar . . .' the lawyer protested, rising to his feet.

'Good day to you, Mr Sinclair. No, I can see myself out.' In seconds she was gone.

'Michty!' Sinclair mopped his brow, feeling as if he had been trodden on by a pair of Clydesdale cart-horses. 'Well, I suppose I'd better write to Elspeth McClure and tell her her fortune has just been increased by £100 per annum.' He picked up his pen and dipped it in the silver ink-pot.

Saturday was busy as ever in Miss Cranston's Willow Tearoom on Sauchiehall Street. Acting manageress Peggy Soutar kept alert, checking that everyone was being attended to. Miss Cranston was very particular about that, as she was about everything.

'Ellen, over there in the corner, dear. See if she's ready now.' She sent a girl for the second time to serve a young woman sitting alone, head bent over a book. A hat in the latest fashion shadowed her face.

'She'd just like a pot of tea. Och, she must be waiting for someone, Miss Soutar.' Ellen came back almost at once. 'I asked if she wanted some cakes, but she said she would have the tea first then maybe order something to eat later on.'

'Just bring the tea then, dear, and leave her in peace. I'll give you a nod if someone joins her, or if she starts to look around.'

Peggy was used to genteel, discreet assignations. Miss Cranston's elegant establishments were places where 'Mamas' allowed 'approved' meetings to take place. They knew young ladies would not get a bad name for being seen there with a suitable escort.

The tearoom emptied after the lunch-time rush. Tables were quickly cleared and reset in the lull before afternoon customers began arriving for high tea. After an hour or so, the young woman summoned Ellen and ordered more tea and finally some scones, then sat on, reading avidly, till there was no one left but the staff.

'Miss Soutar, the young lady says she wants to have a private word with you.' Ellen looked anxious. 'I haven't done anything, neither I have, Miss Soutar.'

'Oh, I'm sure you haven't, Ellen,' Peggy said reassuringly, but imagined it might be a delicate matter of a scone that wasn't perfectly shaped, not enough jam, or a tea-pot that hadn't been topped up instantly. Ellen was only fourteen, perhaps she had been inadvertently rude. 'I'll see to it. Now don't worry.' Peggy knew it was best to avoid any unpleasantness, Miss Cranston was always furious if a customer complained and was not dealt with instantly and courteously.

'What shall I do?' The little waitress hovered anxiously.

'Show her into the office, Ellen, I'll be there in a tick.' Peggy quickly totted up a bill and gave the last customer change. At once, the doorman opened the shining glass and oak doors and called a carriage.

'Can I help you?' Peggy politely asked the elegantly clad young woman who stood, back to her, in the office.

'I think so.' Slowly she turned round, showing the livid red mark which everyone noticed first before they saw the fine symmetrical features and glowing grey eyes. 'You are Margaret Soutar, I believe?'

'I am.' Peggy stiffened, instantly suspicious of the use of her full name for the second time in as many weeks.

'I am Elspeth McClure.' She held out her gloved hand.

'Miss McClure,' Peggy's voice was icy and she ignored the proffered hand. 'I don't know why you're here but I would like you to leave, please. I have nothing to say now, or at any time, to you . . . or to anyone who bears your name.'

'Please listen, Miss Soutar.' Elspeth dropped her hand and spoke urgently. 'I'll say what I have to as fast and as simply as I can. If you don't want to hear any more when I've finished, then I'll go without fuss and never bother you again. But let me speak, I beg you.'

Peggy looked at the earnest young woman standing in front of her, head proudly erect despite the disfigurement.

113

What on earth could have made her come? Curiosity won. 'Say what you have to, then go, please.'

'You turned down my mother's bequest because of what my father did to your family?'

Peggy nodded. 'What did you expect?'

'Just let me say this – the money was my mother's alone. It's McKelvie money not McClure. My father never owned nor earned a penny of it. And, Miss Soutar, he led my mother a life of cold hell because she gave him no heirs, only a useless, disfigured girl whom he could not even trade with advantage on the marriage market.' Elspeth's voice carried the note of bitter truth. 'The sight of me is anathema to him. And, by God, the feeling is mutual.'

Peggy felt the grey eyes compelling her to believe. Face expressionless, she listened as Elspeth hurried on.

'The day the Will was read, my father almost died of apoplexy! Within a few minutes, it seemed as if I was made free and the name Soutar thrust back into his life.'

'But why are you telling me this? I gave your lawyer my decision, Miss McClure,' Peggy broke in stiffly.

'I am trying to explain that if you hate him, then, you should take the bequest . . . even if you chose some strange trade and never practise it. Taxidermy, if you like! But, I beg you, take the money. It will drive a knife through my father's heart every day he lives, to know a Soutar benefits through his family, even indirectly.' Elspeth drew breath and then rushed on, 'He took me to court to deprive me of Mama's money and my independence, and almost won. It took the hatred he felt for your father to reveal his true nature in front of everyone. If you turn it down, he will have won, at least in part.' In a characteristically self-contained gesture, Elspeth leaned her back against the office wall and stood watching Peggy's reaction.

'Is this true?' She asked in a sharp, staccato tone. 'Now don't lie to me, Miss McClure!' This was no time for petty niceties.

'On my mother's soul.'

'Why did she do it?'

'She married when she was eighteen and he turned her existence into a lonely, barren waste. It wasn't only your

114

parents who suffered at my father's hands, nor those who live in misery in the mining rows and work for a pittance. We who were closest were also blighted.'

'You're still not answering my question,' Peggy insisted quietly. 'Why did your mother do this? There are mining charities which would be glad of the money.'

'It's not easy to explain, but I'm trying.' Elspeth took a deep breath. 'Miss Soutar, you and I were born within weeks of one another. I heard from my mother's own maid that in the sensitive time after my birth, it revolted Father even to see me. In her misery, Mama became obsessed with the parallel tragedy, the death of Kirsty Soutar . . . and hence the fate of her daughter. In later years this obsession grew to a torment. This legacy is both an attempt at restitution and the only revenge she could think of which would really hurt my father and go on hurting him, maybe forever.'

Peggy turned away and stood motionless for long, silent minutes, staring through the office window. Unseeing, she watched as the waitresses carefully placed cups and saucers on the white linen cloths. Finally, she swung round. 'I agree to take the bequest.' She sounded decisive and confident. 'But on one absolute and non-negotiable condition.'

'What condition?'

'That your lawyer allows the money to be used towards my training as a doctor. I want to take up a place in the medical school at Queen Margaret's College in October.'

'What did you say?' Elspeth McClure's pale face flushed, engulfing her mark. She took an involuntary step back.

'You heard,' Peggy said shortly. 'Oh, I'm sorry if I've shocked your genteel sensibilities,' her anger spilled out, 'but I believe women *should* become doctors. They are desperately needed. And, Miss McClure, I want to be among the first – maybe the very first – working women to become a medical graduate. I have the qualifications for the course already, but not the money.'

Elspeth stood still, not saying a word. Bitterly Peggy rushed on, 'Och, I see! For all your fine words, perhaps you would prefer to see me sewing gowns for you and your well-heeled friends instead?'

'Not at all! I was just taken totally by surprise. And why

115

should you have shocked me of all people?' Elspeth's face broke into a radiant smile. 'We'll be classmates!'

Mr Sinclair shook his head in utter disbelief. 'Och, no, Miss Elspeth. What on earth is this nonsense? A doctor? Margaret Soutar? Madness is a better word! What woman of her estate in life could even think of such a thing? It was bad enough when you decided to go ahead with the idea yourself. I've had an awful job with the Trustees. I had to persuade than it was just a fancy to study, not a career you would likely take up . . . but the daughter of a miner? Never!'

'This one can think of it, and she has. She's even got the right qualifications. They're better than mine!' Elspeth smiled at his discomfiture and astonishment. 'And I approve. The bequest is just big enough. Och, why not, Mr Sinclair?' Elspeth didn't approve of cajoling, but this was an exceptional situation. 'You're a fair man. I want to become a doctor, so why shouldn't she? The bequest doesn't state what kind of apprenticeship she should take. Medicine's as good a trade as any!'

'Hmmmm, I don't know about that!' Sinclair had strong private opinions on Elspeth's eccentricities, but with her brave spirit and sense of irony, she had worked her way into his affections over the last year or two. More and more he found himself seeing her point of view despite his natural reservations.

'Come on, what do you say?' Elspeth leaned forward, grey eyes compelling.

'Och, I admit the bequest is wide open as to the choice of occupation,' he said slowly. 'And since such a situation was not envisaged, approval lies simply with me.'

'So if you agree, then no one can legally stop her studying medicine if that's what she chooses?' Elspeth demanded.

'Aye.' He got up and wandered round the room thoughtfully, Elspeth's eyes following him every step of the way. 'Och, no, it's impossible!'

'It's not impossible, Mr Sinclair,' she insisted. 'You've said so yourself. And the sum was incredibly generous for an apprenticeship. In practical terms, it could cover the medical

116

school fees if they don't go up from the sum I showed you. Four hundred pounds for five years, wasn't it?'

'Aye, well . . .' he faltered.

'Yes. Say yes!' Elspeth encouraged. 'Mama would have wanted it, I'm sure she would.'

'Well, I have my doubts about that!' Despite himself a smile pulled at the corners of his mouth. 'Och, I suppose we could place the money in the bank.' He took refuge in hard figures. 'To be released in units coincidental with the payment of fees each year. In that way it could last five instead of the four years your mother imagined.'

'You agree then?' Elspeth was triumphant.

Sinclair stopped looking bewildered. 'Aye, I suppose I do, though reluctantly, I may say!' he qualified his decision. 'And the young lady must realise that there will not be one penny over the four hundred pounds available.' He went back to the desk and picked up the papers. 'And she'll have to realise that if she embarks on this unwise course, there won't be funds for books, clothes or equipment.'

Elspeth nodded. 'Yes, she knows that. I've said she can borrow my books, but she refused. "I'll use the lending libraries," she said. Apparently she still intends working part-time in the tearooms. I admire Peggy Soutar, Mr Sinclair, she is a very determined young woman.'

'Aye, and not the only one. Spare us from this terrible new generation of unladylike ladies! Wanting the vote as well, what next?' Sinclair muttered, but resignedly began to draw up the appropriate documents for Elspeth and the Trustees to sign. Hamish McClure will fall down in a choleric fit when he hears about this! Och, well, there's a silver lining to every cloud. The little lawyer allowed himself the pleasure of that uncharitable, but thoroughly enjoyable, thought.

Chapter 10
Here's a hand my trusty friend

Clutching her worn satchel, Peggy stood looking at the notice-board, trying to find where her lectures were being held. All around, long skirts swishing, the young women of Queen Margaret's College hurried into lectures, chattering and laughing. QMC buzzed with pride and confidence.

'What is it, hen?' An officious porter hurried up. 'If yer looking for the kitchen, just go round the back to the staff entrance, ye'll see it right away.' He waved across the courtyard.

'No, thanks.' Peggy smiled ironically. 'I'm a medical student, looking for the lecture room.'

'A medical student? Are ye sure, hen?' The man gawped, taking in her shabby clothes and boots.

'I'm sure.'

'Aye, well, over in that building then.'

'Thanks.'

As he watched her go, head held high, he scratched his head in bewilderment. Medical student, imagine that! Are they sending paupers to university these days?

'You will need determination to succeed and dedication beyond anything you have so far experienced in life,' the Principal warned the six women medical students. 'Whatever you have done before will be insignificant in comparison with what is ahead of you. Historically, physicians have had a special place in society, but female physicians have still to take their place in history. You will be walking along a trail, blazed but not yet well-trodden, by the few brave women who have preceded you in entering this great profession.

Make sure you are a credit to them and an inspiration to those who will follow you.'

Peggy sat apart from the others during the welcome speech. Covertly she looked around her. I knew I'd stick out like a sore thumb, she thought. She glanced down at her well-washed cotton blouse, knitted cardigan and cheap grey calico skirt, trying not to let them matter.

During a brief break later in the morning the six women introduced themselves. Three were straight from school, daughters of missionaries. 'The Church of Scotland Mission funds are supporting our candidature,' they explained like a Greek chorus. 'We will be going back to India as soon as we are qualified.'

Three wise monkeys. No chance of them straying from the Paths of Righteousness anyway! Peggy kept the uncharitable thought to herself.

By tactic agreement, neither she nor Elspeth admitted they knew each other. Peggy mumbled her name to the group as a whole and refused to look the other woman in the eye.

'I'm Fiona Moffat.' The sixth woman, who was about Elspeth and Peggy's age, spoke brightly, trying to cover her shaking hands and obvious nervousness.

'Moffat? Are you related to Alexander Moffat?' Elspeth warmed to Fiona at once and tried to put her at her ease.

'Yes, he's my papa.' The young woman relaxed at Elspeth's kind tone. Alexander Moffat was a well-known physician of radical attitudes and comfortable means. 'He was so pleased I decided to take up medicine after finishing school, he helped in every possible way. Tutors, books, everything . . .'

Lucky Fiona Moffat. Peggy felt a stab of bitter resentment against all of these women, comfortable in their middle-class cocoons and so certain of their future.

'And you're Margaret Soutar, isn't that right? I wasn't sure I caught your name when you introduced yourself,' Fiona said shyly to the shabby woman, sitting apart, pointedly reading some notes.

'Yes.' Peggy looked up. 'My name is on the class-list!' she

119

replied more rudely than she'd intended. Fiona recoiled, but said nothing.

'Good morning, ladies.' The lecturer bustled in and work began again.

Och, I knew I would be the odd one out before I came. Not that I care a bent bawbee anyway! Peggy felt angry at herself for not handling the situation better. It's just daft to bother what folk think. My fees are guaranteed. I've as much right to be here as any of them ... Och, but it's a shame Hughie took it so hard. I never meant to hurt him.

The night before she had finally blurted out to him that she was starting medical school next day. 'I'm really sorry,' she'd said as horrified incredulity dawned on his good-looking face. 'I'd have told you before, but I didn't think you'd understand, Hughie.'

'And you think I understand now?' He looked at her as if she had struck him. 'How could ye do this to me, Peggy? Ye've led me on all these years, hopin' for ye, waitin' for ye. I've just come out of my time. I was plannin' for us, so I was. And all the bloody while ye had this up yer sleeve! A doctor? I've never heard the like, neither I have!' He shook his head as if trying to wake up from a nightmare.

'I didn't think I'd make it ... I never expected to get the money ... it was just a dream ... then this happened with the bequest like I said ... and I've never said I'd marry you.' Peggy tried to explain, to defend herself.

'Aye, but ye kenned I was waitin' for ye, wantin' ye. What was I suppose to be, a spare in case ye were stuck on the shelf?' Suddenly his eyes filled with tears. Seeing his sorrow, Peggy felt more distressed than if he had shouted or yelled. 'And now yer dream's come true, hasn't it?' Hughie went on bitterly. 'And where does that leave me, eh? I'll tell ye, Peggy, it leaves me exactly nowhere! Ye'll never marry me now, will ye? Doctor Peggy Soutar! Who the hell would have imagined that? Christ!' He blundered out and she heard the door slam next door, then nothing.

Afterwards she slept badly; nerves and the aftermath of Hughie's incredulous reaction kept her awake. For hours she lay gazing at the cracked ceiling of the single-end, thinking about the next day, as the noises of the tenement slowly died down. If they turn up their noses at me in Queen Margaret's College, so what? I've neither time for friendships nor the need to be accepted, she told herself firmly before falling into a troubled sleep.

'Elspeth McClure! Dear girl, how wonderful!'

'Mhaire MacPherson!' Elspeth was delighted to see a familiar face from Miss Lovat's as the class broke for lunch.

'So you made it?' Mhaire embraced her.

'Of course! I always said I would, once I got out of the terrible finishing school in Châtillon. Establishments like that are a curse to thinking women! How is your own degree coming along?'

'Oh, fine, this is my last year.'

'Then what?'

'Teaching, I suppose. Miss Lovat has asked me to come for my probationary year to her. Naturally I'd love to. Are you going to the refectory?'

'I think so.' Elspeth nodded cheerfully. 'Though I'm not entirely sure where it is ... Oh, and this is Fiona Moffat who is on my course. Fiona, meet Mhaire MacPherson.'

'How do you do, Fiona?' Mhaire welcomed the new girl. 'Come on, I'll initiate the pair of you.' Laughing and exchanging news, the three young women headed off. Briefly Elspeth glanced around for Peggy, but she was nowhere to be seen.

The relationship between the two Ayrshire women was loaded with unanswered questions and restraints. Worse still, Peggy held herself apart from everyone, not just Elspeth. Anyone who tried approaching her had their head bitten off. After a tense week, Elspeth decided to act. The warm friendships of Miss Lovat's had been her own salvation and she was determined to break down the barriers that Peggy had so resolutely built around herself.

'Are you on your way to the library?' She cornered Peggy after class at the end of a gruelling first week.

'Yes, I told you I'd have to use the college books,' Peggy replied distantly and made to pass.

'Good, then you can show me where it is!' Elspeth's long legs easily kept up with her smaller companion's. 'I had to leave straight away each evening this week. Suffrage meetings, you know. We had a special series of lectures in the Kelvin Hall. But now I'll be able to study here sometimes after class. Where exactly is it located?'

Peggy was trapped neatly. 'Haven't you got all the books you need at home then?' she snapped.

'Most but not all, Margaret. May I call you Margaret?' Elspeth smiled disarmingly.

'It's Peggy! Och, I'll show you if you like.' Her acquiescence was grudging.

'Thank you ... Peggy.' Elspeth smiled again. 'What do you think of the refectory?' she asked casually as they crossed the courtyard. 'I looked for you once or twice but couldn't see you. Of course, it's a big room.'

'I haven't been.' Peggy's reply was abrupt.

'Oh, where do you eat?' Elspeth asked without thinking, then could have bitten off her tongue.

'I bring a piece and eat in the Kelvin Park, it's cheaper.' Peggy's chin lifted, defying the other girl to comment.

'Listen, Peggy,' Elspeth was determined to clear the air, 'I don't intend mentioning to anybody about the link between the two of us.'

'Which link, the old or the new?' Peggy's face was inscrutable and her tone expressionless.

'Either for that matter. It's nobody's business but ours.'

'Good.' The answer gave little away, but Elspeth felt at last she had said the right thing.

'What do you think of the course so far?' That, she prayed, must be safe ground.

'Too soon to tell.' Peggy considered the question seriously. 'The syllabus looks well planned, but I'm a bit concerned about the practical side of things. If we are only allowed access to the West End annex of the Glasgow Maternity Hospital and a few other general practice clinics, how can we possibly compete on equal terms with the men at Glasgow University's male medical school when it comes to exams?' Her tone was scathing.

'You're right! Our clinical experience is going to be far more limited than that of the men,' Elspeth agreed. 'Did you see the article about it in the *Glasgow Herald*? It was good stuff. Maybe they'll relent before our finals. They're five years away.'

'Possible but unlikely,' retorted Peggy. 'Men give up none of their privileges without a struggle.'

'Are you interested in women's rights?' Elspeth stopped and looked at her questioningly. 'I'm in the Scottish Women's Suffrage Society.'

'Obviously I believe in the right of women to study and take up a profession or I wouldn't be here,' Peggy replied dryly and walked on. 'Instead, I'd be working in a tobacco factory at the Saltmarket . . . or scrubbing floors in some big house like Bargeddie!' The words flew like darts over her shoulder.

'Why don't you join one of our groups?' Elspeth refused to rise to the bait. 'I hold women's suffrage meetings in my house every weekend. You could come to one of them and see how you feel.'

Elspeth's enthusiasm sounded genuine even to Peggy's jaundiced ear, but she answered curtly: 'Sorry, no.'

'We have some excellent speakers,' Elspeth pressed on, 'and usually finish up with an outdoor meeting. They can be really exciting. Christabel Pankhurst comes up when she has the time. Have you heard of her?'

'I've heard,' Peggy grunted, unimpressed.

'And Helen Fraser, Margaret Billington . . . all the crowd from Glasgow try to come. Folk from Edinburgh as well. There's a fine suffrage group over there that I've known since my schooldays.' She touched Peggy's shoulder tentatively. 'Oh, do come along. The meetings are lots of fun as well as worthwhile and interesting.'

'I don't think I would fit in among your middle-class friends.' Peggy drew away and glanced down at her shabby clothes. 'Twice this week already I've been directed to the kitchens or the housekeeper's room by the porters. You haven't, have you?' She looked pointedly at Elspeth's elegant brown skirt and high-necked, tucked and embroidered cream blouse, edged with fine broderie anglaise.

'Oh, clothes don't matter among suffragettes,' she insisted. 'It's not a tea party, Peggy! We are women fighting for a serious cause, not a meeting of the Parish Guild. Anyway

123

in England some of the best people are from the working class. Take Annie Kenny . . . maybe you've heard of her too? She's a factory girl from Manchester but stands shoulder to shoulder on the platform with Mrs Pankhurst, a woollen shawl over her hair.'

'How picturesque,' Peggy replied in a sardonic tone. 'Clothes and appearances may not matter to you, but then you're not the odd man out.'

'Peggy, do you know what you're saying?' Elspeth touched the livid mark on her cheek. 'We're all odd in our own way.'

'Sorry, Elspeth.' Peggy used the other woman's name spontaneously for the first time as she realised her faux-pas and flushed as red as her hair. 'Och, I just haven't the time,' she went on, sounding less belligerent. 'I have to work at Miss Cranston's at weekends to pay for my rent and the books I can't borrow from QMC. So, no thanks. Anyway, here we are, this is the library.'

The women fell silent as they entered the huge dim room. Peggy went to work at once, while Elspeth made her way to the desk to get a lending card and be instructed in the use of the facilities. At nine o'clock, eyes stinging with tiredness, she rose stiffly and collected her coat. Turning at the door she lifted her hand to wave to Peggy, but dropped it again. Oblivious of everything else, the young woman sat deeply engrossed in her studies. She would be working at Miss Cranston's all day Saturday and helping with the baking on Sunday. She had to finish almost all her work that night before the library closed at ten.

With deliberate patience, Elspeth McClure wore down Peggy's habitual wall of resistance as they met day by day. It was not in her nature to give up easily, and anyway she genuinely liked and admired Peggy. From their very first meeting in Miss Cranston's, Elspeth had recognised a kindred, free and independent spirit in the miner's daughter. Most of all Elspeth had no reason to hate the Soutar name, unlike Peggy who had every justification to detest the McClures.

'Peggy, don't go off on your own all the time. We must

124

stick together, especially in the clinics, or the men will walk all over us.' Elspeth began applying overt pressure.

'I'm not the pally kind!' Peggy refused to give way.

'That's nothing to do with it,' Elspeth insisted. 'There's only the six of us. "United we stand, divided we fall"!'

'Hmmm . . .' Peggy shrugged, but after a while began to see the sense in Elspeth's argument. The women were barely tolerated at times in the clinics and hospitals. Och, I suppose she's right, we have to support one another or we're sunk come the exams! Peggy had to make excuses to herself as she slowly capitulated and became less standoffish under Elspeth's unrelenting onslaught. But it was still hard to see her as the person she was, not just the daughter of Jamie Soutar's worst enemy.

A crisis came towards the end of their second year when some of the serious laboratory and clinical work began.

'Oh, I see you and I are partnered, Peggy.' Elspeth looked at the board. 'That means we'll be together in labs all this month. Good, you're so much better than me. I'll learn twice as much!'

'Och, are we?' For a moment Peggy thought of asking one of the others to change.

'Listen, Peggy, there's something I want to say.' Elspeth sensed her hesitation. No one else was around and she resolved to speak her mind. 'You are being asked to partner Elspeth McClure, not her father. Will you stop punishing me for something I am innocent of? It hurts, Peggy! It really hurts!'

Peggy flushed and looked down at her worn boots.

Elspeth went on: 'You have reason to hate my father, but be fair, Peggy, what have I ever done against you?' Peggy stared intently at the noticeboard. 'Look, I'm offering you my friendship,' Elspeth went on doggedly. She held out a slim hand. 'This is mine not his, please take it. If you refuse, you refuse me not him.'

Peggy slowly turned towards the other woman, who held her gaze without flinching. Elspeth's intelligent grey eyes were quizzical and vulnerable at the same time. Suddenly Jamie's last words came back to her: 'If the hand of true friendship is extended, don't ever turn away. Judge folk for

125

what they are themselves, not where they come from.' Would he have included McClure's daughter? Peggy thought of her father, of his just and generous nature. With a deep sigh, she finally raised her hand and took Elspeth's. 'I'll try to accept what you are offering,' she said quietly. 'Please forgive my lack of experience, I'm not much used to friendship.'

With each subsequent year it grew easier, until without noticing Peggy had accepted Elspeth's compelling, enthusiastic personality as a natural part of her life. Rarely now did she think of her connection with Hamish McClure. Anyway, up to the elbows in blood and gore in theatre, dissecting corpses or learning to deliver babies in dreadful conditions, there was no place for barriers.

'God, that clinic is an abomination!' Elspeth mopped her brow as much in reaction to their experience as to the June heat. 'Come on or we'll miss the tram.' The little group left their practical session and straggled back wearily towards town.

'At least the clinic exists . . . that's progess,' Peggy reflected as they stood at the tramstop in a huddle. 'Years ago those women got no care at all. Prostitutes, or the poorest of the poor, or lassies thrown out of service pregnant . . . they were just left destitute and died in the streets having their bairns.'

'But there's not even a doctor in charge.' Fiona Moffat shook her head in disgust. 'One visiting nurse and a bunch of half-trained midwives just isn't enough.'

'The ILP is fighting for an improvement in conditions like those,' Elspeth broke in, then turned to Peggy. 'I know you're busy getting miraculous marks, miles ahead of everyone else, but I'm still surprised you're not more active in politics?'

'Och, I've told you till I'm black in the face, Elspeth,' Peggy bantered back in another example of the lively sparring that had grown between them, 'I was brought up on Socialist Soup by my father, but it killed him in the end and I'd prefer to last a while longer.' A weary grin lit up her face. 'Maybe the Socialists are right enough in their ideas, but for the time being I'll leave working-class politics to rich middle-class folk like yourself.'

126

'Peggy Soutar, sometimes I think you're just an inverted snob!' Elspeth riposted.

'There could be something in that!' She nodded with a smile. 'But what on earth do folk like you, Helen Fraser, and your other suffragette friends who dabble in politics, really know about the lives of working people? I mean, really know! If you lot are the face of today's socialism, forget it!'

'Oh, you stubborn, pig-headed woman! That's why you should be in there telling us! Anyway, what on earth are you on about "face of today's socialism"?' Elspeth snorted. 'The ILP is full of ordinary people like your own father. And surely you're not trying to call his old friend Keir Hardie, who is an absolute pillar of the movement, middle-class?'

'No, but the whole movement is hoaching with genteel do-gooders.'

'Come on, Peggy, be fair,' Elspeth protested. 'It's only the Fabian Society and groups like that you can accuse of not being working-class. And what's so wrong with being middle-class, Peggy Soutar? If you become a doctor, the very people you identify with just now will call you that too!'

'Oh, michty me! I hadn't thought of that!' Peggy gasped, and the rest of the group doubled up with laughter at her aghast expression.

'So, Miss Soutar,' Elspeth went on relentlessly, 'are you coming or aren't you?'

'God, how you go on, woman! You know I'm not,' Peggy groaned. 'I'm far too busy.'

'Well, how about joining the WSPU? You don't have to take part in everything we do.' Elspeth was like a blood-hound following a favourite scent.

'The what?' Peggy pretended ignorance.

'Don't wriggle! You know as well as I do – the Women's Social and Political Union.'

'Elspeth, I've told you, I don't want to get involved.' Peggy shrugged. 'My one goal right now is to get my degree with as good marks as I am capable of. Maybe when I finish there might be time for other things.'

'Not if you think of the hours newly qualified doctors work,' sighed Fiona. 'Especially residents. What are you going to do, Peggy?'

'Well, I won't be heading off for India, like those three.' Peggy nodded in the direction of the younger women who were rushing off to a Bible meeting. 'I'd have thought they could find enough squalor and poverty here in these clinics without having to look for it on the plains of the Punjab.'

'True.' Fiona smiled. 'But I hadn't really imagined you would go to the missions . . . your views on religion would shock even my father! What then?'

'I want a couple of years' residency in a city hospital, get as much experience as I can, then maybe try for a position of responsibility in an Infirmary.'

'Impossible . . . or nearly.' Elspeth shook her head. 'Women never get promotion, not even in Poor Law Infirmaries. I hate to say this, but it will be a miracle if you even get a residency unless you know someone.'

'Defeatist talk, Elspeth! Isn't equal rights what you are supposed to be fighting for with the WSPU?'

'Yes, we are, but it takes time.'

'Well, I may not be willing to join you, Elspeth, but if I get good results, I'll have the weapons to fight prejudice in my own way. I'll damn' well beat them at their own game.'

'What if you get married?' Fiona looked at her pretty colleague. Shabby or not, Peggy turned heads, though she consistently repelled male advances.

'Married? No, I don't expect to.' Peggy tossed her bright head. 'Men are fine, but not for me. I want to stay free.'

'One more thing we agree on,' Elspeth laughed. 'Oh, do come to a meeting . . . just one, Peggy,' she coaxed. 'You'd love it.'

'All the more reason why not. Anyway, here's my tram, I'm off to the physiology lab for some extra practice. Anyone coming?'

'No.' Fiona shook her head. 'I'll wait for the next tram, it goes to the centre. I'm exhausted after the clinic. My God, some of those poor women. And what conditions do they go home to?' she sighed. 'If they have homes.'

'I can tell you if you have the time to listen?' Peggy said

128

quietly, as she stood back waiting for the passengers to get off.

'Please don't, Peggy. I don't think I can take any more today.' Fiona mopped her brow. 'Oh dear, I hope I've the stamina for this work.'

'Of course you have.' Elspeth gave her a sharp nudge. 'No back-sliding, Moffat!' The women encouraged each other through moments of doubt and difficulty. 'It's just this heat, and we're tired, all of us.' She dragged at the stiff, unyielding collar of her heavy day-dress. 'Well, I've a pamphlet to write, so I'd better get home and get on with it. Don't forget the special lecture tomorrow, Peggy!'

'As if I would!' she grinned and jumped on to the platform. Like a beacon, her red head bobbed towards the front seats, away from the pall of pipe smoke at the back.

'Cheers, lads! Watch the wee birdies! Tweet! Tweet!' Next day a wave of guffaws and ribald comments greeted the six women as they joined the male students in Glasgow University's main medical school. QMC women were usually allowed to listen to important visiting lecturers. They took the opportunity eagerly, despite the invariable gauntlet of verbal abuse.

'Leading the fillies in the field is Little Miss Moffat and the evangelising sisters!' a wag bawled as, red with embarrassment, Fiona and the three younger women filed in first.

'Isn't it amazing how gentlemanly manners never seem to apply within the jealously guarded portals of a male-dominated university?' Elspeth remarked loudly and sarcastically.

'Oh, look, chaps, bringing up the rear as usual we have Cinderella and the Ugly Sister,' a languid voice drawled from the back of the vast room. Laughter rose to a roar.

'You'd think they'd come up with something new. That's the second time we've heard that one,' Peggy whispered to Elspeth as they found a place together near the front.

'Och, they don't bother us, the silly laddies, do they?' Elspeth shrugged.

'No! As long as we can hear the lecturer, who cares?' Peggy agreed. 'Look at them, packed like stale bread in a pig-bin.' In the boisterous, boyish traditions of medical students, the men had crowded into the back benches of the terraced lecture hall where they could disrupt things if the lecturer failed to keep them entertained. 'I just hope they shut up when he starts, though they should this time with Professor McCall – I've heard he can be a right terror.'

'Oh, well,' Elspeth hissed. 'The little lambies need something to pass the time. Most of them don't do much else but go to the races and prop up the bars!'

Silence fell immediately Professor McCall entered. He was a specialist in the relatively new field of anaesthesia and commanded great respect. Peggy sat totally enthralled as he explained the development of chloroform and the recent advances being made in its use and application.

' . . . And the medical profession's need for and use of anaesthesia is virtually boundless, both in times of peace and in war. It has already revolutionised surgery and even childbirth, though it is not yet widespread in this field.' He dismissed that application, then went on with more enthusiasm, 'The South African War at present raging has shown anaesthesia's vital use in another great and terrible arena. Gentlemen and, er, ladies, it is up to you, the aspirant members of this profession, to nurture and increase the applications and use of anaesthesia in the future.'

Professor McCall sat down to a round of ear-splitting applause. 'Questions, gentlemen . . . oh, and ladies too, of course.' He bowed courteously towards the small huddle of women.

'Will there be other types of anaesthesia freely available soon in your opinion, Professor, or is chloroform enough?' The languid voice drifted from the back again, but this time far more respectfully.

'In the light of past experience, one discovery invariably leads to another, young man . . . McBride isn't it?'

'Yes, sir.'

'Hmm, know your father. Spent some time abroad myself. Fine man. Hope you'll be half as good a doctor as he was a soldier!'

Peggy raised her hand. 'Yes?' Professor McCall's brows rose in surprise.

'Chloroform has been available for some time, and the Queen herself was among the first to benefit from its use in childbirth.' Peggy's voice rang out clearly. 'But we have seen little evidence of its use in the clinics and hospitals we have visited and worked in, Professor.'

'Ah, well, young lady . . . Miss . . . er . . .' Professor McCall began with an avuncular smile.

'Soutar.'

'Miss Soutar. Female students, as we both know, are limited in practice to certain hospitals. Perhaps those establishments are somewhat less advanced than others in Glasgow. But I can assure you that chloroform is certainly in use in the larger women's clinics, even on occasion in childbirth. Any more questions?' He looked beyond her up at the rows of men.

Irritated by his condescension, Peggy cut in again without waiting to be asked, 'But do you not think, Professor, that its use would be even more appropriate in the run-down places we are allowed to visit?' Ignoring a warning nudge in the ribs from Fiona Moffat as the Professor's brow darkened, she rushed on, 'Many of these women have deformed pelvises from rickets brought about by poor diet. Their suffering in childbirth is often terrible and increases the mortality rate greatly among both mothers and babies. Chloroform could help by relaxing the pelvic muscles and, of course, simply ease the pain.'

'It is not for me to discuss the provisions of health care in the City of Glasgow with students, young lady,' McCall replied dourly. 'There are only limited funds available. Training personnel in the adminstration of chloroform is expensive.'

'And human life is not?'

'Madam!' The Professor was shocked and offended. 'Kindly leave the room at once.'

Amidst deathly silence Peggy stood up. 'Professor McCall, I do not wish to leave because your lecture so far, and what you have still to say, is very important to me in my desire to be a good doctor. If I have offended you, I apologise.'

The Professor still looked annoyed. He was known to detest being contradicted . . . and by a woman! The men sat in silent, avid rows enjoying every minute of Peggy's imminent total humiliation. If McCall threw her out, she would have to make a public apology through the board of governors before being allowed into any lecture at all and could be asked to quit the faculty altogether. 'It will take more than a quick apology, young woman!' The Professor's face hardened and Peggy's heart sank further.

'Cinderella is about to be turned into a pumpkin,' Robert McBride hissed to his neighbour, Douglas Munro.

Elspeth stood up. 'My name is Elspeth McClure. Please try to understand, Professor McCall,' she spoke with a confidence gained on a hundred suffrage platforms, 'we female sudents hear all too few specialists and your contribution is exceptionally interesting. Forgive Miss Soutar for being carried away. It might have been any of us who accidentally trangressed because of our genuine enthusiasm. I throw us all on your mercy and condescension.'

Embarrassed, he looked at the two women standing shoulder to shoulder, one pretty but terribly shabby, the other expensively clad with understated elegance in a fine grey dress with a neat lace collar. Pity about the birthmark, she's otherwise quite handsome, he thought as so many had before him. For a few long minutes silence reigned, then gallantry won. 'All right, I accept your apology, Miss Soutar. You may stay this time.' He bowed graciously. 'But kindly never doubt my respect for human life. It is the prime motivation of every doctor, whether the patient be rich or poor.'

Peggy murmured a thank you and sat down, nodding in numb gratitude to Elspeth, shaken by the nearness of catastrophe. But her thoughts were still mutinous. Respect is one thing, giving equal treatment another. It's true all the same, what I said! Diplomatically this time she kept her opinion to herself.

'Bit too clever for your own good, eh, Cinders?' Robert McBride's Edinburgh public-school drawl stopped her halfway down the corridor. The other students had dispersed immediately the lecture ended, but she had stayed on reading extra notes made from the professor's blackboard scribblings and charts.

'Have you nothing better to do, Mr McBride, than to talk such nonsense?' she said icily. 'I'm surprised you're still here. You're usually first in the bar, from what I've heard.'

'Well, I prefer bars to tearooms, certainly.' His dark eyes laughed at her. 'Still serving shortbread and scones, Cinders?' Robert McBride had come in to Miss Cranston's with some friends the week before. After his initial jolt of surprise at seeing her working there, surprisingly he'd said nothing then or since, until now.

'I'll be working at the Willow till I graduate,' she replied steadily, 'though it's hardly any of your business.'

'It could be.' The teasing dark eyes took in her neat figure, green eyes and glowing red hair.

'Mr McBride, you are presumptuous and overfamiliar,' she snapped. 'One more remark like that and I'll report you.'

'To whom and for what?' he drawled. 'Come, come Cinders, I don't know how you're paying for being here, but it's clearly not from working weekends in a tearoom. Some of the men think you're being ... now how can I put it delicately? Oh, yes ... sponsored.'

'No man alive, nor woman either, is paying for my studies, McBride.' Peggy's eyes flashed emerald fire. 'Tell your fine friends that! Now, if you don't mind, I'm trying to get to the library.' She pushed past.

'Peggy!' He caught her arm, still smiling wickedly. 'Why not come with me to the theatre and have supper afterwards? Or just afternoon tea if you prefer, eh?'

'Not even for a glass of water if I was dying of thirst in the desert!' Wresting herself free, she marched angrily along the corridor and out of the door, the picture of outraged fury.

Pity she's from the gutters. Robert McBride, only son of the Empire's most decorated Brigadier, shrugged. I could have enjoyed having her hanging on my arm – and more. Dressed in something better than those rags, of course. He watched as the well-worn coat and hat bobbed indignantly across the street.

'What are you grinning at, Rob?' Douglas Munro asked as his friend caught up with him in the courtyard.

'Thinking of how Cinders would look at the Ball.'

'Oh, give the girl a break, man. It can't be easy for her, or for any of them for that matter.' Douglas sounded uncharacteristically sharp and his cheerful face was flushed.

'Never thought of you as the female emancipation type, Dougie Munro.' Rob dug him in the ribs. 'If I didn't know your tastes ran more to actresses, I'd say you were soft on one of our intellectual ladies. Who is it then, Little Miss Moffat? I can't believe it's the Ugly Sister!'

'None of them,' Douglas replied. 'Just being fair, that's all. And as for actresses, that was all your idea. Supper after the show . . .'

'But you didn't object when the show went on after supper!' Rob laughed.

'Now why should I do that?' Douglas said with mock solemnity. 'As budding doctors, it's our duty never to flinch, even in the face of that naughty new French dance.'

'Oh, la, la! The Can can,' Robert chortled. 'Wonder what the Ugly Sister and her suffragette friends would say to that?'

'I can guess.'

'Or Cinders. Quite the little prude. Pity . . .' Rob said with a meaningful leer.

'You're not trying . . .' Douglas looked astonished.

'Why not? She's not bad-looking despite the rags. I'm working on breaching the "I'm just an honest working-girl" resistance. It's a challenge, Dougie, and you know I can't resist a challenge!' His dark eyes danced. 'Want to bet on me getting there . . . quite dishonourably, of course?'

'I think she might be a lot harder to get in to bed than your actresses, Rob.' Douglas smiled and answered in kind, but suddenly the brave slight figure of Peggy as she stood defying the professorial might flashed into his mind's eye and the words soured in his mouth. 'But, no, my friend, no bet.' He walked on, leaving Robert McBride looking thoughtfully after him.

Chapter 11

The rank is but the guinea's stamp

'Doctors at last . . . or almost!' The six women hugged each other when the lists went up and they had all graduated successfully.

'Margaret Kirsten Soutar, First Class Honours. You're a genius!' Fiona Moffat was lavish in her praise and the rest agreed. Peggy had achieved the highest marks of any woman so far in Scotland.

Three weeks later they attended the graduation ceremony and met as a group for the last time. Peggy hadn't wanted to come, but the others pleaded solidarity so strongly she could hardly refuse. Faced with insurmountable costs and no hiring facilities, she reluctantly approached the QMC governors who loaned her robes for the day. Peggy's results were too good for the college not to flaunt. No one came to see her receive the diploma and Elspeth happily relieved her of extra guest tickets.

'Elspeth Janet McClure, Lower Second,' the Principal announced. Elspeth was delighted with her solid but unspectacular degree. Four of her closest suffrage friends sat in the family seats, clapping enthusiastically as she went up. Another half a dozen waited outside the hall, cheering and chanting 'Votes for Women!' till they were evicted from the University grounds amid jeers.

'Oh, there you are, Peggy!' Elspeth searched anxiously in the crowds after the ceremony was over and caught her as she was slipping out of the gates. 'Have you seen Fiona?'

'Yes, I've just said goodbye. She's over there by the stairs.'

135

'Listen,' Elspeth linked her arm, 'can you come round to my house this evening? I must talk to you.'

'Not this evening.' Peggy shook her head. 'I have to work.'

'My God, woman.' Elspeth gawped at her. 'You have just swept the board! Highest commendations possible for clinical. Honours for your anaesthesia papers, which are murder . . . and for written work too. You can't serve scones tonight! Please come home and have high tea served to you for a change?'

'I can't,' Peggy insisted.

'Look, I'll send somebody round to Miss Cranston's with an excuse, so you don't have to tell the lies yourself. Come on, the WSPU women are organising a celebration dinner. We can both be quests of honour.'

'Elspeth, I confess it's really tempting,' Peggy sighed, 'but I have to work today to eat tomorrow. Miss Cranston would guess I was skiving off, especially on graduation day. It would be too obvious.' She shrugged. 'I can't risk losing my job while I have nothing else to go to. But I'll come tomorrow about two-thirty if that suits you? I'm free then.'

'Oh, all right, I'll be there.' Elspeth knew there was no point in arguing but added with an anxious, enigmatic smile, 'There is something quite important to discuss.'

'Fine . . . and intriguing. Till tomorrow then.'

'Tomorrow.' Elspeth waved and ran to join her WSPU friends outside the gates. Hair escaping from its neat chignon, grey eyes glowing, she felt on top of the world.

'What are you going to do now, Peggy?' Elspeth asked as they sat comfortably next day in her sitting-room. Outside the handsome bow window, a giant horse chestnut waved huge pink candles in the gentle summer breeze.

'Well . . .' Peggy began, then stopped as Libby knocked sharply at the door.

'Are ye ready for tea?' she demanded in her rhetorical way and carried in the inevitable laden tray.

'Oh, yes. Thanks, Libby, just leave it there.' Elspeth pointed towards the sideboard.

'Och, I'd better pour or you'll just let the tea go cold. Ye always do, Miss Elspeth. And they scones are fresh off the griddle.' The housekeeper fussed round, setting out little plates of home-made cakes and sandwiches and pouring tea from a fine Chinese willow pattern pot into delicate matching cups.

'Thanks, Libby, your scones rival Miss Cranston's best any day.' Smiling, Peggy took the proffered cup.

'Och, that's nice of ye! And ye did very well in they exams, I heard, Miss Peggy . . . or should I say Doctor Peggy now?' From the outset, Libby had taken a proprietorial interest in Elspeth's odd friend. It was to the older woman's credit that she'd accepted Peggy without a moment's hesitation. Never once had she sniffed at the idea of serving Jamie Soutar's daughter tea in the sitting-room, just like all Miss Elspeth's other friends.

'Thanks, Libby. Och, it's been a long road, and the journey's not over yet. And you can call me exactly what you like, though we really should do our MDs before we use the title Doctor. Without that it's just courtesy,' Peggy explained.

'Och, courtesy fiddlesticks! Ye've all worked hard enough to have earned it! It'll be Doctor Peggy from now on, so it will,' Libby said decisively. 'I like the sound of that.'

'Me too!' Peggy replied from the heart.

'Well, what are you going to do?' Elspeth repeated once Libby had gone.

'Apply, apply and reapply to all the Scottish hospitals. Try to get a residency. But it's very hard. You know what they're like about accepting a woman.'

'It's not obligatory yet to do a residency, Peggy, though they're talking about making it so. You could go straight into general practice, or to a Poor Law Infirmary without one. I thought you wanted to be out there helping the poor to get fair treatment?' Elspeth teased gently. 'At least you'd have an income, though not a very high one.'

'I don't want to start in a Poor Law Infirmary,' Peggy replied. 'I'll likely end up in one but only once I am eligible for promotion, which means I need to have completed a residency. Do you think a Poor Law doctor should be the limit of my ambitions, Elspeth?' she said with more than a touch of her old acid tone.

'Oh, for goodness' sake, you know me better than that by

now, you daft woman!' Elspeth refused to respond in kind. 'I only meant that now Mama's bequest is finished, you will have to get some work that pays enough to keep you. A residency just about would, but no more than that . . . if you can find one.'

'Och, I'll find one.' Peggy hid her tense, set mouth behind her cup. She replaced it gently on the saucer with a tiny tinkle. 'I want to do a post-graduate qualification, first the Doctor of Medicine, then maybe a diploma in Public Health, so I must get a residency . . .'

'You're going to be pretty poor for a long time yet then.' Elspeth shook her head. 'Post-graduate study charges will be just about covered by what you earn. Aren't you fed up scrimping and living off next to nothing? I admire you, Peggy, but I couldn't do it year after year.'

Peggy looked down at her well-worn outfit and many-times repaired boots. 'You've never had to, that's why. I've never known anything else, Elspeth. I'll manage. Anyway how about you?'

'Christabel Pankhurst wants me to move to England for a while to be near the centre of the suffragette movement. They're well established in Manchester and we're dug in up here, but the WSPU is planning to escalate the campaign all over the country, especially in London . . . make life uncomfortable for all the fine gentlemen at Westminster.'

'Won't you practise now you have your degree?' Peggy tried not to sound as disapproving as she felt. Woman's suffrage always took first place with Elspeth.

'Oh, yes,' she replied quickly. 'Despite what you believe, I intend becoming a good doctor.' A smile reached her eyes, then faded as she added soberly, 'It's part of my testimony as a suffragette, even if I haven't your absolute dedication to the job. I've been offered a residency in the New Hospital for Women in London. You know, the one founded by Elizabeth Garret Anderson.'

'How on earth . . .'

'Through friends.' For once Elspeth found it hard to meet Peggy's eyes.

Peggy understood her feelings. 'Och, don't worry, Elspeth, I've never grudged you your money or your connections . . .

well, at least not since I got to know you,' she added honestly. 'You admire my sturdy poverty and independence, Elspeth, and I admire your strong character and political convictions. You can't help who you are, where your heart lies, or what you have, any more than I can. Enjoy your residency, for heavens sake, you've earned your degree . . . if anyone can enjoy virtual slavery!' She looked around the comfortable sitting-room. 'What are you doing with this house if you move?'

'I was just coming to that.' Elspeth suddenly flushed deep red and went on with a hesitancy that sat ill on her forthright face, 'Er, Peggy, I don't want to sell Lansdowne Crescent just now, and above all I don't want to take Libby to London with me. She'll only worry herself to death if I get involved in militant action, as I fully intend doing. And I'll go mad with her fussing and serving tea all day.'

'Serves you right too!' Peggy grinned, knowing how poor Libby tried unsuccessfully to curb Elspeth's 'excesses'.

'But I know if I do take her, she'd be horribly lonely on top of it all, Peggy.' Elspeth leaned forward and took her hand, blurting out suddenly, 'Would you consider moving in here for a year or so to keep an eye on the place and to keep Libby happy?'

'What?' Peggy stared as if she had gone mad.

'I mean it. I am not going to sell and so I'll have to pay for heating and other expenses anyway. Libby would stay if you came. And she can provide food for both of you from the housekeeping allowance I make her. Of course you wouldn't have to eat here . . . just if you wished.' Elspeth knew Peggy's hatred of being patronised.

'Why don't you let it?' Peggy demanded, green eyes wary.

'Oh, I couldn't let the house. I don't want strangers messing about with my things and Libby wouldn't be a bit content. She couldn't go back to being just some sort of servant. We've not been like that, she and I . . .'

'Yes, I think you have a fine relationship with Libby,' Peggy agreed. 'But I still can't see why you want to keep the place at all.'

'Sentiment, I suppose. It's the first real home I've ever had. I'm not ready to give it up,' Elspeth admitted.

139

'But why me? You could get one of your suffrage friends to take over.'

'Libby likes you far more than anybody else who comes here,' Elspeth replied. 'On top of that, the Trust income for your fees now reverts to me. I have had full control since I became twenty-five a few months ago.'

'So?' Peggy insisted.

'So, I don't need the money and I'd love to share it a bit longer with you while you're still studying. This is one way to do that.'

'No, Elspeth!' It was Peggy's turn to blush.

'Please, Peggy. The letter of Mama's bequest might be followed by stopping your money now, but the spirit of it entitles you to something more. I know she would agree with me if she was alive and that's the flat truth.'

'Och, it's charity, Elspeth,' Peggy protested, 'I could never accept.'

'It's not charity! I'm not offering you the money. I know you would just turn it down. What I'm asking is that you become an unpaid house-guardian for me, keep Libby out of my hair, and at the same time make your own next year or two more comfortable. Oh, Peggy, do it for me or poor Libby, if not for yourself.'

Peggy pictured the single-end, the shared toilet, the discomfort, dirt and noise. Struggling to light the rusty old range after long, long hours of work in hospital. These days her isolation was almost total. With every year at university, she had become more and more of an outsider. Though her own attitude hadn't changed, folk regarded her with suspicion. Jamie Soutar's daughter was a cuckoo in the nest. Lassies, or lads from Clancy's Lane, didn't go to places like QMC. What hurt most was that even people she had grown up with all too clearly felt uneasy in her presence.

Maggie Naughton has hardly said a word to me these five years, Peggy thought sadly, ever since Hughie told her what I was doing. And Hughie himself is married to that nice lass from the Co-op and gone these three years past, with two fine bairns into the bargain. God, the offer is so tempting! She looked round the glowing comfort of the charming room. On the next floor was an elegant guest-suite with its own water-closet and a big bath standing on iron legs. Unbelievable luxury for a year at least! Libby's scones and blaeberry jam instead of yesterday's loaf and dripping! Involuntarily her mouth watered.

'Come on, please, Peggy. Say yes.' Elspeth saw her waver and pressed home: 'I would feel so much happier leaving Libby in good hands and knowing I have someone here to deal with unexpected crises. Also it would be a place to come to myself when I need to.' She knelt down beside her and looked up into her face. 'We get on so well, Peggy, don't we? You've become one of my dearest friends . . . we've so much shared past, both good and ill. We understand each other as few can.' Elspeth could be charmingly, devastatingly, honest. 'Can't you bury that terrible pride for once?' She shook Peggy's hands gently.

'Elspeth McClure,' Peggy replied slowly after a long pause, 'you are an incredible creature. When you convinced me to accept your mother's bequest five years ago, I suspected in my heart you could talk me into anything. Now I'm sure.'

'Does that mean you will?'

'Och, dammit, I will!' Peggy laughed. 'It's Libby's baking I can't resist! Though if I get a residency, I'll be most often sleeping at the hospital.'

'That doesn't matter, you can be here in between and Libby can fuss her heart's content. Oh, wonderful, my dear!' Elspeth drowned Peggy's slight form in a bearhug.

'But on one condition?'

'What?'

'Think before you act in London. Don't rush in like you usually do, both feet first!' Peggy's face clouded. 'And please, Elspeth, call on me for help any time you need to. I have a feeling you might be biting off rather a large piece of suffrage pie. A piece big enough to choke you!'

A brusque refusal from the Western Infirmary was followed by a curt note from the Royal Infirmary asking Peggy to provide the name of some senior medical personage, other than a course tutor, who could support her application.

That's where I come unstuck every time! she sighed. With

connections you can get almost anywhere and I'm doubly disadvantaged being female. After a great deal of soul-searching, she decided to approach the only person she could think of with influence in Glasgow's most prestigious voluntary general hospitals.

June 30 1905

Dear Professor McCall,
Please forgive my presumption, but I have no one else to turn to who knows my capabilities. Once you almost threw me out of a lecture for inadvertent rudeness, then you passed my final exam paper in anaesthesia with First Class Honours.

Professor McCall, I need a sponsor to be able to apply for a residency at the Royal Infirmary where you are Senior Physician. May I throw myself on your generosity, and your faith in my future career, by asking you to support my candidature?
Your obedient servant,
Margaret Soutar

Peggy never knew what McCall thought of the letter. His secretary wrote briefly to acknowledge receipt, but shortly afterwards she was accepted for the crucial short-stay post essential to gaining her full MD.

'Well, well, Cinderella got to the ball after all.' A familiar drawl greeted her as she donned her white coat on the first day of residency.

'I can't say I think much of Prince Charming's manners, McBride,' Peggy replied acidly. 'And while we're in the mood for exchanging niceties, I'll thank you to remember we're both supposed to be professional people, not drawing-room sparring partners.'

'Still a prickly little red-haired porcupine.' His eyes were insolent. 'You might find you've taken on more than you imagine here, Cinders. A lot of the men don't want women residents. I've heard one or two say they are going to make life very, very difficult for you.'

'Thank you for the warning, Dr McBride, I'm sure it was

142

kindly meant.' Her voice dripped sarcasm. 'But I've never had much help from any man since I came into medicine. Or, with the exception of my father, before that either. Men in the medical profession are so worried in case women beat them on their own ground, it's pathetic the tricks they try. Och, don't worry your curly head, I'll not cry if the little laddies are nasty to me.'

'Brave words, Cinders.'

Peggy looked squarely at him. 'You know, I'm surprised at you, Robert McBride. You have the makings of a fine doctor, I could see that when we worked together in pathology. What's biting you? You should be far too glad having your own residency to bother baiting a useless woman!'

McBride's eyes narrowed. 'There's nothing biting me!' he snapped, a flush rising on his handsome face. 'I just think, like most doctors, that the profession is better without women dabbling in it. They should keep to their own domains – the drawing-room and nursery!' Turning on his heel, he stomped off.

'I've never met a woman who infuriates me so much,' he confided in Douglas Munro when they met a week or so later. 'You're lucky you haven't any where you are.'

'Well, you can hardly say that.' Douglas smiled. 'The General is full of nurses.'

'Don't be so bloody obtuse, that's not what I mean!' Robert snapped. 'Sorry, Dougie,' he apologised, 'it's just the damned woman gets on my nerves. I can feel her criticising me all the time. As if she has any bloody right! There's no place for women in this profession.'

'I can't agree,' Douglas said quietly. 'Peggy Soutar was the best medical student of our year, Rob, irrespective of her sex.'

'Oh, don't you start!' he groaned. 'I should have known it was no use moaning to you about the woman. You've always stuck up for her, ever since she and the Ugly Sister nearly got thrown out of old McCall's lecture. If I didn't know you better, I'd think you were soft on her.'

'I thought, and still think, that they are two fine women and I can't for the life of me see what you and most of this profession have against women doctors. There's a crying need for them, for God's sake! Anyway,' Douglas went on soberly, 'whatever you feel, Rob, Peggy is every bit as much a doctor now as you are. Whether you like it or not isn't relevant. Give the poor woman support instead of making her life miserable. What's up? Surely you're not still sour over not catching her fancy?'

'Oh, damn that, I never really tried to seduce her. The woman's not that good-looking!' Robert's handsome face flushed bright red. 'And don't start preaching at me Dougie!'

'I'm not!' he protested. 'You started it.'

'Oh, come on, we're both tired, or we wouldn't be arguing like a pair of idiots. Let's see what's on at Ayr.' Robert's usual good humour broke through. 'It's years since we've been to the races. Or at least it feels like it. I've almost forgotten what relaxation is!'

Well honed by her years of study and work, Peggy quickly settled into the routine of exhaustingly hard work and excruciatingly long hours faced by all young residents. On one of their too-infrequent meetings, she and Elspeth compared notes.

'It's the constant parrying of attempts to confine me to certain "womanly" things, like paediatrics, that is most wearing,' Peggy complained. 'I can put up with the male doctors making silly comments and playing childish tricks. My God, Elspeth, after what we went through as students, I'm used to that.'

'At least I escape all that nonsense in a women's hospital.' She nodded thankfully. 'It's just as well. I get less tolerant with each year, Peggy. These days I'd probably hit someone with a chamber-pot . . . a full one!'

'At least they're getting tired of the pranks now,' Peggy went on. 'Even Robert McBride has given up lately. We try to avoid each other when we can.'

'Are you going to stay in hospital work like me, or go into general practice?'

'I'll tell you in a few months when the results of the MD exams come out.' Peggy gave a worried frown.

'You'll do outstandingly as always! On past form, if it was only exams that counted, you could take your pick of the profession!' Elspeth put a comforting arm round her friend's shoulders.

'Oh, I don't know . . .' Peggy said anxiously.

'Come on, forget the hospital, have a look at my pamphlet, tell me what you think about the main articles.' Tactfully Elspeth changed the subject before her friend became thoroughly depressed.

Elspeth was right. Peggy took the prized post-graduate degree with highest honours. Despite their overt hostility on account of her sex, the examiners graciously offered her a temporary post at the hospital.

'Oh, no! Would you believe it?' Peggy's delight turned to resigned cynicism when she saw she was to be assistant to the male colleague who had done next best: Robert McBride.

Two days after the post-graduate degrees had been published he stopped her in the corridor. 'Well then, how do you fancy working for me, Cinders?' He leaned against the tiled wall, grinning triumphantly.

'I don't grudge you the job of junior house doctor, Dr McBride, though I imagine I need the extra money more than you do,' she replied dryly. 'Och, don't worry, I'll work for you as hard as I would for anyone else. But just ask yourself how you would feel if the shoe was on the other foot? You know what your MD marks were . . . and mine. Remember what your namesake Robert Burns said: "Oh wad some power the giftie gie us, to see ourselves as others see us!" ' Peggy turned into the ward, leaving him standing looking after her, expression inscrutable.

He watched her progress down the long open ward, greeting patients and checking nurses at work. Her manner was confident and her touch sure. Dammit, she's bloody right, I'd be furious if I was passed over for no real reason! At long last he began admitting that he might have made a mistake. As he turned to go, the new batch of young residents charged along the corridor and stopped at the noticeboard, craning eagerly up at the list of their first hospital assignments.

'Oh, calamity! Bertie and me are on with a woman! I

heard there was one here. Just our luck. What's she going to teach us – knitting?'

'Hard luck, old chaps, the rest of us are with Doctor McBride,' chortled his friends.

'There he is!' The little group turned towards their supervisor who had heard the exchange.

'Good morning, gentlemen.' The mantle of authority, however limited, sat well on Robert McBride's fine broad shoulders.

'Good morning, Doctor.' The chorus was gratifyingly respectful.

'Er, Doctor McBride.' Bertie grinned cheerily. 'Do you think Chas and I could change to your group?'

'Why?' Robert asked with an enigmatic smile.

'We've been assigned to the lady doctor.' The young student could hardly hide his disgust.

'And?' McBride raised a questioning eyebrow.

'We'd prefer to work for a man.'

'Do you know Doctor Soutar?' he asked quietly.

'No, but . . .'

'I thought not. If you had, you would have been only too damned glad to learn she's looking after you! You're bloody lucky to be working with the best doctor you're ever likely to meet! Report in ten minutes for your instructions. I'll be in the office all morning if anybody needs to ask any questions.' With a look that shrivelled the hapless Bertie to the soles of his woollen hose, Robert McBride left them standing gaping.

Now why the hell did I say that? Christ, I'm beginning to sound like Dougie Munro! Rob shook his head when he closed the door of the office. Going soft, McBride? Defending lady doctors – what's this, eh? His face lit up in a puzzled smile.

I wonder what he's up to? Peggy had expected Robert to take advantage of his superior rank to belittle her. But since their conversation in the corridor he did not seem inclined to do so, either during their briefings or in the rare clincs when they jointly worked with the students. Years of

146

torment at his hands made Peggy brace herself for trouble but it never came.

'Morning, Doctor Soutar.' Bertie and Chas stood up as she entered the clinic.

'Morning, Dr Brown, Dr Wilson.' She smiled back. 'Ready for the rounds?'

'Yes,' they chorused. Their unexpectedly respectful attitude also made supervision easier than she had anticipated. That puzzled her too, but slowly she accepted it with pleasure and relief. Maybe there was a new breed of male doctors coming up after all! This optimistic thought cheered her day as she led out her little team.

'Emergency, Doctor McBride!' Three weeks later, Sister Hay ran into the duty-doctor's office, cap streamers flying and dignity thrown to the winds.

Peggy, handing over her notes to Robert at the end of a long shift, stopped in amazement. 'What's happened?'

'Oh, you're still here as well, Doctor Soutar,' Sister gasped. 'Och, thank God. We'll need everyone from what I've heard – all the young residents too. The Motherwell train mounted the platform at Central Station. It ploughed straight into the poor folk waiting to board. At this time of day the place is packed!'

'Come on!' Robert and Peggy grabbed their white coats and rushed to casualty. Ambulances began arriving at once, horses snorting nervously at the cries and moans of the injured as they were lifted down.

'God, what carnage!' Robert grimaced as they began the gruesome task of patching up the demolition of flesh and bone the maverick engine had caused.

Ten hours later, swaying on their feet with tiredness, the medical team peeled off blood-stained garments and scrubbed themselves clean. Peggy rejoined the men once she had changed and they sat in stunned silence drinking strong, sweet tea. For once the young medics were disinclined to chaff or joke. Peggy could see the stress and built-up tension of the night weigh them down like a black pall.

After a moment she got up and stretched. 'Well, I think I'd better grab a couple of hours' sleep, I'm on again at two.'

She looked at the drawn, tired faces around her. 'Come on, lads, get to your beds as well. You'll see worse before you're finished in this job! Oh, and by the way, knitting lessons start next week, Charles and Bertie. Tonight was just sewing and embroidery and you've passed those with flying colours! Well done!'

Peggy had heard about the comment long ago from a nurse, but had never mentioned it.

'What?' The young men gaped at her and sheepish smiles chased away the shock from their face. 'Righto, Doctor Soutar, one purl, one plain.' Bertie got up and the others followed, grinning. As she had meant to do, Peggy had shaken them out of their shock.

Peggy and Robert could hear the young doctors' tension dispel in fits of immoderate laughter. They would be fit to face the world of casualty another day.

'Well done, Peggy.' Robert looked at her with unqualified admiration. There was no trace of the old sneer on his tired, handsome face. 'I could see they needed something to get them over the horror. The first big casualty incident is always the worst, but I didn't know how to do it.'

'Och, it's an old miner's trick, to get them laughing over some daft black joke as soon as possible.' Peggy blushed. 'They always do it after an accident. There's less damage to the psyche,' she added as she made to leave.

'Doctor Soutar ... Peggy ... I'm sorry,' he said in a low, gentle voice that stopped her in her tracks.

'For what in particular?' she asked with a touch of her usual irony, expecting a jibe.

'For being so bloody stupid.'

'What are you on about?' Peggy gaped.

'You were absolutely right that time in the corridor. If I had got the results you did and been made deputy to a less well-qualified peer, I would have been furious and I'd have resigned. Why haven't you?'

'Where would I go, Robert McBride? What would I do? If I turn down this post, no other hospital would accept me.' Her answer was brutally truthful. 'And having decided to stay, I have a responsibility to the patients not to let pride and anger get between me and their care. Working for you was the price of the hospital experience I need, and I decided to pay it without whingeing.' In her exhaustion, she didn't bother to dissemble.

'You're twice the doctor I'll ever be.' His dark eyes were sincere. 'Please believe me, I've thought long and hard about this since we talked. I'll put no more obstacles in your way. And you were wonderful tonight.' He put a hand on her shoulder and looked into her drawn, weary face. 'I couldn't have coped without you.'

'Och, fiddlesticks, you were fine . . . you'd have managed.'

'I mean it, Peggy. Listen, I can't change what they've ordained here, so I'm technically in charge, but you're at least equal in my eyes from this time on. You once quoted Burns to me, so will I to you: "The rank is but the guinea's stamp, the man" . . . or the woman's . . . "the gowd for all that". Do you believe me? We're partners?'

Peggy looked at him searchingly and moved away. 'You've got the rest of the year to prove you mean it, Doctor McBride.'

'I will, Doctor Soutar.' His face was serious and his voice unrecognisably humble. Stripped of all arrogance, Peggy could see something of the real man. She was surprised at how different the image was to the one he'd presented before.

This will take some getting used to, she thought wryly. If he still means it when he's had some sleep!

149

Chapter 12
Supremely blest wi' love and thee

'Robert, I have to leave. I need to do another full residency,' Peggy explained as she handed in her resignation just before the summer of 1907. 'The Royal Samaritan specialises in women's illnesses, it's just what I want before working in a Poor Law Infirmary.'

'So it's a pauper hospital for you after all!' Robert teased, but his careful smile didn't reach his eyes.

'They're the only places I have a chance! Wages are so low, men don't apply unless there's no alternative.' Peggy grinned in resignation. 'I'll probably end up spending my entire career in one. Anyway,' she shrugged, 'Poor Law work fits in with my ambition to bring good medical care to ordinary folk.'

'I'll miss you, Peggy.' Robert turned away and stared out of the window across the busy Glasgow streets.

'And I'll miss you, Rob.' Peggy surprised herself by the sincerity of the statement. 'We made a decent team after all . . . though who would ever have thought it?'

'May I call on you?' he asked after a moment's poignant silence.

'Why?'

'Because I would not like to lose touch. I, er, value your professional opinion.' Flushed, he floundered in rare confusion.

'Och, if that's the case, then why not?' Peggy smothered an impish smile at his discomfort. 'I'm still staying at Elspeth McClure's house.'

'Yes, I know.'

'Do you also know where it is?'

'Yes, Lansdowne Crescent. I, er, went past once, I know someone over that way . . .' Robert looked down intently at his feet.

'Well then, leave your card with Libby.' The green eyes danced. 'Lucky I'm not still living in my little single-end, Rob McBride. You would look daft trying to leave a card there.' Her laughter echoed in his head long after she was gone.

Rob McBride, you're getting into dangerous waters, he told himself, as Peggy's image spun endlessly between him and his work over the next few weeks. Finally he confided in Douglas Munro.

'If you want to see her, do it, Rob. You're man enough to make up your own mind over a woman!' Douglas was unusually short with him.

'But that's it, I can't believe I feel like this,' he said. 'Peggy Soutar, for God's sake . . . little shabby Cinders! You know how it's been, Dougie. Why her of all women on earth?'

'I don't see why you're so bloody astounded, Rob, she's a fine-looking lass,' Douglas got up and stared out of the window of Robert's apartment. 'And intelligent, God knows. Now you know her better, why should you be surprised that you've fallen for her? What's the matter, Robert, are you worried she's not good enough for you or your family? I thought we Scots were more democratic than that . . .' he hesitated and Robert butted in.

'I just don't know what I think or feel any more. And you're right in a way. What will Father say, Dougie?'

'He'll have a bloody cheek if he objects to Peggy,' Douglas snapped. 'You told me he's been living with some native woman since your mama died.'

'Still, he won't expect me to marry a miner's daughter, Dougie. God! Is that what I want?' Robert's face registered shocked astonishment.

'Sounds like it.' Douglas kept staring down on the empty street below.

'Oh, Christ, I have to think about this,' Robert muttered worriedly from the depths of his armchair.

151

'I agree it's about time you thought,' Douglas replied dryly, crossing the room and picking up his jacket and a sturdy carpet bag. 'Well, I'll be off, I have to catch the London train in less than an hour.'

'Good luck with the surgery interview,' Rob said mechanically as he opened the door.

'Thanks ... and good luck to you. I'll call when I get back.'

'Are you going on to Italy?'

'Yes, I need a break.' Whistling an old air softly under his breath Douglas left his friend, bemused and thoughtful at the revelation of his own heart.

For two months Robert held off, refusing to give in to the gnawing desire to see Peggy again. Once, in darkness, he stood outside the house in Lansdowne Crescent, feeling utterly stupid. For a good hour he looked up at the lit window above him, then, heavy-hearted, turned and went home.

Dammit, this time I will! Robert left the hospital mid-afternoon and took a carriage directly to Elspeth's house. He gave the driver the exact address, knowing that would oblige him to do something more than hang around like a callow youth.

'Good afternoon, ma'am.' At the door, he raised his hat and handed his card to Libby, fetched from her sitting-room by their wide-eyed tweeny. 'Would you please see that Doctor Soutar receives this card and ask her if I may call at her convenience?'

'Certainly, sir, I'll see she gets it the minute she's back from the hospital.' Libby bobbed a curtsy, taking in the dark curly hair, handsome face and elegant cut of waistcoat and jacket. Now that's what I call a dashing suitor! Oh, Doctor Peggy! Her sentimental heart did a little jig.

'This is for you, Doctor Peggy!' Libby was all agog, presenting the card as soon as she got in, tired and weary after a three-day shift at the hospital.

'Oh, Robert decided to brave it at last,' Peggy commented enigmatically, looking at the card.

'Doctor McBride said to let him know when he could

call,' Libby persisted. 'Och, he seemed a nice gentleman, so
he did, and from the cut of his jacket he's no short of a
bawbee or two either. Now, listen to me, Doctor Peggy,
you've a wee bit free time coming up this weekend, haven't
you? Shall I send a laddie round in the morning?'

'And you're a terrible romantic, Libby Purdie! Robert
McBride is only an old colleague.' Peggy smiled as the
housekeeper's face fell. 'Anyway I'm too tired to think about
it just now.' She put the card on the hall-stand and made
her way upstairs. Despite her exhaustion, she found it hard
to sleep. Surprise that Robert had got in touch, mingled
with unexpected pleasure. It was hours before her weary
mind relaxed and her eyes finally closed.

'Ye haven't invited over your old colleague yet,' Libby
nagged a week or so later.

'I'm too busy!' Peggy's reply was laced with uncharacteristic sharpness.

'Och, that's not right. You're that hard-working, Doctor
Peggy, and the hours expected of you are far too long, but
you could make a wee bit of time to see an old friend if you
wanted to . . .'

'Well, we'll see.' Peggy refused to discuss the question
further. Robert McBride may have proved himself a good
colleague in the end, but Peggy balked at introducing com-
plications into her personal life. His dark eyes and charming
smile haunted her more than she would ever admit, but
there was a long road ahead to achieve her ambitions and
it was best tramped alone.

Libby sighed and shook her head. Och, that one and Miss
Elspeth are two peas in a pod when it comes to it! Not a
romantic bone in either of their bodies. What did I do to
deserve the pair of them?

Robert came back after a month, this time in the evening.
'Is Doctor Soutar at home?' Uncertainty hid behind his
languid manner.

'The doctor won't be back for another good hour, sir.'
Libby eyed him shrewdly, saw beyond the bravado to the
anxiety in his eyes and made a decision. 'But you're welcome
to come in and wait for her. Would ye like a wee cup of tea,
or maybe a sherry, in the drawing-room?'

'Thank you very much, tea would be excellent!' Robert handed her his hat and a conspiratorial look of complete understanding shot between them.

'Ye've a visitor, Doctor Peggy.' Libby was at the door, ushering in her mistress before she had the chance to draw breath.

'Who?' Peggy was astonished. 'It's a bit on the late side, Libby. You should have asked whoever it is to call back, not wait till I got in.'

'Oh, please don't blame your housekeeper, I insisted.' Robert emerged from the drawing-room where Libby had been plying him with endless trays of tea and cakes.

'Robert McBride!' Peggy gaped in astonishment. 'What on earth brings you here at this time of night?'

'Can we talk?' His eyes swivelled meaningfully towards Libby's back.

'Yes, all right. Thanks, Libby.' Peggy handed over her coat and led the way into the warm room, firmly closing the door after her. 'What can I do for you, Robert?' She raised a quizzical eyebrow.

'Did you get my card and message?' He hoped he didn't sound as nervous as he felt.

'Yes.' Peggy's face gave away nothing of her thoughts, or her emotion at seeing him again.

'But you didn't reply.'

'I didn't think you meant me to take the message seriously. I assumed it was only a politeness.'

'It wasn't a politeness. I've missed you, Peggy. I wanted to see you again. I would like us to be friends. Please.' Robert looked pleadingly at her. 'I mean, I want to call on you. You know . . .'

'Robert, you and I worked together like good professionals should during that last year.' Peggy sat down, trying to chose her words carefully. She noticed that her hands were shaking. Self-consciously she tucked them primly in her lap. 'I really appreciated your change of attitude towards me. And, honestly, I'm glad to see you too, but I think we should leave things as they are. I don't want to start any entanglements.'

Robert looked longingly at her, at last not trying to hide

his feelings. 'It's too late for me to leave things as they are, Peggy, I'm already entangled.'

'Well, I'm not!' She got up and walked to the window, fiddling with an imaginary wrinkle in the long plush curtains.

'Are you sure about that?' Tentatively he laid his hand on her shoulder.

Peggy stood stock still. Everything she had fought for was in jeopardy. Her obsessive desire to be a doctor had cost her dear. Clancy's Close, night after night of weary study and days of exhausting work, the gaping loneliness after Jamie's death . . . these had been only part of the terrible price she had paid. And now, when fulfilment was within her grasp, this man who had wilfully made her path even harder, Robert McBride of all people, was threatening it with the very emotions she had resolved never to allow to stand in her way.

'Peggy, please. Look at me. Tell me to my face,' he whispered.

If he had tried to hold her then, she would have flinched away, but the vulnerability in his voice and the gentleness of his touch unseated her resolve. Slowly she turned to face him, raising troubled green eyes to his dark ones. 'No, I'm not sure.' The answer was whispered.

'Can we meet tomorrow?'

'I'm working tomorrow and Saturday.'

'Sunday then.' With a touch as soft as thistledown, he ran a finger along the contour of her cheek. 'Please don't change your mind. I promise we'll go at your pace. There's no need to avoid me. I've been the bane of your life at times, but I'm learning. I'm belatedly growing up, Peggy.'

She was pale and solemn. 'No, I won't change my mind. I always keep my word, especially to friends, Robert McBride.'

Arm in arm they walked through Kelvingrove Park that Sunday, talking as if they had just met. Now they had admitted the depth of feeling that lay between them, their latent love burned like a dozen flames.

'Did you hate me?' Rob asked her as they found a sheltered spot on the banks of the Kelvin and sat side by side.

155

'Hate you? When?'

'At Medical School? Afterwards in the Royal?' He threw little stones into the gently flowing river, watching them ripple and disappear in the dark waters.

'No, I've never hated you.' Her bright curls danced. 'It just seemed so unnecessary that you were forever blocking my way . . . when you weren't making improper suggestions, that is,' she added with a touch of fine malice.

'Ouch! I deserved that!' He turned and smiled full at her. Peggy held his gaze and was lost in the depths of tenderness she saw there. Try as she might, she could not remember any longer how it had been between them in the old days of conflict and mistrust.

All that glorious autumn they made the lovely Kelvingrove Park their own, escaping when they could from the hard, committed work of the profession they had both chosen, to the trees and gardens which laced the banks of great Clyde's tributary. It was a time of discovery, of harmony, of pure undemanding love. Robert was surprised at his own restraint. Without flinching, he kept his promise to go slowly, but found he had an insatiable need to know everything about her and to open his own soul as never before.

Under his gentle probing, she told him of Kirkowen, of Kirsty, of Auntie Lizzie, of Tam Laird and the curlew's nest, of Jamie and the struggling isolated years after his tragic death. But she never betrayed the secret of her friendship with Elspeth, nor the source of the bequest that had brought her so far on her chosen path. Even to beloved Robert, some things could never be explained. Deep in this new found love, he never noticed the omission.

'From what you've told me, Rob, it would seem as if you had no real family life either,' she said as the gloaming fell across the city one fine evening. Behind them the dying rays of the sun touched the lacy stone towers of the University.

'I've told you, my father followed Queen and Empire and my mother followed him! I was an irrelevance . . . expect to keep the McBride name going, of course.' His words were tinged with bitterness when he spoke about his parents. 'Father was always running some bloody border campaign

156

and Mama couldn't be bothered with me. She'd done her duty when she gave Father a son and that was that. God knows what she would have done if she'd had a quiverful of daughters instead of the required heir. It was her idea to send me away so young.'

'But you went to school in Edinburgh. Surely there were relatives in Scotland, or friends to visit?'

'I had an elderly aunt in Kilmarnock who hated children like poison, especially boys. "Nasty little creatures!" she called us.' Rob gave a wry shrug. 'If it hadn't been for the Munros, I would have been stuck at school most of the holidays.'

'And that would have been so bad?' She tried to remember what Elspeth had told her about Miss Lovat's, but could only recall the happiness the place had given her friend.

'It was cold, strict, puritanical, and bullying was rife.' Rob shrugged. 'But I was a big lad, good at sport and good at my studies, despite being lazy at heart.' He smiled. 'I got by, more than that if I'm really honest, but it would have been a blow to stay alone there during the breaks.'

'So you went to the Munros – Douglas Munro's family?'

'Yes, to Dougie's. Glorious, freedom-filled weeks at Ardgartan on the banks of Loch Long where his family have a fine house still. Tickling trout in the burns, climbing the Cobbler Mountain, running bare-foot in the heather with the gamekeeper's bairns. Eating great slabs of bread spread with honey that tasted of heaven on earth! God, those were the happiest times of my life.'

'I can believe it.' Peggy thought of the heathery cliffs and the wild free sea-birds that wheeled over her own childhood, despite poverty and want. 'How did you meet Douglas?' she asked.

'Dougie and I were pals from the moment we landed in the same cold first-year dormitory. They used to call us "The Twins", though Doug has never been as tall or as dark as me. Mind you he's a strong lad and a bonnie fighter!' Rob added with touching pride in his old friend. 'We stood shoulder to shoulder against the second-year bullies, played in the same teams at everything, and rowed in the same boat at the annual race on the Firth of Forth. We were inseparable. Still are when we get the chance! But you should have seen his face when I finally admitted that I was soft on you, Peggy! He nearly fell off his chair!' Rob put his hands behind his curly head and leaned back with the carefree grin that turned her heart over.

'Did he approve?' she asked softly.

'I think so. You know, it's strange, the only thing he and I ever disagreed over in our lives was the female medical students, but especially you and Elspeth. He always took your part. I once teased him for being sweet on you . . . it certainly couldn't have been Elspeth.'

'Robert McBride!' Peggy's eyes flashed. 'Elspeth is a lovely person, inside and out! Don't ever say a thing like that again.'

'Sorry!' Rob knew he had trodden on sacred ground and backed off, 'I just meant she's not Dougie's type. Mind you, I'm not sure what that is.' He paused thoughtfully for a moment then went on slowly, 'No, I think he was only worried that I wouldn't treat you right.' He said nothing of the long-abandoned bet.

'I'm sure that was the only reason, Rob, your imagination runs wild at times.' Peggy laughed. 'Och, poor Douglas. Tell him I can well take care of myself and so can Elspeth McClure.'

'He knows that.' Rob smiled and got up, holding out his hand to her and drawing it gently into the crook of his arm. 'Walk down Sauchiehall Street and then tea?'

'Why not?' Peggy had stopped working at Miss Cranston's when she began her first internship, but was still welcome. Miss Cranston had been surprised, but pleased, when she first brought in Robert. He was definitely from the genteel classes to which the formidable lady herself belonged and a fine catch for Peggy for whom she still had the greatest affection. A visit there was a favourite finish to many of their first outings as they tentatively broke through old barriers of misunderstanding.

But, despite his honourable behaviour and his resolve, Peggy knew Robert was becoming restive. It was clear that he wanted more from her in every sense. The thought kept her awake more often that she cared to admit. The crisis came in the festive days between Christmas and New Year when the world relaxed and looked forward to fresh beginnings.

'Whew, what a crowd!' Robert flopped wearily on to Elspeth's settee after a cheerful walk through the busy city centre.

'What do you expect?' Peggy said as she unpinned her hat and hung it on the rack in the hall. 'Did you notice Elspeth's friends from the suffrage movement were busy too?'

'Yes, er, the suffragettes, I noticed.' Robert was non-committal. He had quickly learned that Peggy would jump to Elspeth's defence if she detected a hint of criticism.

'I'm just away out to my cousin in Milngavie, Doctor Peggy.' Libby stuck her head round the door. 'Will you and Doctor McBride be wanting any supper? I can ask wee Phemie to stay and fix it for you. Otherwise I've said she can go home to her parents till tomorrow.'

'We had late tea and we're eating out after the concert, Libby,' Robert broke in. 'I've promised to take Doctor Peggy to the new restaurant in St Enoch's Square.'

'Oh, just let Phemie go, Libby. When will you be back?' Peggy asked as the housekeeper buttoned her gloves. 'Are we likely to be late, Robert?'

'I don't think the recital will be finished before ten,' he said. 'There's always a fine pianist and at least one solo singer, maybe a quartet as well. It would be a shame to miss the end.'

'Och, you'd better take your own key, Doctor Peggy,' Libby advised. 'I usually get the nine-thirty train from Milngavie. It gets into Glasgow about ten-fifteen and I'll take a cab straight here. But I'd be worried sick thinking of ye standing on the doorstep if anything went amiss. It's cold enough for snow, so it is! Don't forget your scarf!' With that dire warning, Libby wrapped her own muffler firmly round her neck, pulled on knitted Fair Isle gloves and headed off to her sister's.

Robert and Peggy sat companionably for a few minutes in the quiet house after Libby and the maid left. Rob finally got up. 'I better go home and change.' He lifted her hand and touched it to his lips. 'Is seven o'clock too late?'

'No, that's fine.'

'Till seven then.' Resting both hands on her shoulders, he pulled her to him, kissing her forehead lightly. 'Oh, and will you marry me, Peggy?'

'What?' His tone was so conversational, she thought she had misheard.

'Will you marry me?'

'Good God, no!' Peggy jumped as if she was stung.

'Why not?' Robert sounded deeply hurt.

'I want to stay free to get on with the job I struggled to train for.'

'I wouldn't stop you.'

'Maybe not, but I prefer to be my own person.'

'Peggy, I want you.' His voice became low and thick and he forgot his carefully cultivated resolve. 'It's eating my guts out! I can think of nothing but you, day and night. I've tried not to pressurise you ... you know I've showed restraint, but it's getting more and more difficult the longer we are together.'

'And you see marriage as the only way to get me?'

Her expression was unreadable.

'It's the usual way,' he admitted honestly.

'And if I say want you too, Robert?' The green eyes were steady.

'Then you *will* marry me?'

'No.'

'For God's sake, woman, what then? I can't bear being near you and not feel free to touch you, to kiss you, to love you.'

'Then do it.'

'Do you mean what that sounds like, Peggy? I'm offering you marriage and you're suggesting a clandestine relationship instead?'

'Och, if you want we can have a Scots marriage.' Her half-embarrassed giggle broke the tension.

'What do you mean ... "by habit and repute", like in the old days?' Rob demanded, looking as if she had taken leave of her senses.

'Something like that.' Now she had thrown her habitual caution so unexpectedly away, Peggy sounded carefree as the wind from the sea. 'Tell you what, we can write down our intentions towards one another, if it makes you happier. Then if something happens, we can formalise it. Rabbie Burns and Jean Armour did that. Mind you, I think he was doing the same thing with his "Highland Mary".'

Rob couldn't follow her sudden change of heart, or believe she meant what she was saying. 'But that's not the done thing these days. We're in the twentieth century now, not the eighteenth! Just when I think I understand you, Peggy, you astonish me all over again!' He shook his head in bewilderment.

She laughed at his confusion. 'Och, it's still legal if we want it to be.' Her green eyes darkened and she took his hands, looking up at him, face still and serious. 'I don't want to lose you either, but I'm just not ready for the usual kind of marriage with kirk, minister and all the palaver yet, Robert.'

'But are you ready for love?' He pulled her to him and whispered against her hair: 'Are you, Peggy?'

She leaned against him, conscious of his nearness. 'Yes, Rob, I am ready for love. Your love!' Peggy felt her body contract with desire as his hands tightened round her.

'I'll marry you any way you want: kirk, Scots . . . both!' Robert murmured passionately, and kissed her till her breath came raggedly.

Suddenly he let her go and Peggy stood utterly still as he began loosening the front of her blouse and untying the belt from her skirt. Gently he opened her chemise and slid in his hands, cupping her breasts. Her breath came faster, but she did not move. Deftly he unfastened the buttons on her skirt and helped it fall round her feet, then lifted her bodily from the floor and laid her on the chaise-longue.

'Robert!' The word was filled with all her unashamed longing.

'My darling, my darling!' He buried his face in her neck, then stood up and took off his own clothes.

Peggy watched every move. Many times as a doctor she had seen men naked and had felt no lust. But Robert was

161

utterly beautiful. When he stood completely ready, she held out her arms and drew him to her.

Five times that year he asked her to marry him in the kirk. 'I want to be sure you're mine, that one day you don't just disappear . . . take a job in Timbuctu and say "Goodbye, nice knowing you, Rob McBride!"'

'Och, I thought it was only women who worried about their lover disappearing,' she teased. 'I promise I won't do that to you. But I'm still not ready for marriage.' Despite her refusal to declare their relationship to the world and be blessed by the kirk, their closeness and commitment were complete. There was little they did not know about one another.

'I can talk to you like I've done to no one else in my life since I left my Indian nurse,' he whispered across the draped darkness of Elspeth's drawing room. 'I loved living in India, but once I was sent away they never brought me back, not even once. I never saw my nurse again. Mama didn't even let me say goodbye to her. She said I might blubber and that wouldn't be fitting for a McBride and the son of a Brigadier Sahib! Love and emotion were never fitting in my mother's book. I think she made me hate women for years . . . except for pleasure, of course.'

'I noticed that exception,' Peggy said dryly. 'But I would never send a child away from folk they love.' She stroked his dark curly hair gently. 'I stayed with old Auntie Lizzie when Daddy worked with the Miners' Union in Glasgow, but she had helped care for me all my life. I always knew the people around me in Kirkowen, at least till we moved to the city, and by that time I was older and Daddy was there. He would never have let strangers look after me when I was only seven. Children need to feel that someone loves them.'

'Peggy, please can't we be married?' Robert begged yet again a few months later. 'Skulking round like this in my apartment or here when Libby is visiting her sister is undignified for two distinguished doctors!' His grin was uncertain. 'And it would make me feel happier, more secure. Dearest girl, try to understand, I'm terrified of losing you now! Life would have no meaning at all!'

'Och, my darling Rob,' she replied, holding him close, 'you know I understand, but you know too that your father would object, and your fine relatives. I've no intention of being the object of their scorn or pity!' Peggy was adamant.

'I have no fine relatives. They were all old maids or crusty bachelors . . . and they're mostly dead.'

Peggy refused to give in. 'No, I have too much to do yet, marriage is too much to cope with right now! Och, you know there's no danger of me leaving you, Rob . . . come, love me again.' She drew him into her arms and as they lay back together in the soft depths of the huge sofa, Peggy gave a great sigh of contentment. There was never any disharmony in their togetherness.

Despite her refusal to legalise their love, Peggy sometimes worried about what they would do if she conceived. She wasn't afraid he would desert her, but she knew it would affect her career. For all their intimacy, a it was something they never properly discussed. Robert would ask occasionally whether she was 'all right'. Nodding dismissively, she would go on to another subject.

At first they tried to use thick, rubbery condoms Robert got through some friends. Amid gales of embarrassed laughter they abandoned the idea. Peggy took some simple precautions of her own though she knew they were unreliable. But the sponge soaked in vinegar solution she used after he had gone seemed to have worked again this time, for she bled a couple of days later. There was no child yet to betray their relationship.

In spring 1908 she became pregnant. 'Now we have to get married,' Robert said, holding her close.

'I can manage alone,' she insisted. 'You don't have to marry me, Robert.'

'Don't deprive me of my child, Peggy. And above all don't deprive me of you any longer. I love you. I'll hold you to our Scots marriage anyway. Oh, please, my darling, let's make it official.'

'Och, maybe you're right!' Smilingly she acquiesced at last. 'I'll carry on working and cross the other bridges when

I come to them, she thought as he laid her head against his heart.

They were married quietly in late-May by the Minister of the Kirk on Great Western Road. An astonished Elspeth, and Douglas Munro, their closest and oldest friends, were witnesses. There were no guests except Libby who came in her best coat and hat and sniffed emotionally into an enormous handkerchief throughout the simple ceremony.

Peggy bought a smart green velvet dress for the occasion, which gave the housekeeper a fit of superstitious vapours.

'Ye should never get married in green, Doctor Peggy, what on earth are ye thinking about?' she protested. 'It's not lucky!'

'Blethers!' Peggy answered, glowing with pure happiness.

Both witnesses left after a celebratory drink at Lansdowne Crescent, Elspeth for a demonstration at Westminster and Douglas to an urgent appointment in Edinburgh.

The honeymoon was a month spent in Robert's bachelor apartments. Being together was enough. They gave themselves up to loving and sharing every minute, as if time was rationed – as indeed it was, for at the end of the too-brief interlude, Robert left for India to face the music with his father. They hoped he would be back for the birth if the Brigadier took the news of his marriage well.

Peggy resigned her post at the Samaritan when her stomach began to swell out of the white doctor's coat. She stayed on in Robert's apartment, waiting for the birth in December. But it felt strange and empty without him.

After Robert left, Libby wrote daily to Elspeth, insisting she was lonely and pressing her to persuade Peggy back, at least while Robert was away. Fed up with Libby's relentless moaning, Elspeth came up to Glasgow and put a very different solution forward to them both.

'I've decided to leave medicine for a while, Peggy,' she explained shamefacedly, knowing her friend's opinion of doctors who didn't practise.

'Why, for God's sake?' Peggy shifted clumsily in the deep armchair.

'I've agreed to make a lecture tour in the States with Emmeline. We'll be presenting the case for women's suffrage

164

all over the land. We expect to be away six months or so. The audiences are very enthusiastic there and it helps our cause enormously here ... not least with funds.'

'Do what you feel is right!' Peggy grunted grudgingly. 'You seem to be completely obsessed with Votes for Women! Anyway, I have no right to interfere in your life any more than you have in mine. How are you going to fund this? You're not badly off, but it'll cost a fortune, Elspeth.'

She leaned forward, face alight with enthusiasm. 'I know, so I'm thinking of selling this house. The capital will come in very useful and I still have the flat down in London. I've worked out that I have enough already for the first couple of months and then I'll have the money from here to pay for the rest!' Problem solved, she leaned back happily.

'What about Libby?'

'Er, yes. I was just coming to that.' Elspeth blushed. 'Could she, er, stay with you till I get back?'

'I'd be happy to have her ... and her scones!' Peggy had missed the older woman's cheery, down-to-earth company. Over the previous years they had become deeply fond of one another, but frequent visits had not made up for their companiable closeness at Lansdowne Crescent. 'I just didn't like to ask her while she was looking after the house for you. Och, there's plenty of room in Robert's apartment for us both until he comes home.'

'And after that?'

'Then we can all move into a bigger place, since that's what Rob intends anyway. We'll need a housekeeper and Libby adores him. There won't be a problem if she wants to stay with us permanently, Elspeth.'

'There you are then.' Elspeth smiled with overt relief. 'Let's tell Libby.'

Rawlpindi, November 1908

My darling Peggy,

A short letter to tell you that Father has now accepted our marriage and far better than I expected. In fact, he seemed almost relieved that I had settled down. He said he didn't give a fig for your lack of 'credentials'!

However, my dearest, he wants me to stay on and sort out some papers concerning my inheritance. The crafty old devil has put a price on approving our marriage. It is to be measured in the transfer of some shares and capital to my three young half-caste brothers and one sister. I met them briefly at Father's country house the day after I arrived. All I can recall is four pairs of big brown eyes, darker even than my own, staring at me from coffee-coloured faces.

Father keeps that side of his life well apart from his habitual round of tiffins and drinks at the club. Oh, Peggy, I smile sometimes at the rampant hypocrisy here. It is almost worse than in our own noble native land! Elspeth would be enraged! A man is allowed his native mistresses and may even acknowledge the little black-haired results of his indiscretions, though they should be kept in the shadows, of course. For a woman to live with a native man, even discreetly, means instant expulsion from 'gentle' society.

Dear girl, the old man is as yellow as a Chinaman! He knows his liver is completely shot and he can't have too long left. With eternity staring him in the face, he has suddenly become aware that the world is not kind to half-castes, especially in India. Now he wants to safeguard their future and that of his mistress. Money is a wonderful buffer in all societies! Since funds are not unlimited in the McBride coffers, this means I will be a lot less well off when the old man goes than originally anticipated. I know that sort of thing does not worry you greatly and I am glad not to have to feel guilty on your account. In any case, my own income will soon be more than sufficient to keep us and our child(ren) in reasonable comfort.

Did I say this was to be a short letter? Please take care of yourself, my lovely lass. I dare not ask after your health, but hope in my heart all is progressing well. Oh, how I long for you every day and especially every hot, Indian night.

Your loving husband,
Robert

Peggy was saddened by Robert's delayed return, but wrote agreeing at once that he should do as his father wanted. Secretly she applauded the Brigadier's perspicacity in seizing the chance to protect his second family.

Lansdowne Crescent
16 December, 1908

My darling love,

Robert, you have a daughter. She was born at nine o'clock yesterday evening, delivered by your own closest friend, Douglas Munro!

Poor man, he just stopped off to say goodbye to us (he thought you would be home by now) on his way to New Zealand, when I went into labour right there and then. What a shock for him! Libby had been warning me the day before that I had a 'look about me' and the child was surely about to come. Dear superstitious, caring Libby. For all my medical training, it was she who was right!

Douglas delivered our child here at home. What a wonderful doctor he is . . . though he kept moaning throughout that he was a surgeon, not a midwife! Still, I had made sure there was plenty of chloroform around just in case, and surgeons at least know how to use that!!

Our girl has your dark eyes and a mass of rich auburn hair all over her head, not a sparse covering like most babies. Fortunately she will not be ginger like me! Maybe between us we have produced something better-looking than either of us can claim. I have called her Kirsten Roberta McBride, as we agreed should we have a daughter.

Come back soon my dearest.

Lovingly and longingly,

Peggy

Despite the cost of such a long message, she decided to telegraph the entire glad tidings to Robert. He replied at once.

My dearest Peggy,

I cannot wait to see you and my little Kirsten. What luck Dougie was around! We can book him to help with the rest as they come! I have told Father and he's agreed I can arrange my passage home at once.

Your own,
Rob

But Robert McBride never saw his child. He contracted a virulent form of cholera and was dead within a week. All Peggy had left was a broken heart, her memories, a wedding certificate and a bonnie daughter with her father's lovely dark eyes.

Chapter 13
Fortune's fell cruel decree

After he buried his son, Brigadier McBride's heart as well as his liver gave out. His old regiment took care of the funeral and sent him on his way with full military honours. Four orphaned children and their shadowy, veiled mother were allowed to visit the grave once all the pomp and ceremony was over and the bands had gone home.

'Och, I'm sorry, Mrs McBride, really and truly.' Robert's lawyer, Graham Stewart, apologised over and over, managing to shake his head and wring his hands all at once. 'The Will is such a mess, God knows how long it will take to sort out. You know your husband and his father had just superceded the simple Will I have here with one in India?'

'Yes, I know that.' Peggy nodded, black hat and dress in stark contrast to her flaming hair and pale, sad face.

'Because your husband died before his father, a greater portion may go to the children in India than was maybe originally intended. I think the Brigadier expected Robert to come here once he got back and we would then sort out final details by telegraph. Naturally his death stopped all that. I'm afraid the Indian Will is probably the one which is valid.'

'That's logical.'

'But there's an added difficulty.' Stewart dropped his voice so low she had to bend forward to hear. 'It would appear the Brigadier managed to contract a marriage with the mother of his illegitimate children in the week between Robert's death and his own untimely departure. As you can

169

imagine, that complicates matters greatly since they would now also be legitimate heirs.'

'Where does that leave Kirsten and myself?' Peggy asked, head beginning to throb painfully.

'Well, so far as you are concerned, I'm not sure. You are not automatically entitled to anything from his father's estate. Robert clearly thought he would be keeping you both, so there may be no provisions for you at all. That's still to be established.' He didn't quite meet her eye. 'But the child is different. Robert's daughter cannot be entirely disinherited simply because her grandfather remarried ... unless she was deliberately cut out of the Will. And I shouldn't imagine the Brigadier would do that to his first grandchild. Och, it's a mess!' The lawyer sighed. 'The whole business could take a long time to sort out. We must check on the validity of Brigadier McBride's marriage to the, er, native woman for a start.' Mr Stewart found it hard to hide his partisan distaste.

Peggy longed to get out of the office, to grieve in peace instead of talking about all this, but she gritted her teeth and said, 'And in the meantime?'

'In the meantime I can make you a small allowance for Kirsten, but very small indeed, until we at least establish the extent of the inheritance. Your late father-in-law took an unusual attitude to money. Despite his last-minute arrangements for the, er, half-caste bairns, Brigadier McBride told me many times that he intended spending liberally on his own comforts. He claimed that your husband had had a good education and could fend for himself. Whatever residue there was left he said could go to Robert, who was his only legitimate child at the time I spoke to him. So there might not be much left to divide.'

'Well, the man was entitled to do what he wanted with his money, there's a deal of justice in that idea.' Peggy smiled despite her sorrow. 'I'll try to go back to work as soon as I can. Kirsten and I will have to manage.'

'Work? Oh, dearie me, do you have no alternative?' The lawyer was shocked. 'What can you do? Governess perhaps? They sometimes don't mind a widow with a bairn, er, born in wedlock.' Stewart had heard young McBride had married beneath him, but he had been surprised and impressed by his wife's educated accent and confident manner. When he sent for her, he'd half expected some chorus girl or music-hall singer.

'I'm a doctor, Mr Stewart, like Robert was, so that's what I'll do.'

'Och, michty me! A doctor!' The lawyer forgot his manners and gawped for a moment. 'Aye, well, right then, I'll be in touch as soon as I can, Mistress, er, Doctor McBride!' He accompanied her to the door.

'Thank you.' With a nod she was gone.

Peggy thought till her head almost burst all the way home to Robert's fine rented apartment. She walked the long way down by the Clyde, trying to sort out some plan of action.

We'll have to find somewhere much cheaper to live almost at once. The apartment is far too expensive for me. The wee allowance from Mister Stewart would just about keep us in food, little more. She knew Robert had paid the landlord till the end of this month, but had expected to be home before the next instalment was due. There was only ten days left till the next was to be paid. Oh God! she thought wearily as she turned into the elegant entrance. Back to the beginning! And I don't even have the single-end any more. That safety net had been given up when she married.

'Are ye all right, Doctor Peggy?' Libby took one look at her white face and defeated expression. She had never seen Peggy so down.

'Och, I'm fine, Libby,' Peggy said slowly, but her slumped shoulders belied the brave words.

'Tell Libby, lass.' The housekeeper knelt beside her and cradled Peggy's icy hands in her rough warm ones.

'Kirsten and I have to leave here almost right away. I must find somewhere cheaper,' Peggy blurted out. 'Then I'll have to try and find somebody to look after her while I get a job. Brigadier McBride's Will could take months, even years, to sort out. The lawyers can only let me have five shillings a week for the baby. I'm sorry, Libby, you'll have to find somewhere else as well till Elspeth gets back.' She stifled a sob that rose despite her iron self-control. 'I wish we could contact her, but she's on the move all the time.

171

Can you stay with your cousin in Ayr . . . or maybe your sister in Milngavie?'

'Och, you've not to think about me, you poor wee lassie.' Libby spoke from the heart, for she had come to love Peggy dearly. 'It's you and the bonnie bairn we have to think about. I can look after my wee love while ye work, Doctor Peggy.'

'Libby, I can't pay a housekeeper,' Peggy replied sadly. 'Kirsten will have to go to a childminder, though I must be careful.' Her voice shook. 'Some of them are terrible.'

'Childminder?' Libby was aghast. 'They'll be no childminders for that bairn while there's a breath in Libby Purdie's body! Now listen, Doctor Peggy, Kirsten will be as safe as houses with me. Libby has always been there since the little love opened her big brown eyes. She knows Libby and loves her, doesn't she?' Libby got up and lifted the baby who crowed happy agreement. All the old maid's pent-up maternal feelings had fastened on to the fatherless child.

'See!' she said triumphantly. 'Bonnie wee thing, canny wee thing – she kens every word Libby says, so she does!'

'But, Libby, we've nowhere to go. We'll be living in some cramped tenement till I get a job and get on my feet.'

'What are ye on about, woman?' The housekeeper shook her head firmly. 'I've got my income from Elspeth's dear mama. I've hardly spent a penny of it since she died and that's nearly ten years ago. We can find a respectable wee place to rent for the three of us. Then you get on with yer doctoring and I'll get on with baking the scones and loving the wee angel.'

'Do you mean that, Libby?' Peggy looked at her in astonishment.

'Of course I do. You don't think I would walk out on the pair of ye! What do you take me for woman. Come on, have a cup of tea then get yer coat back on. I'll fix the pram and we can start looking. Where do you think? Anniesland is nice and not as dear as folk imagine.'

'Anniesland would be wonderful.' Peggy got up, tears in her eyes. 'And so are you, Libby, so are you . . . och, Libby, Libby!'

'That's the way. Come on, cry it out, you poor lass.'

Libby put down the baby. A great sob racked Peggy's slender body as she gave way at last to the terrible grief bottled up since Robert died. Abandonedly she wept in the older woman's arms.

'Peggy! My love, are you bearing up? I'm so sorry about Robert, so very sorry.' Three months later, fresh from America, Elspeth arrived at last. She found their modest hideaway easily from the letter Peggy had sent to her London address.

'Of course I'm bearing up, Elspeth, hard work's the best therapy! Come in.' Peggy drew her into the tiny hall.

'Whew, I'm exhausted!' Elspeth threw her hat on to the sofa and sank down. 'Where's Libby?'

'She'll be down in a minute.'

'Well, what an awful state of affairs! I was shocked to get your letter. You should have tried to contact me in America, Peggy,' Elspeth chided. 'I'd have come home at once. What's going on now? Why are you living here in this poky place?'

'It's not that small. We have three rooms and a kitchen. Whole families have less in Cowcaddens,' Peggy replied with a grin. 'I couldn't afford Robert's apartment because of the mix up with his father's Will. There was no choice but to get out.'

'Yes, you said that in your letter. You must have been distraught!'

'Elspeth, I was going mad with desperation and grief. It was like being back in the old days after my daddy died. All alone, facing a struggle for every penny, and probably living in some stinking single-end with poor little Kirsten. But dear Libby saved the day. This wee house is rented on the money she inherited from your mother.' Peggy spoke with pride of the other woman's sacrifice. 'I work to provide the food and the upkeep. The furniture came from Robert's apartment and we polish our own floors these days!' Peggy smiled.

'Good for Libby. Does she know I've arrived?' Elspeth sounded puzzled. 'She's usually down right away when she hears my voice.'

'I'm sure she knows, but she was with the baby when the door went, that's why I answered.'

'Oh, I expect she'll be here any second with the eternal tea-tray, telling me off!' Elspeth cocked an ear. 'What did I tell you?' Her smile broadened as the door opened and a laden tray poked round the corner with Libby carefully manoeuvring it in.

'Miss Elspeth, welcome home. I've made a pot of tea. And ye'll be wanting some of my nice warm scones. Och, look at ye . . . as thin as a stick, not a pick on yer bones! Ye don't take care of yerself, neither ye do!' Libby arrived in full fettle.

'What a lovely tea, Libby. You're wonderful and I've been thinking about your scones all the way round America.' Elspeth was rewarded with a glowing smile from the house-keeper.

'Has Doctor Peggy told ye everything?' The beam faded suddenly. 'Och, dearie me, I'll just away. Ye can manage the tea yerselves, can't ye? I think I can hear my bonnie wee love crying again. It's the wind!' Libby dumped the tray unceremoniously with a clatter on to a butler's table that had belonged to Robert's grandmother, and shot off in the direction of the wailing.

'Well, you've lost out there, Elspeth,' Peggy teased. 'She has hardly any time for anybody since the little tyrant in the back room took over.'

'Thank heavens for that!' Elspeth spoke from the heart. 'Anything that will keep Libby from driving me mad with worried letters full of admonitions, cuttings from newspapers about suffragettes in prison and endless anxious questions, is good news!'

'She dotes on Kirsten, I assure you.'

'Well, I have a vested interest myself in Kirsten, since I'm going to be her godmother . . . that's right, isn't it?'

'If you insist.' Peggy smiled affectionately. 'Though I hadn't thought to christen her. Och, I'm that glad to see you again, Elspeth.' She hugged her. 'It's been a rotten time.'

'I know, my dear, but the worst is surely over.' Elspeth laid a comforting arm across her shoulders. 'And you must take me to see the baby once I've revived a little.' She sighed. 'God, it's a long journey from London via a couple of suffrage marches in Manchester, even by express train.' After a moment, Elspeth looked hard at Peggy over the rim of her teacup. 'What are you going to do now?'

'What we're doing, I suppose, for a while yet,' she replied crisply. 'I would have gone back to work even if there had been no pressing reason to do so. Kirsten is wonderful, but life is so empty without Robert. I hardly dare think more than a little while ahead, it hurts so much. Och, Elspeth, the idea of life without him . . .' Despite the brave words earlier, Peggy's eyes filled.

'Well, now I'm back, I want to help, especially since I intend staying down in London for the time being. Unfortunately I'm rather short of funds right now so I can't plan anything too radical, though I do have my income.' Elspeth nodded vigorously. 'Yes, that's the best thing . . . why don't we just share what I have and keep each other company at the same time? Oh, my poor dear girl.' She saw a tear slide slowly down her friend's cheek and got up, putting her arms round her. 'Am I being too crass as usual? I really am sorry about Robert, Peggy, though he and I were never close. We never really knew each other at all. It's such an awful waste!'

'It wasn't anything you said, Elspeth, I just can't talk about him yet without making a complete fool of myself by crying,' Peggy said quietly, head bowed. 'It's all beginning to feel like a dream . . . the last year, our marriage, his absence, that terrible telegram saying he was ill, then just the next day one to tell me he was dead. I look into little Kirsten's eyes and see him staring back at me. I'm still trying to understand that he will never come back . . . never.'

'Well then, Peggy, why don't you and Libby come to London? Bring the baby and stay with me like I said. Just take things easy. If you prefer, I can make you a small independent allowance on top of the pittance the lawyer has given you. I'm well past my majority and can do what I want with my income . . . except touch the Trust capital, of course.'

'Elspeth McClure.' Peggy kissed the fine-boned, serene face with its unjust mark. 'I'm not going to do anything of the sort, but I must tell you that you're the most wonderful friend anyone could have. Many's the time in the last nine years I've blessed your stubbornness in forcing me out of my isolation. My life would have been a lot bleaker without you, so it would.'

'Och, fiddlesticks!' Elspeth reddened. 'You'd have been fine without me bumbling in and out, nagging at you to join this and that and then dumping all my responsibilities on your shoulders while I do exactly as I please.'

'What responsibilities?'

'Libby and the house, while I had it.'

'God, those were and are pleasures! Libby's an asset, not a liability. Look what she did for Kirsten and me. No, you've been generous enough.' Peggy made a visible effort to regain control of herself. 'Robert is dead and I have to make a fresh start for myself and Kirsten. I fought to become a doctor, so I had better get on with it. If Libby wants to go with you, I'll have to make other arrangements for the baby, otherwise I'll carry on here. Now I'm working, I could just about afford to pay the rent and a nurse myself.'

'We'll see what she says, but the other offer remains,' Elspeth said firmly.

'Would you mind if Libby stayed with me and Kirsten . . . if that's what she chooses, of course?'

'Mind? Not a bit!' Elspeth's face broke into a broad smile. 'It would be the best news I've had since Australian women got the vote in 1902! Where are you working?'

'I got a temporary locum position in Greenock. There are no permanent openings for women just now, at least none I've been able to locate. I didn't want to work in a Poor Law Infirmary while Kirsten is so young.'

'Hmm, yes, it wouldn't be fair on the baby to risk bringing home some dreadful fever. General practice might be safer for a while.' Elspeth gave a crisp professional nod. 'Was Greenock the only place? It's a bit of a journey, isn't it?'

'There was a post in Ayr, but I prefer Greenock. It's not so far really, and anywhere in Ayrshire holds too many memories for me.'

'As for me,' Elspeth agreed. 'But you wouldn't have to work near Kirkowen, would you?'

'No, the post was in Ayr itself. Have you heard anything

of your father?' Peggy regretted the spontaneous question as soon as she had asked. Tacitly they never talked of Hamish McClure.

'Actually, I have,' Elspeth replied without hesitation or embarrassment. 'That's another reason why I came post-haste to Glasgow ... though not the main one, of course. The fool has been trying to get Sinclair to stop my income from the Trust. There was a letter about that too, awaiting my return.'

'Can he do that?'

'Not under normal circumstances, but he claims I'm insane!'

'What!'

'Yes, he regards my militancy in fighting so publically for women's suffrage as incipient madness. And I don't suppose he's the only man in Britain who thinks the same.' She gave an ironic guffaw.

'Has he a chance of winning?'

'I hope not. It is 1909, after all. Twenty or thirty years ago almost definitely he would have. Sinclair wants me to come and discuss it, though he assures me that my father cannot touch the capital nor the Trust income unless the court rules it.'

'Why does he want to make such a stupid accusation now? You don't meddle in his life, why should he meddle in yours? You haven't even met for years. And you've not exactly been discreet about your past suffrage activities.'

Elspeth looked grim. 'Flora has produced only one child so far – another girl, Louisa. And I heard she has lost at least two babies since, poor girl. Father will keep going till she manages to produce a son, or dies in the attempt,' she said brutally. 'But the main reason for his sudden interest in me, according to what Sinclair has been able to glean, is financial. Father gambled heavily on South African gold investments which were weakened by the Boer War. Coal mining in Ayrshire has not been doing too well either lately. There is no mystery about it, Peggy, he wants my money.'

'But it's held in Trust.'

'Yes, but like most Trusts, my proven insanity would allow him to use it "on my behalf". Failing that, and he will fail,'

177

her face became grimly determined, 'he needs another war to stimulate sales so he can recoup his losses.'

'I see. When are you going back to London?' Peggy changed the subject, unable to trust herself even to go on thinking about the detestable man.

'As soon as possible. We're planning a new London campaign and maybe a "Suffrage Fair" early next year to bring our case back before the Government. We hope that 1909 will be the year women finally get the right to vote. We need to make people sit up and listen!'

'Suffragettes have been doing that quite enough this last couple of years with "Women's Parliaments", demonstrating in the Lobby at Westminster, going to prison, and God knows what all else,' Peggy commented wryly.

'It's still not enough for the Pankhursts, nor me either, for that matter. We won't stop till we get the vote, whatever sacrifice it takes!' Elspeth's eyes gleamed. 'If some of the colonies have female suffrage, why not the Mother Country? Ludicrous!'

'Talking of the Pankhursts, the more scurrilous newspapers have been making much of Mrs Pankhurst's friendship with Keir Hardie. Is it true?'

'Certainly not!' Elspeth laughed at the idea. 'It's Sylvia who is Keir's paramour . . . has been for years, but don't tell the reporters.'

'Sylvia? Keir Hardie must be well past fifty now and she can't be more than twenty-six?'

'Sylvia claims they are "twin souls and divine confidants" . . . met in another life . . . all that twaddle!' Elspeth was sceptical. 'I don't know why she needs him. Women make far more faithful and sensitive friends, on the whole.' Just in time she remembered Peggy's bereavement.

'Oh, well, good luck to them. What's Lillie Hardie saying about it all?' Peggy wondered about Keir's patient wife who lived quietly in Cumnock with their children. 'Is she still keeping out of his public life?'

'Yes, completely. Oh, I can understand Keir's being attracted to Sylvia. He's a lonely man and his wife is just not up to his intellectual level. I don't think there is much left of that marriage but habit. Sylvia is very communicative and bright. Perhaps she needs a father-figure. Obviously they have something to offer each other.' Elspeth gave a nonchalant shrug.

'Well, it's up to them, I'm not going to point the finger.'

'Actually I spoke to him in London the day before yesterday just before I left,' Elspeth added. 'He was sorry when I told him you had been widowed.'

'I'm surprised he remembers me.'

'Oh, he certainly does. It was years after I got to know him that he discovered first who I was and then that I was friends with Jamie Soutar's daughter. You should have seen his face!' Elspeth gave a jaunty grin 'Especially since he suffered at the hands of Hamish McClure himself. It says a lot for the character of the man that he accepted me without question.'

'What did he say about you and me?'

'Nothing! I told him we both could look beyond the mistakes of the past, and of others. He agreed that was the right attitude. He always asks after you when we meet at rallies: "How is that bright lass of Jamie's getting on?" ' She imitated Hardie's rolling Ayrshire accent. 'It's a shame you didn't take up your father's interest in politics Peggy.' Elspeth forgot to be sympathetic for a moment. 'You would be an asset to the WSPU.'

Peggy smiled. 'I was too occupied with surviving and too obsessed with becoming a doctor, Elspeth. Now I have Kirsten to think about, the chances of my becoming involved are even slimmer.'

'I know better than to force you where you don't want to go, Peggy. But for now, lead me to this amazing child. I expect Libby will send me a letter each week, describing every burp and ounce gained in weight . . . if she doesn't decide to come home with me, of course.'

'Come on, then, Kirsten will need a feed anyway,' Peggy led the way up to the little alcove next to Libby's room that they used as a nursery. The older woman was sitting by the cradle, crooning gently as the baby stirred.

Elspeth put an arm round her shoulders. 'Are you coming to London, Libby or do you want to stay here with Peggy?'

'Och, you don't need me, Miss Elspeth,' Libby replied

179

without a moment's hesitation. 'And ye always come like a homing pigeon to Doctor Peggy when you're in Scotland. I can see ye then. Anyway, you're never down there from what I hear. I'd be on my own all the time in that heathen place among all they foreigners.' She bent over and tickled the baby's little feet. 'Och, no, I couldn't leave my bonnie wee lambie, now could I? Anyway you'll be glad to get me off your back.' Libby knew her old mistress well. The offer was dismissed and the case closed.

'Maybe you're right!' Duty done, Elspeth breathed a sigh of relief then turned to Peggy who had watched the exchange with amusement. 'By God, I hope when this child is a grown women, we will have had the vote for decades!' She looked down at the waking infant, jaw set in determination. 'Just think, Peggy, Kirsten could be a parliamentary figure. Or the head of a great corporation. Why not?'

'Why not indeed?' Peggy smiled and opened her blouse in preparation for the feed. Kirsten had wakened fully and was gazing at Elspeth with big dark eyes. 'And somebody else agrees with you.' Peggy smiled, picked up the baby and gently turned the auburn head to her breast.

On the train back to London, Elspeth sat alone in the first-class carriage, thinking of Hamish McClure's attempt to have her declared insane. Sinclair had been more worried about it than she had expected, but he assured her he and the other Trustees would do what they could to quash the case before it reached court. He's exaggerating the risk, Elspeth told herself till she almost believed it.

Before long she tired of thinking about the whole business, opened her case and drew out a folder, then sat single-mindedly drafting a pamphlet to spearhead the next stage of the campaign. After a couple of hours, writing in the jolting train began to give her a headache. Sighing, she put down her pen, leaned back and watched idly as the last miles flew past.

It's getting nigh on impossible to summarise exactly what all the different groups within the movement want! Logical Elspeth felt a surge of exasperation. If we go on like this there will be another split in the WSPU! It's a pity all the leaders are so at odds with one another. We have the same goal, why dissipate energy in rows and divisions?

Elspeth's own loyalties were torn since the Pankhurst family itself had divided. Charismatic, dictatorial, efficient Christabel, with her First Class degree in Law, was pushing hard for controlled militancy rather than the dramatic gestures favoured by equally charismatic, artistic, emotional Sylvia and her friends. On the whole Elspeth agreed with Christabel, even if her manner was hard to take at times.

'Paddington!' The train pulled in with a final belch of steam and cinders.

Elspeth got up stiffly and packed the sheaf of papers into her portfolio. At least the cause is worth the struggle, she thought. Though maybe I'll be eating those words soon in Holloway! In consideration for Peggy's grief, she had glossed over the risk of going to prison. But Elspeth knew that the demonstration she was about to take part in meant that fate was almost certain.

Chapter 14
This partial view of humankind

'Christabel, listen to me, for heaven's sake! We've known each other such a long time, you know I'm objective, it's my hallmark!' Elspeth tried to talk her old friend out of causing yet another split in the ranks of the WSPU.

'Elspeth, you mean well, but there can't be a whole tribe of leaders. Mother and I are quite sufficient!'

'I know that. I've never disputed your ability to lead and lead well, either of you, but expelling Teresa Billington last year, constant rows with Sylvia : . . and now the break with our old friend Keir Hardie. You're isolating us too much. Since they started this horrible practice of force-feeding in September, we need more than ever to present a united front in protest!'

'Of course, we are all opposed to force-feeding.'

'Well, why don't we try to reunite the movement? For goodness' sake, we can surely accommodate differences of opinion on means if we achieve our ends quicker.'

'Rubbish! It's better that we have a small core of totally dedicated people than dilute it with those who are willing to compromise on our goal.' Christabel's face set in determination. 'Adult suffrage is not enough! We want Votes for Women now!'

'Och, you're both right,' interjected Fiona Drummond, the cheery, stout little Scot nicknamed 'the general' from the uniform she habitually wore. 'Here, take these, lassie dear!' She thrust a pile of pamphlets at Elspeth. 'But I do think it's a pity to break with Keir, Christabel . . .'

'You're biased, Fiona,' Christabel said acidly. 'You think

the sun shines out of the man. You even called your son after him. I admit he's been a great supporter of women's rights all along, but he's wavering about how it should be achieved.'

'Exactly, that's the point. The arguments in the WSPU are only about how we reach our goal, not what the ultimate goal is,' Elspeth insisted. 'People are beginning to say that you're too dictatorial, Christabel.'

'So what if I am?' She shrugged. 'Better that than have no clear direction.'

'Well, lately you've opposed all demonstrations you haven't planned yourself, even if they're sound.' Despite her admiration for Christabel, Elspeth wasn't afraid to speak her mind.

'If everyone comes up with their own schemes, we'll get nowhere!'

'That's generally correct, but you could at least consider Sylvia's plan. We have to protest against force-feeding with all our might. The King has personally sanctioned it. Every prison medical officer in Britain has been instructed to go ahead.'

'Hah!' Fiona sniffed, 'I'm surprised the selfish old rake took time off from flaunting his mistresses in Marienbad to write that vicious letter to Herbert Gladstone.'

'Well, he did. We must bring matters to a head at once. I believe Sylvia's idea is an excellent way to do it. The press will be present and can get a story right away,' Elspeth concluded firmly.

'Oh, go and join the stupid demonstration if you want, Elspeth,' Christabel replied icily, 'but don't blame me if you end up in prison being force-fed yourself. You've been lucky to escape so far.'

'I know that. And I also know this time is likely to break that run of luck. But you've been in Holloway before now and you used to organise schemes just as daring. What's gone wrong?'

'Nothing's gone wrong. When I was in Holloway, Sylvia made a mess of leading the WSPU and that's why I'm determined to avoid that happening again. Mother says she is willing to go back to prison and be force-fed if necessary, but that I shouldn't. We both feel a permanent leader working outside prison is essential. It's vital that someone holds the movement on course just now, with Mother heart-broken over poor brother Harry and touring America much of the time.'

'I know all that and I agree in principle...' Elspeth broke in.

'1910 will be the year women get the vote,' Christabel went on, ignoring her. 'So I have to be in charge, making sure we get it, not sitting in solitary confinement waiting for tubes to be stuck down my throat or up my nose. Sylvia is much better at making such gestures!' Christabel turned her elegant back, bending over a pile of papers spread over the desk. 'Oh, please yourself, Elspeth,' she finally threw her half-hearted agreement over her shoulder.

'I'll certainly do that,' Elspeth said quietly. She had known the other woman too long to expect any further concessions.

'All right, let's get on with the plans for the campaign. I'm thinking of asking the Pethwick-Lawrences to coordinate another window-breaking campaign in the West End for the autumn. What do you think, Elspeth?'

'I prefer demonstrations and rallies to any violence, but all right, I won't oppose you.'

'Fine.' Christabel rarely bore grudges and quickly got over her chagrin; now she was all charm, putting her arm around Elspeth's shoulders and accompanying her to the door. 'I'll discuss it with you and the others next week at the WSPU meeting – that's if you're not scrubbing floors alongside prostitutes in Holloway,' she teased.

Elspeth beckoned a cab standing at the corner of the square. As it clattered smartly through the darkening cobbled streets towards her comfortable house in Chelsea, she thought of what lay ahead. In her heart she knew she was doing the right thing joining Sylvia's protest against force-feeding suffragettes, but her stomach tightened with nervous anticipation all the same.

Keeping her head bent well forward, scarf and hat shading the tell-tale mark that could give her away to the stewards, Elspeth slipped into the High Court. As agreed familiar faces were dotted round the room, but the women dared not acknowledge each other for fear of discovery. All were lightly disguised with scarves, glasses or wide-brimmed hats. The trial of their two colleagues from the league was just drawing to a close.

Little Zelie Emerson and Norah Smyth defended themselves as vigorously as they could in the witness box, defiantly denying the charges of resisting arrest and verbal abuse to the police. But they were not allowed to put their case fully and were cut off in mid-stream. The verdict was a foregone conclusion. Only sentence had still to be pronounced.

'Two months' imprisonment.' The judge barely managed to say the words when, at a signal, all the WSPU women stood up and threw off their coats. Everyone was clad in white and purple suffrage dresses with sashes over their shoulder. Immediately they began shouting: 'Votes for Women!' 'Stop force-feeding!' 'Votes for Women!' 'Stop force-feeding!' Stewards rushed forward amid the chaos, to evict them from the court room.

'Let go of me!' Elspeth struggled as three men seized her arms and unceremoniously bundled her into the corridor. Her hat fell askew and her long hair began slipping from its confining bun.

The women waiting outside took up the chant 'Stop force-feeding!' 'Votes for Women!' as the noise of the fracas drifted out. Furious, the judge ordered the arrest of the five who had been inside and charged them at once with contempt of court.

Judge Smith was well known for his hard line against suffragettes. 'You women must be shown such behaviour cannot be tolerated!' he thundered as they were brought back into the dock.

Since it was Elsepth's first offence, she was given one month without the option of a fine. Sylvia, as a persistent offender, was sentenced to double that, as were the others. Judge Smith insisted that each of them should spend fourteen days of their imprisonment in the Third Division at Holloway among the common criminals. 'For such are these women proving themselves to be. Their actions strike at the very fabric of law and order!' His face was severe and his voice solemn.

'Remember what we agreed!' Sylvia yelled as they were bundled into a fleet of Black Marias with other women who had been sentenced that day. 'Hunger strike at once while you are still strong, but only for the two weeks in Division Three this time! We can nod to each other in chapel. Keep in good spirits. Votes for Women!'

'Right, you, this way. There's a space left in van 405.' Elspeth found herself separated from the others to make up the complement in the first van to leave.

'Bastards . . . effing swine!' Some of the female convicts in Elspeth's prison van screamed and yelled, hammering on the back of the van till the court was out of sight, while others wept or sat silently grim-faced.

'Oh, you must be a fuckin' suffragette?' A skinny young woman with matted hair, looked assessingly at Elspeth's neat, expensive coat.

'Well, she ain't a high-class whore!' Another nodded meaningfully at her birthmark.

'Yes, you're both right,' Elspeth said quietly, trying to come to terms with what had happened. The smell of sweat and ingrained dirt in the Black Maria was oppressive. She was glad her early experiences as a student doctor in the poor clinics of Glasgow meant she didn't flinch.

'Fuckin' mad, gettin' arrested for that sort of thing!' commented another.

A dozen other pairs of hostile eyes glared across the van. As it clattered its way towards Holloway, the women were tossed against one another at every corner. Elspeth expected she would end up covered with lice and fleas by the time the journey was over.

'It takes all sorts,' she replied evenly, realising that hostility would be the wrong reaction. She would have to spend the next month with women like these and learn to rub along, or it would be impossible to survive.

'Yer right there, luv,' an older woman sighed. 'But I can't understand why the likes of you does it. Here's me walkin' the streets for twenty years and tryin' to avoid being nicked all the time. You lot go out and ask for it!'

'Fuckin' mad, like I said,' repeated the younger woman.

'It's a matter of principle.' Elspeth smiled gravely. 'We think that men are no more entitled to make important decisions than women. Why shouldn't we have a say in running the country, we work hard enough? "Women should vote for the laws they obey and the taxes they pay!" ' she quoted a popular WSPU banner.

'You've got a point there, ducks.' The older woman nodded. 'The men I've met in my time couldn't be trusted to look after a plate of whelks, let alone the country.'

'I fink they're jest fuckin' mad.' Her companion was still not convinced.

Once the Black Maria stopped within the gates of Holloway, the women were taken immediately to reception. There was no sign of the other suffragettes in the grim prison yard; Elspeth assumed they must be arriving later. Her van seemed to have been the first to leave the courtyard.

'Name!'

'Elspeth Janet McClure.'

'Address!'

'Care of McBride, 2 Riddrie Lane, Anniesland, Glasgow.' It felt like a life-line to have at least some outside contact through Peggy and Libby. There was no one at all at the London flat.

'Sentence!'

'One month.'

'Right, medical inspection! Line up. Strip to the waist,' the wardress ordered curtly.

God! Elspeth slipped off her outer dress and began unfastening her chemise.

'Hurry up, you.' She was proded unceremoniously in the back.

'Lean forward. Cough!' The elderly male doctor walked up the line and palpated the breasts of each woman. Elspeth winced as his hands grabbed her before he moved on.

'Baths!' She looked in disbelief at the huge cold room with its rows of big iron baths.

'Come on, luv.' The older woman nudged her. 'Drop 'em and get in or they'll lift you in!'

She looked at the grim-faced wardresses and realized the

truth of the advice. Dropping her clothes in a pile, she climbed into the filthy water, scummed with the dirt from other bodies.

'Ready?'

'Yes.' She climbed out as quickly as she was allowed and dried herself on the rough towel. Following the others, she pulled out a pair of calico bloomers and a dark brown serge prison outfit from the piles on the floor. With difficulty, she managed to find a pair of shoes in approximately her size from the racks round the room. Many others had worn them before her.

It was worse being a doctor and knowing what could be caught. Elspeth suppressed a shudder and hoped no one with foot-fungus or warts had worn that particular pair.

The cell was small with a bare electric light bulb attached to the wall. Elspeth could see there had recently been a gas jet there instead. 'Progress,' she muttered ironically.

A round badge made of dull yellow cloth hung on a nail. The cell number, prison block and letter were printed on it. 'Pin that on. You'll answer only to the cell number from now till you're transfered,' the wardress rapped out curtly. Impatiently she waited while Elspeth fumbled to obey, forcing the pin through the thick brown serge of her uniform.

'You roll your bed like this.' She was shown how to make the whole parcel of sheets and blankets into a tight sausage and warned she would be punished if it was not done properly. 'These three rags are to clean out your pint.' The wardress handed her two pieces of frayed brown serge and one of calico. Elspeth tried not to gag, the rags had obviously been well used before her.

'Is there water?' she asked politely.

'No. Soap one of the brown rags with that.' She pointed to the cake of yellow soap Elspeth had been given for her own use. 'Then take that bathbrick and fold the rag round it, rub it on the floor to get some dust and use it to scour the pint clean.'

'Then do I wash it?'

'You don't wash it at all!' the other woman said irritably.

'Wipe the dust off with the other brown rag then polish the pint with the calico.'

God, Elspeth thought wearily, so much for hygiene!

'I'll be back in a few minutes.' The wardress left, clanging the door shut and locking it.

Right, Elspeth McClure. You're going to make this a positive experience, she told herself firmly when the woman had gone. Ouch! The mattress on the bed was hard as a rock and filled with what seemed to be straw. Fourteen days here and then fourteen in the luxury of the Second Division. Och, it'll pass. Elspeth took refuge in reciting a favourite poem:

> *'Along the solitary shore,*
> *Where fleeting sea-fowl round me cry,*
> *Across the rolling, dashing roar,*
> *I'll westward turn my wistful eye.'*

'Right, Number 14, scrub the floor, shelves, bed and floor.' The door clanked open and a pail of water was thrust in, together with a scrubbing brush. 'You'll usually be doing this before breakfast.' The door slammed shut again and the key turned.

'Empty your slops, Number 14.' Next morning, after a restless night, Elspeth was waiting when the wardress unlocked the cell door. She had already washed as well as she could in the little tin basin and got dressed. Half an hour earlier the bells had rung and the electric light had been switched on automatically.

'Where's your pint, 14?' a gruff voice demanded and she handed over her tin. Some watery gruel was poured into the pint and six ounces of dry bread were handed over. As agreed with the other suffragettes, the food went back untouched. Then Elspeth began the rough sewing that was part of her sentence. Just as well I learned ordinary seam-stitch and not just fancy embroidery, she thought ruefully. Otherwise I'd be hard pushed to sew fifteen of these things a week.

Elspeth found the five days of solitary confinement that

189

began her sentence hardest to cope with. In the bare cell the only book, the Bible, was impossible to read in the poor light. The print was far too small. I'd love a walk . . . a breath of air. A wave of unexpected nostalgia swept over her for the clear air of her native Ayrshire. Och, what I would give to hear the cry of sea-birds on Kirkowen cliffs. The third day dragged to a close. But at least it's not hard to go on hunger-strike. Ruefully Elspeth looked at supper. The food is appalling!

On the fourth day, the prison doctor came in with two of the wardresses carrying a bowl of gruel and a long tube. Elspeth knew they were about to force-feed her. Her heart sank. She had seen the results of this on other prisoners.

'I must tell you at once, Doctor' she said firmly, 'I'm a doctor myself and I do not accept the need for force-feeding. It is dangerous.'

'Oh, doctor indeed? And where do you practise?'

'I'm was house-doctor at the Women's Hospital.'

'Well, Doctor, or Number 14 as I should call you,' he said heavily, 'in that case you know what the result of your refusal to take food will be. But in the light of your superior experience, I'll give you a couple more days to change your mind.'

'Thank you, but I won't.'

'Please yourself.' He shrugged and signalled to the wardresses to remove the bowl and the equipment they had brought.

As promised, they were back in a couple of days. Elspeth was weak and tired after her continued hunger-strike, but defiant as ever. 'If you countervene any of the regulations concerning force-feeding of prisoners, Doctor, I will write immediately to the *Lancet* when I get out of here.'

'Nonsense! The *Lancet* doesn't like women doctors, so I doubt they'll publish!' the elderly man said sourly. 'And I may as well tell you, neither do I. Now open your mouth and eat this or we'll get it down you one way or the other.' He looked sternly at the determined, marked face of the young woman in front of him. The port-wine stain glowed livid in the dim light, but her eyes were calm and steady.

'Aggrahh!' Elspeth could hear herself scream and she felt

her whole body arch in agony as the steel gag he had forced between her teeth bit into the flesh and held her jaws unnaturally far apart. Dribbles of blood ran down her chin and on to the sheet they had covered her with.

'Sit still! Hold her steady, you stupid women!' The doctor hissed at the wardresses. They tried to obey, twisting her arm till she felt it would break.

'That'll do for now.' The doctor wiped his hands and withdrew the tube from down her throat.

Immediately she gagged, but her stomach refused to throw up all of the food.

After he had gone, two of the wardresses stayed behind and tried to comfort her kindly enough, but all Elspeth wanted to do was die.

As she lay on her bed, tears dripping silently on to the hard straw pillow, she heard the horrible sounds of her friends suffering the same fate.

The process was repeated the next day, the next, and the next. 'Tut-tut, Doctor McClure,' the doctor said sarcastically. 'Three times now and still you ask for more. Vomit it up and we'll put it straight back again.'

Bastard! Elspeth thought, but had no voice to speak with even had she wanted to; the four feedings through the tube had bruised her throat so much that speech was impossible for hours after each session.

'Now be sensible. You're going over to the other side soon. Start eating and we'll all be far better off.'

Only two more days, she told herself as she sipped water and nursed her swollen face. Thank God we've agreed only to hunger-strike for part of this time. I don't think I could take much more. How does Sylvia cope with this over and over again?

Peggy was worried to death when she heard Elspeth was in Holloway. In a fit of moral cowardice, she decided not to tell Libby, but she immediately contacted Keir Hardie.

Defying the ILP, which was trying to keep a low profile on the whole business, Hardie stood up in the House and objected to forcible feeding. To his disgust, the women's sufferings only seemed to amuse many of the men. Furious, he protested in a long letter to the *Daily News*, which they published on 29 September. It finished with: 'I was horrified at the levity displayed by a large section of the Members of the House when the question was being answered . . .'

Keir Hardie could not get the sentences shortened, but he managed to have Elspeth's last two weeks spent in the First rather than the Second Division of Holloway. Here the women came under the category of political prisoner and their treatment was dramatically different. Elspeth wrote a relieved letter at once to Peggy.

> Oh, the bliss of being able to send out for food, to read and to write. But it is shocking to meet up again with some of my fellow suffragettes. All of us have blood-shot eyes from the force-feeding and our bodies seem to have shrunk in just two weeks.

'Elspeth!'

'Zelie! What have they done to you?' Zelie Emerson, already weak and thin from a previous hunger-strike, seemed to have almost disappeared. 'It's just as well we agreed not to go on for the month, or there would be nothing left of you at all!'

'You should have seen me the last time,' Zelie smiled. 'But poor Sylvia has been transferred to the hospital block – she began to haemorrhage. They ruptured a bloodvessel in her nose and nearly punctured a lung.'

'My God!' Elspeth was aghast. 'Will she be all right?'

'I hope so.'

'Have you any more news?'

'Christabel has gone to Paris.'

'Why?'

'Emmeline came back from New York last week and Christabel feared she would be arrested herself soon. Emmeline thinks she should stay abroad till the risk is lessened. We all agree that someone has to carry on writing and publishing *The Suffragette* and organize overall tactics. The leader must live to direct the fight another day,' Zelie said with conviction.

'Well, there's something in that, I suppose.' Elspeth sounded less convinced. 'Does Sylvia know?'

'Yes, I got word to her. She wasn't too pleased – you know they're always at loggerheads. Sylvia wants to go off on another direction altogether . . . to start a section of the WSPU for slum-dwellers in London's East End.'

'Hmmm.' Elspeth remembered the slum-dwellers she had treated in hospital and was doubtful of Sylvia's potential success.

'Och, this has got to stop, Miss Elspeth!' Libby nearly had a fit when, gaunt and weary, Elspeth appeared in Glasgow after her release. 'Doctor Peggy just told me where ye've been yesterday when she knew ye were out and on your way here. I wondered why we'd heard nothing from ye for a few weeks, and the papers kept disappearing and coming back with bits cut out. I thought it was medical stuff she was collecting. Now I know what she was hiding – it was your daft antics!' The older woman did not mince her words.

'Och, I'm fine, Libby.' Elspeth hushed her with a hug. 'Now don't fuss. When is Peggy due in?'

'Any minute. And ye can sleep in my room like ye did the last time. I'll manage in the alcove with my bonnie wee lassie. Och, the bairn has a sight more sense than you, Elspeth McClure, so she has!'

'You're a gem, Libby, has anybody told you that?'

'I'd rather hear that you were giving up your activities.' She sniffed and fussed, shaking her head and muttering under her breath. 'Prison, of all things!' And: 'Daft lassies that should be big enough to ken better!'

'Oh, my dear Elspeth, how are you?' Peggy came home tired, shocked to see Elspeth's condition, but glad above all to see her and agog to hear the latest news. Elspeth had already warned her that part of the reason for coming was a worrying letter from Sinclair.

'Glad to be out, but worried!' She was direct as ever. 'While I was in prison my father decided to go ahead with his old plan. He's going to try to have me committed to an asylum.'

'Oh, no!' Peggy sat down heavily.

'I'm afraid so. Sinclair says that now he is motivated more by revenge than money, for the mines are doing well again.'

'Why, for God's sake?'

'I don't know. Maybe Sinclair has found out something new. I do hope so.' The birthmark burned on her pale, drawn face. 'Apparently this episode in Holloway is being used as evidence of my degenerating mental state. Also my selling the house in Glasgow and spending the money on lecturing in America is to be used to show I cannot be trusted to handle my own affairs. According to Sinclair's letter, an agency has been collecting information for months on Father's behalf. They even have pictures of me being hauled off by police. Very undignified.' Elspeth tried to smile, but couldn't.

'When is the case coming up?' Peggy felt the colour drain from her face.

'God knows. That's part of the trouble. It depends how quickly my father decides to act and when the court can do it. Sinclair says the case is low priority since I'm not considered a danger to anyone's life and limb but my own.' Elspeth gave a wry grimace. 'Father will have to wait his turn if there is a lot of work before the Ayrshire courts. In a way I'd rather get it done with, it's hanging over me like the sword of Damocles.'

'I can appreciate that,' Peggy agreed.

Elspeth paced the room like a caged lioness. 'The idea of looking over my shoulder for years, afraid to do anything in case someone will drag it up in court as further evidence against me, is horrifying. Och, I'll maybe know more when I see Sinclair tomorrow.'

'Are you worried?'

'More than I was the first time round,' Elspeth admitted. 'There's a lot of ill feeling against suffragettes just now. An unsympathetic judge wouldn't hesitate to have me committed. And once you're inside an institution, there is very little you can do to get out.'

'Go abroad for a while! Join Ellie in Florence, or Christabel in Paris if you prefer.' Peggy felt a shiver of fear for her friend.

'I may go to Christabel later,' Elspeth nodded, 'but not now. It could detract from my own defence if I run. And I can't stay away forever. If judgement was made against me in my absence, I would be virtually desitute.'

'You could go back to being a doctor,' Peggy teased gently. 'Och, Elspeth.' She got up and embraced the gaunt figure. 'Be careful.'

'Of course I will.' Elspeth gave her lovely smile.

A month later, Peggy had another welcome visitor at Riddrie Lane. Douglas Munro, fresh from New Zealand, called without warning one Saturday afternoon.

'Peggy! What a job I've had finding you! Are you all right?' His normally cheerful face was clouded and the anxious words tumbled over one another before she could greet him properly.

'Yes! No! Och, Douglas, what on earth are you doing here?' She hugged Robert's old friend. 'Man, it's great to see you! I thought you were still in New Zealand. Och, don't stand there, come inside!'

Douglas followed her into the tiny hall.

She took his coat and noticed at once how he had changed. His stocky figure was solid muscle now and he carried himself with an air of confident authority. 'New Zealand seems to have been good for you,' she smiled.

'A glorious country, Peggy, I spent every moment I had free roaming the mountains and exploring great valleys with steaming hot springs . . . just glorious. But we'll talk about me later. What a job I had to find you!'

'How did you trace us?'

'Well, it was no thanks to you, Peggy! Why didn't you write when you moved? I finally found you through the medical register. It said you were working for a Doctor MacDougall in Greenock and I followed the trail from there.'

'Oh, so you've met my dear employer, then?' Peggy grinned wryly.

Douglas laughed. 'He's a bit of an old terror, isn't he? At first he refused to help at all, then I invited him out for a drink and that did the trick. By goodness, he fairly loves his dram!'

'He does that!' Peggy's grin widened. 'When I got the job,

I wondered they were willing to appoint a woman. Then I discovered how little he does. MacDougall has gone through five male locums in the last year!'

'Well, you seem to be sticking it out, and he thinks highly of you . . . at least when he's in his cups!' Douglas's shrewd, intelligent eyes twinkled.

'Good to know! Though serving the area and its patients, not to mention coping with the peculiar ways of old Mac-Dougall, hasn't been easy.' Peggy said with feeling, 'Trudging through snow to dying old men . . . riding out to confinements in the middle of the night. Great stuff! Now give me that coat.'

'I'm afraid I can't stay long this time, Peggy, I'm on my way from London to a meeting in Edinburgh, but I couldn't pass by once I knew you were here,' Douglas said apologetically as she led the way into a cramped sitting-room.

'I hope it won't be the last visit.' She smiled. 'You're always welcome, you know that . . . if I'm here, which is all too seldom just now.'

'I don't envy you the job of Locum,' he replied thinking how thin and fragile she looked, 'it's hard graft.'

'You can say that again!' Peggy agreed. 'Never less than twelve hours, six days a week, sometimes all night too. And for £200 a year! But the experience is wonderful, Douglas, and the people I help make it worthwhile. At last I have a sense of what I was trying to achieve when I struggled all those years to get qualified.'

'Your dedication made the rest of us seem immature and frivolous . . . still does.'

'Fiddlesticks!' she said with a dismissive wave. 'Now I want to hear all your news. Och, it's that good you came.'

'I wasn't sure if I should,' Douglas said quietly, watching her reaction intently. 'Since you hadn't sent your new address, I thought maybe you didn't want to see me.'

'Why not, for God's sake?' Her eyes widened in surprise.

'Because I was so close to Rob. Because it might open wounds that haven't had a chance to heal yet.'

'Och, it wasn't that,' she replied shamefacedly. 'Look, I'm sorry I didn't write, but it has been a struggle here. There's been time for nothing more.'

'You did get my letter?' he asked.

'Yes, it was forwarded to me from Robert's old apartment.'

'If I had been any nearer than New Zealand when Rob died I could have come at once, but I was bound by contract. I did try to get out of it, to explain how close he and I had had been. But they refused to release me even on extended leave, there was nobody else to take over what I was doing . . . it was a bit specialized, I suppose.' He ran a hand through his hair. 'I couldn't believe it. It was a terrible shock.' He shook his head. 'I loved Rob as a brother . . . we had shared so much. Och, I still can't believe he's gone.' Douglas went on softly, pain in every word, 'But when I became too immersed in my own grief, I only had to think of what you must be suffering to feel ashamed.'

'Douglas Munro,' Peggy said, blinking back tears, 'always thinking about somebody else.'

'Now it's my turn to say fiddlesticks,' he retorted with some of his old familiar heartiness. 'I'm not as altruistic as you believe, young woman, but I am pleased to see you're managing.'

'With a lot of help from Libby. We're partners in renting this palace, you know.' Peggy glanced round the cramped room. 'And she takes marvellous care of Kirsten. They're out in the park right now. In fact, she'll be furious she wasn't here to make you a cup of tea.' Peggy got up. 'So I'd better do it.'

'Sounds fine.' He smiled.

'Are you back in Scotland for good?' she called from the kitchen through the rattle of porcelain and pots.

'I think so. I've just been appointed specialist in surgery at Edinburgh,' he replied modestly.

'Congratulations! You'll do it brilliantly, if your old form is anything to go by.' Peggy handed him a cup. 'I remember you used to show the rest of us how in surgery classes at university. That's when you weren't holding up the bar with Rob and the rest, chasing music-hall actresses, or tormenting female students.' Her eyes twinkled.

'Och, Peggy, don't remind me!' Douglas's ruddy complexion deepened. 'I'm ashamed of the rough time we gave

197

you in those days. Despite it all, you showed us the stuff you were made of. And you can tell Elspeth McClure that living in the Antipodes has certainly changed my attitude to women's rights and aspirations.'

'I certainly will, she'll be delighted.' Peggy grinned and sat down. 'Now you promised to tell me, how was New Zealand?'

An hour later Douglas stood up. 'I must go if I'm to make it to Edinburgh this evening, but I'll try to see you again once I've settled in, if I may?'

'Like I said, the door is open to you always.'

'Peggy, dear girl.' He lifted her hands and looked solemnly down into her eyes. 'If there is ever anything I can do, anything at all, just let me know.'

'Thank you, Douglas.' She was touched at his obvious concern and sincerity. 'Just come and talk to me sometimes, that's enough. It's comforting to speak to someone who was so close to Robert. For a little while it's brought his presence back into my life, I thank you for that.'

'Remember you have a friend, Peggy. Rob would have expected me to help, but I want to do it anyway.'

'I will. Now safe journey and good luck.' Sadly she waved him off, then turned and went into the makeshift nursery and stood looking down at the empty cradle. 'Och, Robert, Robert, this was not a bit like we planned.' For a few rare indulgent minutes she gave way to the deep grief carried day and night in her heart.

Chapter 15
The last time I came o'er the moor

'Ah, Mistress McBride, come in, come in.' Robert's lawyer ushered her into his office eighteen months later. 'This is my partner, Andrew Graham, who runs the Kilmarnock office.' He drew foward a handsome man in his late-thirties. 'He'll be handling your portfolio from now on. So, if you approve, I'll leave you to it.'

'How do you do, Mrs McBride?' Graham offered his hand with a pleasant smile.

'Mr Graham.' Peggy shook hands and sat down, folding her long skirts neatly round the chair.

'I'm sorry we took so long to sort this out,' the lawyer apologized profusely. 'But never in my time as a lawyer have we had such a complicated situation on our hands. Hopefully it's now resolved. The allowance we made you was not generous, Mrs McBride, you couldn't possibly have lived on it?'

'As I told your colleague, Mr Graham, I'm a doctor. For the last year or so I've been working, and with the help of good friends we've managed.'

'I heard that you were something of the sort.' His tone was dubious. 'Well,' he said briskly, 'the result of our efforts is rather mixed. Your deceased father-in-law had never met you, or I'm sure he would not have made such provisions as he did in the Will drawn up while Robert was in India. Also he had not expected his son to pre-decease him, other- wise you and your child would have benefited much more than I am afraid is the case.'

'Do you mean he cut us out of his Will?'

'Not exactly. He had left his houses in India and his wealth in that country to the children of his native mistress. Or widow, I should say. The Rawlpindi marriage was valid after all. They were married by a Church of Scotland missionary minister. It was binding if rather unorthodox . . . oh, perhaps that's not the most tactful phrase to use.' Mr Graham looked momentarily embarrassed at the slip.

'And Kirsten?' Peggy demanded. 'What about her?'

'Kirsten McBride inherits the family home in Kilmarnock which was transferred unconditionally to Robert and his offspring in the new Will. You have the right to live there, but it is hers. The house has been empty for years, though an agent has been keeping it cleaned and in good repair. It is regularly inspected and I believe in decent habitable condition,' Andrew Graham added with a touch of professional pedantry.

'But what does that actually mean for Kirsten and myself?' Peggy asked. 'Can I sell the house if I want?'

'No. It means you can live in the house for life if you choose, but you are not permitted to sell it, even to invest the money for her. Of course, on her majority – she can dispose of it . . . if you are willing to leave.'

'I see, but what about the upkeep?' The idea of finding funds to maintain some mausoleum of a house, till Kirsten was old enough to sell, appalled her.

'Ah!' The charming, professional smile was back. 'I'm pleased to say that, as is often done in such cases, there is a small Trust fund associated with the bequest for the maintenance of the house. But,' the smile disappeared again, 'it is really only enough for that.'

'I see.' Peggy's head was spinning, trying to work out exactly what impact this was going to have on their lives.

'However,' the lawyer continued, 'Kirsten will also inherit some capital directly from Robert's mother's estate. It's not much, but if it is wisely invested, there should be enough for education, food, a maid and other normal expenses for the child of gentlefolk. In other words, the bairn is provided for but not her mother. I'm sorry.'

'Oh, don't worry, Mr Graham. In the odd circumstances of Robert's and his father's deaths, I didn't count on any-

200

thing at all.' Peggy smiled at his obvious dislike of such an untidy situation. 'I'm not disappointed. In fact, if I understand you correctly, it's a lot more than we have now. But I'll have to go on working, that's obvious.'

'You really don't have to,' he protested. 'Kirsten's inheritance is not much, but with sound administration it could be improved. As her financial guardians through the various Trust provisions, we would have no objections to your using the money while she is small for general family expenses. Mind you, that's about the best we can do,' he added with an aplogetic shrug.

'Oh, that won't be necessary, I intend working anyway. When can we visit the house?'

'As soon as you wish.'

'Then we'll do so this weekend. Now you wanted to discuss your plans for augmenting Kirsten's income, Mr Graham?'

'Yes, indeed.' The lawyer was impressed by her air of confidence and independence. 'Would you like to do it now or on a later occasion?'

'Now, please, I'm a busy woman.' Suddenly she smiled and her green eyes glowed.

And too lovely to remain a widow, doctor or not! Andrew Graham thought, but kept his opinion discreetly to himself.

'Och, it's an awful size, Doctor Peggy.' Libby stared at the forbidding dark red sandstone building when they went to inspect Kirsten's inheritance that Saturday.

'You're right, Libby.' Peggy pushed open the big iron gate and led the way up the front path to the door. 'But at least it's been well looked after.' She pointed to the neat garden and big rhododendron bushes surrounded by wrought-iron railings.

'Aye, and it's handy for Kilmarnock station.' Libby began warming to the place.

'That's true, Libby . . . the town centre too.'

'Och, it's better than I feared when ye told me about it, Doctor Peggy.' Libby placed the pram outside the door, lifted Kirsten and followed Peggy into the vast hall.

'Kirsten inherits the furniture as well,' Peggy answered

Libby's unasked question as she opened doors and peeked into cupboards.

'Just as well,' Libby snorted, 'it would take a fortune to furnish a house this size. Our wee bits and pieces would rattle about like dried peas in a jar!'

'It's amazing.' Peggy looked around her. 'The whole place seems to have been frozen in time. Look at that.' She rubbed a finger across a window ledge. The surfaces were clean and hardly dusty at all, only the clocks stood eerily at different hours. 'Robert's own family haven't lived here for the last thirty years, maybe even longer. Rob visited sometimes with the lawyer, but I never followed him down. It didn't seem right somehow, before we were married. Then there was not time . . .' She swallowed hard.

Libby saw her distress and tried to distract her. 'That lawyer said it was kept cleaned and aired, did he no?'

'Yes, and it has been, well and truly.' Peggy sniffed the air. 'It's amazing – there's not a trace of damp or must. My God! Look at this, Libby!' The calendar on the wall was edged in funereal black and showed a picture of Prince Albert, the old Queen's late Consort, issued less than a month after his death in December 1861.

'Och, surely somebody has lived in the place since 1862?' Libby gawped unbelievingly.

'Oh, certainly! I know an unmarried great-aunt of Rob's stayed here. Maybe she just liked the picture!' Peggy laughed and the sound echoed through the empty house. 'She died about twenty years ago. Rob spent occasional holidays with her from boarding school but hated it. He said she was a right old dragon, and I gathered the antipathy was mutual! He usually went to friends instead, especially Douglas Munro's family.'

'Aye, Doctor Munro is a fine lad, so he is. It's a pity he doesn't live a wee bit nearer, Kirsten dotes on him.' Douglas was a great favourite of Libby's and she fussed happily during his occasional visits from Edinburgh.

'I think it's Libby who dotes on him,' Peggy teased.

The elderly housekeeper blushed. 'Och, the stuff's good and solid, so it is.' She hid her embarrassment in practicalities. 'Aye, good and solid!' She poked approvingly at the heavy furniture and drank in the general atmosphere of Victorian gentility.

'Well, it is Kirsten's home, so I suppose we had better move in,' Peggy said after they had looked the place over thoroughly from cellars to attics.

Libby nodded. 'It'll be a sight less cramped than where we are at any rate and Doctor Elspeth can have her own room when she comes to stay. Och, and don't you worry, Doctor Peggy. A wee embroidered tablecloth, a few lace doilies here and there, some nice aspydisters or whatever they call they big plants and we'll have brightened up the place in no time!'

Peggy, Libby and Kirsten moved to Kilmarnock within weeks. Peggy applied for the job of supervising doctor not far from the town, at Greenwoods Poor Law Infirmary where there was a long-standing vacancy. Bluntly she was turned down on grounds of her sex. They readvertised. In August she had to leave Greenock, when Dr MacDougall retired and sold the practice. With great reluctance she took a locum position in Ayrshire. The practice covered Maybole but not, thankfully, Kirkowen, the last place she wanted to work.

It's not that I'm afraid to go back, she told herself. Och, maybe it is! I sometimes wonder if I have any real place left in life, any roots at all. Wee Peggy Soutar has gone forever, that's for sure, but who is in her place? The question bothered her more and more these days. Och, I'm not dwelling on that! Nobody associates the barefoot lass, Peggy Soutar, with Doctor Margaret McBride. And why should they? I don't exactly advertise the connection.

The new job meant she could see Kirsten a little more often. That was a bonus for them all. Maybe something will come up soon nearer Kilmarnock, I'll keep a weather eye open, she consoled herself.

Unexpectedly, in January of 1913, Greenwoods Poor Law Infirmary contacted her and called her for interview.

'Er . . . we have not been able to find a suitable male candidate for the post.' The Chairman had the grace to look embarrassed. 'So on reflection we are offering it to you, Doctor McBride. Here are the conditions.'

Peggy took the papers he offered and read them carefully. 'Well, it's hardly surprising that you haven't had them queuing up at the gates at this salary,' she commented wryly.

'This is standard Poor Law pay – £120 per annum.'

'It was standard two or three years ago,' Peggy retorted, 'and not many men wanted the job then either.' She decided to gamble on their obvious need to fill the post. They would never have called me back if they weren't desperate, she thought, watching their reaction.

'You're not turning it down?' The stout leader of the board gaped incredulously.

'At that salary, yes.' Peggy's eyes didn't fall.

'Oh!' He looked dumfounded.

'And what was Doctor McBride thinking of asking instead?' volunteered the Treasurer nervously in the deathly silence that had fallen. 'Greenwoods is a Poor Law Infirmary, not a voluntary one. We have to think of the taxpayers' money, ye ken, Doctor.'

'I know that.' Peggy tried not to laugh at their affronted, bemused expressions. 'But I cannot afford to take a drop in salary for this appointment. I am a widow with a child to keep, gentlemen, as you know.'

'Och, aye. Tragic that, tragic.' The Chairman nodded. He had known the McBrides by reputation, but it was so long since any of the family had lived in Scotland, let alone in the house, he could not put a single face to the name.

'So, er, what might your present salary be, Doctor McBride?' queried the Treasurer.

'It is £200 per annum. Full Locum pay.'

'Nonsense! Don't agree! We could get a man for that!' The Chairman nearly burst his buttons in astonishment.

'Well, you won't get as well qualified a doctor for the price. You've seen my dossier.' Peggy knew her worth. 'Think about it, gentlemen.' She rose to leave, forcing them to their feet out of courtesy. A week later they acquiesced and she began working out the last few weeks of her time in the Maybole practice.

'I'm sorry you're going, Doctor McBride,' Doctor Abernethy, the senior partner, sighed when she told him. 'You're a right good doctor. We'll be hard pushed to replace you. I must admit both myself and Doctor McTaggart were a wee bittie nervous about taking you on. In fact, it was only because the shoe factory women up the road are covered nowadays by this new-fangled work insurance that we considered a lady doctor at all.'

'I know. Women are usually the poorest patients of any general practice,' Peggy said bluntly. 'Few of them have independent incomes to pay the doctor. Even now hardly any are fully covered by health insurance under the new Act.'

'Aye, well, that's the way of things,' Doctor Abernethy replied with a shrug.

'Anyway you didn't lose income by taking me on,' Peggy went on with a dry little smile. 'The men started coming to me too after they got over their shyness.'

'Aye, it was that time you went down the pit and treated the men who'd been injured in the roof-fall at Crossburn mine. Doctor McTaggart suffers that badly from claustrophobia, poor soul, he just couldn't do it. Still he did a fine job at the pit-head once you'd patched up the lads and they were winched to the surface. Of course, I'd have been down there myself right away, if I'd not been away in Ayr at the time,' he added stoutly.

'Of course.' Hiding a grin, she eyed his ageing, portly body.

'Aye, Doctor, we'll miss you right enough,' Abernethy continued his lament. 'Still, I suppose you have to make this move if you want to better your prospects.'

'Och, I'd be quite happy staying as a GP, though not as a Locum of course, Doctor Abernethy, but with Poor Law experience I'll have more choice later on. I might eventually be able to buy into a partnership, though the chances of my ever having enough capital are slim.' Peggy swung round. 'Is that the door?'

'It'll be Ellen. Come in, lass!' Doctor Abernethy called.

His elderly housekeeper bustled in carrying an envelope on a silver tray. 'This has just come for ye, Doctor. A laddie brought it over on the pony from Maybole station.'

Abernethy opened the letter and read, then turned to Peggy with a worried frown. 'Can you manage alone this weekend, do you think, Doctor McBride?'

'If I have to, but I thought you were on duty with me.' She paused, seeing his expression. 'What's the matter? Have you had some bad news, Doctor?'

The frown deepened. 'I don't know if you would call it bad news. It looks as if I have to go to Ayr and stay till Sunday. There's a special Elders Synod over that wee problem with the Gannock Kirk finances. Irregularities, you know. Och, you must have seen the palaver about it in the *Post*. A terrible business, terrible,' he tutted.

'Haven't they sorted that out yet?' Peggy remembered reading about the local scandal that had set tongues wagging from Troon to Girvan.

'Apparently not! Och, this would happen when Doctor McTaggart is up at that conference in Edinburgh. I don't know what he needs to go to things like that for. Waste of time in a country practice. Poultices for bronchitis and senna pods for the bowels, that's what our work is all about.'

'Advances in anaesthesia application are important too, even out in the wilds of Ayrshire,' Peggy reprimanded. 'It was a godsend to be able to operate with it after that accident at Crossburn. Anyway, you know my obsession with that subject. I just wish it was me that had gone.'

'Och, one at a time is enough, and you're leaving anyway.' The old doctor shook his head. 'Young doctors! Never content, neither they are! But if you're sure you can manage . . .'

'Of course I can.' Peggy gave him a reassuring smile.

'Well then, I'll leave you to it,' he said cheerfully. 'The Ayr train goes in an hour or so. I've just got time for Ellen to pack my things.' Peggy's competence was well established and he left without a moment's worry.

Friday evening was spent as expected, dozing in her clothes between calls to patients in the immediate vicinity of Maybole. In the small hours she had to make an emergency call to one of the farmhouses in the outlying countryside. A farm worker had injured himself sharpening the plough share and had put up with the pain till he could bear it no longer. It was a tiring but otherwise not extra-ordinary incident.

In some ways weekend work is a pleasant change from the round of regular visits and queues of walking wounded with cuts, coughs and sniffles every weekday at the surgery, Peggy thought as she rode back in the dawn light.

'Doctor McBride!' The housekeeper shook her awake from a catnap on Saturday afternoon. 'Can ye go out to Cairrybing cottages? A lad has come to say his faither is worse. A TB case, ye ken. Rintoul's the name.'

'Is the lad still here?'

'No. I ken ye know where the cottages are, ye went to old Mistress McNab there last week. I gave the pair wee lad a roll and jam and sent him back to his mither.' The housekeeper sighed. 'Och, the bairn was blue with the cold, he'd hardly a shirt on his back and not a shoe on his foot . . . and it February!' Sadly she shook her head.

Poverty is still the main enemy, Peggy thought bitterly as her horse ploughed through the mire, up a dreary lane. Pockets of old snow lay in filthy drifts in ruts and on north-facing banks. She dismounted in the mud in front of a huddle of dilapidated miners' cottages and was directed at once.

Rintoul was badly tubercular and bleeding intermittently from his lungs. Peggy could see he needed hospitalization.

'I think you'd be better off in the Poor Law Infirmary at Ayr, Mr Rintoul.'

'No, I don't want to go!' The man was terrified of the idea. 'Once they get ye in, ye never come out again. Can I no' stay here, Doctor?' he pleaded.

'You'll not get any better lying in this damp cottage,' she explained sadly. 'At least in the Infirmary it's dry and they can treat your illness easier as well.'

'Whit's the use?' Sunken eyes burned in fever-red cheeks and he broke into another fit of coughing. 'Ye ken as well as I do that I'm finished. Can ye no just give me some medicine to take away the pain a wee bit? Let me die here in my own bed in peace, not among strangers? Och, for God's sake, Doctor.'

Peggy looked at the bundles of ancient blankets on a straw pallet he called a bed. Ragged children stood silently gawping at her from the corner of the one room they all shared. An open coal fire smoked and hissed as drops fell from the big pot and kettle hanging over it, suspended on twin hooks. This was a miners' row like the one she should have been born in. A thought struck her.

'Are you likely to be evicted if you don't work . . . which you can't now, of course?'

'Naw, we're safe enough. My eldest laddie is down the pit since June. We can stay as long as he works.' Half-focused eyes swung over to the group where a boy who must have been fourteen, but looked a stunted ten, was standing a little apart from the rest, preserving his dignity as breadwinner. 'He'll get the rent-book when I go.'

'Och, Wullie, dinnae talk like that.' Rintoul's worn-out wife threw herself down beside the pallet. 'Ye'll be fine. Go wi' the doctor, laddie. They'll gie ye medicine in the Infirmary, and ye'll be right as rain. We'll come up and see ye when we can.'

'I'm not goin'!'

'Don't upset yourself, Mr Rintoul,' Peggy said softly. 'I can't move you tonight anyway. But I will give you some medicine now to help you rest and we can talk about it when I come in tomorrow.'

'I'm no' goin',' he insisted weakly.

She rummaged in her bag for a sedative draught. 'Give him a spoonful of this every two hours, Mrs Rintoul.' She handed the bottle to the distraught women. 'Remember to keep it well out of the way of the bairns – it's dangerous if you don't stick to the dose I've just told you. Can you manage that?'

'Och, aye, Doctor. And thank you very much for comin',' the poor woman replied courteously. 'Er, can we settle wi' ye next week when the laddie gets his pay?' She flushed with shame. 'I've nothin' in the house now.'

'There's no charge for my visit, Mrs Rintoul. I can please myself on this kind of call,' Peggy lied, smiling. 'Now, I'll be back tomorrow about three o'clock and we can see how you are, Mr Rintoul. I think you should come into the Infirmary for a bit anyway. It's not so bad, you know, and it's free.'

'Ye've been awful kind, Doctor, are you English?' Mrs

Rintoul ventured diffidently at the door of the rundown cottage. 'Ye sound it.'

'Och, no, Mrs Rintoul. I'm every bit as Scots as you.' Peggy smiled. And I can speak the Ayrshire dialect just as well. That thought she kept to herself.

'Wullie looks a wee bit better already for your visit, don't ye think so?' the poor woman went on hopefully as Peggy mounted her horse.

'He does that,' Peggy lied consolingly. She glanced in disgust at the shabby houses and the filthy, flooded path in front. 'It's time some drainage was put in here. Who's your landlord?'

'Hamish McClure, of course.' The woman was surprised at the question.

Peggy rode back to Maybole, thanking heaven that she had only a week left in the area. Mention of Elspeth's father had felt like a kick in the stomach. And the situation she had just left was too close to her own parents' tragic story for comfort.

In fact, I'm glad I'm going, it was getting me down being here. With every day at Maybole, so near to where she had been born, Peggy had felt increasingly torn, despite her efforts to remain detached. Seeing again the beautiful coast-line and the hills she had known as a child, breathing in the clean sea air, listening to the cries of the sea-birds on the cliff-tops, gave her pleasure far beyond words. But the continued alienation from her past was painful. She had kept away from Kirkowen, but now and then memories broke through unbidden to tease and torment, carried on the smell of fresh-baked griddle pancakes, or a local turn of phrase.

I don't feel I belong here any more. I've been away too long . . . put distance and education between me and all this. These are not my people now, this is not my home. Her mind spun as she rode. But I don't know where I do belong. The increasingly familiar confusion rose to haunt her. Och, I'm glad folk think I'm English, or from Edinburgh. Nobody associates me with wee Peggy Soutar. She sighed aloud: 'I couldn't face talking about my parents, or Hamish McClure . . . and everything that has happened since. I just

209

want to be Doctor McBride and get on with what I'm trained to do. Some day I might sit down and think about who I am and where I came from, sort it all out, but not yet.'

At last she swung the horse off the narrow lanes and on to the broad road that ran the last few miles to Maybole. Feeling a better surface beneath its hooves, the big bay took the short home stretch at a fine canter. Peggy thought pityingly of the family she had just left in squalor. How can Hamish McClure go on letting folk live like animals? She tried to think objectively but failed. There was only one answer. Och, he just doesn't see them as human at all.

Tired and wet, she handed over the animal to Doctor Douglas's groom. Then she changed out of her soaked riding clothes and lay on the chaise-longue for a quick nap. Like all doctors, Peggy had learned how to sleep to order.

'Doctor Abernethy! Doctor Abernethy!' Peggy woke in darkness to the sound of shouting, hammering on the door, and the bell being pulled simultaneously.

The housekeeper was never expected to answer the door late at night. Peggy glanced at the clock. It was 2 am. She had slept for four or five hours, but felt stiff and unrefreshed. 'All right, I'm coming!' Wearily she struggled to her feet and clattered downstairs.

'Get Doctor Abernethy, woman!' a distraught man demanded, mistaking her for the housekeeper.

'I'm the duty doctor, Doctor McBride.'

'Och, naw!' His eyes rolled in his head as if he was terrified out of his wits.

'Take it easy, man.' She tried to calm him down to a state where they could communicate. 'Now what's the matter?'

'Och, not a lassie! We need a proper doctor!' In his consuming panic he was beyond politeness.

'Well, I'm all the doctor you're likely to get,' Peggy replied dryly. 'The others are away and the next practice is in Kirkowen. Go there if I won't do.'

'I've come from Kirkowen, from Bargeddie. Doctor Bain is out on a call somewhere over at Fernieclough. That's right over the other side of the practice. Some old woman that lives in a farmhouse away up in the hills is dying. The housekeeper says she's not expecting the doctor back before morning. We can't reach him . . . there's no time!'

Peggy froze, spine tingling with eerie presentiment. 'Is there nobody else?' She knew the answer before he replied.

'Naw, Doctor Bain is the only one in the practice. Kirkowen isn't that big.'

'What's the problem?' She put on her coat and hood and picked up the bag packed at readiness.

'It's Mistress McClure . . . she's started with the bairn. They've lost the last two and it looks as if she's on the way to losing this one as well!'

'Who?' Peggy stopped in shock.

'Mistress McClure. She's having trouble wi' the bairn,' he repeated impatiently. 'Have ye a horse, Doctor? The road is too bad for the carriage the night. Anyway the quickest way is to ride over the moor.'

'I have a horse,' Peggy answered shortly and followed him out.

Sleet drove in from the sea as they galloped the dark miles across open moorland to Kirkowen. The man knew every inch of the dangerous way, avoiding moss and rocky outcrops where a horse could sink or stumble. Riding like the devil, Peggy stuck close behind, trying to think only of her profession and not her emotions.

As they reached the top of the rise, the scent of the sea hit her full in the face, carried over on the salty, icy rain. Suddenly she was a child again, running down the lane to meet her father coming from the pit. Tears joined the water dripping down her cheeks and on to the sodden riding cape.

They swung inland again and down, down, down to Kirkowen. Peggy could have taken the route blindfold. Every turn, every step came back. Skirting the sprawling little town, they rode up the valley side till Bargeddie House came into sight.

Lights were blazing at the front of the house. As they dismounted, the housekeeper, dishevelled and distraught, came running out. 'Oh, thank God, Ritchie! Have ye brought the doctor?' she shouted at the dark figures handing over their sweating, shivering mounts to the grooms.

'Aye,' Peggy's companion answered shortly. 'But I'm no sure Mr McClure will be that happy. It's a lady doctor.'

'Michty!' the housekeeper gasped as Peggy emerged from the darkness. 'I'd heard there was one at Maybole, but I never thought . . .' she trailed off.

'Where's the patient?' Peggy asked briskly, handing her sodden cape and coat to the housekeeper.

'Upstairs, the Master is with her. The poor Mistress is in a bad way.'

'Take me up.' Peggy followed grim-faced behind the swirling black skirts.

'Doctor?' Hamish McClure's face froze when he saw Peggy enter. 'I sent for a doctor, not another midwife!' he roared, florid face infused with rage. 'We've got a midwife already. Where is that idiot of a messenger?'

Peggy tried not to look at the man she had been brought up to hate most in the world. Out of the corner of her eye, she shot a glance at the pitiful sight on the bed where Flora McClure tossed, whimpered and intermittently screamed like a tortured cat.

Peggy made the only decision possible. 'I am Doctor McBride, Locum at the Maybole practice, Mr McClure. I will do what I can for your wife. Now please leave the room. Your shouting can only make her situation worse.' The green eyes were icy.

McClure stood in dumb astonishment for a moment, but knew she meant it and had no choice but to agree. 'As you wish. But if there has to be a choice, then you save the child.'

God help anyone that is wife to McClure, Peggy thought as she rolled up her sleeves and joined the midwife at the bedside.

'The baby is lying wrong, Doctor,' she explained. 'It started as breach, like the last one. The bairn has one foot stuck up and I'll dislocate the whole leg if I can't get it round, but the contractions are stopping me. They're coming so fast it's hopeless. Poor woman, she's in terrible pain. But if we can't move the baby soon, it's going to die. That's how the other one went.'

'Right.' Peggy drew out her bottle of chloroform and a

212

pad of lint. 'I'll show you how many drops to put on this and exactly where to hold it. It's easier with a proper cup, but this will have to do. Leave the mouth free, but hold it closed with one hand. Remember to count how long you keep the lint over her nose, we don't want to suffocate her. Watch carefully now!' She demonstrated the technique.

'Like this?' The midwife had never administered an anaesthetic before, but Peggy could see she was quick and intelligent.

'Excellent!' She sighed in relief as the agonised woman on the bed instantly stopped her terrible moaning and fell back on to the pillows. 'Now, I'll be as quick as I can ...'

She felt deep into the uterus and found the baby to be bent almost double as the contractions had forced down the little body, still trapped by its foot. 'The leg is already slightly dislocated.' Peggy gasped with effort as she firmly pushed against the natural birth-trend downwards and slid up the other greasy little foot, which was already showing, to join its neighbour. For a moment she thought it wasn't going to work. If I have to perform an emergency caesarian, I'll lose the woman, she thought despairingly. Surgery is always risky, even with chloroform, but after a protracted birth the dangers of post-operative infection spell sure death for the mother.

'Can I give her another drop?' the midwife asked anxiously as Flora began to stir and moan.

'Once more,' Peggy instructed. Grimly she went on manipulating the child as it desperately tried to escape from the suffocating womb. 'Got it!' Suddenly the other little foot appeared and the child shot into the world, silent, blue and bloody. At once she cleared the mucus from its mouth, but still no breath came.

'Give me some of that warm oil! Quick!' Peggy grabbed the still little form, turned it upside down and slapped its tiny back. No sign of life.

'Just like the others,' the housekeeper said sadly. 'Here ye are, Doctor!' The midwife handed her a dish of oil that had been used to massage Flora's stomach in the early stages of labour to ease the pain.

'Hold him!' Peggy thrust the child, suspended by the ankles, at the midwife.

Deftly she soaked her hands in the oil and began a swift massage of the child, gently shaking, slapping and rubbing his chest and back.

For a few agonising minutes the boy remained like an inanimate doll, hanging grotesquely by his tiny feet. Suddenly, with a sucking gulp, he spewed out a globule of thick mucus and let out a mewling wail. Peggy worked on till Master McClure howled steadily in protest.

'He'll have a fighting chance now.' She turned him up, his little body shining with oil. 'Don't wash him yet. I'll splint the leg in a minute, just wrap him in a cloth for now . . . not too tight . . . and let him sleep. Tomorrow you can get your own doctor to check the leg. It will take careful handling if he's not going to be crippled for life. But there's still work to do.' Grave-faced she turned towards the still figure on the bed.

Flora McClure would bear no more children, her son had seen to that, but she would live if infection did not set in. Peggy stitched her up, washed her hands and gave strict instructions to the housekeeper on care of both patients.

Totally exhausted, she picked up her bag and opened the door, knowing Hamish McClure was outside waiting anxiously. She had not allowed him in, even when she was sure the baby lived.

At once he rushed over, slack flesh wobbling. 'Does the child live? Is it a boy?'

'The child lives and so does your wife.'

'Is it a boy?' he insisted.

Peggy looked in silent disgust at the fat body and florid complexion of the man she loathed. The man who was trying to have his own daughter committed to a mad-house. Then with a horrified jolt she realized that, despite his signs of over-indulgence and creeping age, Elspeth resembled her father far more closely than Peggy had ever expected. There was the same stubborn chin, the shape of the face, the high cheek-bones belonging to her best friend. Even the grey eyes were his. Once he must have been a strikingly handsome man.

214

'Is it a boy?' he repeated.

'It's a boy.' Her voice sounded tight and cold. 'But he will need medical attention tomorrow. I've made a temporary support for his leg, it was trapped during the birth and is slightly dislocated. Doctor Bain must deal with it at once.'

'That's nothing . . . I can pay for any treatment he needs! A boy.' Hamish McClure rushed into the room and over to the cradle where his son lay.

Peggy was about to mount her horse when he caught up with her. 'Er, I'm sorry about the little incident when you arrived, Doctor McBride.' McClure was magnanimous in his joy. 'I just didn't expect a lady doctor. And you maybe know that my wife has lost two boys already and there have been many late miscarriages in between?'

'Well, that will be the last child she will bear, Mr McClure,' Peggy replied. 'No more births are possible. She should not really have had this one.' Desperately she tried to remain as professionally detached as she could. The Hippocratic Oath spun round and round in her head.

'Well, perhaps this one will have to do, I'm getting on myself,' he said with heavy jocularity. 'Now how can I thank you?' It was customary for wealthy patients to make a decent donation to the practice after special service. 'I feel greatly in your debt. Greatly!' The man was obviously completely sincere. 'The midwife said the child would have died if you had not saved him.' His face crumpled with emotion. 'Name your fee. Within reason, I'll grant it. I mean that.'

'That's between you and Doctor Abernethy.' Peggy watched him coldly.

'Oh, now, let me reward you personally, Doctor McBride,' he pressed on. 'You've done a wonderful job, and a lady doctor is such a rarity . . .'

'Less rare than before. Your daughter is one.'

'Do you know Elspeth?' The puffy eyes narrowed suspiciously.

'Oh, yes, Mr McClure, I do indeed. Medicine is a small world, especially with there still being so few women practising. In fact, Elspeth McClure is my dearest friend, one of the people I love and respect most in this world.' Peggy's own pent-up emotions were coming rapidly to the surface

215

and waves of tiredness broke down her resolve to remain detached. 'I'll try always to think of the child I saved tonight as her half-brother, not your son.'

'What do you mean?' McClure's face registered shock and horrified incredulity.

'I would have tried to save the child and mother anyway. Above all other feelings or allegiance as a doctor, I am bound by my oath to save life. I'd even save one as worthless as yours if I had to.' Despite her inner turmoil, Peggy's voice was so even, he thought he had misheard the uncompromisingly insulting words.

'Who the hell are you . . . No, by Christ, I don't believe it!' His face blackened in sudden comprehension.

'Poor neglected, opium-sodden Janet McKelvie has given you your heir after all, Hamish McClure. It was your first wife who made my presence here possible.' Peggy gazed straight into his face without flinching. 'And it was your own daughter who persuaded me to forget the taint of the McClure name associated with her mother's legacy.'

'You're . . .'

'Yes, you know, don't you?' Expressionless she looked at his astounded face. 'I'm Peggy Soutar, Mr McClure. The child who was born on straw in a barn on a winter night and whose mother died because of your inhumanity. You'll have to spend the rest of your life knowing that it was Kirsty and Jamie Soutar's daughter who saved your name from the extinction it deserves. By God, I only hope I can live with the knowledge myself!'

'Soutar's daughter,' he repeated, stunned. 'Och, no . . . no! What will folk say? My son delivered by Soutar's daughter. Coals of fire! I'll never be able to lift my head.'

'Aye, it would make a fine story in the *Ayrshire Post*, wouldn't it?' Peggy turned the knife. 'Well, I'll tell no one that it was Kirsty and Jamie Soutar's daughter who was here this night,' she went on slowly, as if each word caused her pain. 'Doctor Margaret McBride is known here only as Doctor Abernethy's Locum . . . it can stay that way, but on one condition.'

'What?' McClure's eyes showed hope and fear.

'That you stop persecuting your daughter. Show your

gratitude for a son, Hamish McClure, by leaving *her* alone! Elspeth McClure is the sanest person I have ever met.'

Peggy grasped the reins and mounted her horse. 'Walk on!' Turning, she kicked its flanks sharply. The animal started forward and broke into a canter, leaving Bargeddie behind.

Dawn light began spreading silver fingers over the distant cliffs above the sea. Last night's wind had blown the sky clear before it spent itself. February had ended and March begun. Suddenly Peggy wanted to be away from everything. She needed to think, to cry, to shake off the happenings of the night and set free the pain that filled her heart to bursting point.

Instead of riding up the moors to Maybole, she cantered straight on towards the coast. It was eighteen years since she had been along this path, but she had not forgotten any turn or twist of it.

Tying up the horse in the shelter of a rocky outcrop, she wandered across the headland where she had played so often as a child. The eerie early-morning light made her feel she was stepping back in time.

Under her feet, damp grass became scrubbier and gave way to clumps of sea-pinks and thrift. This will be a mass of colour in a month or so, she realized. The gentle memory intruded into her bitter confusion.

Beyond the cliff-edge, seagulls wheeled and screeched in a raucous dawn chorus. Below, far below, the smooth-surfaced sea fell and rose in majestic surges.

Last night it would have been a mass of white horses and crashing waves, Peggy knew. With great deep gasps, she breathed in the clean air and began at last to feel a sense of melancholy peace fill her. Och, I did the right thing going to McClure's. No doctor could refuse. But I wish I'd never had to do it. How is it possible for a rotten man like that to have a fine daughter like Elspeth? Even as she asked herself the question she knew the answer. Elspeth was like her father, strong-willed and single-minded. But there was enough of gentle Janet McKelvie in her for those character- istics to be untainted by selfishness and greed. Elspeth and Hamish were alike in their stubbornness too. Whether he dropped the case against her or not, there could never be a reconciliation between them.

Feeling cleansed, she began walking back to the big bay horse, her riding cloak trailing wetly in the dew. The animal was calmly eating grass, stamping and snorting gently now and then.

Peggy jumped as something moved just ahead of her. Almost from under her feet a bird rose, startled from its nest, long curved beak open as it called its plaintive protest. *Cureee . . . cureee . . .* The pure voice of the curlew wept across the salty air.

Och, how many times did I dream I heard the curlew cry and long for just a wee breath of sea air, when I lived in that rotten old tenement in Glasgow? Peggy smiled to herself. And how many times since? Maybe there's part of me still in Kirkowen, despite my struggle to leave it all behind.

For a moment she paused and watched the bird wheel and call anxiously. Not till she was safely past did it settle back down on the half-hidden nest.

I remember Tam Laird showing me the curlew's nest. Och, poor wee starveling Tam, not a pick on his bones. But what a gift for music! He could make that old mouth organ talk. I wonder what became of him? '*Why weep ye by the tide, lady? Why weep ye by the tide?*' Under her breath she began singing *Jock o' Hazeldean*.

The wind rose as she walked and snatched at her neat bun, dragging out flaming strands of red hair to dance madly. I should think Tam is living in one of the farm cottages now and raising a baker's dozen of his own. I just hope he feeds them better than he was fed himself!

Mounting her horse, she resolutely shook off the past and rode steadily northwards towards Maybole, not once turning back to watch as the sea faded from sight. The curlew's cries died on the breeze, drowned out by the steady drumming of the horse's hooves.

Chapter 16
Wild war's deadly blast

True to her word, Peggy mentioned nothing of the night's work at Kirkowen to anyone except Doctor Abernethy, and then without comment beyond the professional.

'Mr and Mrs Hamish McClure of Bargeddie are proud to announce the birth of their son, Hamish Lachlan.' The proud announcement was in all the Ayrshire papers. Peggy could hardly avoid being reminded.

The last I heard was that Elspeth's case has been set for January next year. We'll see if Hamish McClure thinks better of going on with it, otherwise I'll keep my threat, even though it will be nearly as painful for me as for him, Peggy told herself grimly.

A week later she left Maybole and threw herself into the job of medical officer in charge at Greenwoods Poor Law Infirmary. As a woman, she had to prove herself worthy of the post over and over again. Confident and competent, she set about reorganising the hospital, which had become neglected in the interregnum period. After a while her hard work began to show results. The Infirmary had never been run so economically, despite vast improvements in patient care and conditions. Even the Scottish medical journals began to mention Greenwoods as a model for similar establishments.

'It's just a matter of good management,' Peggy explained to the delighted board at the annual meeting in December 1913, after nine months in the job. 'There was a lot of waste and doubling of resources. I've worked with the administration to sort that out and free resources to provide better facilities.'

'Aye, maybe a woman's hand on the housekeeping was what was needed.' The Treasurer rubbed his hands happily. 'Ye ken what they say: "Look after the pennies and the pounds will look after themselves." ' Joyfully he pored over the neatly kept books.

'Well, the results so far have been excellent, gentlemen,' the Chairman admitted.

'Indeed!' The Board nodded collective agreement and raised sherry glasses proudly. 'Here's to a prosperous and healthy 1914, Doctor McBride.'

Peggy hurried home from the meeting that evening in eager anticipation. Elspeth was due off the six o'clock train from Glasgow and Peggy wanted to be there to meet her. Time was running out for McClure to withdraw his charges. If there was no news soon, Peggy would have to decide how to carry out her threat. Though she feared the inevitable consequences on her hard-won privacy and independence, she was determined to do it.

'Over here, Elspeth!' Amid the chaos of bags and people pouring off the Glasgow train, Peggy spotted the tall figure struggling on to the crowded platform.

'Peggy!' They embraced warmly and, arms linked, headed out of the station.

'This all you have, ma'am?' The porter looked astonished.

'That's all!' Elspeth nodded.

'Not much of a tip in this! Not much luggage for a lady, neither it is!' The despondent porter muttered glumly as he carried the small trunk which was all she had.

'Elspeth, you're even thinner than the last time!' Peggy had been shocked at her friend's gaunt appearance. Tall like her father, she needed to carry some flesh to avoid appearing emaciated. 'Have you been ill or worried? Or is it just those terrible hunger-strikes?'

'Maybe a bit of all three.' Elspeth shrugged. 'Thank you.' She tipped the porter more generously than he'd expected.

'Och, thanks, ma'am. Guid New Year.' The man touched the peak of his worn flat cap and cheerfully loaded her trunk on to the carriage.

'Cannock Road, please, driver,' Peggy instructed. Clattering across the cobbles, the carriage bore them towards the McBride house, with the two women chattering without pause all the way.

'You know, Peggy McBride, you're beginning to sound like Libby, mithering about my health every time I appear,' Elspeth teased. 'Tell you what, I'll put some flesh back on my bones at New Year. Or at least Libby can with her Black Bun and Dundee cake. May I stay that long? It's been nearly a year since I saw you.'

'As long as you want, my dear. The door is always open to you.'

'I know that. Oh, Peggy, I so feel the need to be with dear friends. It's been a challenging twelve months,' Elspeth replied with uncharacteristic weariness. 'And have you heard, I have a half-brother?' Her tone became carefully neutral. 'Born the last day of February, according to Sinclair.'

'I heard.' Peggy's heart began thumping with anxiety.

'I thought you might. And there's other news from Bargeddie too ... good news for me. Sinclair sent a telegram yesterday to say that my father decided at the eleventh hour not to go ahead with trying to have me committed. After all the time and trouble gathering a case together, suddenly he's dropped the whole project. Nobody knows why. Maybe getting the longed-for son cured him of some of his neuroses, though it took eight months to filter through to conscious action!' Elspeth sighed wearily. 'God, I'm so glad. It's been hanging over me for years. I never thought such a thing could get me down but it has. And now it's all over! I can hardly believe it.' She leaned against the leather carriage seat, closing her eyes.

'That's great news, Elspeth.' A secret surge of happiness flowed through Peggy from head to foot. McClure had acted just in time. The decision must have hurt for him to wait until the last minute. Peggy hoped it still hurt.

'How are Libby and Kirsten?' Elspeth asked suddenly changing the subject.

'Fine. And waiting on hot bricks for your arrival.' Peggy was relieved Elspeth seemed disinclined to speculate further on her father's change of mind. 'Look, there they are.' She pointed to the two beloved figures at the gate as they pulled up: Kirsten jumping up and down, hand firmly in Libby's protective grasp.

'Kirsten, you're growing like wildfire. And, Libby, why, you get younger every day!' Elspeth hugged her god-daughter and the housekeeper affectionately.

'Aye, well, ye know what I'm going to say about you, Doctor Elspeth. You're like a walking skeleton!' Libby shook her head. 'Och, you're an awful worry to me, so ye are. Always have been, always will be!'

'Some things never change, Libby.' Elspeth smiled wryly. 'But here's some French lace I brought for you to trim your best blouses with. I got it the last time I went over to see Christabel Pankhurst. And this is for you, darling, carried all the way from Paris.' She handed Kirsten a china doll.

'Och, it's beautiful, Auntie Elspeth, so it is. Look, it has bloomers trimmed with lace!' The child peered underneath. 'Thank you,' Kirsten bobbed a curtsey and turned to the housekeeper, 'Libby, are you going to trim your bloomers with the lace from Aunt Elspeth?'

'Lace bloomers? Never in a month of Sundays! Respectable ladies don't do that sort of thing in Scotland. Lace bloomers . . . michty!' Libby went bright pink.

'Oh, there's always a first time!' Elspeth and Peggy chortled at her embarrassment.

'I'm away back to the kitchen. Come on, Kirsten.' Libby regained her composure. 'Now mind the cakes, lovely lass! Watch that shortbread, the tray's hot!' They could hear her admonishing an excited Kirsten as they went into the sitting-room. Libby had turned the kitchen upside down in utter delight at having the three people she cared about most in the world altogether at the same time.

They passed a quiet holiday, celebrating the advent of 1914 with sherry and Black Bun in the little drawing-room Peggy had turned into a private den. All over Kilmarnock the bells rang in the New Year. Laughing and singing, folk tumbled out into the streets carrying bits of coal, bun and whisky to first-foot neighbours and friends.

Peggy, Elspeth, Libby and Kirsten raised their glasses and toasted 1914, whatever it might bring. After the toasts, Libby carried a sleepy Kirsten back to the nursery and left the two women alone.

'Did Douglas Munro say he called on me in London?' Elspeth asked as she sipped her sherry, looking relaxed and far more healthy than she had been when she arrived ten days before.

'No,' Peggy looked surprised. 'When?'

'A month or so ago, he was speaking at an international conference on new techniques in surgery.'

'But how did he know where to contact you?'

'Oh, that was simple.' Elspeth waved a slender hand. 'He often works with Doctor Elsie Inglis, an old friend of mine in Edinburgh.'

'Oh, yes, you've mentioned her.'

'Elsie asked Douglas to give me some articles she had written on women's suffrage. He's quite sympathetic to our cause.'

'I didn't know that,' Peggy said.

'Oh, yes. In fact he even wrote to *The Times* explaining the more enlightened attitude to female suffrage in the Antipodes.'

'Did he?' Peggy thought guiltily of the many times he had come all the way to Kilmarnock, always cheery and always bearing thoughtful little gifts. Even Libby usually got a box of her favourite Edinburgh Rock. Peggy and Douglas had talked for many companionable hours since he came back from New Zealand and she looked forward to every visit. Yet how little she knew of the man's real interests or opinions. 'Sorry, what was that, Elspeth?'

'I said, what a nice man Douglas Munro is as well as a brilliant surgeon,' Elspeth repeated with an enigmatic look on her face.

'Yes, he is that, Elspeth,' Peggy replied, feeling unexpectedly disorientated. 'I just didn't know he was interested in votes for women, though. I'm ashamed to admit, I mostly talk about Robert when he comes here. Maybe I'm being too self-indulgent. Och, surely he would have said if he minded?' She could hear a defensive note in her voice. 'I never really ask much about what he does when he's not here and he hardly ever mentions it himself . . .'

223

'Don't you want to remarry, Peggy?' Elspeth changed the subject abruptly. 'Wouldn't you like to have a brother or sister for Kirsten while time and nature are still on your side?'

'Not a bit.' Peggy shook her head. 'I've had offers. And some have been rather importunate at times.' She grinned. 'Menfolk imagine a young widow must be desperate for male company! But it's not hard to refuse. I was telling Douglas, the last time he was here, that my work is so consuming I don't feel the need for more children and I could never replace Robert. Never.' Her head went up in a defiant gesture.

'And of course Douglas understood,' Elspeth said dryly.

'Of course.' Peggy shot a puzzled look at her friend. 'I didn't say this to him in so many words, Elspeth,' she went on, 'but I would be terrified to love anyone like I loved Robert ever again. I thought I would die of sorrow when he left me.'

In the firelight Elspeth could see tears shining in her friend's eyes. 'But you need not love someone else with the total passion you had for Robert. He was your first love and they say that's the most intense. Love can also be built on friendship, respect, shared interests . . . strong qualities that last,' she said softly.

'Elspeth McClure, I never thought to hear you speak like that. Well, when you show the way to the altar I might think again!' Peggy smiled suddenly, snapping out of her sad mood. 'Och, but the pair of us are chasing thirty-five and catching up in a hurry. Goodness, woman, we're almost middle-aged.' The green eyes twinkled. 'And Kirsten is soon six. No, my dear, it's too late to start again.' She failed to mention Andrew Graham, the handsome lawyer, to Elspeth, though she had laughingly told Douglas about his decorous attempts to persuade her to marry him. Afterwards she wondered about the omission.

'You'll be waiting forever then if you wait for me to show you the way.' Elspeth touched her mark with a slim finger. 'I've been spared all that nonsense by my talisman. Well, almost.' She looked thoughtful for a moment. 'And in the suffrage movement it's regarded as a positive advantage not to have a man in charge of your life.'

'Be careful, Elspeth dear.' Peggy felt a sudden flicker of superstitious anxiety and foreboding. 'I would hate anything to happen to you. This business with your father might have receded, but there are other dangers out there. I've read the reports of this terrible Cat and Mouse Act where they let you starve yourselves and then release you under orders they know you are bound to break.'

Elspeth shrugged. 'It eases their consciences. Unfortunately the public doesn't yet realise the effects of those measures on our health, though I'm afraid they soon will.' Her tone became grim, 'I wouldn't be surprised if there are fatalities soon.'

'Why don't you try less dangerous tactics?'

'If deaths mean suffrage for women, then most of us feel martyrdom is justified.' Elspeth sounded more overtly fanatical than Peggy had ever heard her.

That wouldn't have gone down well in court. Just as well Hamish McClure backed down, she thought worriedly.

'None of us will rest till women have the vote, Peggy,' Elspeth continued, voice ringing with conviction. 'It's our right.'

'I still think it's daft to to kill yourself for it.'

'Well, let's hope it's not necessary, I want to be at the party to celebrate getting the vote,' Elspeth replied with a flash of her old humour. Then she saw the frown descend on Peggy's face. 'Oh, stop worrying, you're worse than Libby at times, Peggy! I'm sticking with Christabel's suffrage group and not following Sylvia in her breakaway league. Her methods are too extreme even for my taste. And I was so saddened by the death of Emily Wilding Davison at Ascot, she was a great friend. No, my dear girl, I'll keep a low key in 1914.'

'Thank God for that!' Peggy gave a relieved sigh then leaned forward anxiously again. 'Do you think there will be war, Elspeth? Everyone up here does. Douglas thinks it will be sooner than we expect and I fear he's right.'

'Almost certainly he is, but Sylvia, Keir Hardie and some

225

of the International Socialists in the Labour movement, are sure International Brotherhood will prevail.'

'They'll be disappointed. The Kaiser seems bent of trouble and the Balkan States are in such turmoil.'

'Oh, if there is a war, I expect it will be sorted out quickly.' Elspeth got up and stretched her long frame. 'I must go to bed, there's that wretched long journey south to face tomorrow. Goodnight, my dearest Peggy.' She bent down and kissed her affectionately. 'Thank you for a wonderful holiday. And don't worry, a war won't have much effect on our personal worlds. You're working wonders by all accounts at Greenwoods and I'm soon off to meet Annie Kenney and Christabel. There are too many articles to write for *The Suffragette* and railings to chain ourselves to, before we bother about men's nasty games. War will have to wait!'

'Sound sentiments.' Peggy laughed and rose to her feet.

Elspeth turned with a smile as she mounted the stairs. 'And neither you nor I have a man in our lives who might be called up, so there's even less chance of war being any more to us than headlines in the evening paper.'

'Och, you're right as usual.' Peggy caught her buoyant mood and went smilingly to bed.

The declaration of war in August 1914 split the women's suffrage movement deeply. Some decided to follow Sylvia, Keir Hardie and others in their opposition. Instead of continuing with their active suffrage campaign, Sylvia and her breakaway movement turned to the social problems of London's East End. They feared unemployment would mount among women in factories making peace-time goods.

Elspeth stayed on in London for a time, becoming more and more appalled at the carnage reported in Belgium as the German invasion was resisted. Christabel came back from Paris for a meeting with the editorial staff of *The Suffragette*. They decided to replace it with a broader-based magazine, *The Common Cause*, to publicise women's commitment to the war effort.

In November, troubled and unsettled, Elspeth left for Scotland to see Elsie Inglis. Elsie, almost twenty years older than her and one of the first Edinburgh-trained women doctors, was a committed supporter of women's rights. She had helped found the Queen Margaret College suffrage association in Glasgow to which Elspeth had belonged. Elsie was a charismatic, pioneering woman and an outstanding leader.

'Elspeth, the War Office is simply refusing to accept any female medical volunteers! Have you ever heard the like? Such stupidity!' she said furiously before her visitor had time to take off her hat and coat. 'After all the work volunteers did in the Cinema and the Boer War too.'

'But they have the VAD and they'll be taking on volunteer nurses as usual in army units, won't they?' Elspeth was a little confused by Elsie's anger.

'Oh, yes, but as usual there will be no women in positions of real responsibility. It's the old story. Women can do the dirty work but not make the decisions.'

'Well, what can we do about it? If women don't join the normal volunteer groups, there's no alternative?'

'Now there is!' Elsie's voice rang with triumph. 'Last month I started a group called the Scottish Women's Hospitals.'

'All women?' Elspeth asked.

'No men at all . . . expect a few temporary cases here and there. But in principle all are women. I offered our services to the War Office, but they turned us down. Then I wrote straight to the Entente Allies asking if they want to use us, on the understanding we would serve as independent volunteer units.'

'Have they replied?'

'Oh, yes. They jumped at the chance. The present medical services at the front and the back-up behind the lines are horribly overstretched. Men are dying for want of care, in Northern France and down in the Balkan States, especially Serbia.'

'When are you mobilising?'

'Now. I am sending two units over straight away and I hope to send more as soon as I can organise them. They are self-contained field units, run completely by women.'

'You mean that? Completely?'

'Stretcher-bearers, nurses, sisters, doctors . . . who also act as the commanding officers.'

'Elsie!' Elspeth's face lit up. 'When do I go?'

'Och, Elspeth! I was shocked enough when Douglas came to tell me he was off to Belgium, but at least he's a man and men go to war. I thought women had more sense!' Peggy said bluntly when Elspeth came to say goodbye. 'God, you must be crazy!'

'You've always thought that anyway . . . you and my father.' The fine grey eyes danced at Peggy's horrified expression. 'Oh, maybe I am, but I feel this is the right thing for me to do. I'll be working at my profession again, so you should at least be pleased about that.'

'Work in hospitals here.'

'Help is desperately needed in the field, Peggy. And I can make another type of statement about women's abilities and women's rights.' Elspeth had lost none of her fire.

'I suppose so.' Peggy sighed. She knew that tone of old. Elspeth wouldn't be dissuaded now.

'The SWH is affiliated to the suffrage movement and we'll be sending regular reports to *The Common Cause* for publication.' Elspeth smiled happily. 'Just let Asquith, Lloyd George or that young idiot Churchill say we don't deserve the vote after this!'

Peggy was still doubtful. 'I hope you realise it'll be quite a change from gynaecology and women's ailments. It's some time since you've practised medicine at all, Elspeth.'

'So? I hardly expected the soldiers to start having babies, Peggy. VD perhaps! Medicine is like riding a horse. Once you learn how to do it, you never really forget.'

'Och, Elspeth, you know what I mean!' Peggy threw up her hands in exasperation. 'Do you really have the experience to treat war wounds?'

'Not right now. But from what I've been able to find out so far, the injuries in this war are often caused by gas and chemicals.' Elspeth had done her homework. 'They're outside everybody's experience. Elsie tells me that all field-doctors are having to learn new aspects of their trade. I'm a trained general practitioner like you. I'll learn what I have to.'

'I'm the last to dispute that.' Peggy gave up. 'Oh, well, you've nearly killed yourself with protests over the last few years. You might as well go to war and finish the job completely!'

'I'll survive.' Elspeth smiled wryly.

As she left, Peggy watched her beloved, tall figure stride confidently down the station platform. Suddenly she envied Elspeth's single-mindedness, her sense of purpose. Like I used to be myself, she realised with a shock. Now I've achieved most of my old goals, I don't really know what I want! Douglas and Elspeth are at least doing something they believe in. What am I aiming for these days? There's no real vision left. Thoughtfully she turned back into the big house and stopped in the hall, listening as Kirsten played the piano in the nursery suite above.

'Too much thinking is bad for the brains, Doctor Peggy. I'm forever telling you and Miss Elspeth that!' Libby bustled past, carrying a plate of fresh-baked biscuits and glasses of milk upstairs.

'There's something in what you say, Libby.'

I'm redundant here. Peggy watched the housekeeper disappear into the nursery. Lucky I have a demanding job, even if it is becoming a grind.

Kirsten's annual allowance had just been improved yet again through shrewd investment of her small capital by Andrew Graham and his colleagues at Sinclair's. The child was more or less financially independent and her future increasingly assured.

Not redundant if you marry me . . . Unbidden Andrew's voice broke into her thoughts.

But that's not what I mean – or want. The inner restlessness persisted. Andrew would have to wait a while longer.

'Doctor Peggy, Doctor Peggy!' Libby came running upstairs in a fine tizzy one morning in May 1915.

'What is is, Libby? Has something happened to Kirsten?' Peggy buttoned her pegnoir with trembling hands.

'Och, no.' Libby stood panting and puffing on the landing. 'We've a letter from Miss Elspeth!'

'Oh, at last!' Peggy took the envelope and ripped it open. The two women sat side by side on the stairs and Peggy began reading aloud. As always a letter from Elspeth brimmed with understatement, humour and observation.

17 March 1915
From Valjevo, Predstrazia Serbiski (The Serbian Outpost)

My Dearest Peggy, Libby and Kirsten,
Now admit that you have wondered over and over again if you would ever hear from your utterly mad friend again? Sometimes during the forty-five days of our journey from Cardiff I thought Father was right after all! But here I am at last in Valjevo. I do hope the little card from Valetta reached you and quietened your worst fears.

'Hah!' Libby snorted. 'One wee card and it took five months to get here.'

'Well, at least this letter arrived within a few weeks.' Peggy looked at the date. 'Now, listen.' And she went on reading.

Our brave ship *Ceramic* left Cardiff amid bands playing and crowds cheering on 30 November. It would have taken a heart of stone not to be touched.

After all the problems of placing our personnel in cabins (cooks absolutely *refused* to share with washerwomen or, horror, scullerymaids!) the journey to Malta was uneventful. Most of us were horribly sick. A cruise in December to the Mediterranean is not to be compared with one in June! But we were not torpedoed as so many gloomy prophets had forecast ... though I admit, my dears, that we all slept with our clothes on and one ear open as we passed through the danger zone.

When we reached the lovely ancient island of Malta, we were dispatched up the narrow winding streets towards the Cameretta barracks in ass carts, scattering goat and vendors alike before us. Our accommodation was clean and airy despite a distinct lack of furniture. Better by far than Holloway!

Malta was rife with rumour, and for a time it seemed as if we would never reach Serbia at all. In fact, dear girl, if we had been delayed any longer we would almost certainly had been sent to the Dardenelles where so many poor souls have perished. I expect you have seen the lists of casualties? Terrible! Instead, while we waited, we did not idle away our time. Our nurses worked hard patching up the boatloads of soldiers shipped in from all over the area to Malta, many hideously wounded. It was a sharp and necessary introduction to the horrors we had all taken on ourselves so freely.

None of us will ever forget the bravery of those soldiers. I particularly remember one Australian captain, a doctor like you and me, who was wounded tending injured men in action. In terrible pain, he cheerfully led the singing every evening in the old grey templar courtyards of the Knights of St John. *Who's your Lady Friend?*, *Tipperary*, or the latest rag-time. How those jolly voices chased the shades of ancient Gregorian Chants sung by ghostly monks!

Water was scarce in Malta and kettles few, but we learned on those sunny slopes valuable field lessons we have used many times since.

With little warning on the first day of February (my thirty-fifth birthday) we were dispatched to Greece. After all too short a time eating wonderful chocolate eclairs in Athens, we sailed further up the archipelago to Salonika. Prices were high and food scarce. Can you picture your good friend, together with our brave Scottish unit Treasurer and Mrs Scott, the little Adminstrator, standing guard over one hundred boiling eggs which were to feed our girls? There we were, in the garden of what had once been a fine house of the Jewish quarter, surrounded by murderous-looking – and probably quite innocent – Turks. Our job was to ensure they did not substitute old eggs for new!

After Salonika, our train ambled through meadows glowing with the scarlet of poppies, the gold of trefoil and the purple of vetch. It was difficult to imagine we were journeying relentlessly towards ravaged little Serbia, fighting the might of the Austro-Hungarian Empire for the right to retain its nationhood.

Many wayside stations were thronged with soldiers, ragged and battle-worn, but with Serbian good manners, smilingly polite and ready to fill our water bottles, which we appealed for them to do at every stopping place. Shell-shattered buildings scar every hillside. Our unit grew very quiet and reflective as the journey progressed. I thought again and again of the beauty of Ayrshire and the peaceful farms that nestle in every hillside. More than once I wondered at my native caprice that never allows me to rest in tranquility.

For a time we were based in Nis which is not an inviting town. It lies in a flat marshy plain where ravenous mosquitoes breed . . . a dreadful pest to us and the wounded alike. In the distance we had the privilege of seeing a glorious range of mountains over which the sun set in splendour each night.

Now we are quite at home in our Valjevo base and the long journey is almost forgotten. Elsie Inglis is coming soon for a visit. It will be wonderful to see the dear woman and to show her, with not a little pride, how hard we have worked to fulfil her vision of care for the many, many wounded. The conditions were so primitive when we arrived, I thought guiltily of my complaints in the comparative luxury of our British clinics!

My dearest friends, I will write again when I can but days rush wildly into one another and the pressure of command is greater than I had expected. Dr Evelyn Philipps, our commander, has been forced to give up through ill health. The poor woman was infected with typhus in Nis and she and three of our nurses have gone back to Malta to recuperate. Her burden fell on my shoulders for want of anyone else. I hope I have the strength and courage to carry it.

With loving thoughts and wishes to you all and to my dear colleagues in the Glasgow suffrage union.
Your loving,

Elspeth

P.S. Have you heard from Douglas? Is the dear man well?

Libby got up, looking satisfied. 'Och, I'm that glad to get a wee word from her, so I am. It sounds as if she's fallen on her feet as usual.' She paused with a hopeful, speculative look on her face. 'Ye better write and tell her that Doctor Munro is fine and doing his bit in Flanders for the poor laddies out there. In fact, ye could sent her his address. Ye ken, I wouldn't wonder if he and Miss Elspeth don't make a match of it some time. She always asks after him and he after her.'

'Do you think so?' Peggy folded the letter, and with a thoughtful expression on her face, went back into her bedroom and closed the door.

Andrew Graham left his card with Libby later that morning while Peggy was at work. 'Please remind Doctor Peggy to send a messenger confirming our outing on Saturday, Libby.'

'I'll do that, Mr Graham.' Libby smiled as she closed the door. Andrew was Libby's great romantic hope for Peggy since they had moved to Kilmarnock and she had to bite back annoyance at how off-handedly she treated the poor man sometimes. Still holding a candle for Robert McBride, Libby thought with a touch of fond irritation. It's not healthy for a young woman to make a god of a dead man, however worthy! But she bites my head off if I so much as mention the word marriage.

Peggy was still distracted when she came home for lunch and Libby had to remind her twice about Andrew. 'Oh, right, send someone round, Libby, or the man will surely get upset. He loves to keep his precious diary in order.'

That letter from Miss Elspeth has unsettled her, she's not herself, neither she is, Libby fretted as Peggy went back to work after picking at her food and hardly saying a word.

What's up with me? Peggy asked herself as she arrived at the hospital still preoccupied. But she couldn't find an answer. The rest of the day was disturbed and unsatisfactory. Everything went wrong. Thoughts of Elspeth in Valjevo and Douglas in Flanders destroyed her concentration. Rounds

233

were made in a state of distraction, till she was forced back to reality by a petty crisis.

'Doctor McBride . . . a wee word!' The Treasurer of the Board hurried officiously after her just as she was finishing a routine inspection of the women's ward.

'Yes, Mr Alexander?' Peggy raised a quizzical eyebrow. 'Not more problems with the cost of gruel or the number of times I've ordered the bedclothes to be washed?' The honeymoon relationship with the Hospital Board was a thing of the past, and Peggy was beginning to tire of their petulant complaints.

'Och, not at all.' He missed the irony of her tone entirely. 'It's just that the Board thinks the wee comforts you've been ordering for the patients are a wee bittie unneccesary and a wee bittie on the dear side. This is a Poor Law hospital after all, Doctor, not a luxury hotel. There's a war on. Funds are limited, ye ken.'

Peggy looked round at the austere wards with their long lines of simple beds. The temperature was about bearable for the season, no more. Whitewashed walls and scrubbed wooden floors gave little joy. Toilets and sluice rooms were cold, serviceable and stank of disinfectant. Notes on the walls curtly stated exact times of the few strictly regulated visiting hours per week. Save for a picture of the King and a religious homily, there were no other decorations to rest the eyes. Patients lay or sat passively in their iron-framed beds. Some walked about helping the nurses and orderlies to clean and attend the others. Nobody fit enough was allowed to be idle. Those were the rules and even Peggy could not change them, had she wanted to.

'No, you're right, it's not a luxury hotel,' she agreed grimly. 'What comforts were you thinking of?'

'Well.' His small eyes shot over to a nearby table.

'Oh, you mean those?' She pointed to a vase of bright daffodils, the only splash of colour in the grim room.

'Aye, the flowers for one thing. And chocolate drinks for another. What's wrong wi' Parish cocoa?'

'It was too thin and with so little nourishment it was hardly worth giving out.' Peggy kept her tone even, but the irritation rose almost to choke her. 'They gain strength from

234

decent food and beverages and that means they can be discharged earlier. It makes financial sense, you know.' Irony deepened to outright sarcasm. 'We save money in the end if we get rid of them quicker. Oh, and the daffodils were free. Libby picked them from our garden.'

'Aye, well, ye could be right, I suppose,' he admitted grudgingly, 'but the Board doesn't like it.'

Damn the Board! Peggy thought with a surge of irritation. They're getting more and more penny-pinching by the minute. If they go on like this, I might look around for another post. With the war, there are a few more places willing to consider women than before.

'Ye'll be at the meeting on Tuesday?' the Treasurer asked.

'Of course, Mr Alexander.'

'Fine. The Board would like your half-year report, Doctor, and a forecast of spending for the next half.'

'Certainly. Now, if you'll excuse me, I have to do my round of the men's TB and fever wards. I don't suppose you'd care to join me?'

'Er . . . no, thanks. I just came to say what I've said. I'm a wee bittie busy.' A notorious hypochondriac, the Treasurer shot off down the ward as fast as his bandy legs would carry him.

Peggy watched him go with a professional eye. Rickets. Poor nutrition as a bairn. She turned back to her work, but the irritation wouldn't go away. I'm getting to loathe these Board confrontations, she muttered beneath her breath and made her way to the crowded TB ward.

'Peggy, my dear, lovely as ever.' Andrew took her hand and gallantly helped her into his carriage when he came to collect her on Saturday.

'Thank you, Andrew.' After the challenges of her work, normally she quite enjoyed being cosseted by him. Today it merely got on her ragged nerves, but she made an effort. 'Are we going to ride out in your new automobile, Andrew? Shall I fetch my cape and scarf?'

'Not today, my dear. It's having something done to the pistons. No, I thought since the weather is so lovely, we might ride down to Alloway in the landau and take refreshments at the Burns Tearooms.'

'Wonderful.' Alloway held no sad memories for her. Peggy always enjoyed the chance to see one of Ayrshire's finest monuments and, like most Scots, loved the poet Robert Burns. Her spirits lifted for the first time in days.

'Come, tell me about your week.' Andrew noticed the tension round her mouth and eyes and kindly gave her the chance to unburden. 'Was it hard?'

'Difficult rather than hard.' Absently she gazed out as the lovely countryside rolled by, glowing in early May sunshine.

'What do you mean?'

'I got a letter at last from Elspeth.'

'Wonderful! Or is she ill?' His face clouded in concern.

'Not at all, she's as indomitable as ever and leading the SWH group all alone now in a place called Valjevo. There is so much to do for doctors in Serbia. In fact, everywhere in this terrible war. I've told you about the carnage poor Douglas Munro is dealing with daily. And, Andrew, did you read the latest list of dead from Gallipoli in the *Post*? There were hundreds from Ayrshire alone. Most of the men and women in the hospital had someone they knew or loved killed. Every day there's a death that touches them. Poor folk, it's terrible.'

'I know, Peggy. I would have liked to join up myself, but with no military experience and being over forty, they wouldn't have me,' Andrew said defensively.

'Robert would have been an army doctor. He and Douglas would have joined up together, that's for sure.' Peggy bowed her head and blinked back sudden tears. 'Sorry, Andrew.' She dabbed her eyes in embarrassment. It was rare for her to show emotion in front of anyone.

'Oh, don't apologise, Peggy. We're friends enough to be natural with each other, are we not?' Andrew was quick to reassure her with a comforting pat on the arm. 'I believe it is mainly the shadow of your husband that makes you refuse my suit,' he said slowly after a minute. 'And though I respect your fidelity, indeed I do, I would like to think there is hope one day for me.' He spoke in a stiff formal voice which masked the emotion behind the question.

For a while the only sound was the hum of the landau wheels on the metalled road and the jingle of the harness. 'Andrew,' she finally replied, 'I can't answer truthfully. Though I've accepted Robert's death, the memories are still precious. I just cannot see myself replacing him. Maybe one day I'll feel differently, but not yet . . .'

'I'll try to be patient, my dear, till the wounds heal more fully,' Andrew sighed and flicked the whip lightly across the horse's rump.

'Well, don't throw your life away waiting for me. I have to be honest with you, Andrew,' she added, 'it's not just Robert, there is also uncertainty about giving up my independence now I've learned to live alone. That and my maverick nature. Something Elspeth and I have in common, I fear!' A smile hovered. 'Anyway, I'm getting too old, thirty-five, you know. Get a young lass that can give you bairns. You'd make a wonderful father.'

'Och, no. I don't feel a great need for children, Peggy, or I'd have married years ago,' he replied. 'Little Kirsten would be enough for me. And I'd not expect you to give up your job altogether and stay at home waiting all day for me, if that's your worry,' he added magnanimously. 'Though I would advise you to take on something a little less demanding. Part-time in a nice wee private clinic, perhaps?' Andrew turned to her with a wry smile. 'And as Mistress Graham you would want for nothing material. I'm more than comfortably off, Peggy.'

'I've just told you that I like my independence,' she said crossly. 'Now don't spoil the day with proposals, Andrew Graham, or I won't come out with you again!'

'In that case, I have no alternative but to agree.' The lawyer raised his hand in mock submission and drove on at a smart trot towards their destination.

The high tea was delicious and the sun shone. As the light carriage sped swiftly back along the coast road to Ayr and then on to Kilmarnock, Peggy felt relaxed and comfortable. Andrew was marvellous company: intelligent, amusing, kind. Maybe one day . . . She allowed the thought to creep in after all.

On Tuesday she went to the Hospital Board meeting

armed with facts and figures. There was no sign of the previous years's magnanimity. Instead the mood was carping and mean. War seemed to have soured everyone's attitude.

'And we think the food bill is too high, Doctor McBride . . .'

'Properly fed patients get better quicker. Look at the discharge rate and the low relapse figures,' she argued.

'Why do pauper women seem to need so much chloroform in childbirth? Medications cost, Doctor, and it means having an anaesthetist on hand.'

'Many of them have bone defects as a result of their poor diet as children. Births are often long and complicated. Anaesthesia saves lives.'

'Look at this item. Number 10.' The Chairman pointed down the list. 'Ye've asked again for extra staff. I can't see the need for a night-nurse per ward?'

'Aye, the Chairman's right,' the others chorused.

'I think there is a need, at least in the TB wards, with so many very sick patients,' Peggy said firmly.

'And this business of babies being lifted and fed by their mothers when they cry.' The shocked protest came from a Board member who owned grocery and general provisions shops all over Ayrshire. 'It's far too indulgent. They should be left in the nurseries and just taken out at set times for feeding. Once they're cleaned they should be put straight back in. It would teach them discipline!'

'Discipline at two or three days old?' Peggy raised an eyebrow. 'Babies thrive on contact, gentlemen, it's a medical fact. Anyway, each infant's nutritional need is unique. Our mortality rates are among the lowest now in the West of Scotland Poor Law Hospitals. You saw the national report yourselves. I thought you were proud of it?'

'Aye, well . . .' They went on and on, the same old complaints, chipping away at her, Peggy was heart-weary of it.

'Oh, gentlemen, have you discussed the matter of my official status?' she asked briskly at the end of the meeting. 'I still think I should be made Superintendent. At the moment I do the job but without the proper title, which weakens my authority.' She looked round the table at their

238

stubborn expressions. 'Why not? It's not as if I'm asking you for more money.'

'No, we haven't talked about it, Doctor McBride. None of us sees the need for further discussion,' the Chairman replied. 'Women don't usually get made up to Superintendent.' He drew himself up to his full height.

'That's the point, isn't it?' she snapped. 'Even after all this time . . . after all the good results I've achieved here . . . you still see me as a stop-gap.'

'Och, not at all, Doctor McBride,' the Chairman said placatingly, but none of the Board could meet her eye. 'It – ahem, just wouldn't be fitting.' It was clear he spoke for them all. 'Meeting closed, I think, if that's all, gentlemen, Doctor McBride. I have an appointment at twelve.'

The Board dispersed rapidly and Peggy worked the rest of the day in an all too familiar state of irritation. At seven she went home wondering yet again what she was doing with her life.

'There's a letter from Edinburgh. It came this afternoon. I don't recognise the writing. Ye don't think something's happened to Doctor Munro?' Libby handed her a slim envelope as she came in the door.

'If Douglas had been injured I don't think we'd be informed, we're not related,' Peggy snapped, and then felt ashamed. 'Och, sorry, Libby.'

'Aye, well, you're not yerself,' Libby forgave her with a understanding shrug. 'Away and have a few minutes to relax, I'll bring ye a cup of tea.'

'Thanks.' In the quiet of her study Peggy opened the letter.

Edinburgh
10 May 1915

Dear Doctor McBride,
You may have heard my name from our dear mutual friend Elspeth McClure, who is doing such wonderful work for the SWH in Serbia. She does not know I am contacting you, but your name came to mind when I thought about my present dilemma. I am sure she would approve my action were she here.

239

My main concern has been to organise and equip female medical units for active service in all the war zones of Europe. Where possible we try also to train local women to take over and carry on. Reflecting this principle, I have asked Elspeth to organise a training hospital for Serbian nurses at Kragujevatz in Northern Serbia, not far from the Bulgarian border. Because of this project, I am trying to organise another SWH unit to take over her work in Valjevo and complement the staff at Kragujevatz.

The SWH has now twelve active units in France and Serbia. You may know that our other mutual friend, Douglas Munro (who often spoke most highly of you when we worked together in Edinburgh), is one of the few men who is helping out temporarily in Belgium before transfering back to his 'official' unit. We have a lady doctor now able to replace him. However, we desperately need more personnel and doctors are in particularly short supply. Two of our senior physicians in Serbia, Doctor Soltau and Doctor Holloway, have succumbed to typhus fever and are recuperating at base in Salonika. Their departure and the needs of new projects have left a huge gap in our resources.

Because of this terrible loss, may I ask if you would be interested in joining us? Your reputation and work in Greenwoods is well known. I would be proud to welcome you to the SWH. If not, would you please help me find a female doctor who could come? Perhaps you still have contact with former student colleagues. Doctor McBride, I am sorry to press you but the matter is urgent. The Balkan people are suffering terribly in these unhappy times.

I remain, your colleague and servant,
Elsie Inglis (Doctor)

Peggy sat for a long time deep in thought. Downstairs Kirsten laughed and chased a kitten in the hallway.

'Your tea's ready, bonnie lass!' Libby's voice drifted up the stairs.

'Ooohh, clootie pudding!' Kirsten cried in delight. 'Libby,

are you taking me to the park after?' Peggy heard her demand.

'Of course, my sweetheart, we must have our wee walk.'

'*Ye banks and braes o' bonnie Doon . . .*' the little scullery-maid sang as she polished the dining-room table. Then the song stopped and the kitchen door swung shut. The house settled into comfortable quietness. It was like a well-ordered ship under Libby's careful guidance. But would it be fair to remove the captain's hand from the helm altogether? Peggy wasn't sure.

After a time, she got up and walked with decisive steps over to her writing desk.

Chapter 17
Lines and tented fields

'Done!' Peggy leaned back. The letter had taken only a few minutes to write, but its contents were momentous, for herself and everyone associated with her.

Kilmarnock, 17 May 1915

Dear Doctor Inglis,
Your letter touched and inspired me. Please send me instructions as to how we can meet and begin my preparation for joining your proposed Valjevo/Kragujevatz unit. Thank you for thinking of me as a suitable candidate.
    Yours sincerely,
    Peggy McBride (Doctor)

Peggy's unit sailed direct from Southampton to Salonika without the detours suffered by Elspeth. But the voyage was long enough for her to consider the folly of her actions and the shock of family, friends and colleagues.

'Michty me! Ye'll drive me to an early grave, you and that other one!' Poor Libby could find nothing else to say, but went around tut-tutting under her breath. Kirsten, at six, was too immersed in her own life to bother a great deal. Once she was sure nothing would greatly change for her, she was happily nonchalant even as she waved Peggy goodbye just a month after she had dropped the bombshell.

'Aye, well, you realise we will be unable to hold the position open for your return, Doctor McBride?' The Chairman of the Poor Law Hospital Board took her decision in the nature of a personal insult. 'You'll have to look for another one when you come back. Assuming you *do* come back. Och, war is no place for a woman!'

'I expected that would be your verdict,' was Peggy's only reply. Under Andrew's stewardship, Kirsten's increasing financial independence meant she had no worries over support for her daughter, the household and Libby. Anyway, her basic salary was being covered by the SWH charity fund.

Andrew, appointed temporary guardian for Kirsten, was sad but remarkably unsurprised. 'I had a suspicion it would not take much for you to up and do something unusual.' His charming smile was wistful. 'I've known for a long time that a provincial lawyer's protestations of devotion weren't enough to hold you.'

'Och, it's nothing to do with that, Andrew.' Peggy touched his arm gently and hoped she was not lying. 'I just want to go where I'm needed.'

'You're needed here. Even the medical papers have mentioned your work with the sick in Greenwoods, especially pauper women and children, plus the improvements you've made in all the wards.'

'Tell that to the Board,' she said dryly. 'And my replacement, Doctor Brown, seems an enlightened enough young man and says he's keen to continue my work. I expect the Board are so relieved they don't have to appoint another women that they'll listen to him. For a while anyway.'

'But why Serbia?' Andrew was trying hard to understand. 'You've no connections with the place.'

'It's not a question of connections. As far as I'm concerned they are just people who desperately need medical help and I can give it. I'd probably do the same for the Germans if I had to.'

'Good God!' For a moment Andrew was stunned into silence.

'Och, Andrew, don't take everything I say so seriously and literally.' Peggy smiled at his expression. 'Anyway, connections or not, the Serbs are our allies and that's where Elsie needs me most right now. It could just as easily have been Belgium or France.'

'But I still can't see why Greenwoods isn't enough for you, Peggy,' Andrew went on, his expression utterly puzzled.

243

'Listen, Andrew,' she said, trying to make him understand, but knowing it was impossible. 'I used to chide Elspeth sometimes when she was deeply involved with the suffragettes. I accused her of not using her medical qualifications as she should. Now she's doing that . . . and more.' Peggy got up restlessly. 'Och, I feel so confined these days, as if I've done all I can in life and now I'm just going to mark time fiddling round the edges forever.'

'That's nonsense, you wouldn't be marking time.' But his protest fell on deaf ears.

She picked up the *Ayrshire Post*. 'Look at that, all the good Scots names in the lists of dead every time they're published. The lads need doctors. *I'm* a doctor. I'm going.'

'There are few Scots troops in Serbia,' he replied stubbornly.

'You've missed the point. But who can blame you?' Peggy reached up and kissed his cheek. 'Take good care of my bairn and Libby for me, Andrew dear, especially if I don't make it back.'

Apart from one torpedo scare in a calm, summery Bay of Biscay, the journey was uneventful. During long weeks at sea, boredom was the biggest enemy. Peggy used the time to train the women in her unit, using materials and information provided by Elsie. At Salonika they saw no more than the rooms in their fine sea-front hotel. Next morning they boarded a train to begin the long journey northwards, first to Valjevo and then, for some, eastwards to Kragujevatz.

'God, Elspeth was right!' Peggy was shocked by the burned-out farmhouses and villages they passed by day. At night they stayed in towns where displaced peasants mingled with wounded soldiers and, most bizarrely of all, Austrian prisoners who wandered about freely. Everywhere there was chaos, adding to the risk of disease, especially the feared killer typhus.

'Are they serving us coffee? It would be too much to hope for a cup of tea! Maybe it's hot milk? Oh, look, they've set things up beautifully!' Weary nurses and medical staff gasped in pleasure as they changed train at Mlanovitch.

244

Right beside the station, tables had been placed under trees in what had once been a lovely garden.

'We'll soon know!' Peggy led her little troop over to sit in happy anticipation. With full ceremony, smiling local orderlies carried trays of steaming liquid round on huge trays.

'Thank you. How nice!' Peggy needed all her reserves of self-control not to show the shock she felt when she sipped the brown stuff. It tasted highly peculiar and had a kick like an Athens mule.

'Delicious is it not, *dobra doktora?*' The head orderly waited expectantly for her response.

'Delicious.' Peggy gave her most charming smile. 'And what is it?'

'Infused lime leaves and rum.'

'Ah. Oh, well, ladies. "Here's tae us, wha's like us?" ' Peggy raised her cup in the old Scots toast.

' "No' many and they're all dead!" ' chorused her colleagues, and downed the lot.

The women accepted slices of thick black bread spread with goat's cheese and forced it down with more rum and lime tea.

'Now I've seen it all! Where in the name of all that's holy did these come from?' Peggy whispered to Chief Staff Nurse, Betty Anderson as more refreshments appeared.

'Don't ask me, Doctor McBride, just be grateful for small mercies that it's not more black bread!' Stifling giggles, they nibbled Huntley and Palmer tea-biscuits, served graciously on a fine china plate.

Half-drugged from the alcohol, the women dozed and sang to pass the rest of the long winding train journey north. Some miles before they were due into Valjevo, they spruced up as best they could and sat out the final hours impatiently.

'What the heck is that abominable racket?' Peggy stuck her head out of the window as the train pulled into town.

'It's a band, Doctor,' giggled a nurse. 'I think they're playing a Serbian folk tune for us.'

'Serbian folk tune, my granny!' Philomena the little kitchen-maid chortled. 'It's supposed to be *Tipperary*!'

'What a reception!' Sister Katherine Bailey struggled with

her hand-luggage. 'There'll be no room to get off the train. Look at the platform, it's packed.' Peasants, soldiers, prisoners-of-war and townspeople craned to see the arrival of the *Englezi*. Resident SWH staff had long ago tired of explaining they were Scots, not English, and being met with blank stares.

'Och, mighty me!' A giant of a man with enormous moustaches grabbed Kate Bailey's bag and tossed it on to the nearest cart, then lifted her up to join it. Amid incredible noise and chaos, the rest of the bags and women were loaded on to rickety open carriages, pulled by dilapidated horses of every shape and size. 'Will they horses, donkeys, or whatever they are, make it, do you think, Doctor? They're awful skinny!' yelled Nancy the cook.

'Doubtful. Those patients look beyond medical help! Och, it's like the Kirkowen miners' whippet-racing day!' Peggy was nearly doubled up with laughter at the sight of her unit perched on the carts. 'Oh, jings!' she yelped, and clutched her hat as she was lifted on to the place of honour at the front and the crazy cavalcade set off at a fast trot.

'They've put dynamite in the horse-shoes!' Betty Anderson gasped as the animals gathered speed and charged up the hillside towards the town, sparks flying on the cobblestones. 'God almighty!' Sisters, nurses, cooks and orderlies forgot rank or decorum as they clung to handbags and each other. Stones rattled under the shaking wheels and they swayed, rocked and jolted to the sound of cracking whips and the fearsome yells of the drivers.

'Peggy! You've made it!' a familiar voice greeted her as the carts finally pulled up in front of the hospital and the women staggered off.

'Elspeth!' The two old friends threw themselves at one another and hugged in delight.

'It's wonderful to see you, but what are you doing here?' Peggy demanded. 'Elsie thought you would have left for Kragujevatz by the time we arrived.'

'The school got underway faster than we anticipated and I was needed urgently back here for a few days because of another typhus scare.' Elspeth's grim expression lightened. 'Fortunately it wasn't typhus this time. For now we seem

246

to have won that battle. I've handed over temporarily in Kragujevatz to an Australian colleague, Captain Brian McGonagle. That meant I could stay here till you arrived in Valjevo with our reinforcements and supplies.'

'A man?' Peggy was astounded. 'I thought the SWH only used females?'

'It usually does,' Elspeth agreed. 'But Elsie sanctioned this temporary appointment herself. The man in question is the Australian captain from Salonika I told you about in my letter. He's a field doctor, and suffered terrible wounds under fire during a skirmish. As soon as the poor man was more or less recovered, he was posted up north with an Anzac unit on its way to Northern Albania.'

'Anzac? What's that?' Peggy had never heard the term before.

'Anzac is what they call the Australian and New Zealand divisions. They're rough and ready but wonderful soldiers, and great characters most of them.'

'Why is this captain . . . what's his name . . . still in Serbia?' Peggy asked as she followed her friend into the cool building.

'Authorities never change!' said Elspeth. 'They suddenly decided he might be best deployed back in Salonika, so they cancelled the poor man's orders and he was left hanging about helping out as a volunteer till they could make up their minds. Dithery dolittles!' She threw up her hands in disgust.

'As always and everywhere,' Peggy agreed wholeheartedly, thinking of Kilmarnock Hospital Board.

'Then they said he could go with his unit to Russia,' Elspeth went on. 'But at the last minute they changed their minds yet again. No wonder the war isn't going as well as they expected!'

'Do you mean that? Mostly we're fed positive propaganda at home, though they can't disguise the terrible losses. The figures tell their own story.'

'It's tough down here and I've heard from the men that it's no better elsewhere.' Elspeth looked worried. 'The Serbs have managed to push back the Austro-Hungarian Army for the moment. You must have seen the abandoned guns as you passed through Southern Serbia on the train?'

'I did. It was a real reminder of why we're here,' Peggy agreed.

'There's even more wreckage on the way to Kragujevatz,' Elspeth said. 'But despite the abandoned guns, we all know they'll be back. German and Turkish allies are holding on. Gallipoli solved almost nothing, despite the carnage . . . oh, do come in.' Elspeth led the way to the offices.

'You hear so little, just that victory is round the corner!'

'It's far from over yet,' Elspeth sounded grim.

'I suppose not.' Peggy changed the subject, deciding not to dwell on the horrors of war. 'So this is it?' Curiously she gazed round the whitewashed building she would soon be running.

'This is it,' Elspeth said with a note of pride in her voice. 'It didn't look as clean when we arrived, I can tell you.'

'Och, it's fine. But listen, this Australian you mentioned – is he staying on in Kragujevatz?'

'No, he'll leave when I get back. It was lucky for us that Elsie persuaded the Anzacs to loan him till you got here.'

'And then?'

'Then he'll probably head back to Salonika to take over one of the field-hospitals again.'

'My goodness, Elspeth McClure, he must be exceptional right enough,' Peggy teased. 'Just a year ago you would not have voluntarily handed over anything to a man, let alone charge of your precious hospital.'

'Ah, but in wartime everything changes. And, yes, he is different,' she added so quietly Peggy almost missed it.

'Different?'

'Captain Brian McGonagle is different from most men I've met,' Elspeth said with a touch of defiance.

'Australian . . . Irish name. Catholic, is he? Surely you've not fallen for him, Elspeth, and you a good Presbyterian?'

'What? Oh, don't be ridiculous!' Elspeth coloured up to her bright red mark. 'Fiddlesticks and blethers anyway, I haven't time for religious nonsense, these day Presbyterian or otherwise, you know that. No, no, Brian is a good col-

248

league, nothing more, Peggy. And talking of good colleagues, have you heard from Douglas?'

'Indeed I have, just before I left. He's gone to his own unit now, says the casualties are terrible . . .' The women sat amidst the chaos of the war hospital and chatted as if they had never been apart.

Over real tea brought in with the precious supplies from Britain, Elspeth spoke proudly of the training school she had created in the other base. 'We adapted a building which had once been the finest boys' school in Kragujevatz. The locals helped with whitewashing, cleaning and so on, then our girls soaked the place in disinfectant.' A brilliant smile lit up her fine eyes. 'I don't suppose any self-respecting germ would dare come within a mile of it now.'

It was amazing how well Elspeth was thriving in this strange environment. Peggy could see her friend had regained the old *joie de vivre* lost during the hard years of fighting for women's rights. She asked, 'How many trainees have you, Elspeth?'

'Six of our nurses are teaching hundreds of vounteer women from all over the country.' Elspeth was full of enthusiasm. 'We have more applicants than places. And now, my dear, I have to get back. I'd love to have a little longer with you,' she said apologetically, 'but there is so much to be done. I can't leave poor Brian stranded there forever.'

'Send me a message with the extraordinary captain when he comes through. And I must hear how my girls are settling in,' Peggy reminded her.

'They'll be fine. I've told you, conditions are far better than when we arrived, though still very primitive. The spirit and cheeriness among the staff is wonderful and the local people are very grateful. I'm more concerned about leaving you here, Peggy.' Elspeth's face clouded. 'Valjevo has had a terrible time with war-wounded and typhus. It's hard to keep disease at bay with no running water or source of power! But as you've seen, Peggy, it's not much better anywhere in Serbia. This is their third war in quick sucession and it's taken a toll on the entire country.'

'Och, don't worry, Elspeth, I'll manage. I've had plenty of practice living in primitive conditions!' Peggy thought wryly of Lizzie's cottage in Kirkowen and the tenement she had shared with her father in Cowcaddens.

'Actually my main worry these days, other than typhus fever, is invasion.' Elspeth bit her lip. 'Kragujevatz is a bit too near the Bulgarian border for comfort or safety. It's even worse at Nis, they're just a stone's throw from the enemy. You've got the Austro-Hungarian allies just to the north of you here. Oh, I do hope you'll be all right!'

'You've a nerve, Elspeth McClure, after all the lost nights' sleep you've caused me over the years.' Peggy grinned and got up. 'Now come on, let's get you and my lassies to the train, you said it was due to go at four.'

Amid the usual turmoil at the station, Peggy said her farewells. The reduced unit waved cheerfully to their travelling companions as they boarded the train with Elspeth, though their hearts were sore at losing them.

War is all about goodbyes, Peggy thought sadly.

Elspeth gradually faded into a dot as she stood waving from the open back of the carriage platform. Gradually the ancient train disappeared in a cloud of flying cinders and eldritch whistles.

Three days later Peggy was supervising the unpacking of precious medical supplies when a tall man in his forties, with a thin expressive face, arrived, escorted by Sister Bailey. 'Good day. You must be Doctor McBride. I'm Brian McGonagle.' He held out a sunburned hand. 'Elspeth McClure said to come to see you the minute I got in from Kragujevatz, so here I am.'

'Welcome to Valjevo, Captain, and sorry about the mess.' Peggy waved at the boxes they had brought with them and which were strewn across the reception area of the hospital.

'Oh, don't worry, it always feels and looks like Christmas when supplies come in!' A broad smile flashed in his tanned face. 'I left Elspeth doing the same, just like a kid with a box of tucker. Luckily I met Sister at the station and she knew exactly where to find you. She's been telling me all the way here what a good job you've been doing since Elspeth left.' Shrewd blue eyes assessed her.

'Thank you.' Peggy flushed at the praise, thinking what

250

an agreeable person he was. 'The local staff and the prisoners are very cooperative. That helps.'

'Yeah! The prisoners sure have a lot of freedom.' Brian nodded. 'It struck me as bloody weird when I first came up here from Salonika where they are held in camps, but I take it for granted now.'

'It doesn't matter to me, this isn't my war . . . if you know what I mean?' Peggy shrugged. 'I find it hard to separate friend from foe, prisoner from guard, in my own mind. It might be different if one or other lot were British.'

'Sure, but that'll change after the first skirmish. Under fire you soon sort out who's your enemy, Doctor McBride,' the Captain replied. 'Though with a bit of luck you'll not be involved directly in anything like that. By the way, anything I can do to help? I've a little discretionary time in hand before I go on.'

'No, we're fine.' Peggy shook her head. 'Elspeth has set up everything so perfectly, it hardly takes any running at all. Luckily things are quiet at the moment too. I've had an easy time so far.'

'As you wish.' If he was offended at her refusal, it didn't show.

'When are you leaving?' Peggy hoped she didn't sound as if she was trying to push him out.

'Well, it's clear you don't need me here!' His grin widened as she flushed to the roots of her red hair. 'I expect to leave tomorrow . . . assuming the train comes.' Seeing her embarrassment, he said, 'Don't worry, I know you have a lot to do. I won't get in the way. I was only joking about the train. They're pretty reliable, and my unit command would prefer me back in Salonika as soon as possible. I'll just stop at Mlanovitch for a day on the way down to pass on some scout information we got from the Bulgarian border.'

'How is Elspeth's training school shaping up?'

'The school is going great guns. Like everything she fixes. That's one marvellous woman! In fact, she's just bloody brilliant! The time I've spent working with her has been like ro other.' The Captain's obvious admiration and sincerity took Peggy completely by surprise.

'Doctor McBride?' a voice called from the corridor. 'Can

251

you check this burn? I dressed it yesterday, but I think it's threatening gangerene.'

'Excuse me then, Doctor McBride.' The Captain held out his hand. 'I can see you're busy. Well, I'm off to visit some old friends in the town.'

'Thanks for calling in. Oh, and I think Elspeth is wonderful too,' she called after the tall figure, limping across the courtyard. Elspeth had told her he had suffered leg and stomach wounds. Poor man, he should really be convalescing, but wartime is different, I suppose. Well, if he and Elspeth have become a mutual admiration society of two, that might put Libby's plans for her and Douglas in jeopardy. Hope she was wrong about Douglas, though. Peggy couldn't bear the thought of his being hurt, especially not by Elspeth. That would strain all our loyalties.

Valjevo,
July 1915

My darling Kirsten and Libby,

Now everything is spick and span in the hospital. We've unpacked all our medicines and bandages and stored them neatly. Fortunately we don't seem to need them just yet, so I am able to sit with a precious cup of tea and write to you.

Kirsten, lovely lass, yesterday I waved goodbye to a friend of Auntie Elspeth at the funny old station we have here, then I walked through the quaint cobbled streets of Valjevo back to the hospital. Suddenly I heard the sound of a street organ. It drew me like the Pied Piper of Hamelin. I hurried towards a little square, from which the gay melody was coming.

What do you think I found there, Kirsten? An old man was turning the handle of a finely painted organ, and playing such lively music that I wanted to dance. Oh, but that would be no way for the doctor in charge of Valjevo SWH to behave, would it? At least not in the streets in front of all those fearsome-looking Serbian warriors. (Though you and I have danced many happy times up and down the big hallway at home.) But the funniest thing of all, my dearest, was the organ-grinder's little monkey who went round collecting coins from the passers-by.

Quite without warning, he jumped on to my shoulder and I had to stifle a cry of shock. He stuck his wise little face almost into mine, bright eyes shining like black buttons, and thrust a worn hat under my nose. How could I refuse to add to his collection of coins? The little chap grapped my coin and at once bit it, as if to test it was true. Then he hopped, chattering loudly, on top of the organ while the old man played a new selection of tunes. How I wished you could have seen them with me, both of you. How we would have laughed!

Are you practising your piano scales, Kirsten, and doing your very best for the teacher at school? Oh, I am sure you are, with dear Libby there to keep you in order. Kisses to you both and remember you are always in my heart and thoughts. Please send my kindest wishes to Uncle Andrew.

Goodnight, darling girl.

Your loving,

Mama

Two days after Brian left, all hell broke out in Valjevo. Without any warning, cart and train loads of seriously wounded men began arriving from north and the south. Skirmishing on the northern borders had turned bloody and intense. Wards were filled with patients lying on mattresses on the floor, so close they could hardly walk between them. Corridors, landings, every inch, of floor was covered with groaning and bleeding wounded. Out in the courtyards, they laid them in rows, erecting rough shades to keep the sun off the suffering men.

Peggy and her staff worked round the clock. The nursing sisters converted the ballroom of a nearby manor house into a room for dressing the less serious wounds. Long tables were set up for them to work on. Round the room, patiently waiting their turn, were queues of pain-racked men. Most were Serbs but some were Austrian and Magyar prisoners. Racial hatred seemed to be totally set aside within the confines of the hospital. Walking wounded on both sides helped nurse both comrades and enemies.

'Ask him if he wants us to give a message to his mother?' Peggy urgently asked an interpreter, as she finally gave up the unequal fight to save a young Serb with terrible stomach wounds.

'*N'ama maika, maika ye mura.*' The dying man shook his head weakly.

'What did he say?'

'I have no mother, my mother is dead.' The young man muttered something else.

'What is it? Is there maybe someone else we can tell?' Peggy felt a wave of terrible sorrow as she watched the young life ebbing fast away.

'He can see the tears in your eyes, Doctor. He says not to be sad, he will soon see his mother and many of the others he loves again. He is dying for his country ... he is proud to die. Will someone stay with him for a moment?' The nurse got up. 'I have to get the priest, he wants to confess.'

'Yes, I will.' Despite the pressure, the noise and confusion, Peggy sat down, holding the young man's hand, till the Orthodox priest arrived and absolved him from his sins. Later she saw the boy sink slowly, holding tightly on to the hand of Ellen Fraser, a young nurse from the gentle hills of Galloway. Within half an hour, his eyes closed forever.

Seven long hours later, Peggy went into the starlit night, exhausted, knowing there would be many, many more poor souls to tend before this war was spent. Suddenly she longed to feel the clean sea breeze in her hair on the Kirkowen cliffs. War was so evil! She looked above her at the innocent summer night sky and asked aloud, 'Why does humanity do this over and over again?' The distant stars gave no answer and she could think of none either. After a time, she glanced down at her blood-stained white coat and, sighing, went back to the hospital.

'Typhus!' The nurse supervising the admission of a new batch of sick and wounded Austrian and Magyar prisoners sent the dreaded word to Peggy a few days later.

'We have to get moving or the disease will go round the town again like wildfire, folk are so weak and depleted. It may even be too late already,' the old hands warned her.

Peggy acted instantly and decisively.

'Typhus! Oh, in the name of God, not another outbreak! What can we do?' Anxious town officials wrung their hands in dread. They remembered all too clearly the last time, when the dead had been carried in cartloads by night to be buried outside the town.

'I want the old palace as an isolation hospital,' Peggy ordered. 'Sitting on that little rise away from the town, it's ideal.'

'Of course. It's still in reasonable condition and nobody is using it now.' Fear made them cooperative.

'We'll knock it into shape,' she said. 'Is there water?'

'Not running water, but there is a deep well in the court-yard. It's good and clean.'

'Excellent. And a kitchen?'

'A whole cellar full of them. They're old-fashioned, of course.'

'Better than here, whatever they are.' Peggy nodded over to the converted school that was the main hospital, with its tent-kitchen and pitiful water supply piped in through makeshift open runnels.

Dozens of locals set to work under the direction of orderly and dispenser Alice Campbell. Scrubbed, disinfected and whitewashed, the palace was soon in use. Bedsteads were carried into every room and mattresses laid on the floor when those ran out.

'Fine, good work, but far too stuffy. Stale air increases the risk of cross-infection,' said Peggy, inspecting the new wards.

'The windows won't open, Doctor McBride,' Sister Bailey, said worriedly. 'I thought the same myself, but the locals say they've never been opened in all the years the palace was lived in by the lords of the manor. Fresh air wasn't a priority, it seems.'

'Well, it is now! Get the men to force them. If they still won't open, break them!' Peggy was beyond compromise or sentimentality. 'We have to have air circulating or it's death to anybody we send here, including the nurses. And tell

255

your staff to get the men outside as much as the weather allows.'

'We can lift them into the gardens,' the nurses agreed enthusiastically.

'Right. Fresh air and cleanliness is our only hope. Thank God it's not winter yet. We must get this business under control before the cold sets in. Doctor McClure has told me it's terrible. And there's virtually no firewood left round the town. Drifting snow and low temperatures are a terrible hindrance to providing decent ventilation!'

It wasn't enough. Peggy comandeered a couple of inns, even some stables, and they laid mattresses out in the scrubbed stalls. Most of their sick comrades' 'nursing' had to be done by healthy Austrian and Magyar prisoners.

'They'll murder us all in our beds,' shrieked a terrified Serbian nurse when the first contingent was installed with the minimum of supervision. 'The sick ones are all right, but these are soldiers.'

'Marija is right.' Her collegues crowded round anxiously.

'They've been walking freely around the town for months, why on earth should they suddenly decide to harm us?' Peggy squashed the panic before it began. 'All prisoners, including those who are helping by doing the nursing, are restricted to their compounds at night. Their officers are keeping tight control. If there are any incidents, they know they will all be confined to prison camps.'

Even with extra help, at first the struggle seemed to be lost. Every morning bells rang for the funerals of important victims in the old town cemetery. In the afternoon the Crown Prince's own band played Serbian heroes to their graves in the new military graveyard outside town. The Austrians and Hungarians buried their own dead with full honours and dignity. At night lesser folk were trundled to mass graves in silence.

But within a month or so, the women slowly began to win the fight against the disease. Another temporary lull in the fighting gave them a chance to regain some of their own depleted strength, though by that time they had lost three nursing sisters from typhus fever and others were forced to return home because of ill-health. New staff arrived from

Britain, including a couple of doctors. This took some of the burden off Peggy's shoulders, but it was a tough, demanding life.

One glorious autumn morning, when the sun shone on the Montenegran mountains and reflected golden fire, Peggy looked at herself in the mirror. A woman of 35, her red hair still glowed brightly and clear green eyes stared back at her. About her mouth was a look of solid determination that took her by surprise. I'm turning into a right tough old medic! The idea didn't worry her. But maybe I'm a wee bittie on the thin side. She turned sideways and peered into the blotchy glass. Hmm ... Peggy had never carried much weight, but now her slight frame was decidedly meagre. The white doctor's coat, belted round the middle, showed off a tiny waist. 'Poor Andrew wouldn't be happy,' she remarked aloud to the image. 'He likes women to be shapely and feminine.' Andrew! With a shock she realised this was the first time she had thought of him spontaneously since she'd arrived in Valjevo.

As she combed her hair into its tidy chignon, she noticed fine lines had begun etching themselves round her eyes and mouth. You're getting on, Peggy McBride, right enough! she teased herself. But even so, in the months here you've done a worthwhile job, enough to justify your medical training, even if you never lift a stethoscope again in your life once this is all over. The thought was deeply comforting.

In October fighting intensified, bringing with it the threat of imminent invasion. The Austrians, furious at having been driven out of Serbia, decided to cauterise the 'Ulcer' between them and their allies by reinvading. On 5 October 1915, Austro-German allies attacked from the south and, in a flanking movement, across the Drina.

Before Franco-British reinforcements could arrive from Salonika, Bulgarian troops swept westwards into Southern Serbia, driving a wedge between the Serbs and their allies. The whole of Northern Serbia was cut off. To add to their troubles, the autumn turned wet and cold. Heavy rains turned the roads round Valjevo to mud and made fuel and food harder to get by the day.

'Thank God for the railway!' Peggy sighed with relief

257

every week when the little train chuffed up from the south, bringing contact with the outside world and carrying essential medical supplies.

'We'll freeze to death in this place!' Kate Bailey moaned as, by the beginning of November, winter began sending vicious warnings of what lay ahead.

'At least the snow isn't lying yet,' Peggy said comfortingly. 'Even where it fell in drifts, it's melted.'

'For the time being!' Kate refused to be consoled.

At night temperatures plunged to well below freezing. Fuel became scarcer still and some days they had to do without a fire at all. Tramping from hospital to hospital, usually on foot, Peggy was wrapped from head to toe in a long fur coat given to her by the Mayor's wife. It had been her mother's in happier times.

'If we cannot boil water, wash clothes or heat wards, even a little, then typhus is bound to return!' the nurses warned grimly.

'I'm doing what I can.' Peggy rubbed a weary hand across her forehead. Part of each day was now spent cajoling, threatening and persuading the local authorities, themselves stretched beyond measure, to provide more wood and food.

Trains from the south became fewer. As Serbia was being squeezed from almost all directions, supplies were no longer coming in from the Entente Allies to the depots. There was little to bring.

'Will we be all right?' Betty Anderson asked anxiously one evening at supper after a rumour-filled day.

'I hope so.' Peggy tried to sound calm, but it was not easy. Sometimes, when she listened to the locals talking about the threat of invasion, she felt a chill of fear in the pit of her stomach.

'Have you noticed, Doctor McBride?' Kate Bailey's voice shook a little as she and Peggy crossed from one hospital unit to another in the town.

'Noticed what?' Peggy asked nervously.

'There isn't a single man of an age to carry a gun, left in Valjevo,' Kate whispered.

'You're right!' Peggy looked round the silent, fearful streets and shivered involuntarily. Only old men and women with babies, scuttled here and there. Over the next few days the tension grew worse. Austrian and Magyar prisoners began ignoring the night curfew and strutted round the town, or else sat chatting in the town's cafes, patiently awaiting their freedom.

'What will happen if the enemy comes?' Nurses waylaid Peggy, to enquire anxiously.

'Don't worry, the SWH won't leave us in danger,' she replied with more confidence than she felt. They all knew that the Bulgars, positioned both to the east and west, were trying to join with the Austrians to the north in a pincer action. If that happened, the only way out would be over the mountains of Montenegro. In mid-winter few could survive such a journey.

'They're getting closer . . . they'll soon be here!' A week later, vague fears became urgent reality. Terrifying news, full of stories of atrocities, trickled in as town after town began to fall. Since October, pathetic columns of starving civilians had drifted frantically south behind the units of soldiers, keeping just ahead of the enemy. Now it was a full-scale exodus. Many of the hospital units joined them in the march towards the Albanian border via Pristina and on to Pec, which was still in Serb hands.

'I've received a letter from Doctor Inglis in Krusevac with instructions for all SWH units,' Peggy announced, having called her team together. 'She advises those who are fit enough to join the organised treks over the mountains before winter tightens its grip.' Grim-faced, she looked round the group of nurses and helpers. 'I'm obliged to tell you that the journey is already hazardous because of the terrible mud and the passes are made no easier because of all the folk flooding out. Some are taking fearsome risks.'

'What's the alternative, Doctor McBride?' Betty Anderson asked quietly.

'Stay and be captured if Valjevo is invaded.' Peggy was in no mood for dissimulation.

'Och, I'm used to mountains,' broke in a little nurse from a quiet glen near Loch Lomond. 'They're no bother to me.'

'Well, I've never been up one in my life, but ken I prefer mountains to they Bulgars any day!' her friend from Gallowgate agreed with a cheery grin. 'Aye, we'll cross the mountains, Doctor McBride, so we will!'

'We all will!' The unit chorused agreement, terrified of what might happen if they were taken prisoner.

'What's Doctor Inglis doing?' Kate Bailey asked when the noise died down.

'She has decided to stay on at her post.' Peggy's expression was unreadable. 'She'll try and negotiate the safety of very ill patients who can't be moved.'

'Are you coming with us, Doctor?' somebody called from the back.

Peggy shook her head. 'Doctor Inglis said it was up to the individual doctors and nurses in all units to make that decision for themselves. I'm staying here.'

'I hope the Austrians will show us more mercy, than the Germans did poor Edith Cavell,' Elsie Inglis said with a worried frown to Elspeth, who had come to Krusevac on one of the last trains. 'And I hope that I'm not sending you all to your deaths in the mountains.' The poor woman could not hide her anxiety. 'But what choice do we have now we are totally cut off from the Entente Allies?'

'Elsie, you're not sending us, we're choosing to go. We're made of good Scots stuff, woman!' Elspeth replied robustly. 'We'll make it! And the Serbs going with us are tough as old boots, they're used to the mountains.'

'Well, I don't know, I've heard a lot of them are plainsmen and afraid of the mountains,' Elsie worried.

'We have to leave,' said Elspeth. 'Other than falling into the hands of the Austrian or Magyars, or even worse the Bulgars, what else can we do? Anyway, it's not just escape, Elsie, we all know that. Most of the men will need medical attention on the journey. Poor souls, I fear many will not make it,' Elspeth contradicted her previous optimism. 'Half of them should still be convalescing.'

'I know, but they have little choice.' Elsie got up and paced the room she used as an office. 'I've sent word to doctors round the country, advising them and the nurses to leave ... by the way, I mentioned to Peggy that someone should stay with the very sick from both Kragujevatz and Valjevo.'

'In that case, I'll take our patients over there and stay at Valjevo,' Elspeth volunteered. 'It's nearer the Austro-Hungarian border than Kragujevatz, so it is likely to be occupied by Austrians rather than Bulgars. They've got a kinder reputation with prisoners. Peggy can take my place on the trek, Elsie. There's time if I do it now.'

Doctor Inglis looked doubtful. 'It's a good idea to send your very ill patients to Valjevo, Elspeth, but you should get out if you can. You're needed elsewhere. Try to get back to Salonika and set up the Serbian nurses' training school there. More than ever we need to be able to prepare them for the outposts where their soldiers are still fighting.'

'Let me think about it. Anyway, I must be off, there is so much to do.' Elspeth stood up, towering over the little doctor. 'Goodbye, my dear friend, and good luck.'

'Good luck to us all, Elspeth,' Elsie said softly. 'We're all going to need it!'

'Peggy! We always manage to meet in a state of crisis these days.' Despite the gravity of the situation, Elspeth's face lit with pleasure when Peggy arrived unexpectedly at Kragu-jevatz with the refugeee train.

'What do you expect in a war, woman?' They clasped each other for a long, emotional moment.

'Why have you come from Valjevo?' Elspeth asked. 'Have you had second thoughts about my offer to change places . . . we still can do it?'

'No.' Peggy shook her head. 'I came down to wave off our folk who're joining your trek and to escort the sick back to Valjevo the minute you leave. They say this will be the last train to go through.' She took Elspeth's hands in hers. 'Also I felt I had to see you if I could. I wanted to say goodbye and take back what little medical supplies you cannot carry with you. God knows when we'll get any more. They say the Austrians will be in Valjevo within a week or two at the most.' Her eyes betrayed none of the fear she felt.

'Maybe you should come with us anyway?' Elspeth held

261

her at arm's length, searching her face for a trace of uncertainty.

'No. If I go there is no other qualified doctor left in Valjevo.'

'Then if there is a God up there, may He be with you.' Elspeth did not try to dissuade her, though her heart was heavy. They had always respected each other's right to choose their own fate.

'And with you. Elspeth, will you take this for me?' Peggy held out a thin oilskin package. 'It's letters for Kirsten, Libby and Andrew. Send them as soon as you reach a place of safety. And try to contact Douglas if you can, he must be wondering what's become of me. I haven't answered his last two letters. Och, it's been so busy . . .'

'Peggy,' Elspeth broke in, 'about Douglas. Have you thought about your place in his life, what you really mean to him?'

'Of course.' Peggy looked at her in astonishment. 'I know exactly what I mean to him. He was Rob's best friend and carries that on in a way, through visiting Kirsten and me. We always talk about old times. I've told you so, Elspeth.'

Oh, Lord!' Elspeth took a deep breath. Oh, well, it's hardly the time or the place, and we've never meddled in each other's lives.

'Och, Elspeth, are you bothered in case I'm jealous?' Peggy smiled. 'Was Libby right for once?'

'Now we're really talking at cross purposes, I haven't a clue what you mean! Dear girl, let's discuss this at a more appropriate moment. How stupid of me to bring up such matters now.' Elspeth looked round at the final touches being put to horses and mules. 'We had better get the column started, the Bulgars are only a day's march away to the southwest. Listen, can you hear the guns?'

'Yes, I think they're getting closer. Please don't let me keep you,' Peggy said anxiously.

'You aren't. But, yes, there's a lot still to do.' Elspeth pointed to the train load of soldiers disembarking to begin the long trek overland and onward through the Montenegran mountains. Before the train was completely empty, stretcher-bearers were already loading on the very ill who were to go with Peggy. 'Where are you putting our folk when you get to Valjevo?' Elspeth asked.

'The very sick will be put into the main hospital once we've cleared the wards. We've decided to keep the Serbian wounded together rather than spilt them up. Have you any fever cases?'

'Only one or two.'

'That's a relief!' Peggy sighed. 'All right, they can go to the fever hospital with ours. There are still quite a few patients there.'

'Do you expect a peaceful surrender?' Elspeth tried to sound optimistic.

'I think so.' Peggy nodded. 'The Serbian command and fighters have already left. They've decided it's best to let the Austrians walk in and take the town without unnecessary bloodshed. They'll regroup in Montenegro and fight in units from there and Albania. So long as the Austro-Hungarian command realize there are no fighters left, the town should be saved from destruction. I'll try to meet the senior commanders when they come.' Her chin went up bravely.

'How will they know you're no threat?'

'Och, we've draped the hospitals in white flags and red crosses. The whole town looks ready for a kirk garden fête. All we need is some home-made jam and knitted tea-cosies!' Peggy's laugh broke the tension for a moment, then she became grave again. 'Let's just hope the invaders respect our immunity when they recognise the Red Cross.'

'Doctor McBride, where shall we put the amputees?' A young nurse ran over, white-faced. Behind her the station was a seething mass of men, stretchers, carts and horses. Supplies and boxes of ammunition were being loaded and unloaded in apparent chaos across the lines of wounded waiting for placement.

Muffled booms from Bulgarian guns echoed eerily round the curve of mountains, definitely louder than half an hour before. The tiny medical train would have to leave for Valjevo, Red Cross flags hanging from every window, as soon as Elspeth's column moved out.

Peggy watched as medical supplies and provisions for the

263

journey were carefully packed in oilskin and hung on pack donkeys and horses of every shape and size.

'What do you think of our trousers?' Elspeth twirled round laughing. 'I've tried to make sure that patients and nurses are as well equipped as possible for the mountains. Mr Asquith would surely say they were unwomanly!'

'Fiddlesticks to Asquith, they're straight from the latest mode magazine for lady cyclists!' Peggy called after her.

Running about checking lists and dressings, dressed in the warmest clothes they could find, Elspeth and the nurses were almost indistinguishable from the men. They each wore padded breeches and balaclavas that could be pulled up over their faces against the bitter cold. Every woman wore her nurse's blouse with its red cross on the front under thick wadded jackets. Elspeth had told them to show the cross in case of capture and gave them each another they could tie on the outside if needed.

Band playing defiantly, the motley caravan pulled cumbersomely out of town in an incredible hullaballo of cries, drums, snorting horses and the clattering hooves of draught oxen.

'Goodbye, Doctor McBride!' There were tearful waves from the women she had worked beside in conditions that forged strong memories and bonds.

'Goodbye, safe journey!' Peggy forced herself not to shed a single tear. Her jaw ached with the strain of it.

Elspeth rode ahead with the officers, long slim figure upright and confident. It was vital for morale that she should appear unafraid, when all the time her stomach was churning. The tortures of hunger-striking in Holloway had been a useful training-ground for hiding fear.

Peggy watched as they disappeared gradually from sight, light flurries of snow quickly covering their tracks. Eerily the cacophony of sound disappeared into the gloom of the early afternoon. By tomorrow night, with luck, they would have left the plain behind and started up the mountain tracks on their horrifying trek to neutral territory.

Oh, my dear, dear friends! Peggy wondered if she would ever see Elspeth again, or any of the brave nurses she had so proudly led. How many of you will survive the journey?

Will I survive what lies ahead? And my poor wee Kirsten, what did you get for a mother? A sob rose in her throat. Och, stop mithering, woman! Peggy told herself sharply, and turning away from the town, ran to the station and climbed on to the waiting train. Immediately the whistle blew and they headed uneasily back up the track towards Valjevo.

As soon as they arrived, the soldiers who had ridden guard rushed to carry the wounded into the main hospital and unload the supplies. Then they left, heading south again, hoping to catch up with the main caravan before the mountains swallowed it.

'The next train into Valjevo will probably be Austro-Hungarian,' Peggy thought finding an overwhelming sense of desolation in the realisation.

She called the two remaining Scottish staff to her office that evening. Nancy the cook, had simply refused to go with Elspeth. 'Och, I'll die here among my pots, instead of up there in the cold. I've never been able to tolerate mountains, neither I have! And I'm fifty past, I've had a good innings anyway. If they kill me, they kill me!' Now she received her instructions impassively and went back to the kitchens.

Little Philomena, the Irish kitchenmaid, had just recovered from typhus fever. In her weakened state she would not have managed the journey. 'I'll pray to my patron saint,' she explained firmly to Peggy. 'Saint Philomena will see me all right, she always does. Anyway, most of the Austrian prisoners seem to be Catholics. I don't know about the Magyars, though. Oh, sure, the Lord and his Blessed Mother permitting, there's bound to be some good in them.'

Peggy wished she shared the girl's innocent faith. Later she spoke to the Serbian nurses who tried to be brave, though terror lurked in their eyes. They had heard stories of what the Bulgars had done further south. Many of the younger nurses had gone with the convoy. Only those with very strong family reasons, or who were too old to make such a journey, had stayed. Responsibility weighed heavily on Peggy's shoulders as she instructed them to stick together and stay within the hospital grounds as much as possible.

'Doctor McBride, may I come in?' The most senior of the

265

former Austrian prisoners, a young captain, knocked and entered when the last of the nurses had gone.

'Captain Schmitt, what can I do for you?' Peggy asked in the halting German she had learned of necessity since she came to Serbia.

'I think it is best if we agree on the reception of my countrymen when they arrive, Doctor.' Schmitt stood smartly to attention, any trace of his former role as temporary nurse to sick comrades gone completely.

Peggy nodded. 'What do you suggest?'

'As you've already done, keep the wounded Serbs together. It helps identification and makes – protection easier. I will try to stop any revenge killings or other unpleasantness, by being with you at the hospital when our troops arrive.' He permitted a dignified smile to soften his expression. 'Be glad you treated me and my comrades well, Doctor. Otherwise I would not be so concerned over your well-being, or that of the prisoners.' His words showed quite clearly that the boot was now on the other foot.

'Thank you, Captain. I hope I treat all patients fairly.' Peggy's red head with its neat chignon bobbed briefly. 'Can you also make sure the old men, townswomen and children are not mistreated?'

'Austro-Hungarian troops are not barbarians, Doctor. But I can guarantee nothing. Men in wartime, you know . . . Of course I will try.'

As the boom of the guns drew closer, the tension rose. Peggy kept a brave front, but noticed her hands shaking when in the privacy of her office she riffled through records to make sure there was nothing which would help the invaders. Carefully she checked that the tiny gun she kept in her desk drawer was loaded. I hope Captain Schmitt keeps his word, she thought, fighting down a wave of sickening terror, or I'll maybe have to use this.

That afternoon the Austrian command rode up the main street in full uniform. White flags hung from every building. Kragujevatz had been taken, she heard, with relatively little bloodshed but other towns like Brace were in flames. It seemed to be a matter of luck and the attitude of the commanding officer. Peggy prayed that Valjevo would be spared the worst excesses of invasion.

Serb guns had been silent now for some days. Resistance was carrying on from the hills to the north and columns were regrouping in Salonika and Montenegro to fight their country's conquerors.

Peggy stayed at her post and waited. As the day wore on, she tried not to wince at the occasional scream of a woman's terror or wonder at the object of a sudden burst of gunfire. But on the whole the cobbled streets were eerily silent. None of the wholesale slaughter or rape she had feared was taking place. Yet. In mid-afternoon the din of military bands and marching men grew to a crescendo as the invaders established their presence. Finally she heard them clatter into the hospital grounds. Quietly she picked up the little gun and slipped it into her pocket.

Chapter 18

I see thee gracefu' straight and tall

In later years Elspeth still dreamed of precipices where men and pack-horses slid screaming in terror to their death. Sometimes it was frozen faces or blackened hands and feet that appeared to haunt her. Experience had taught her to tolerate the pain and suffering of war, but this was a different horror. She felt physically ill when men, mad with cold and fear, wandered aimlessly into the dark days and night, were swallowed by snow drifts and then gone in an instant for all eternity.

She and her colleagues tended the sick when they could, but after a few days she had to leave them to their officers. The state of her own staff, those women who had come so bravely from Scotland, became critical. With each long, dreadful day it was a terrible battle to stay alive in this dark, icy, never-ending hell.

'Get your nose covered, if you don't want to lose it!' she barked abruptly at a nurse, stumbling on in the rough path broken through the drifts by the pack-animals.

'Sorry, Doctor.' The young woman fumbled to pull the wool balaclava safely up again. 'Och, I'm so tired. Can we not take a wee rest?' she mumbled pitifully.

'Not yet, girl!' Elspeth snapped, knowing that sympathy would lead to instant tears and increase the risk of frostbite as they ran down her face.

One of the nurses was already slung across the back of a pack-pony like a load of hay. Her feet had become too painful to carry her and were infected. She floated deliriously in and out of consciousness. The rest stumbled along, encouraging each other. 'They show enough raw courage to shame a charge of wild Cossacks,' a Serb sergeant said with awe.

'How much longer?' Elspeth dared to ask that night as they made rough camp in the shelter of a cave.

'About two more days,' the guide replied.

'You said that two days ago.'

'But you didn't believe me.'

'Nor should I have.'

'No.' He grinned through the rim of ice round his mouth. 'But you can now. Dark eyes peering out above a frost-rimmed balaclava crinkled with unexpected humour.

'So we really are almost there? Oh, thank God for that!'

'Come on, lassies, we're on the last leg, the downward path! Let's show these Albanians what stuff the Scots are made of!' Elspeth herded her exhausted group together on the last day, urging them to rally for the final stage of the dreadful journey.

'Last leg right enough,' a tired voice was heard to mutter, but they found the reserves of strength to stumble after the men down the rocky Montenegran mountains towards the Albanian coast and salvation.

" 'Scots wa hae wi' Wallace bled, Scots wham Bruce had often led, welcome tae yer gory bed, or to victory . . .' " Sturdy Albanian peasants gawked in astonishment as the little troop of trousered women led by Elspeth marched or limped, singing, into the rescue camp. Even poor Lizzie Barclay managed to raise her voice, if not her head, from the pack-pony's back.

They were exhausted, ill, and suffering from delayed reaction. One or two would lose toes or fingers. Lizzie's leg might not be saved. But they wanted nothing more than to get back to Salonika as fast as possible. The Austrians, Germans and their Bulgarian allies were threatening to close the remaining sea-exit south down to the Ionian Sea. Time was too short to spend more than a few glorious days in the balmy comfort of Corfu, where they were taken from Albania. There they heard the good news that Dr King-May, with sixty British women medics and the other units which had left Serbia before them, had reached Scutari safely and were already on their way to Salonika or to England.

'This place must have looked much the same to the Ancient Greeks, including the buildings!' Elspeth commented as their boat sailed into the bay at Salonika. Fine white hotels glistened incongruously, framing a harbour full of warships and docks swarming with soldiers. 'At least it looks exactly the same as when we landed a year ago en route to Serbia,' she qualified the exaggeration with a laugh.

'Happy Christmas, Doctor McClure!' a familiar voice called as she disembarked amid the usual chaos.

'Brian McGonagle!' Elspeth's ice-burned face lit up with pleasure.

'Stay put, I'm nearly through.' Her old colleague from Kragujevatz fought his way through the tangle of people, guns, vehicles and animals on the quay.

'I'd love to shake your hand, but mine are in a bit of trouble.' Elspeth held up her bandaged fingers as he reached her.

'Frostbite?' Brian knew the terrible story of the women's trek from earlier arrivals.

'Luckily only mild in my case. I'll keep them all at any rate, but not everyone has been so fortunate,' she answered.

'Then I'll have to hug you instead!' Before she could protest, he grabbed her and held her close against him, pushing his way forward till they managed to get to the edge of the crowd. For once she did not object.

'How did you know I was coming today?'

'I've been asking every day.' Brian's blue eyes danced. 'They were so used to me haunting the quay, some of the guards thought I had set up a special mobile medical clinic and started bringing me all their aches and pains every time I appeared.'

'But why?' Elspeth's face was puzzled.

'Because I was worried sick about you, Elspeth.'

'That's kind, Brian. But you needn't have been, I'm used to looking after myself.'

'Oh, I know that. And looking after everyone else as well.' He had drawn her up a slope away from the quayside and they sat together on a huge boulder by an olive tree, watching the continuing chaos below. 'But I did worry.' He put a tentative arm round her shoulders and felt her stiffen. 'Elspeth, I've missed you like hell since I left Serbia. Really missed you, and I don't just mean as a colleague. I've been crazy with worry while you were crossing those bloody mountains.'

'Brian, are you serious?' Instinctively her hand went up the the mark on her face.

'Oh, don't start on about that thing.' He noticed the movement. 'You've told me all that bloody rubbish before about being unattractive to men. Well, that's not true at all . . . and I'm a man, believe me.' He smiled but his eyes were serious.

'I told you how I felt about my birthmark in confidence as a friend in Kragujevatz . . . the night we talked before you left for Salonika. I trusted you, Brian. Trusted you too much it would seem.' Her voice shook. 'My words were not meant to be used as a taunt.'

'I'm not taunting when I say I find you attractive . . . oh, hell, more than that, Elspeth.'

'Stop this, you're being cruel!' To her shock and disgust her eyes filled with tears. She couldn't believe this conversation was happening. And now she was about to cry to top her humiliation.

'Elspeth McClure.' Brian took her face and held it so she had to meet his eyes. 'I wonder how many other men would have loved you – maybe did love you – if you hadn't rejected them by hiding behind that birthmark. Stop punishing us all for your father's cruelty. Or at least,' his face lit up in a lopsided smile, 'stop punishing me . . . you can do what you like with the rest!'

'Brian, I think you've gone completely mad!' Elspeth protested, pulling away. 'Look, I'm tired, I'm emotional, I have nurses to look after and arrangements to make for a school for Serb nurses. Let me go. They're waiting for me, I have to get back. I can do without this nonsense.'

'Not till you promise to marry me.'

'Now you're definitely not serious.'

'I am.'

'My God!' She made to get up. 'I'll answer you some other time.'

271

He reached up and caught her arm. 'Tell me now.'

'Then the answer is no. Anyway, I'd never move to Australia.'

'Why not?'

'Women have the vote there.'

'What? I thought that's what you wanted!'

'It is, and I intend staying in Britain till we get it too.'

'Oh, come on!' he said incredulously, and let her go. 'What a bloody woman!'

'Brian let's leave this daft subject. It's beginning to sound like a music-hall comedy.' Elspeth's sense of the ridiculous broke through. 'You know, you should be locked up as patently insane!'

'Oh, hell, all right. I've been so worried about you, I guess I've made a pig's backside of handling the thing tactfully. I forgot how thick that protective hide you've developed round you is. Come on then.' He got up and led the way back to the others, gathered by the cart waiting to take them to their quarters.

As soon as Elspeth rejoined the unit, the military band started up in their honour and led the way through the town. Elspeth and her little group of stalwart nurses were celebrities. Tomorrow the papers on sale in Britain would be full of stirring reports about the 'Angels of the Montenegran Mountains'. It was the stuff wartime propaganda thrived on.

It'll make my father choke on his porridge when he reads the *Ayrshire Post* tomorrow. And knock a few more years off his life with rage that I managed to survive. Elspeth smiled grimly to herself as the cart shook and rattled triumphantly up the narrow streets.

Have you heard from Peggy, or about her? It's been months,' Elspeth wrote for the fifth time to Elsie Inglis who was recuperating briefly in Britain after her release from Austrian captivity.

'Not directly. But don't worry, we've been told she's fine,' Elsie wrote back reassuringly. 'Nancy and Philomena are well too. Their release is expected any day. I'll be going back to join the Serbian Unit of the Russian Army at Dobrudja soon. If I have not heard any more by then I'll start agitating and pushing for action.'

Elspeth sent a baldly realistic note full of her own fears to Douglas at his Flanders base. Then she composed a bright, hopeful letter to Libby and Kirsten, playing down the dangers and promising them that Peggy would surely soon be free. In the total absence of any further news, she resolutely settled into her new, peculiar life in Salonika.

The Greek town was still in the hands of the Entente Allies but was closed off from the rest of Greece and Serbia to the north by the Bulgars. Greece's neutrality wavered as the British, French, and their allies seemed to be making little headway anywhere in Europe. Salonika was left high and dry in the middle of hostile territory. 'Our largest internment camp', the Austro-German alliance called it ironically.

Leaders of the British allied forces wanted to evacuate the troops trapped in or around the port to use them more profitably elsewhere. The politicians said no. It was a matter of prestige. Terrible losses at the Dardanelles and Greece's virtual defection were humiliation enough. Instead, more French and British reinforcements were poured through the narrow channel the Allies managed to keep open into the already overcrowded town. Most of the troops were to remain stuck there for the next two years. As many died of disease as wounds.

'Damn these effing mozzies! No wonder they call this place the Valley of Death!' Doctor McGonagle waved away huge clouds of mosquitoes as he dressed the wounds of the soldiers he had been called out to help.

'Doctor, these mosquitoes are killing me!' Men groaned in as much agony from the attentions of the insects as from the wounds they had received skirmishing with the Bulgars.

'More victims for your Serb girls to practise on, Doctor McClure.' Brian handed the lists to Elspeth.

'Thanks,' she replied dryly, passing them on to the staff nurses. 'Next month this lot will all have malaria, I suppose. Did you take your quinine, Doctor McGonagle? If not, you'll be next.' Her grey eyes danced.

'Yep, I took it!'

Brian had never repeated his outburst of the day Elspeth

273

had arrived. She assumed it had been just the weird kind of thing that happens in wartime where emotions become heightened and distorted, and was far too fond of him to let it stand between them and their old relationship. They had become close colleagues again, natural allies and firm friends who hardly needed to talk to communicate. Today they walked a little apart from the group of nurses and orderlies who were checking the field-dressings. The wounded were being carefully allotted wards, according to their injuries. 'Not bad this time,' Brian called back over his shoulder as they left the rows of wounded. 'You'll all live to be blown to bits another day, lads.'

'Thanks, Captain,' the men chorused amid cackles of grim laughter.

'Look at their faces.' Brian smiled. 'Most of the buggers are glad to be in the SWH training hospital, being cosseted by lovely nurses. So long as they're not too badly injured, of course.'

'Why on earth would they want to be in hospital?'

'Usual problems.' Brian watched a young New Zealander make sign-language love to a trainee Serb nurse. 'Too much bully-beef and biscuits, nothing to do and no female company! Pity the poor lads in Salonika.'

'Better than being stuck in the mud of the trenches in France,' Elspeth replied crisply, remembering Douglas's last letter.

'True. Say, Elspeth, can you come for a ride with me up the ridge this evening? I promised to show you the view over Mount Olympus, and if we're lucky we can see Pelion and Ossa too. If we leave an hour or so before sunset, it should be exactly right.'

'Why not?' she agreed. 'I feel so trapped in Salonika at times. So many people, Brian, so much sickness, and I'm worried about Peggy. I keep telling myself that she's fine, but it hardly helps.'

'I believe we'd have heard if the situation had got worse for her, Elspeth. She'll turn up, you'll see.'

'But when? I just wish we knew something definite!' She paced about like a caged animal then stopped abruptly. 'God, yes, a ride out of this place would be marvellous.'

'It should be peaceful up there.' Brian gazed at the surrounding hills. 'And there are no Bulgars left in the hills
after that skirmish. The business was all confined to the
river plain.'

'Come for me then.'

'I will.'

They left before sunset and rode at a smart trot away
from the town with its Greek churches and gleaming white
buildings. As Elspeth glanced back, the curve of the sea-
front, lined with once fine hotels, became a crescent of
glittering stone reflecting the rosy light.

'Before all this, Salonika must have been a paradise.' She
stopped and looked down. 'Damn war!' She felt a spurt of
impotent anger. 'Wait for me, Brian!' She spurred her horse
after her companion.

'Look at that!' The snow-topped peak of the Mountain
of the Gods, suddenly caught the rays of the setting sun and
turned a brilliant, translucent pink.

'Brian, it's so magnificent.' Her breath caught in wonder
as they dismounted. When he put his arm across her
shoulders, she did not pull away. This was a moment to
share with someone beloved.

'Elspeth, have you thought any more about my question?'
The glory had gone and they walked slowly back down the
ridge, leading their horses. Spring was as balmy and warm
here as summer in Britain. They revelled in its gentle heat.

'What question?' Her eyes narrowed.

'About marrying me, what else?'

'Brian.' She gazed at the path ahead. 'I thought you'd
given up on that? It's just a wartime illusion. You'll go home
when this is over and forget me. I'm just an old maid doctor
with a life time of work ahead of her and an obsession
to see women enfranchised. Let's just enjoy each other's
company, be good friends. Forget this silly romance stuff.'

'No!' He swung round, blocking her path. 'This is nothing
to do with wartime emotions or adolescent romance. We're
both doctors. I'm almost ten years older than you and I
don't feel middle-aged yet. Why the heck should you? We
have years ahead of us. Years we could be together, Elspeth,
years we could share.'

275

'Oh, this is all rubbish!' She shook her head, moving away dismissively.

'Rubbish, nothing! Listen, stop a minute. I want to talk this out properly.' Brian took the reins of both horses and tied them to a stunted olive tree, drawing her over to a rocky outcrop which formed a wide ledge by the side of the path. 'Elspeth, come.' He put his hand on her arm. 'Please, we have to be straight with each other.'

'All right, I'm listening.' She sat beside him, feeling his nearness and warmth without flinching.

'I was married once,' he began quietly.

'You didn't tell me that when we talked in Kragujevatz . . .'

'No, I haven't told anyone. It was a long time ago. We were young, both of us. My wife died having our first child. That's not so unusual as you know, and at the time we lived in the outback where they were no medical facilities other than those I provided myself. I'd set up a clinic for aborigines and the few farmers in the area as soon as I finished medical school.'

'What happened to your wife?'

'Mary had a terrible time with the pregnancy. I wanted her to go back to her mother in Sydney, but she refused to leave me. The birth was mercifully short but impossible. The baby was strangled by the cord and Mary must have had a weak heart, it just stopped.' Brian raised a hand helplessly. 'For all my medical training, I could do nothing for either of them. Nothing.' His face was bleak under its tan.

'Oh, Brian.' Elspeth touched his arm. 'And you didn't want to marry again?'

'I'm one of ten. A big Irish Catholic family. I was the bright kid who won all the scholarships. My parents are dead now, but they were so proud of me. And of the others too. I might be the doctor, but the rest of their kids presented them with a total of forty-six grandchildren . . . that was real achievement in their eyes!' He smiled wryly. 'With all those nephews and nieces, I felt no pressure to remarry and perpetuate the McGonagle line.' His hand reached towards hers and clasped it in a firm grip. 'Nor had I any inclination to, till now.'

'I see.' Elspeth pulled away her hand and looked at her

feet in their sturdy boots. Nervously she smoothed imaginary creases from her cotton riding skirt.

'No, you don't bloody see!' Brian burst out. 'Unless it's work or Votes for Women, you never bloody see! As a real person, I might as well not exist.' Desolate and angry, he got up, but she caught his sleeve and pulled him down beside her again.

'What do you mean?'

'I bloody love you, woman! And you're too bloody pig-headed to accept it.'

'No, I'm bloody not!' she replied, leaning over and meeting his lips with hers. Long ago at Miss Lovat's she had decided to open her heart to friendship. Now she did the same to love with the whole of her generous spirit. And in the moment of capitulation she forgot to touch the birth mark, glowing like fire on her cheek in the last lingering rays of the sun. She never touched it defensively again.

'Elspeth ... Oh God, Elspeth, how I love you!' Brian drew her towards him, and there on the dusty ledge of ancient rock, as a last glow of rose-pink lingered over Mount Olympus, they made love.

'Imagine losing my virginity at 36, lying on a slab of stone in Greece.' Elspeth smiled gently and traced a line on his tanned face with one finger.

'Better late than never, and where could be more romantic than in the home of the Ancient Gods?' His throaty laughter warmed her heart. 'Now will you marry me? Or do I have to prove this wasn't a one-off occurrence until you agree?'

'You can prove it any time.' Elspeth's grey eyes shone, 'Inside or outside the official state.'

'The army doesn't like illicit relationships.'

'I'm not army.'

'But I am.'

'Oh, well, I guess we'd better do something about it before I'm caught sneaking into your quarters or you into mine!'

'So you will marry me?' He sat up, face alight with happiness.

'Dammit, why not? As long it's not taken for granted that we'll settle in Australia?'

'I promise that's open to negotiation. Votes for Women in Britain first, OK?'

'Yes. But do I have to marry you in your Church?'

'Religion died for me with Mary. Any army chaplain will do.'

'Then I'll speak to the authorities, they can arrange someone neutral to do the honours.' Elspeth got up and unselfconsciously rearranged her clothes, tying up her long hair once more into a neat bun. She laughed aloud. 'I wonder what Christabel would make of this? Not to mention my father.'

'Who's going to ask their opinion?'

'Not me!'

Brian and Elspeth were married by a judge that week. In war time all rules were flexible. But they waited till the simple ceremony was over before letting anyone else into their secret.

'Gee, what a great team you'll make!'

'Topping, old man.'

'Congratulations, Doctors.'

The medical staff rustled up a spontaneous celebratory meal, but soon things settled down again to the uneasy chaos of their work. Elspeth kept her own name, so there could be no confusion in the hospitals. And despite the war, the deprivations and the interminable wait for Peggy to be released, she glowed as never before with deep happiness.

Chapter 19
Tho' I were doomed to wander on

'I leave shortly after you, Doctor McBride,' the Austrian Medical Commander told Peggy when he bade her goodbye.

'Where are you going?'

'The front.'

'Which?'

'That I'm not allowed to tell the enemy.' A wry smile belied his harsh words. 'But before you go, I wanted to say that I came to respect you during our time together. I will never again think women unfitted for work as physicians. I apologise for my initial lack of judgement.' His heels clicked sharply and he gave a bow.

His unexpected words brought a flush to her cheeks. 'And in turn I thank you for treating us well and allowing me to continue my work . . . after your initial lack of judgement!' Peggy smiled and held out her hand. 'When this is over, maybe we will meet at some conference in London or Paris on anaesthesia or on treating war wounds.'

'Or Vienna.' He smiled back. 'Doctor McBride, I sincerely hope so. And may God be with you.' He bowed again.

'Ready?' Peggy ran down to the little convoy waiting below to take her and Nancy to the border and on to Switzerland.

'Doctor McBride!' Philomena ran over as they started moving.

'Have you changed your mind?' Peggy asked. 'Come if you want, lass.'

'No, Doctor, I'm staying here with Erich. He got the sergeant to fix new papers in my married name. I'll go with the regiment when it leaves and live with his mother in Graz till the war's over.

'Are you sure, Philomena?' Peggy had attended the little maid's wedding the week before in the Austrian Catholic field chapel. 'Will she make you welcome, lassie?'

'Sure she will. Erich is her only child. Just imagine,' the girl's eyes glowed, 'he used to be a waiter in that big Trocadero Hotel down in London. We might move back and take her with us when this rotten war ends. The poor woman is all alone, Doctor. I'll be a daughter to her. And since I've no one of my own, she can be a mother to me. Erich is teaching me a lot of German.' Philomena was full of the confidence of love.

Peggy looked at the young woman standing so bravely before her, willing to face a new life in a hostile, foreign country without language or experience, all for her handsome Austrian corporal. 'Good luck, Philomena.' She blinked hard.

'Good luck to you too, Doctor McBride, and dear Nancy.' The girl hugged the older women, eyes filling with tears.

'Och, the lassie might as well marry the lad and follow him home.' Nancy sniffed emotionally into her handkerchief. 'Enemy or not, he's a decent sort. And she's had nothing but miserable orphanages in Ireland, skivvying in Scotland, and God knows what all else in her short life. She's got courage, that wee thing, so she has,' Nancy said. 'Otherwise she'd never have come to the Balkans with us in the first place.'

'You're not short on courage yourself, Nancy.' Peggy patted the cook's shoulder and waved as cheerfully as she could to Philomena.

'Och, blethers, Doctor McBride.' Nancy blew her nose loudly. 'I'm just an ordinary cook that's wee bit daft and a wee bit stubborn, that's all. I'm not sorry I came, neither I am.'

'Neither am I, Nancy. Neither am I.' Peggy swung her horse resolutely forward and rode to join the officers leading the escort.

The Medical Commander stood at the window watching the convoy leave. It would not have been proper to wave openly. Ah, what a woman. If times had been different and if she had not still been in love with her dead husband . . . He sighed as Peggy's neat figure faded from his sight.

Peggy passed through the southern corner of Austro-Hungary, stopping overnight at the town of Sarajevo where the trigger had been pulled that started the whole terrible conflict. She and Nancy were then sent to Bludnez near the Swiss border, and from there on to to Zurich.

'Nancy, look at the casualty lists!' Peggy was horrified when they got their first glimpse of British newspapers on their way through France to the SWH unit at Royaumont.

'Och, it's carnage, just carnage. Aye, there's work to do yet, so there is,' Nancy sighed. 'But I need a wee rest before I can do any more, so I do. I'm going home to Edinburgh for a while. And so should you, Doctor Peggy.'

'Maybe you're right. Och, I just don't know.' She suddenly felt too weary to decide anything.

When they arrived at Royaumont, Nancy continued on to Le Havre, but Peggy decided to stay for a few days and take stock.

'Go back to Britain for a spell of leave, Peggy,' Elsie Inglis insisted in a letter sent from the Russian front. 'It did me the world of good and you must be deeply exhausted by now.'

Sitting in the old herb garden of Royaumont Cistercian Abbey, which the SWH was using as a hospital, she argued to and fro with herself that these few days were rest enough and it was unnecessary to go back just yet. There was so much still to do here. The sounds of the busy, crowded wards travelled on the soft, summery air. But I should go and see Kirsten, it's a year and a half already since I left, Peggy thought. She'll have grown so much. Och, I'm missing her childhood.

'Thinking, Doctor Peggy?' Sister Katherine Bailey had come out in the first batch from Valjevo, then been posted to France. With a swish of her starched skirts, she sat down beside her former boss.

'I might go back to Scotland for a month or so right enough, Kate.'

'You should. I went home for a couple of weeks when I came out of Serbia. It made me mad-anxious to get back to the action, but the change was refreshing, despite the circumstances.'

'Was that after . . .?'

'Aye, it was after our Alec was killed. My mother needed me home for a bit,' she added simply.

'Imagine, Kate, they said the war would be over by Christmas. Which Christmas, eh?' Peggy said bitterly. 'It's almost the end of June 1916 and there's no let up at all. So many young men dying. Och, it's not right!'

'Well, at least we're doing our bit to ease their suffering,' Katherine Bailey replied philosophically. 'And it's not without its brighter moments either. Talking of which, are you coming to the "at home" this evening?'

'I thought of giving it a miss.'

'Then you do need a break, Doctor Peggy. I've seen this kind of downheartedness set in too often . . . and so have you. Go back, have a wee rest, and then you'll be your old self again: efficient, optimistic and full of beans!'

'Maybe you've got something there, Kate . . . I wrote to Doctor Munro to ask what he thought, but I've heard nothing. I feel as if it's all just buzzing round in my head. I can't seem to make a decision about anything.' She shivered. 'Och, you're right, I'm letting myself get depressed. I'll come to your daft social, Kate.'

The wounded soldiers dressed up in anything they could find, especially nurses' uniforms, and did hilarious skits based on hospital life. Even Matron's severe expression cracked into a smile as she recognised herself and her colleagues being caricatured mercilessly.

How can they do it? Peggy thought as she watched the men, some of them recovering from horrific injuries, sing, laugh and even dance. Then they finished off the show with a sentimental song which was highly popular with the men in the trenches.

There's a long trail a-winding
Into the land of my dreams,

282

Where the nightingales are singing,
And a white moon beams . . .

Outside, Peggy could hear the new motorised ambulances trundling past. This morning she had watched lines of young men marching to the front. Tears filled her eyes, but she bit them back. A doctor could never be seen to cry. The same did not apply to the nurses, some of them only girls fresh from school. Muffled sobs added a bass line to the swelling voices of the men, filling and spilling through the hall into the balmy summer night.

Next day she packed her meagre belongings and her precious medical kit and caught the troop train going north to pick up another load of recruits from Britain. On the way up it was packed with wounded and shell-shocked soldiers being sent home for treatment or to recuperate. The accompanying VADs and orderlies were delighted to have a doctor on board. Peggy was kept too busy coping with on-the-spot emergencies to ponder her decision, or to feel she was running away. Soon she was on the quay at Le Havre waiting her turn to board the next available ship.

'Doctor McBride, Royaumont telegraphed to tell us you were here. Follow me, please.' Her incongruously slight figure was spotted by a sharp-eyed orderly amid the sea of khaki. As the queue shuffled forward on the quayside, Peggy was ushered in to wait in an ante-room with wounded senior officers. Though a civilian volunteer, she was ranked with the Captains.

'You should be sailing around mid-afternoon,' the young lieutenant explained. 'Why don't you have lunch with the officers while you wait . . . those who are well enough to eat, that is?'

'Thanks.' Peggy found a seat and began looking idly around at the milling mass of young men, hardly out of school themselves. Stretchers were carried in and out. In a corner, a young lieutenant sat twitching. Shell-shock, she guessed. How many of you will ever play cricket or rugby again? Peggy wondered sadly. All these shattered limbs and shattered souls.

'Doctor McBride! Is there a Doctor McBride here?' a

motorcycle messenger yelled across the crowded room. His goggles scanned the gathered men and totally ignored the one woman.

'I'm Doctor McBride.' Detaching herself from the group, she went over, heart thumping, thinking of every possible disaster.

'A letter . . . urgent. Forwarded from Royaumont.'

'Thank you.' It was addressed to her at the SWH centre and must have arrived minutes after she had left. Shaking, she ripped it open.

Somme, Field Hospital 1

My Dear Peggy,

Sorry for the delay but I just received your letter. It was forwarded to me at my new camp, and I think, from the state of it, it went round every field hospital in France and Belgium before finally finding me.

You have known me too well, and for too long, to expect any great fuss about your release. All I will say now, or any time, is that I have slept better (when the chance arises!) for receiving good news at last. And, oh, yes, dear girl, I can understand your mixed feelings about going back to Britain while there is so much to do. That is a battlefield where I have fought many times myself. Neither I nor anyone else can truly advise you. You know in your own heart when the final limits of endurance are reached.

Yesterday they started a push across the Somme. I'm certain you've heard about it. So for me there is no choice but to stay. We can hardly cope with the wounded already and there are more and more and more to come. There is a terrible shortage of doctors and we are using anyone who can change a bandage to do so. Once you have had a well-earned rest, you know where to come. This carnage looks set to continue. I think Keir Hardie was right after all, war is best avoided.

Do write to me when you get to Kilmarnock. As well as worrying myself to death (did I say I wouldn't mention that?), I really missed your cheerful, observant letters

284

during your spell as a 'guest' of the Austro-Hungarian Empire!

Affectionately as always,
Your friend,
Douglas Munro

Cheerful and observant? More like self-centred and moaning! Peggy smothered a guilty smile, then scanned the letter again. For a moment she stood looking blankly at the whitewashed wall of the make shift officers' mess which had suddenly emptied.

A young captain stuck his head round the door, 'Come on, Doctor McBride, the troop ship can't wait.'

'Go without me,' she said. Just as well I didn't tell Kirsten or Libby I was coming home, she thought.

'Where can I get a train to the front at the Somme?' she demanded of the administrative staff.

They didn't seem at all surprised. Personnel moved around crazily all the time. 'There's a troop-train from England leaving any minute. Every lad among them is needed. We've been telegraphed that the injured will be starting to come in by tonight. Thousands of them. Christ, what a war!' The staff lieutenant shook his head.

'Where is the train?'

'Number six depot. But really, Doctor, should you go with that lot? It's a "bantam" regiment, the 16th HLI from Glasgow?'

'Bantam?'

'They're small men, below the regulation height. That's why they're in the "bantams". I'm afraid they're an awfully rough lot. Not really fit company for a lady.' He looked doubtfully at Peggy's slight figure.

'What's the old music-hall joke ... that's no lady, that's my wife? Well, this is no lady, Lieutenant, she's a doctor. I'll manage, especially if they're wee hard men from Glesca!' Grinning at his astonished expression, she grabbed her bags and ran hell for leather down to the train depot, holding her hat with one hand.

The journey to the front was bitter-sweet. The lads were full of bravado and cheery chaff. This and other bantamweight regiments had been formed when Kitchener realised the little Celts of Glasgow and Liverpool, previously excluded on medical grounds because of their lack of inches, slight, ill-nourished frames and rotten teeth, were needed at the front.

' "Fit subject to undergoing dental treatment", that's whit he says to me, Doctor. So I says, "Is that a fact, Sergeant? Do ye think the Huns will ask tae see my teeth before they let me stick a bayonet up their arse?" Och, sorry for the language and that, Doctor!' the soldier apologised.

'Och, I heard worse manys a day in Cowcaddens.' Peggy smiled, wondering if Hughie Naughton was somewhere on the train. Probably not, he might even be too old! she realised with a jolt. 'Don't mind your language for me, lads,' she added, knowing they would try not to offend. It had only taken her minutes to establish her credentials with these men she had grown up amongst. Already they were pathetically proud of her and regarded her as a mascot.

'I'm goin' tae demand it's you that cuts off my leg, Doctor McBride,' a lad from Bridgeton teased with the grim humour of war.

'If she does it the now, ye won't even have tae fight, Boabby,' his mate chaffed.

'Here, Doctor, have a wee swig of this. I've wiped the bottle proper, so I have.' A soldier politely offered her a bottle of cheap whisky produced like a magician's rabbit from his kit bag. 'I'm sorry I haven't a glass.'

'No thanks, you have more need of that than me.'

'Have ye been to the front, Doctor? I cannae wait tae have a go at they Huns.' A voice loaded with bravado spoke from a white face studded with a pair of anxious eyes.

'I have that, in Serbia,' she said softly, knowing only too well what they were in for. 'It's not easy, lads, but you're a tough lot,' she encouraged.

'Aye, we are that, Doctor, so we are.' A tiny soldier grinned, showing rows of blackened teeth.

'Tell him what ye said to the general, Wullie,' his friends urged.

'Aye, a' right,' said Wullie. 'There was this right toffee-nosed General inspected us at Southampton, Doctor. "Ooo,

286

my man!" he says to me, all high and mighty, looking down from away up there. "Could *you* kill a German, my man? You seem rather on the small side." '

'What did you say?' Peggy joined in the fun.

' "Och, aye, sir," I says. "I could kill a Hun no bother, but he wid have tae be a WEE Hun!" ' The diminutive soldier almost fell off his wooden seat in amusement.

'Oh, Doctor, there you are.' An officer appeared anxiously at the carriage door. 'I heard there was a lady doctor on the train. I've been searching for you to invite you up among the officers?'

'I'm fine here,' she said firmly.

'Er – please, Doctor.' The man was clearly ill at ease and intent on carrying out his orders.

'Ye might as well go, Doctor, before the poor officers cry!' the lads chorused.

'Aye, they've got cucumber sandwiches and cups of China tea up there. We can only give ye a bite of bully beef and hard-tack biscuits,' Boabby added, drawing a look of reprimand from the lieutenant.

'Well, all right.' Peggy had been too long on active service even to try fighting the strict hierarchy of military life. 'Good luck, lads. Me and the nurses will be looking out for you with the biggest hypodermic we can find.' She added her bawbee's worth to the grim humour.

'And don't forget my leg,' yelled Wullie as she left with waves and good wishes in her ears.

A month later she heard that most of the 16 HLI were either wounded or killed in action.

The front was a hell of hells in this wasteful, interminable war. Peggy sent word to Douglas, further down the line in yet another new field-hospital, that she had arrived. The courier returned with his reply immediately.

Peggy,
Thank God you came. I couldn't ask you outright, but hoped you would read between the not-too-subtle lines. Please stay where you are in Number 1. We have a couple of people there already, but they have just lost a doctor

and desperately need help. I'm sorry I can't come to greet you myself, but it's chaos here.

Gratefully and affectionately as always,

Douglas Munro

'Is there a reply, Doctor?' the courier asked politely, as if he were delivering tea-dance invitations instead of doing a job renowned for its danger. 'I'm going back to Number 4 position in about an hour.'

'Thanks. Just tell Doctor Munro Number 1 is fine and we'll meet when we can.'

When he left she dumped her bags on the screened-off iron bed she was allotted in the female personnel tent, changed into a white coat and walked through the crowds of injured and dying to the big hospital theatre marquee.

Almost a week later, she had begun to wonder if she had ever been anywhere else in her life. The pace of life was indescribable and the work out of hell. Even Serbia's traumas faded into distant memory.

'Red label him!' Peggy said briskly to the little VAD nurse at her elbow.

'Yes, Doctor, anything else?'

'I've amputated the arm, but he'll have to go back to England. If he stays here he'll die.'

'Right.' The nurse pinned the red warning for haemorrhage on the unconscious man's torn and bloody jacket, slung across his body.

Stretcher-bearers carried him out of the tent and brought in another batch. Peggy worked on. She hadn't slept properly for nights. Though she'd managed to change her blood-soaked coat once or twice, within minutes it was as bad again.

The scale of death and destruction was horrendous. In the first four days, 33,392 patients from casualty clearing stations at the front were sent to Boulogne, Le Havre and Rouen. Hospital ships that had once been luxury liners were berthed in the harbours, lights glaring day and night. Some men were so badly injured they had to travel straight to Britain, there was no point in even attempting field surgery. Many died on the way.

'Saline solution, Sister. Twice if you can do it. And careful with those hands,' Peggy reminded an exhausted nurse who already had a septic infection on her thumb from soaking wounds which were pouring pus.

'I've got a waterproof stall over it now, Doctor,' the girl replied tiredly and staggered off after the stretcher which was carrying her patient.

They continued like this for three weeks till finally it was essential the nursing staff should rest. Some had already succumbed to a combination of exhaustion and infection themselves and had been sent behind lines to recuperate. The others battled on, hoping additional help would arrive soon.

Somewhere in the midst of the chaos, she finally met Douglas. He looked older with touches of grey in his light brown hair, still muscular but thinner, tougher, honed by the horrors he had lived with for so long. But the sight of his old familiar cheery grin and steady grey eyes gladdened Peggy's heart. They had only time to hug and exchange a few words before he went off to yet another dangerous frontline post and she back to the gore of casualty.

At the beginning of August, Peggy's casualty unit was relieved by a complete medical group sent from a war hospital in England.

'Thank God you're not rookies.' Peggy handed over her responsibilites with a huge sigh of relief.

'No, we've been based in the South of England for the past six months, and handled a lot of the poor lads from here,' the doctor in charge said. 'We've seen most of it. My God, you look utterly shot.' He took in Peggy's lank hair tucked under a bloody cap and her drawn, grey face.

'Understatement, Doctor. And to think I was just going to take a spot of leave when this happened.' She rustled up a wan smile.

'Are you off to Blighty now?'

'No, I'm worried about what disease I might have picked up here. A lot of the men have dysentery and there was an outbreak of typhoid over in Arras. I've a young daughter in Scotland, it would be terrible if I passed something on.'

'So where will you go?'

'I'll rest a while up near the Belgian border and then maybe . . . och, we'll see. I'm too tired to think at all just now.'

'Is that really the best place to rest? Most of poor old Belgium is frontline.'

'Well, I'm not going to Flanders, just to a lovely château near the coast in the unoccupied zone. You can probably still hear the shelling. At least I won't get homesick, will I?'

'Good luck!' He waved cheerily as she climbed into the armoured truck waiting to convey her to the coast.

'Good luck to you too!' she called back. Poor man, your need is greater than mine, she thought wearily. Now, Peggy, rest, rest, rest . . .

Peggy arrived in Rosendaele in such a deep state of exhaustion she had to be carried off the train, fast asleep. Cannily she had stuck her money and precious ID in the pocket of her bloomers and tied a name-occupation-destination label round her neck. No one could waken her, so they loaded her, asleep, on to an armoured car and drove her to the Château de Tieds.

For almost a week she slept, waking only to sip some soup and try to chew the bread she dipped in it. After a few minutes, she would simply keel over and sleep again, despite the efforts of the VAD nurses to keep her awake and feed her.

'Now I know what the lads went through when they came to casualty and we made them answer all sorts of daft questions,' she groaned as some bright-eyed nurse yelled: 'Soup time, Doctor McBride, wakey, wakey!' in her ear.

Sometimes in her sleep she saw lines of young men, led by Hughie Naughton, cheerily marching along singing Glasgow street songs. It was always the same. She would be standing waving when suddenly the rows of happy faces would start to twist and distort. Eyes fell out and cheeks were blown away; legs fell off; bodies crumbled; blood ran everywhere. Songs became shrieks which rose higher and higher to be swallowed in the crash of guns and the cries of battle. Then she started screaming and had to be wakened.

By the early autumn of 1916 the Somme offensives had

dwindled to the euphemistically termed 'leisurely progresses'.

'Futile charges now and then still bring bunches of bloody injured for us to patch up, but it's not like before. Rest while you can, dear girl, for I don't think the deadlock will last,' wrote Douglas.

I bet the army chiefs are up to something, she mused. Between getting the invention of the devil they call the tank in September and hope that the Americans will soon be in, the Entente Allies are like laddies with new toys. That means more trouble for ordinary soldiers and medics alike! The thought of Douglas and the others still working made her feel guilty. Och, I can't malinger here, especially if things get hot again, she angrily told the darkening sky.

Peggy was right, new offensives were being secretly planned and conscription to feed them was proving bountiful. Boatloads of previously exempt married men under the age of forty-one came to join the younger volunteers in manning the trenches. It was hard for anyone to escape service, even by pleading conscientious objection.

'Ah, Doctor McBride, you're looking much better.' The owner of the château, Baron de Tieds, joined Peggy in the garden one day.

'Thanks to your wonderful hospitality.'

'A pleasure, Doctor, a pleasure,' he said. 'Look, there. Isn't nature peaceful and uplifting?' He pointed to where the last glowing rays of the October sun lit the flat landscape.

'It is lovely.' Peggy smiled. 'But I've had enough peace, I'm ready to go back to the front.'

'No! You cannot mean that,' he protested. 'You are still very pale and very thin.'

'Red-heads are always pale, and I have never carried much weight, Baron. No, I've been thinking about some Scottish lads I met in the train from Le Havre. I'll stick this war out as long as they do. This evening I intend writing home to tell my family of my decision. I hope they understand.'

'You could be here for years.' The Baron lifted his shoulders expressively. 'The war shows no signs of abating.

'However long, I will still be here.'

'Well, I think the rigours of the front would be too much in your present condition. You need longer away to recuperate completely. But don't just take the word of a layman,' he raised his hand as she began to protest, 'those who are treating you agree with me.'

'No, I'm sorry, Baron, but I cannot sit here wasting my time while a war is raging. I'm a doctor and my duty is to tend the sick.'

'Yes, yes, I thought you would take that view. So my dear doctor,' he bent forward, 'I have a suggestion.'

'Suggestion?'

'Would you consider becoming supervising doctor here at Rosendaele . . . just for a time?'

'What?' Peggy was taken aback.

'Our resident doctor has also decided to go back to the field-hospital service. Perhaps he told you that?'

'Yes, to the Western front.'

'And we must have someone qualified here, not just nurses, dedicated as they are. Very sick people are sent to us from all over Belgium and France as you know. Oh, you've seen the poor creatures – not just the physically wounded, but those who have nervous disorders or terrible exhaustion like you. We really cannot run things properly without a trained doctor.'

'Let me think for a few days.' Peggy got up. 'I won't reject the idea out of hand, but I had more or less decided to go straight back.'

As always when she couldn't make up her mind, she sent a note to Douglas asking his advice.

'Great idea! Stay there over the winter and get back all your old vigour,' he replied at once. 'You'll be doing worthwhile work at Rosendaele and building up your strength at the same time. We miss you, but we're managing quite well here for the moment. I've a feeling that things will suddenly get worse, then I'll be yelling for you.'

'I'll stay, but the minute you need me, I'm on my way,' she wrote back with a deep sense of relief. Peggy knew the Baron and Douglas were right: her constitution, strong as it was, had been stretched almost to the limit.

292

Peggy was lucky to be in Tieds. The winter of 1916/17 was the hardest in living memory. Men died of cold in the trenches. Injuries from frostbite were horrific, especially when combined with foul, rotting 'trench foot'. A few of the officers who had lost fingers or toes made their way to the Château de Tieds at Rosendaele for brief spells of treatment. Peggy was kept well abreast of the dismal war from them and from Douglas who wrote regular cheery notes, playing down the terrible work he was doing. As they toasted New Year 1917, every patient, medical attendant and soldier in the trenches wished in their heart for peace.

The call came in early-March. Douglas sent a telegram saying simply, 'The Germans are using gas again. We need you.'

'Why don't you let them send for new doctors? You are doing fine work here!' the Baron demanded in the face of her determination.

'I have experience with gas casualties, new doctors don't.' Peggy's expression brooked no argument.

'Ah, well, I can see you will not be dissuaded. Let us hope this time the offensives are short and decisive. There are strong rumours that the Americans are at last joining the Entente. That should surely tip the balance.' Baron de Tieds tried to sound optimistic.

'I would like to think you're right, but my past experience weighs against it.'

Her pessimism proved right. On 6 April the Americans joined the Allies, but there was no immediate improvement on the Western Front.

'This new offensive feels like some nightmarish *déjà vu* from the Somme,' Peggy said to Douglas on the short walk in the camp they always tried to take together each day now they were working side by side. It was a lifeline to sanity for them both.

'We'll see how fast they push across the Ypres Canal. Maybe it will be shorter at least than the Somme.'

'No.' She shook her head. 'I'm not a defeatist, Douglas, but I can't help fearing this sacrifice of lives will be just as futile as the others.'

'Can't argue with that, I'm afraid, Peggy,' he sighed.

Grimly the volunteer medical staff began coordinating field-hospital and casualty clearance arrangements with those of military medical staff as the new offensive gathered pace.

'God, the bloody rain! It's all right for the men up on the Pilckem Ridge, but down below it's a nightmare!' Douglas yelled to Peggy as he stripped off his dripping wet khaki cloak and immediately began helping her operate on the latest batch of casualites.

'So much for medical school training,' she shouted back, scraping mud from wounds. Decent standards of hygiene were impossible. Men seriously injured and half-drowned in the swamps behind Ypres could not be properly cleaned in the primitive conditions the two doctors and their teams of nurses were forced to work in.

'I told you it was like the Somme,' Peggy muttered wearily as they grabbed a five-minute respite and drank some foul-tasting cocoa.

'You were bloody right! Surgery is my speciality,' Douglas agreed, 'but this is just butchery, Peggy. I won't insult you by asking how you can stand it?'

'No, don't.' She smiled grimly. 'I'm a hardened old medic. These wee nurses are the ones to admire. Most of them had hardly seen a cut till they came here. They're wonderful.'

Douglas stood up and stretched. 'Well, if women don't get the vote after this, I'll personally put my stethoscope where Asquith and Lloyd George won't miss it.'

'I'll hold you to that.' Peggy put down her tin cup with a rattle. 'This war has made a suffragette of me at last! Well, back to the butcher's shop, Doctor Munro!'

'They can't be serious!' Peggy threw up her hands in protest at the medical corps emergency meeting in October. After months of devastation, word had just come in that, despite the continued rain and appalling conditions, the men were being sent into battle again over the same terrible swampy territory.

'I think we should talk to HQ,' suggested Jean Lecroix, a Canadian doctor. 'Our lads are being asked to join in this time to reach that bloody little village on the other side of the canal. What's it called?'

'Passchendaele,' said Douglas.

'That's it.'

They sent a despatch to HQ, signed by all the senior medical staff. General Gough hesitated as the protests poured in from all the hospital services and from many others. He wanted to wait till the weather improved, but both Plumer and Haig insisted that the offensive should begin at once. It went ahead.

'The whole bloody campaign was based on dammned inexcusable ignorance, self-delusion and arrogance!' Peggy wept out her anquish on Douglas's shoulder after the first offensive in pouring rain across a sea of mud. 'They didn't bloody listen, they didn't bloody want to know!' Her voice rose to an almost hysterical scream.

'Peggy, Peggy!' He cradled her gently, rocking her to and fro. 'I'm really sorry it was you who had to see first-hand proof of how stupid and ignorant they are. I admit, I'm completely shocked myself.'

'I wanted to show them where the field-hospital was, Douglas.' Peggy scrubbed her eyes like a child. 'That's why I detoured to the edge of the battle-field. It's so rare for anyone to come from HQ, but I still believed that they knew what they were doing when they gave the orders to the men. But they bloody well don't!'

'I know,' he crooned, letting her pour it out.

'It was the tears that finished me. There they sat in the armoured car, weeping when they saw the sea of mud and swamp, with arms and legs still sticking up where we haven't managed to get the bodies out. They'll be there till the mud hardens enough to drive carts over and dig.

' "Did we really send our men to fight in that?" one of them says, crying like a baby. None of them had been here before. All this time we've been telling them they were wrong to go on sending men to a foul death, and they wouldn't listen!'

'Maybe they will now.'

'I hope so, before there are more and more useless deaths. Sorry, Douglas.' Slowly she dried her eyes.

'Come on, let's get back to work.' He pulled her to her feet. 'You've been so brave, Peggy, I wondered when you'd break. Don't be ashamed, I've done it myself a few times. It's necessary now and then.'

'Have you?' She looked into the grey eyes that always seemed so calm and steady.

'Of course I have.'

'Never in front of me!' She felt an unexpected stab of resentment.

'It happened when you weren't here, either before you came or when you were at Tieds. There you are, Peggy,' he grinned, 'your presence is enough to keep me sane!'

'Och, Douglas.' She managed a reluctant smile. 'Sometimes I feel such a fool.'

'That you're not,' he said softly. 'Lassie dear, that you're not.'

Two days later Surgeon Douglas Munro and Doctor Margaret McBride were decorated by the Belgians for their work at the front.

'I don't want damned medals, I want peace!' Peggy began weeping again in great gasping sobs when she heard about the award.

'Well, you and I are Chevaliers de l'Ordre de Leopold whether we want to be or not.' Douglas shook her roughly, bringing her back from the edge of hysteria. 'Now stop it, Peggy. Stop it right now! You've wept enough.'

Chapter 20
Human weakness has come short

'I'll have to go back to Ayrshire.' Elspeth ran her fingers down Brian's lean body, following the line of the still livid scar on his stomach.

'Do what you have to, darling girl.' He held her close. 'I understand that you must sort out this business.'

'I still find it hard to believe that my father is dead . . . and in such circumstances. It was a terrible shock.'

'Are you sad?'

'Why should I be? You know we hated each other. I'm not a hypocrite, Brian, to pretend affection now he's lying in the McClure vault.'

'What else did Sinclair say? Is your father's estate complicated?'

'I wouldn't have thought so. Though maybe poor wee Hamish dying too alters matters. I'd always assumed he would take on the mines and Father's other business once he was older. Och, Sinclair was cryptic as ever, but is adamant that I should come if possible. You saw the telegram and the letter for yourself. I wonder what really happened that day on the cliffs, Brian?'

'What do you mean, Elspeth? Witnesses saw your father go after the boy when his pony broke away and galloped towards the edge of the cliff. They fell over together. There's nothing strange in that, just tragic . . . the child's death anyway.' Brian felt no regret about the father-in-law he had never met, nor ever wanted to.

'Oh, I know it must have been an accident, but father had so many enemies, one wonders . . .'

'Oh, rubbish, woman!' Brian stilled her speculation with a hug. 'When do you think you'll leave? Did you ask at the office?'

'Yes, last night while you were still at the hospital. I can get the *Cleland* tomorrow afternoon. It's carrying troops and a group of nurses to Southampton and aims to be back in England the week after Christmas. I might even make it to Scotland for New Year. That should please Libby.'

'When will you come back?'

'As early in 1918 as I can.'

'The sooner the better, my Elspeth.' His lips sought hers and they clung together in a passion fanned by the prospect of forthcoming separation.

Boxing Day, 1917
Aboard the *Cleland*

My dearest Brian

Christmas on board, lying off the coast of Egypt. What a strange occasion! I thought we would have been much nearer England by now, but no, storms have kept us rolling about the Mediterranean a long week after we should have left.

Yesterday festivities were celebrated with great gusto by the young nurses and soldiers. Someone hung a bunch of mistletoe (where on earth it came from, I cannot guess) above the entrance to the dining hall. Can you imagine the fun, laughter and chaos? Not everyone was amused! Matron in charge of the girls is exactly the type of dragon you and I know well. She tried to stop 'frivolous fraternising' as she put it, sniffing icily when anyone attempted to jolly her out of the sulks.

After a time the officers and nurses organised a little impromtu dance when one of them sat down at the piano and rattled out some popular tunes. Matron went mad, yelling that it was against regulations for nurses to dance in uniform and they should 'Stop this cavorting at once!' The captain and I finally took her to one side and told her off quite firmly, upon which she burst into tears and ran off to her cabin.

The nurses and officers moved the dance on deck.

298

Hours later as I lay thinking of you and longing for you in my own cabin, I could hear the jollity still going on. Poor Matron will never be quite the same again!

My dearest husband, take your quinine, take care, and think of the time you can take me in your arms again. I dream of nothing else. I will write from France or England, whichever we reach first. Tomorrow we join a convoy coming out from Alexandria for the rest of the journey across the Mediterranean. The waters between here and Gibraltar are infested with U-boats, I have been told. Let's hope the enemy are still too full of Yuletide cheer to attack a convoy as small as ours!

Till we meet, my darling Brian, I think of you day and night.

Your loving wife,
Elspeth

Elspeth sent the letter to shore with the pilot boat that led the escorting convoy out of Alexandria to join them. Slowly six boats swung into position, the *Cleland* among them. Cautiously they headed into the most dangerous part of their passage. The first two days passed quietly, but the jolly mood of Christmas had given way to a nervous silence.

'Once we get through the Straits, Doctor McClure,' the captain told her, 'things are usually much safer. The convoys have been a great help against the U-boats in the Mediterranean, but every so often our ships get "zonked", convoy or not.'

'Wonderfully reassuring,' Elspeth replied with an ironic lift of her brows. 'Shall we have an "abandon ship" practice soon, or whatever you call it?'

'Certainly.' His reply was unnerving. 'We usually do about now.'

Elspeth was standing by the rails next morning after breakfast, exchanging professional chat with the ship's medical officer, when a torpedo struck the *Cleland*. There was a terrific crash and she was flung headlong across the deck, grabbing a rope which brought her to a jerking stop. Struggling to her feet, she managed to seize a life-belt from a pile nearby as the boat listed and heaved. The medical officer had disappeared, but all around her sailors, soldiers and nurses yelled as they ran for the life boats. The noise of sirens, splintering wood, cries and screams was deafening.

Gathering her scattered wits and telling herself to stay calm, she stopped for a second to take stock instead of running aimlessly about in blind panic. To her right some sailors were just starting to lower a boat which was crammed with men in khaki.

'Over here, Doctor, come on!' One of the men saw her hesitate and beckoned.

'Right!' Elspeth ran full pelt for the boat and found herself lifted bodily in, just as the winch began dropping it into the water. With an almighty splash they hit the sea and she was thrown on top of half a dozen soldiers. For a moment it looked as if the heavily loaded lifeboat would capsize, but it rocked wildly, steadied then floated.

'Man the oars! Get the hell away from the hull!' The men grabbed what they could and began to row for their lives as the *Cleland* tipped crazily, threatening to drag them down in the fierce undercurrents it created.

After a few minutes they were far enough away to take stock. Bodies were everywhere in the sea, some swimming, some clinging desperately to floating debris. None was near enough for them to help, but the other ships in the convoy circled, trying to pick up survivors. Elspeth's boat kept as far back as possible so they would not hamper rescue attempts.

A sudden blinding light and a deafening crash caused huge waves to rock the fragile life boats and another of the merchant ships in the convoy began to list and sink. The U-boat pack had scored another hit. Figures in khaki and blue ran about like crazed ants, scrambling into boats or sliding helplessly into the water as the angle of the deck increased.

'Oh, the bastards! That boat had just picked up survivors from the *Cleland*!' a soldier yelled in anger and frustration.

'Oh God, where are all the poor lassies?' Elspeth remembered the happy faces of two days ago.

Silently they watched as the whole process they had just escaped happened over again. A body covered in oil floated face down nearby. Elspeth bit her lip. This helpless onlooking was worse than the traumas of tending the injured. But she did not have time to think or mourn.

'Christ, they're at it again!' Another torpedo, and yet another hit upon the stricken vessels, finishing the job and causing havoc among the flotilla of life boats and makeshift rafts dotted everywhere.

Elspeth's boat was hit by a raft in the crazy confusion and within minutes she was in the water, desperately fighting for her life. The life-belt just held her head above water, but she was hit chokingly in the face over and over again by the swell. An oil slick from the sinking ships started spreading slow, deadly tentacles across the water. Get that stuff on you, McClure, and you're dead, she thought in terror, vainly struggling to move away but hampered by her long skirts which were pulling her down.

'Rip off your skirt, for Christ's sake!' a naked man swimming alongside bawled to her. 'Then kick like hell with your feet away from that lot.'

Fumbling with the wet swollen eyelets, she finally managed to loosen the heavy folds. It felt like a miracle when the skirt floated off. I'm keeping my knickers on anyway, she thought with grim humour, and kicked hard, trying to push herself out of immediate danger. 'Keep going, McClure,' she muttered through gritted teeth as the December sea began to chill her limbs and sap her will-power. Think of Brian, think of Peggy, think of Votes for Women! Slowly she edged away from the oily black death.

'Over here, lass!' A broad Yorkshire accent penetrated her single-minded determination to stay afloat and away from the deadly oil.

Over where? Elspeth thought she'd shouted back, but hadn't. A solid lump of something came into view and for a second or two she almost panicked, thinking she had swum into the oil-slick. She lifted her arm in an automatic gesture, cracking it hard on the side of the life-raft.

'Give me your hand!'

Panting and exhausted, she was pulled on to the raft and lay face down for minutes on the flat deck before she had the strength to even look up or take stock. The half a dozen men on board were sailors from the *Cleland* who had left

301

the sinking ship at the last moment. The Captain was among them. 'Welcome aboard, Doctor McClure.' He bowed. 'I told you we might need that practice.'

'There was someone else near me in the water,' she mumbled anxiously, but the man who had shouted to Elspeth to kick off her skirt was nowhere to be seen.

'Keep on your life-belt, love,' a sailor advised as Elspeth sat up, dazedly fumbling with her right hand for the ties which were biting into her flesh.

'Aye, he's right,' another added. 'There goes another torpedo. We're not out of it yet.'

Elspeth put her aching head between naked knees, and tried to steady her nerves. Her throbbing left arm hung uselessly, and she realised it was probably fractured. The raft rocked wildly as debris landed all round from yet another torpedo strike. She would not survive one more session in the water handicapped like that. Oh, Brian, she thought with sad resignation, I hope you're not going to be a widower all over again.

Passchendaele was taken by the Canadian 1st and 2nd Divisions in November. Totally exhausted, Peggy and Douglas spent Christmas and New Year recuperating together at Tieds. The two old friends passed leisurely days walking in the beautiful grounds and talking about the past, never dwelling on the horrors they had left.

For Douglas it was a bitter-sweet time. Constantly by her side without the pressure of work to distract and occupy him, his grey eyes followed her everywhere. But Peggy, reminiscing about Robert and the love they had once shared, couldn't see what everyone else had known for years, and what the Rosendaele staff took for granted! Douglas Munro was totally in love with her. The way she always sought his company, her nearness and genuine affection, gave him some measure of compensation, but it also brought refinement to the torture he felt in her presence. Only in the height of the field-hospital carnage was the pain eclipsed by greater urgency. Still he dared not speak his mind for fear of damaging the precious closeness they had, and in respect of the memory they both held so dear.

Peace in yet another New Year was toasted, but nobody believed in their hearts that 1918 would bring it. Though the Americans were now fully engaged, the Entente Allies were too busy squabbling to be effective. The German allies seemed as invincible as ever.

Peggy wondered sometimes where the Austrian medical commander was. And if little Philomena was safe somewhere with Erich's mother.

They were at Tieds when the newspapers reported the sinking of the *Cleland* and other ships from the Alexandria convoy.

'Oh God, Douglas – Doctor Elspeth McClure. Look here! Elspeth was on the *Cleland*.' Peggy read her friend's name on the list from the torpedoed convoy.

'Let me see.' Douglas grabbed the paper and the two of them gazed in horror at the report.

'She's listed under those missing. Och, Elspeth! Elspeth!' Peggy shook from head to foot.

'I'll telegram HQ!' Douglas rushed off, leaving her sitting staring into a past only she remembered.

After two anxious days and a series of frantic telegrams, they discovered that Elspeth had been located in a hospital further down the Egyptian coast and would soon be on her way to England. Their relief and happiness were sealed with a bottle of Baron de Tied's best champagne brought up from the cellar.

Later that evening, Peggy, tongue losened by the alcohol and emotion, finally asked Douglas a question which had preyed on her mind for a long time. 'How did you feel when you heard that Elspeth had married Brian?' She sat at his feet, gazing into the dancing flames.

'About Elspeth's marriage? Delighted, what else?' Douglas looked puzzled.

'Och, Libby thought you and she might make a match of it one fine day.'

'Oh, trust Libby,' Douglas guffawed. 'I admit I admire Elspeth greatly and we have been the best of friends for years. I suppose she has told you all about my fringe involvement in the suffrage movement?'

'Yes.'

'And in fact she's a fine-looking woman, despite that birth mark she flaunts,' Douglas went on, 'but we were never on those terms at all.'

Peggy smiled suddenly. 'Poor Libby. None of us lives up to her expectations, but I do know she is happy that Elspeth has married at last.'

'And you, Peggy?' Douglas asked gently. 'Will you remarry?'

'Replace Rob? Never!' The answer came without hesitation. 'How could you of all men ask me that?'

Douglas didn't answer.

The following week Peggy and Douglas left Tieds for a military camp in Flanders, providing temporary relief for the team there. Half afraid of his own motives for asking her to work with him, Douglas suggested she rejoin the SWH. 'Think about it, Peggy. Don't stay with me out of loyalty. As volunteer doctors you and I are both free to decide within reason where we operate.'

'I don't really want rejoin the SWH,' Peggy replied. 'Now poor Elsie Inglis is dead and Elspeth is on her way to Britain, I have no special SWH contacts, except maybe at Royaumont. Och, it doesn't matter who I work with, I want to do what I can for the poor souls who need it. Are you trying to get rid of me, Douglas?' she teased.

'No objections to continued collaberation with the weaker sex . . . men?' His eyes twinkled.

'Not a bit! The prejudice has never been on my side! Anyway, you and I have always worked well together. But you haven't answered my question. Don't you need me with the unit any more, Douglas?' She felt a sharp stab of rejection.

'Need you? Of course I do!' His face flushed. 'Having another doctor in the team is essential, and having one with your guts, calibre and field experience is a bonus.'

'What are you on about, Douglas Monro?' It was Peggy's turn to redden at the unexpected sincerity and fulsomeness of his praise. 'I just do my job.'

'More than that, lass, more than that.'

'Less of the lass. I'm the same age as you, old man.'

'Whatever you say, Doctor.' Douglas laughed at her indignation. 'So, shall we take our evening stroll, madam?'

'Certainly, sir,' Peggy curtseyed smilingly.

She slung the old fur cloak, a reminder of her winter in Serbia, over her coat. Wrapped up against the icy-raw February chill, they wandered behind the camp and away from the tents. Weak afternoon sunshine played ineffectually against banks of low, grey clouds. 'More snow. Och, maybe we can give it a miss today.' Peggy shivered despite her warm clothes.

'A wee walk is good for the circulation.'

'Maybe that. We'll make it a short one then. Walks out here might be useful, but they're hardly memorable.'

But Peggy was wrong. She was to remember that walk for the rest of her life.

There had been little skirmishing since Christmas though everyone feared this was just another false lull. Men could move freely within a mile or so radius of the camp and there was continual toing and froing to the trenches at the front. Only officers were able to go further away without special permission. Some reluctant conscripts and even men who had come voluntarily were tempted to wander off and try to make their way home. The period after Christmas, when depression and homesickness set in, was worst of all for desertion. Military Police kept a sharp lookout and punishment was severe. Everyone was war-weary. Soldiers from both sides sat in parallel trenches, longing for action yet fearing it, week after week.

'It's rumoured the Germans are massing troops in Flanders again,' Douglas said quietly as they left the camp behind and began walking into the area decreed out of bounds to soldiers.

'Does that mean another offensive?' Peggy groaned.

'I think so. In fact, they're moving a lot of the men out to the trenches tomorrow. I was told a few hours ago, but I didn't want to say in camp in case we were overheard. The commanders suspect something big is happening. Peggy, you remember my question of earlier?'

'About working together? Yes.'

'Well, before you commit yourself officially, I want you to know that I'll be sticking it out in Belgium. With so many troops deployed on both sides here, there's going to be plenty more blood and gore before this is all resolved.'

'Fine. I'll stay with you like I said.'

He gave a short nod. 'Good. So long as you're sure.' Since her earlier breakdown, Douglas didn't know how much more prolonged pressure she could stand.

'Don't start that again . . . I'm fine now. In fact I felt better for letting go like you said. Och, I'll stick it out if you do.'

'Peggy, is that a soldier?' Peering ahead, Douglas pointed to a figure sitting on a stone.

'Looks like it, but it's out of bounds here. If he doesn't manage to get back with a convincing story for the MPs, he'll be taken as a deserter.'

'Courts martial then prison. At least he's not in action so he won't be shot,' Douglas said glumly. 'Poor lads. Some of them are in such a bad state of nerves, they'd do anything to get out of this hell-hole.'

'Well, clearing off like he seems to have done, isn't the way,' Peggy said. 'Look, stay here, I'm going to talk to him. He'll not be so nervous of a woman.'

'All right, but be careful. Some of these lads are so jittery they shoot or bayonet as quick as look at you.' Douglas found himself a spot just out of sight and tried to shelter from the bitter wind, now blowing hard across the plain.

'You're a wee bittie out of bounds, soldier.' Peggy spoke quietly. 'I'm Doctor McBride from the medical unit,' she added quickly to allay his fears of arrest and surprise at meeting a woman there.

'Aye, so what, missus or Doctor whatever yer name is?' the soldier said dourly, not looking up.

'Well, you'd better head back to camp before someone thinks you're a deserter,' she said bluntly.

'Maybe I am a deserter an' all.' The soft Ayrshire accent, so familiar to her ears, was the last thing she'd expected. Later she wondered why she was so taken aback; the place was full of Scottish regiments.

'Now you don't mean that, soldier.' Peggy had heard this kind of talk before. The realisation of what war meant usually came shortly after these men had come singing and cheering to the front, but by then they could do nothing about it.

'Aye, I mean it right enough.' His voice was so low she had to bend over to hear him.

'Laddie, you'll be court-martialled, branded a coward. You don't want that.'

'I'm not a laddie, I'm a man of 38. I got conscripted in 1916. I'd never have joined up, left to myself. I'd have been a conchie. Ye ken what that is?'

'A conscientious objector. Of course I know what it is.'

'My wife was that ashamed,' he went on bitterly. 'I was handed white feathers every time I went into our wee town. She kept on about it day and night. Finally I said I'd go. Fightin' the enemy began to seem no so bad after all,' he added with a touch of grim humour.

'Why did you want to be a CO?'

'Why? For the same reasons as Keir Hardie . . . he came from near me in Ayrshire, ye ken. Poor man that's died of a broken heart over all the suffering and death. I'm not a coward, Doctor,' he blurted on, 'but I hate killing. I'd never even kill a beast if I could help it . . . and that's hard when you're a farm labourer.'

'It'll be worse now, if you go back branded a coward and deserter. What will your wife say then?'

'I ken that. That's why I'm sitting here trying to decide.' His head was still bowed and she could not see his face. 'Will ye say ye saw me?' He knew she could get him court-martialled already, whatever he decided.

'No, man, that I won't. I respect you for thinking. There's many another in high places that could do with thinking a bit more. I've tended wounded men till the floor ran with blood and thought many's the time how unnecessary it all is.'

The man sat gazing down in silence, then he stood up. 'Och, listen, Doctor, I'll go back! Yer right, it's no fair on the wife and bairns to desert right enough.' He turned and faced her at last, a small man, his sad brown eyes not much higher than her own green ones.

'Aye, you do that.' Peggy smiled as kindly and as warmly as she could.

'What did ye say yer name was?' he asked slowly, his expression oddly intense.

'Doctor McBride.'

'I thought that's what ye said, but I can hardly believe it.'

'Why?' Peggy half-expected some silly flirtatious comment, despite the pathos of the circumstances. Men often said daft things to cover embarrassment at revealing their emotions.

'Because I ken I'll never forget Peggy Soutar as long as there's breath in my body.'

'What did you say?' Peggy froze.

'Do ye remember this?' The soldier drew a worn mouth organ from his pocket and the plaintive air of *Jock O' Hazeldean* drifted across the wind-swept Flanders fields.

'Tam Laird. You're Tam Laird.' She grasped his arm. 'Is that right?'

'Aye.' The man nodded. 'Tam Laird that could never learn his tables but could play his moothie like magic . . .'

'And find curlew's nests! Och, Tam, Tam, tell me all yer news, man? Listen, wait a minute.' Peggy pointed to where she had left Douglas. 'I'll explain to my colleague who's lurking over there in the bushes, freezing to death.' She saw the man stiffen with apprehension. 'Och, Douglas is a dear friend as well as a colleague, he's all right, he'll not say a word about you. I'd trust him with my life, let alone yours! You and I can walk back together. There's less chance you'll be challenged if you're with me. If we are I'll explain to the guards that we know each other and were exchanging news of home. They always believe the doctor!'

'Doctor, is it? Aye, I thought that's what ye said right enough. Ye were always ambitious, Peggy. "Rich and famous" ye said.'

'Well, I'm neither, nor likely to be,' she laughed.

'Ye were the brightest and the best lass – or lad for that matter – Kirkowen School ever had on its rotten old benches. Och, how I cried my eyes out when ye left. Ye were a loss to me, so ye were.'

'Och, Tam!' Peggy was touched and amazed at how the years fell away as they talked.

Sensing that the two old friends wanted to talk, Douglas

agreed at once to go back alone. Head bent, listening intently, Peggy walked slowly to the camp, hearing all about Tam's five children and his struggle to bring them up on a farm worker's pay. Though he told all without a trace of self-pity, Peggy could see that life had been no kinder to him as an adult than it had in his schooldays.

'And my oldest laddie, wee Tam, is 12 now. The youngest is a lassie. She's a bonnie wee thing. I insisted we called her Margaret . . . after you. But I've never telt my wife why. I just said I liked the name. Jessie is no' the type to stand for another woman being put before her. Do ye remember Jessie Buchan, Peggy?'

'Jessie Buchan? Wasn't she a wee dark-haired lassie?' Peggy vaguely recalled a quiet little creature who had a perpetual sniff and snotter candles hanging in the Winter. 'She got the cookery prize.'

'Aye, that's Jessie . . . she looks just the same now, wee and dark-haired. Aye, she was good at cookin'. She still is when we have somethin' other than porridge and buttermilk to put on the table. But she was no better at her tables than me!' Tam laughed. 'I don't expect we've produced any doctors between us, Peggy, free education or no.'

'Well, maybe not, but you might have a decent musician among the five.'

'Aye, maybe that,' he replied proudly. 'Archie, the middle lad plays the moothie right well, and the bagpipes an' all.'

They were safely back behind the camp fence. Recognising the doctor, the guards did not even bother to challenge Tam.

'Well, I'm glad ye turned up when ye did, Peggy,' he shook her hand as they parted. 'I'm being sent to the front in the morning . . . or so rumour has it. But it's better to die doing the job I was sent out for, than my bairns be branded as having a "funky" for a faither. I've got my spirit back.'

'That's fine, Tam, but ye never really lost it. A real man should consider what he's doing.' Peggy hid her sadness, for she knew the danger he faced. 'Good luck, Tam Laird.'

'I'll need it, Peggy Soutar.'

She didn't contradict him.

*
309

Douglas and Peggy stayed on in Flanders, patching up the wounded after the enemy offensives were bloodily repulsed in March. They were still there in April when the Germans began offensive after offensive in Flanders and in France. Entente spirits were low. Haig gave his 'Backs to the Wall' order in April. Doggedly the Allies held on and counter-attacked. At the beginning of August, the tide began turning against the Germans with the Battle of Amiens.

In late-August Douglas was awarded the VC for treating and rescuing wounded men trapped in no-mans-land. Peggy shuddered when she heard what he had done to get them out, but with the discipline of war refused to dwell on the dangers he ran. A few days later he was severely wounded by shrapnel, doing the same again. Peggy didn't find out for two days, because he was treated on the field and sent to Britain the same evening.

As senior doctor, she took charge of the field-hospital, feeling as if her own right arm had been amputated. Douglas's absence left a gaping hole she found hard to explain rationally, since his replacement was competent enough. In any case, for the last month or so Douglas had been constantly at the front and they had rarely worked together. She wrote to him cheerfully but was anxious for his return. He replied that he was on the mend and would soon be back to join her. Peggy carried the telegram like a talisman under her bodice, but the weeks passed without any further word from him.

The field-casualty unit followed close behind the troops as they advanced in September. Every day saw a continuous stream of casualties – it was war as usual. Then influenza began raging among the men and hospital staff alike. To their despair it caused almost as many deaths as the war-wounds. For some the peace that was now coming so tantalisingly near would never materialise.

Armistice was signed at 11 am on 11 November 1918. Four years and one hundred days after war was declared, it stopped. It happened so suddenly and amid such daily carnage that Peggy and her colleagues hardly noticed. They

310

were too far away from anywhere civilised to hear bells ringing or see dancing in the streets.

'Peggy!' The feeble call attracted her attention from among the chaotic throng of new casualties. Among the last batch of wounded was Tam Laird. His right arm was shattered and he was bleeding from shrapnel cuts to his undernourished body.

'I'll deal with this patient.' She waved away the nurse who was cutting off the field-dressings, stuck on with blood and filth.

'Will I die, Peggy? Tell me if I will. I don't mind,' Tam asked softly, trying not to groan in agony as she pulled off the dressings.

'What would you want to do that for? The war is over, don't you know?' she said as she examined the horrible wounds.

'Not for me it isn't! What can I work at wi' no left arm, lass?'

'That's a good question, Tam.' There was little comfort she could give. He would certainly lose part of the shattered limb.

'Let me die, Peggy.'

'That wish is not in my power to grant you, Tam Laird. I'm a doctor, I've promised to save life.'

'Disabled, without an arm . . . maybe other wounds that won't heal right.' He gesticulated feebly at his ravaged trunk. 'There's not a farmer in Ayrshire that will have me.'

'Listen, man, fight to live. We'll cross those humphy bridges when we come to them. Ye've got five bairns and a wife. Ye might not be the man ye were, but yer better than no man at all!' she said sharply in the dialect of her childhood.

'Peggy, can ye hear it?' Tam's eyes began glazing over as merciful unconsciousness crept up and he sank into delirium.

'Hear what, Tam?'

'*Curee, curee.*' Briefly his voice rose uncannily in the plaintive cry of the curlew.

'Aye, by God I can,' she lied, as the sounds of bedlam around them almost drowned out her voice. 'And you're

311

going to walk on Kirkowen's cliffs and hear it again, so ye are, Tam Laird!' She signalled to the VAD who was giving the anaesthetics. As soon as Tam was under, she amputated his left arm just below the elbow.

Chapter 21

Where fleeting sea-birds round me cry

'Flora, it's been a long time, how are you?' Elspeth greeted her step-mother in the lawyer's Ayr offices.

'Fine,' the young woman answered briefly, eyes unfocusing and dull.

'Will you excuse me, ladies?' Sinclair said apologetically as his clerk beckoned from the door. 'This shouldn't take a minute.'

The two women sat in silence till Elspeth finally said, 'Mr Sinclair tells me you're not living at Bargeddie House any more, Flora?'

'Louisa and I live in Dumfermline,' she replied in a low, bitter voice, not looking up, 'I hate that house and all it stands for.' She began slowly rocking to and fro. 'Hamish should never have taken my bairn out riding, he was far too wee. I told him, I told him!' Tragic eyes suddenly fastened disconcertingly on Elspeth, showing the naked depth of her grief.

'Yes, Flora, I understand.' Shocked, Elspeth found herself speaking as if to a child. The poor woman needs help, not to be dragged to a lawyer's office, she thought.

'Mistress McClure hasn't been at all well . . . which is why we've waited till now to sort the estate out.' Sinclair took in the scene with a single glance as he came back. The lawyer was beginning to look ancient, but was as wise and spry as ever. He signalled caution to Elspeth and went on in a light, informative tone: 'Mistress McClure has been back living with her married sister. In fact she and Louisa have been there most of the time since Mr McClure and their son . . . er, died.'

'Well, the delay has been fortuitous in a way since I've just got here, thanks to the kindness of the German U-boats.' Elspeth held up her bandaged arm. 'And if you really do require my presence, matters could hardly have proceeded earlier anyway.'

'Exactly.' The lawyer nodded. 'I asked Mistress McClure if she would like to bring her brother-in-law with her, or some other body to speak on her behalf, but she declined.'

'I don't need anyone,' Flora muttered half to herself. 'I know Hamish McClure made me an allowance to live on. That's all I want: enough to pay my way and Louisa's school. After poor wee Hamish was born,' she went on dully, 'McClure wanted to reward me. Reward me! Isn't that funny? Even the wee doctor wouldn't take a reward for saving the life of his son! The housekeeper saw them from the window. She says Hamish McClure was like a whipped pup when she'd finished with him!' Her mirthless laughter verged on the hysterical. 'I wish she'd let me die!'

'Och now, don't upset yourself, Mistress McClure,' the lawyer said gently.

God, how my father managed to destroy folk, Elspeth thought, looking at the wreck of her step-mother and remembering the bright young girl Flora had been when he married her. Losing all those babies then the boy, couldn't have helped but age the poor soul. She looks 50 not 37. I wonder if Louisa has escaped my father's curse.

Flora bit her lip till a drop of bright blood showed, but then she went on more rationally, 'He fixed the allowance with your partner, didn't he, Mr Sinclair?'

'Yes, yes, Mistress McClure, but there may be other things to discuss in your interest or that of your lass,' the lawyer replied gently. 'That was why we suggested it.'

'Well, that's your job, isn't it?' Flora subsided into her former silence and refused to be drawn any more.

'I was amazed when I got your letter. I thought my father had taken all his business from you, Mr Sinclair,' Elspeth broke in.

'Aye, he did, but for some reason after he dropped the

314

case against you, he brought the Will back here to my practice. Though I never dealt with the man directly myself.' The lawyer drew himself up. 'I have my principles!'

'Mr Sinclair,' Flora said in the same weary voice, 'can we get this over with?'

'Of course, of course. If you're sure you can manage, Mistress McClure?'

'I can manage.'

Sinclair picked up the papers. 'The Will is not so very complicated, but maybe a wee bittie surprising. Hamish McClure died after his son in hospital in Ayr, as you both know, which in the legal sense simplifies matters. The boy never inherited. As his eldest daughter,' Sinclair said slowly, looking at Elspeth, 'you inherit the bulk of the estate and Bargeddie House. Lousia gets virtually nothing. She's not even mentioned.'

'What? But didn't he cut me out of his Will?' Elspeth gasped and winced as she involuntarily jerked her bandaged arm.

'No, he didn't. Knowing your, er, mutual antipathy, I was sure he would disinherit you, especially after the business over your sanity. But he didn't. As I said, I don't even know why he decided to give us the Will back here, after all the bad blood there was between us. I sent my partner down with the papers to be signed and witnessed and never heard a single word from him again.'

'So you've known about this for years?' Elspeth asked sharply.

'Of course I've known the contents of the Will, but it would have been unprofessional to say anything,' the lawyer defended himself. 'Anyway, I thought like everyone else that the boy would outlive his father.'

'So I am the heir to the mines and everything?' Elspeth sounded as shocked as she felt.

'Yes. And the South African gold mines too. Those are worth a fortune now. They were a wise investment after all.'

'Oh, no! I'm not becoming a mine-owner here or in South Africa, I'll sell them!' Elspeth said instantly, flushing to the roots of her hair.

'Well, the value of the estate has gone up again over these

315

past few war years. There may be interest from Dalgleish & Company as a local buyer, but shouldn't you discuss this with your husband?' Sinclair asked.

'Brian would expect me to make this decision myself, Mr Sinclair. We don't have a Victorian marriage,' she replied icily.

Och, I should have known better, Sinclair thought, and smothered a smile. 'Well, you must please yourself of course, Mistress McGonagle.'

'I've told you twice already this morning, Mr Sinclair, address me as before. I kept my own name.'

'Och, you're a terrible woman, Miss Elspeth! I never know where on earth I am with you! I never have!' The poor lawyer shook his head in despair.

'Poor Mr Sinclair, what a trial I am!' His bewilderment drew the old lovely smile from Elspeth at last. 'You should know me by now . . . and know how highly I respect and value you.' Turning to Flora, she asked softly, 'Would you like anything from the house, Flora? Maybe Louisa wants the things from her room? Take your pick. Take the lot, if you want, I have my own mother's things in Glasgow. Nothing else is of sentimental value to me.'

Flora sat plucking at her dress, as if no one else was in the room, and ignored the question, forcing Elspeth to repeat it. 'I want nothing from that place . . . och, well, Louisa might want her things,' she muttered at last.

'Mr Sinclair.' Elspeth stood up. 'I want a word alone with you right now, please.' Without waiting for his answer she left the room.

'What is it, Miss Elspeth? Michty me, this whole business is quite without precedent.' The old lawyer mopped his brow. I should have known Hamish McClure's Will would be trouble, he thought.

Elspeth closed the door behind them and hissed, 'Mr Sinclair, poor Flora is not in her right mind at all. Is the allowance all she has?'

'Yes, they have nothing much else. Her family was genteel but not at all wealthy.'

'Right, I'll sell the mines as I said. See Dalgleish. If he's not interested, advertise. When it's done, see to it that Flora gets a house in Dunfermline near her family and set up a Trust for Louisa so there is enough income to keep them both in decent comfort. In the meantime, make sure they can pay their way. Oh, and check all figures with me before anything is signed,' she added crisply.

'Certainly, Miss Elspeth.' The lawyer nodded, trying to hide his astonishment. 'But you don't have to, you know. They do have the wee allowance. They'll not starve.'

'Of course I don't have to, man! But I'm doing it anyway. You helped me once . . . and you're not the only one. I'm helping her. Sow as ye will reap! And in case you think that's the end of what I intend to do with the McClure business, you're mistaken, my dear faithful Mr Sinclair. I'm only just beginning to see the possibilities!'

'Och, I can imagine.' He gave a resigned smile. 'Are you going back to Salonika?'

'Probably not. My husband's unit is being moved at last, possibly to Europe. I'll wait and see what happens.'

'Don't tell me you're thinking of taking things easy, Miss Elspeth?' The old lawyer's eyes twinkled.

'Not a chance.' She grinned. 'I'm off to London next week to see what will happen to the suffrage movement, now we have Votes for Women almost within our grasp. The Lords have passed the Suffrage Bill with hardly a murmur of dissent. It's amazing, after all the sacrifice and suffering for so many long weary years. Everyone has their eyes on the war effort. Votes for six million women seem to have just slipped onto the statute books.'

'You must be feeling very pleased all the same?' Sinclair said with a shrewd sideways look.

'Of course. We all are. I'm going to a "Women's Party" meeting to celebrate when I get to London. And I've promised an account of the shipwreck for *The Common Cause*. The main struggle might be over but there's still work to do. The present Bill gives the vote to women over thirty. We'll press for a lowering of the age to twenty-one.'

'Och, women are never satisfied! Well, I suppose if you don't go back to chaining yourself to railings and starving half to death, it'll be all right,' Sinclair said doubtfully. 'Are you giving up your medical work now you're married?'

317

'Not a bit of it,' she replied. 'In fact I've offered to help out in one of the south-coast hospitals where they are taking injured from France. I'll start as soon as my arm is better. Have you seen the latest lists?'

'Yes.' Sinclair bowed his head. 'My brother's youngest lad was among the dead last month. Still, they say the war will end this year.'

'Let's hope they've got it right at last,' Elspeth replied from the heart, 'so everyone can come home. Oh, well, we had better go back in and see to poor Flora.'

When they finished their business, Elspeth gratefully left the lawyer's office for her hotel. That evening she wrote to Brian then sat thoughtfully staring into the distance. Something Flora had said, something she had hardly noticed at the time, began to weigh heavy upon her mind.

'Mama? Libby said you were not coming home till tomorrow!' Kirsten's dark eyes were fixed unblinkingly on the semi-stranger walking down the path.

'Kirsten, darling girl! I couldn't wait to see you, so I took a night train from London . . . but at least you haven't forgotten your old mama.' Peggy held open her arms. Ten years old and self-contained, the child let herself be enveloped. 'Did you get all my letters, Kirsten?'

Her expression was solemn. 'Yes, I got the letters and the little doll with the funny hat from Rosendaele. I called her Marie.'

'Where's Libby?'

'Upstairs, seeing that the maid airs your room properly.'

'Oh, how I missed you, bonnie lass, all these long years . . . nearly three of them.'

'But you didn't come back to see me.' She had inherited Peggy's own directness.

'There was so much work to do with the sick and wounded. And sometimes it was from fear of passing on disease. Och, maybe I was just scared I would want to stay if I came back. Who would have looked after the soldiers then?' Peggy held her at arm's length, willing the child to understand. 'It was never that I didn't love you, sweetheart.'

'Och, I know that!' Kirsten suddenly smiled and hugged

318

her round the waist. 'Uncle Andrew said you were a heroine and that you won medals. Is that right, Mama? Libby and me read about you and Uncle Douglas in the papers. And we saw pictures of Auntie Elspeth too.'

'Heroine I wasn't!' Arm around her daughter, Peggy walked up the familiar garden path and through the bare Winter garden. Behind them her few trunks were being unloaded from the carriage. 'Or if I was a heroine,' she added, 'then everybody else was as well.'

'You don't look very different, Mama.' The brown eyes assessed her. 'I thought you might have really grown old or had no legs or something.'

'I feel years older and centuries wiser. But you have changed a lot, Kirsten,' Peggy said with a catch in her voice. 'I left a bairn and I've come back to a lovely young lady!'

'Libby! Mama's back!' Kirsten broke away and ran towards the housekeeper who had come rushing down, once she realised what was happening.

'Doctor Peggy! Doctor Peggy!' Libby hugged her tearfully. 'Och, you and that other one have turned my hair grey between you. But now I've the both of ye back safe and well, the Lord be praised.'

'Is Elspeth still in Ayrshire?' Peggy hardly dared hope.

'Aye, and she'll be over tomorrow. We thought you were coming then instead of the day. She's staying in Scotland for New Year with Doctor McGonagle.'

'Brian too? How wonderful!'

'Och, aye, a fine man she got in the end. Not that the poor soul will have his sorrows to seek, keeping her in order . . . but of course ye ken her husband. I forgot you had all met in that heathen place . . . where was it?'

'Serbia.'

'Aye, that place. Och, you're a terrible pair! What a worry ye've been. Not a night's sleep have I had these three years thinking about ye. Hardly a wink!' Libby was off again, alternately weeping and hugging.

'Well, do I get tasting your scones or not, Libby? Many's the time I've thought of them when I was in "heathen places". I used to sit and dream of scones in a lovely big

319

floury pile, with butter melting all over them and a pot of your home-made blaeberry jam standing by.'

'Och, and here's me keeping you hanging about on the doorstep of your own home.' Libby dried her eyes and blushed in shame. 'Come on into the library, I've the fire roaring up the chimney. Kirsten was doing her lessons there. I'll see to the tea right away. I expect you and our bonnie wee lass have a lot of catching up to do. She's missed you, Doctor Peggy, so she has.'

'And I her.' Arm in arm Peggy and her daughter went into the cosy room and closed the door.

'Oh, my darlings, how wonderful!' Peggy rushed down holding out her arms to Elspeth and Brian next afternoon when Libby let them in.

'Peggy!' Emotion ran unashamedly high as the friends met for the first time in two traumatic years.

'Marriage suits you, Elspeth.' Peggy took in the glow of happiness which lit up her friend's face. 'And you've lost that terrible gaunt look you used to have.'

'Instead *you're* as thin as a stick, Peggy McBride.' Elspeth poked her in the ribs. 'Get some flesh on those bones ... just like you used to tell me to do.'

'Brian, did they give you leave at last?' Peggy teased as they settled down, Elspeth and her husband, side by side on the worn sitting-room settee.

'They had to, my girl. You know, I had no time off in the entire war years, not even when Elspeth and I got married in Salonika. Now the regiment is based in England for a few more weeks, just twiddling thumbs while decisions are made about going home. I had no trouble persuading them to let me go.'

'A few more weeks? Then what?'

'Then I have to go back to Australia and sort out my discharge papers.'

'Are you going to Australia with Brian, Elspeth?' Peggy tried to sound casual.

'We've got the vote in Britain, Peggy. More or less.'

'I know, and it's wonderful, but what bearing does that have on you? Women have the vote in Australia too.'

'Exactly. We had a deal, Brian and I.' Elspeth smiled and linked her arm in his. 'I would stay in Britain till we won, then we'd see. Well, we've won.'

'Australia is under negotiation.' Brian stroked Elspeth's face lovingly. 'Give it a try, Elspeth. I won't insist if you don't settle in.'

'As you say, it's under negotiation. Let's leave it at that for today and enjoy Libby's high tea. What's the betting she's done all our favourites?'

'No bets at all, Miss Elspeth!' Libby, the little maid and Kirsten came in bearing trays laden with pancakes, scones, French fancies, Paris buns, and everything else the house-keeper's loving heart and clever hands could devise.

'Are you going to marry Andrew?' Elspeth asked bluntly as they did justice to the spread.

'I feel I should . . . if he still wants me, that is.' Peggy looked intently at a piece of Dundee cake as if it had suddenly grown horns.

'Have you seen him?'

'Er, not yet. Libby says he's coming over tomorrow. I, er, didn't send word that I had arrived a wee bit early.' Peggy couldn't meet their eyes. 'Och, I wanted some time alone with Kirsten, and then today with you.'

'Hardly the attitude of an eager blushing bride,' Elspeth said dryly.

Peggy's head shot up and she flushed. 'I could never pretend to be that. Nor ever replace Rob. But with Andrew it would be a marriage based on companionship, as you once advised, Elspeth.'

'Did I do that?' Elspeth looked astonished.

'Yes, you did. New Year 1914, in this very room. Och, the man has waited three long years for me to get rid of whatever devils were riding on my back. I owe him something.'

'What the hell are you on about?' Brian broke in sharply. 'Get one thing into that determined red head of yours, Peggy, you don't hand over your life to someone because they chose to hang around and wait for you. If you want to marry the bugger do it . . . not otherwise!'

'Crudely put,' Elspeth laughed, 'but absolutely correct.'

'Well, maybe I'll fall into his arms when he comes

321

tomorrow and I see him again. Feelings get distorted over time. And don't forget, Andrew has been wonderful while I was away. Libby tells me that he takes a real interest in Kirsten and kept their finances, the house, everything, in top notch.'

'Just don't marry the man from a sense of pity or duty or whatever, it's not fair to either of you.' Elspeth leaned over and took her hand. 'Whatever I might have said in the past, Peggy, listen to me now. You know how cynical I was about men . . . still am about most of them. Poor Brian had an awful job persuading me to throw in my lot with him. So far I haven't regretted it.' She blushed with emotion. 'I love him, Peggy. I'd follow him to the ends of the earth, even Australia.'

'The point is that I would follow her too,' he added. 'Elspeth is an exceptional woman, not a doormat or a bit of baggage to be lumped here or there. I respect and love her for the independent, intelligent person she is. We'll always make our decisions together. Are you sure Andrew will be the same with you?'

'Maybe not.' Peggy sighed and looked down at her hands. 'I've always been just as free-spirited as Elspeth, though it shows differently perhaps. Och, we'll see tomorrow.'

'Why do you need to marry anyway?' Elspeth demanded. 'I thought you were happy on your own, valued your independence . . .'

'You're right, I don't *need* to marry, I don't think I even *want* to. Och, I just feel so mixed up.' Peggy leaned back in her chair. 'I guess it's the excitement of coming back, the feeling that the war is over and everything should be just perfect. Folk should be happy, life should fall neatly into place. Women and men should be married . . . but it's not so easy at all.'

'Just promise me,' Elspeth said urgently, 'that you won't make any snap decisions about marrying Andrew?'

'How long did it take you to agree to marry Brian?' Peggy replied dryly.

'That was a lightning strike!'

'Yes, I know. Och, maybe that's the difference. It was like that with Robert,' Peggy sighed. 'Anyway enough of

Andrew, let's reminisce instead. Have you seen any of our old colleagues from Serbia . . . and how about Douglas? He's been unusually quiet. I telegraphed yesterday to say I'm home. Och, I must see the man. Maybe I should ask him about Andrew?'

'Oh, God,' groaned Elspeth, but said no more as Libby came back with fresh tea.

Andrew Graham had put on some weight in the three years since they had last met. Standing on the doorstep, he looked exactly what he was: successful senior partner in an excellent provincial legal practice and a pillar of local society. His handsome face flushed with pleasure when Peggy came down to meet him.

'Peggy! How wonderful to see you, my dear.' He kissed her cheek gallantly. 'But, oh, dearie me, you're so thin!'

'Oh, don't you start, Andrew.' She smiled, 'I think everyone I have met since I left France has told me so! A few weeks of Libby's cooking and I shall be squeezing into my clothes with difficulty.'

'Well, have I been a good and faithful steward, or not?' Andrew followed her into the house, smiling, 'Is everything in order and to your liking?'

'It's perfect. And you've been more than a good steward, Andrew, you've been a wonderful friend to Kirsten and Libby. I'm eternally in your debt.' Her hands lifted expressively.

'Now, Peggy, no talk of debts between us, please.' Andrew raised her hand to his lips. 'But I'm more than glad to see you safe and sound. "Missing in Serbia, prisoner of the Austro-Hungarians" was terrible enough, then there were all those horrific reports from France. I worried about you, my dear, especially when you were decorated for bravery tending soldiers at the frontline and the like. People don't get medals for sitting at tea-parties. Was it horribly dangerous, my dear?'

'Well some folk do get decorated for attending tea-parties.' Peggy thought ironically of idiots she had known at military HQ. 'Though not many, thank goodness. Yes, it was dangerous, Andrew, I can't deny that, but we never dwelled on it, there was too much to do.'

'Your colleague was sent home injured, wasn't he?' Andrew asked with voyeuristic fascination. 'You know who I mean – Doctor Munro, the chappie who received the medal from the Belgians at the same time as you and then won the VC?'

'Yes, Douglas was injured.'

'We read about it all in the papers,' Andrew went on enthusiastically. 'You're a real celebrity. The Chairman of Greenwoods Infirmary told me just last week that they've hung a framed copy of the picture showing you being decorated in the hospital reception. They're very proud of you, Peggy. We all are.'

'Don't tell me they want me back there?'

'I wouldn't be at all surprised! Your replacement has just left for a better job in Glasgow.'

'And I can have the old one back again?' Her tone was ironic. 'Some things, like promotion for female doctors, never change, Votes for Women or not.'

'Anyway, if you marry me, I'd still prefer you to take it a bit easier than before.' Andrew coyly took the opportunity to press his case.

Peggy suddenly felt she had come complete circle and was back exactly in the same spot as before. For a moment she felt her head would burst. Suddenly the tension cleared and she decided.

'Andrew, I said you are a wonderful friend and I mean it, but I don't feel we should marry.'

'Why not?' His face flushed.

'Because I'm not right for you. I'm far too independent, too restless.'

'You said going away would change that,' he protested. 'Surely you've got it all out of your system after all you've been through, Peggy? You've experienced enough excitement to last anyone a lifetime or more.'

'True, but it has changed things, Andrew,' she tried to explain. 'Being in the war has taught me to understand myself far better. Before I went, I thought I was just restless, and that it was my old love for Rob that stopped me loving

324

you. I thought I needed to break out for a while so I could really settle down.'

'Exactly.' Andrew was bewildered.

'But that's not what happened,' she went on gently. 'Instead I know now that I am simply not cut out for a conventional life, especially as the wife of someone so, so . . . och, so respectable! I want to go on working full-time, probably more than full-time. I want to choose my own career, to fight for my right to exercise my talents as a doctor. I won't change, Andrew, not ever. Realising that has been a great relief at last.'

'Do you mean what you're saying Peggy?'

'Yes, I mean it. And I have a few more dragons to slay in my soul before I can even attempt what I've just described.'

'What dragons, for heaven's sake?'

'Och, things to do with Elspeth's father and the whole business of who I am and where I come from. I think I'll find the answers to those dilemmas one day, but inflicting the process on someone as steady and kind as you would be unfair. I am as I am.'

'Maybe someone steady and . . . well . . . perhaps even a wee bittie boring,' Andrew argued, 'is exactly what you need?'

'Andrew, do you love me?'

'You know I do.'

'Would you give up your life and all you hold dear right now and follow me to the ends of the earth . . . to set up a training hospital in Serbia, for instance?'

'Of course not, Peggy, that would be madness.' Andrew was confused and hurt. 'Be reasonable, I have a fine practice here and a good social life. If we married, you could be part of it.'

'Then there's your answer! Anyone I marry would have to feel like that . . . even if I never expected him to do it. And he would know I would do the same for him.'

'But that's not logical. You've just said you wouldn't become part of my life, so why should I make the sacrifice for you?'

'Exactly. Both of us should want to.'

Andrew looked at her, face expressionless, then said

325

quietly, 'I hoped you would have settled down when you came back, but I guessed in my heart you wouldn't.' He got up from the chair. 'Well, here's my hand, Peggy. Let's be the good friends we've always been.' Generous to a fault, he capitulated.

'Thank you.' She blinked back tears, feeling both relieved and afraid for the boats she had burned. Andrew Graham was a fine man and she had turned her back firmly on him. 'Would you consider marrying someone else?' She didn't mean to ask the question but it came out anyway.

'Och, maybe that.' Andrew's sudden smile broke the embarrassment between them. 'My heart will recover. You had me well prepared for a rejection when I think about it. But I could do with a bit of female cosseting in my old age, Peggy, I'm tired of being solitary. Yes,' he mused with a twinkle in his eye, 'there's a very conventional and rather bonnie wee widow just moved up to Ayr from Dumfries. I'm supposed to be helping her sort out her affairs and settle in. You can put in a good word for me if she asks.'

'I will with pleasure, and provide a written guarantee!' Peggy joined in his unexpectedly skittish mood.

'Come to Bargeddie House with me, Peggy,' Elspeth asked a few days later. 'I have a lot to do there and I want your support.'

'Bargeddie? Och, Elspeth, wait till Brian comes back up from London then take him with you. I don't want to go to to that place,' she objected. 'Anyway, I was planning a surprise visit to Douglas Monro in Edinburgh tomorrow. He hasn't answered me yet. Still, it's only been a few days since I telegraphed.' Peggy felt inexplicably uneasy. 'Do you think he's all right? Douglas usually gets in touch right away when I contact him.'

'I'm sure he'll answer when he can. Maybe he's away or something,' Elspeth reassured her. 'And if he doesn't know about your plans to visit, then he can't mind waiting a day or so more, now can he?' Suddenly she became grave. 'But whatever, I want you with me at Bargeddie. I mean it, Peggy, please come.'

'Och, I suppose I'd better then.' Her affection for Elspeth

overrode the instinctive revulsion she felt at the idea of going near McClure's house.

'We won't be back tonight, Libby,' Peggy told the housekeeper. 'Elspeth wants to stay at Bargeddie. God knows why.'

'Miss Elspeth never does anything without good reason,' Libby said with a decisive nod. 'Even if her good reasons are a wee bit difficult for normal folk to fathom.'

'Och, you've got it exactly,' Peggy agreed with a chuckle. 'Are you taking Kirsten to dancing classes today?'

'Don't mention dancing to me!' Libby threw her hands in the air in exasperation. 'That wee madam is a right chip off the block you and Miss Elspeth came from! It's just as well I'm used to it or I'd be worried to bits. The bonnie lass dances like a wee bit of thistledown, but she says it's a waste of time. Instead she wants to fly they new airyplanes they used in the war!'

'I think she's a candidate for Elspeth's precious Miss Lovat's Academy soon.' Peggy laughed, then added soberly, 'But what will you do if she goes, Libby?'

'So long as my wee darling is fine, I'll be content,' Libby said gently. 'There'll be the holidays for me to spoil her, so there will. And I think she'll need company of her own age before long. But you'll still find a corner for me though, won't ye, Doctor Peggy?' Her face became anxious. 'I ken I've got my own money from Miss Elspeth's mamma, but I don't want to live alone and I can't see me taking to Australia, it's that far away, so it is.'

'As I understand it, they've not decided about Australia, Libby, but of course I'll always find a corner for you. We're still partners, aren't we?' Peggy put her arm round the elderly housekeeper's shoulders. 'You can't leave me now. Just think, woman, what would I do without your tea and scones?'

'Aye, right enough,' Libby was reassured at last.

'I'm glad we decided to ride across the moors instead of taking a carriage,' Elspeth shouted. The wind snatched her hair from its snood and blew it like a brown halo around her face.

327

'Smell the sea!' Peggy lifted her face and sniffed the pure air that brought back so many bitter-sweet memories. 'I used to think about this in the Balkans and then in the mud and blood of Flanders.'

'Me too.' Elspeth drew alongside, the two horses slowing to a gentle canter.

'There's Kirkowen.' Peggy pointed down into the valley.

'Yes, there it is.'

Wordlessly they swung their horses away from the little town, roofs glistening from the winter rain, towards Bargeddie House.

'Was it here?' Elspeth asked as they crossed the humphy bridge.

'Yes.' Peggy glanced towards the barn where she had been born. It was hardly more than a heap of rubble now.

'Have you forgiven the McClures?'

'I've forgiven the McClures, but I'll never forgive Hamish McClure for what he did. Can you think of any reason why I should?'

'No.'

'Have you forgiven him, Elspeth?'

'There's no need now,' she replied. 'Everyone in our childhood drama is dead, Peggy... poor Flora has her own sorrows to work through, and Louisa too.'

'What about Louisa?'

'She's an interesting lass. Almost twelve now. I met her a couple of times at the lawyer's office when we were setting up the Trust. We got on very well. Sinclair swears she's like me, God help her! I've suggested she goes to Miss Lovat's in September and she seems keen on the idea. Brian and I will take her to Australia one day, perhaps. The poor girl deserves some chance of a life away from the despair and sorrow my father sowed around him.'

'I'm thinking of sending Kirsten to Miss Lovat's too.'

'Why not send them together? The girls know nothing of our old tragedies, only our deep affection for one another.' Elspeth gazed across the wild moorland and her voice rang with certainty. 'We've broken the legacy of hatred through our friendship, Peggy. It might bear even greater fruit through them.'

'I'd like to think so.'

'Did you deliver my half-brother?' Elspeth asked without warning.

'Yes.'

'You never told me.'

'It was better so.'

'Maybe that.'

'How did you find out?'

'From Flora, though she didn't realise what she was saying.'

'As a doctor I had no choice but to try to save both mother and child.'

'Had that anything to do with my father dropping the case against me?'

'Don't ask.'

'All right. Come on!' Elspeth raced on ahead and Peggy galloped after.

Bargeddie House came into view, stark and handsome in the bleak January chill. A curl of smoke reached up and was swallowed by the low, glowering clouds.

'Is someone there, Elspeth?'

'I sent word that we were coming. The caretaker's wife has left, but she promised to have someone light a fire in the drawing room and air a couple of bedrooms for us. I said to arrange a simple meal for tonight and tomorrow morning, otherwise we can fend for ourselves.'

The women dismounted in the empty courtyard and the caretaker came forward at once to stable their mounts.

'Good evenin', Doctor McClure, Doctor McBride.' The man had been well briefed. 'My wife has gone to her sister's in Ayr as ye ken, Doctor McClure, but she got a local woman to fix a wee supper for ye. Nothin' fancy, just like yer message said.'

'That's fine, Willie, thank you.' Elspeth dismissed him with a nod. 'He's leaving next week,' she said to Peggy as they walked across to the house. 'His wife wants to live near her folk and he's found work on an estate in Alloway.'

'Will you be replacing him?'

'Maybe. We can talk better over dinner.' Elspeth pushed open the door and led the way into the silent hall.

'Hamish McClure must surely haunt this place.' Peggy followed, remembering the last time she was here with a sense of eerie unreality.

'I thought my father's ghost would be lingering at Bargeddie,' Elspeth's words echoed hers, 'but I've been back once or twice alone and there's nothing ... nothing at all. It's as if even the house wouldn't have him.'

'And your mother?'

'Not much of her either.' Elspeth's smile was wistful. 'Here's your room. It's always been a guest room, so there are no resident ghosts.'

'And it's warm and comfortable.' Peggy threw her damp riding skirt over a chair near the glowing fire and changed quickly. Elspeth tapped on the door again as Peggy's cold fingers struggled with the rows of tiny buttons on her blouse.

'I'm going on down to the drawing-room, Peggy, it's on the left at the bottom of the stairs. We'll eat there.'

'Coming!'

Within minutes Peggy had joined her. The drawing-room was cosy. Flames flickered cheerily over a bright coal fire. A table was laid nearby, laden with cold cuts, fresh-baked bread and bannocks. A huge tureen of soup sat warmly steaming on a trivet. The women sat down, famished after their long ride. Just as they settled a small dark-haired woman came in, murmured a greeting, served the broth, then withdrew without further ado.

'Who's that?' Peggy whispered when she left.

'Och, just someone the caretaker's wife knows. Her man was injured in France and is still in hospital in Glasgow. There's a lot of bairns to feed and she's glad of anything she can get by way of extra work.'

'There's thousands like her,' Peggy said sadly. 'And most of the men will have a hard job finding work when they come back. It's bad enough when they're able-bodied, but all those who are disabled ... God knows how many limbs Douglas and I had to remove in France and Belgium. Poor souls, what will they do?'

'I suppose the government will pension them.'

'It won't be much even so, Elspeth, and not likely to keep a family in food, let alone comfort.' Peggy changed the subject suddenly. 'Och, I'm longing to see Douglas. Why doesn't the man get in touch?' she fretted. 'How was he when you saw him last week in the convalescent home? I thought he would have been well enough to come back to France long ago.'

'Better . . .' Elspeth hesitated.

'Did you tell him I was on my way home?'

'Of course. It acted like a tonic to know you would soon be in Kilmarnock with Kirsten and Libby again.'

'But he hasn't answered my telegram!' she insisted. 'And I don't think he's away. His old factotum would have let me know!'

'Maybe he's afraid to see you.'

'Why should he be afraid?' Peggy's eyes widened.

'I suppose I'd better tell you, Peggy, so you won't get a shock when you see him.'

'Tell me what?' she demanded.

'I think Douglas is hesitating about meeting you till you've had a chance to rest and recover yourself.'

'What do you mean, Elspeth? Och, this beating about the bush isn't like you at all. Out with it, woman!'

'Douglas Munro will never do fine surgery again. You know most of the nerves were severed in his right hand?'

'God, no!' Peggy blanched. 'He didn't say a word about that when he wrote. I never treated his wounds, it was a field-doctor. In fact, I never knew he was wounded till he had already gone. It was such bloody chaos out there. Och, I thought he wasn't so bad! Poor Douglas, he should have told me!'

'You were under great strain. Douglas knew what it was like in the hospital. He wanted to spare you more anxiety. He has always tried to protect you, Peggy.'

She took a deep breath. 'Right, I'm not waiting a minute more. I must go to him straight after I get back to Kilmarnock tomorrow. What's he going to do now? Surgery was his life?'

'He told me he'll probably go into some sort of general practice, or else lecture in surgery. Eventually his hand will be reasonably flexible, but never enough for the precision needed actually to use a scalpel.'

331

'Bloody war!' Peggy said vehemently. 'What a terrible waste.'

'People like him will bear the scars forever,' Elspeth agreed. 'Though he can at least go back to work as an ordinary doctor.'

'But he was such a brilliant surgeon.

'Sometimes I wonder what we saved folk for, leaving them disabled for life?'

'That's the dilemma we all faced, Peggy. I've thought the same way myself over the last long years. But enough about Douglas for the moment. One of the reasons I brought you here was to find out what *you* plan to do?'

'Now I've decided not to marry Andrew, I would like to work with folk who are shell-shocked, Elspeth, or else learning how to use artificial limbs.' Peggy gazed thoughtfully into the glowing fire. 'There are so many disabled ex-soldiers now. They need help and somewhere to go to recover their self-respect and dignity, as well as their physical strength . . .'

Elspeth broke in suddenly, 'I've decided to follow Brian to Australia, Peggy. We're going to set up a clinic together doing more or less what you've suggested, but for Anzac veterans. He and I faced the same questions that bother you and came up with our own scheme. Now I'm a rich woman, we have the funds to fulfil the dream.'

'Australia? You mentioned you would go, but are you saying you're not coming back?' Peggy felt a terrible pit of emptiness yawn in the place Elspeth had filled for so long in her life.

'Oh, I'll be back now and then. We'll probably see each other as often as we managed to over the last few years.' Elspeth's smile was gentle and she took her friend's hands. 'But we'll always be together, Peggy. In spirit we're sisters, aren't we?'

'Yes.' She blinked away tears. 'Och, go after that daft Anzac if you want!' Peggy struggled to smile. 'But what has any of this got to do with me?'

'If I finance it, will you set up a centre for the disabled in Ayrshire?'

'A centre?' Peggy repeated.

332

'Just like you said, a place where people can heal body and soul. The government will surely help a bit with money, but even if they don't, I can provide backing enough to support at least twenty patients per year, maybe more.'

'How can you be so specific?'

Elspeth answered without embarrassment: 'The idea has been germinating for a while and I've done my sums.'

'And how did you guess I might be thinking along the same lines as you and Brian?' Peggy demanded.

'I know you.'

'I suppose you do.' Peggy's expression was rueful. 'What money are you thinking about? Nothing that was your father's, Elspeth. I'm sorry, but I still wouldn't touch a penny of his!' Peggy said sharply.

'No, no. I understand that and I thought of using the money from my mother's Trust for this project. It's accumulated well during the last few years I've been away.'

'Would that be allowed?'

'Oh, yes,' Elspeth said. 'The terms of the McKelvie Trust allow income to go to charity, according to Sinclair. I would want to call it the Janet McKelvie Foundation. Please, please, think about this, Peggy.' Elspeth searched Peggy's troubled green eyes. 'Libby could be housekeeper once Kirsten goes off to school. You could get a local woman in as Cook – that wee woman who served us tonight, for instance. And there are plenty more like her. Funds would run to a few other essential staff too. What do you say?'

Peggy shook her head. 'I couldn't run the medical side alone, at least not in the beginning while folk are very sick. Doctors don't come that cheap. Then there's the question of equipment, and above all suitable premises . . .'

'I left you to caretake Lansdowne Crescent and dumped you with the responsibility for Libby, so now will you do the same for this place? It would be perfect for the purpose?'

'Bargeddie House?'

'Bargeddie House.' Elspeth nodded. 'The produce from the estate could support even more poor souls.'

'Elspeth McClure, you must be mad! Bargeddie House of all places, and me living in it? Never.' Peggy's face flamed.

'How could you suggest it? Och, no! There are too many old associations.'

'Please listen, Peggy.' Elspeth gripped her arm. 'Are you going to let the past ruin the future for you?' she went on brutally. 'Making a shrine in your heart to Rob is one thing – though I remember Robert McBride too, Peggy, and he would be the last one to wish it!'

'Elspeth, don't bring Rob into this. Let it be, for God's sake. Forget Bargeddie House. Sell the cursed place if you don't want it!' Peggy protested, face burning.

'No, hear me out,' her friend insisted. 'I agree, Robert is your own affair and I'm sorry I mentioned him. You've never interfered in my personal decisions, nor I in yours, even when I saw someone more than worthy of your love suffer. But this is different. It could bring such good from evil.'

'No, Elspeth.' Peggy's face was set. 'I will not come to Bargeddie.'

'Peggy, no one should live in fear of the past. When I discovered you had delivered wee Hamish, I was sure you had risen above the old sins and sorrows! But I was wrong. You are as tormented by them as if they happened yesterday.'

'Elspeth, you don't understand!' Peggy protested. 'Just being near Kirkowen hurts. You can't imagine how I feel when I ride past the town and see the streets where I ran barefoot. Sometimes I don't know who or what I am, and I can't face any more pain in finding out.' Her desolate expression cut Elspeth to the heart, but she was determined to have this out.

'Nobody thinks of you as wee Peggy Soutar, the Kirkowen bairn who was born in a ruined barn. And if they did, Peggy, it would be with admiration and wonder. You've made your name and reputation as a medical pioneer and a war heroine. Kirkowen can be proud of such a daughter.'

'Och, blethers, Elspeth! And even if it's so, that wouldn't make it any easier to live in Bargeddie House.'

'I know it would be traumatic for you to live in the place your worst enemy lived. But think of things differently, I'm your best friend and I was born here. See it as a chance

334

to go on helping the folk you saved in France to find a new meaning in life. Think of Bargeddie as a place of hope, not sadness. Please, Peggy, don't turn me down without at least considering what I've offered.'

She sat staring blankly, her emotions in a turmoil. Finally she sighed. 'All right, I promise I'll think about it. Maybe I'll tell you my decision in the morning. Just don't count on it being the answer you want.' She got up, face white and drawn.

Elspeth joined her in front of the fire's dying embers. 'Forgive me, Peggy, I go at things like a bull at a gate sometimes,' she said softly. 'Maybe I should have handled this more tactfully. I'll be desolate if you turn the project down because I'm a clumsy oaf!'

'Och, you're not that.' Peggy smiled wearily. 'It's just so many "ghouls and ghaisties" have been raised tonight in Bargeddie after all. I'm bewildered and more than a wee bittie scared, Elspeth. Things as big as this are better slept upon.'

That night in the guest room at Bargeddie House Peggy tossed and turned, dreaming of the past and the present in such a mix that she woke in a lather of sweat more than once. Finally, utterly exhausted, she fell into a deep sleep until thin January light filtered gloomily through the heavy curtains.

'God, it must be late.' Peggy jumped out of bed and looked at the watch pinned to her blouse. 'Nine-thirty! Michty.' Quickly she washed in the little bathroom then dressed, rushing down to the sitting-room where Elspeth had told her breakfast would be served.

'Where's Doctor McClure?' she asked the dark-haired woman who came at her ring. 'Is she still asleep?'

'She went out half an hour ago to Maybole in the horse and trap, Doctor McBride. Said to tell you she'll be back by eleven o'clock.'

'Oh, fine.' Peggy wondered why Elspeth had said nothing the night before about going to Maybole. She ate a solitary breakfast, looking out of the big bow windows across the moors. It was a fine, dry morning, with clouds scudding across the wintry sky. When she finished, she decided to

335

take a ride and think again about Elspeth's proposition for, despite her promise, the decision was no nearer being made.

'If she's back before me, please tell Doctor McClure I've ridden over to the Kirkowen cliffs,' she told the temporary cook and maid-of-all-trades.

'Certainly, Doctor McBride,' the woman replied, bobbing a curtsey.

'Sorry, Mrs . . . er . . .' Peggy smiled as she left. 'I haven't been told your name?'

'Mrs Laird, Jessie Laird.' She bobbed again and disappeared into the kitchen.

Peggy rode with the wind whipping her face, the sharp air making her eyes water. Soon she was at the cliffs. Tethering the horse she walked across the headland to where she once had crawled in the grass with Tam Laird to find a curlew's nest.

Jessie Laird . . . Och, she must be Tam's wife. The thought had been lingering since she left Bargeddie. What will become of them and their five bairns?

'You can't take the sorrows of the world on to yourself, Peggy,' she said aloud. The words blew away on the wind.

But you can use the talents you've got to make your own wee bit world better, the answer came back from her heart.

This place would be wonderful for sick folk to regain their strength instead of lying in damp, grimy tenements, she realised. The cheery Glasgow lads she had travelled with to the Somme, Hughie Naughton in his best suit and cravat standing by her side at Jamie's funeral, nudged at her memory . . . They deserve a chance! But can I cope with knowing who lived here and what it meant to my parents?

Cold and stiff, she got up almost an hour later, still no nearer solving her dilemma. Sea-birds wheeled and cried above her head and the sea tossed white-capped waves into a mad frenzy. Slowly, head bowed, she began walking back to her horse.

'Independent I may be,' she muttered aloud, 'but sometimes decisions are better shared. I'll go to Edinburgh like I said and talk to Douglas. Elspeth can wait a few days more for her answer.' Suddenly she remembered the real reason for going and what Elspeth had told her about Douglas's own terrible situation. 'Och, Douglas Munro! What a self-centred idiot I am.' She felt ashamed to the heart. 'Mithering about my fears and fancies when you have worse to face. Right,' she told the wild wind, 'I'm going to see Douglas and put him first for once. Then I'll decide about Bargeddie and the rest. Och, poor Douglas.' Memories of Flanders and long, long before, of his unstinting support, their easy companionship, his loyalty, the look in his eyes . . . the look in his eyes! 'A man more than worthy,' Elspeth

had said . . . 'I thought she meant Andrew, but she didn't, did she?' Och, Peggy said slowly 'it's me that's not worthy!'

The mad world started spinning around her and her heart lifted like the wild sea-birds on the Heathery cliffs. 'Elspeth is right as usual. The past is over. I have to look forward not back. Rob would have wanted that. He always grasped life with both hands and so should I!' Now she allowed it in, the truth she had denied came flowing through, certain and sure. 'Douglas was wrong, I *am* a fool, and a blind one at that! Och, I just hope I've not left it too late . . .'

'Peggy!' A distant rider called through cupped hands. The sound fragmented on the wind.

'Is that Elspeth?' She strained to see.

'Peggy, dear girl.' Douglas Munro's cheerful, familiar smile went straight to her heart as he rode up and dismounted. Wordlessly, she held her arms open.

'Douglas, what on earth kept you, man? Just when I need you,' she chided unfairly and illogically, forgetting her own good resolutions to put him first, but she wrapped him in the warmest embrace she could.

'That's what Elspeth said,' Douglas murmured into her hair. 'She telegraphed me yesterday before you left Kilmarnock. If I was well enough to come, she said, then I'd better get here . . . I am and I came.'

'How is your hand?' Peggy demanded tearfully. 'Elspeth told me about it . . . but you didn't! You lied!'

'I didn't lie, I just didn't tell you everything. I knew you had enough to cope with in Flanders without my woes.

337

Anyway it's much better. See, it moves.' Bravely he struggled to open and close his stiff right hand with its livid scars. 'Now are you glad to see me, or are you just going to stand here and cry?'

'Glad isn't the word!' Peggy looked up at him, eyes shining with happy tears. 'But in the name of the wee man how could Elspeth have known yesterday what my reaction would be to her proposal? And above all else in the world that I would want to have you with me today?'

'Elspeth McClure is a very special person. There's little escapes those sharp eyes. She knows you better than you know yourself, Peggy McBride.'

'Och, Douglas.' Peggy held on to him as if she would never let go. 'I've missed you, so I have. Nothing's been right! I felt like part of me had been sawn off when you went.'

'I felt pretty amputated myself.' His cheery grin made her heart turn over. 'But with greater cause.'

'I suppose Elspeth told you about her proposal for Bargeddie?' Peggy demanded.

'Yes, on the way from the station.'

'What do you think?'

'If you want to do it and need help from an old friend, then I'm with you. Two doctors are better than one . . . we've proved that often enough.'

'Would you follow me here to Ayrshire?' she asked in surprise. 'You're famous these days. Even with your hand, Elspeth says you could get a practice in Edinburgh as a fashionable GP, making money by the bucketful. If you say no to Bargeddie, I'll understand. Och I'm in two minds about it all.'

'You're not using me as an excuse,' he teased. 'And I'm not a poor man. Even if I was, I'd follow you to the ends of the earth if you asked.' Douglas's smile widened but his grey eyes were serious.

'And I you.'

'Well, then?'

'If you come to Bargeddie, so will I.'

'I'll come.'

'Will you marry me, Douglas?'

338

'Why not, Peggy? After all, I love you'

'And I love you, Douglas Munro, though it's taken a while to admit it ... but will you feel that Rob stands between us?' she added anxiously.

'Rob loved us both. I know he would be glad to see us together and with his daughter. But I could ask the same. You've always said you could never put anyone in his place, Peggy, that's why I never pressed my suit. What changed your mind?'

'Elspeth finally made me see sense with her bluntness,' Peggy said ruefully. 'I suppose I've been fighting how I felt about you for a long time, especially in Belgium when we were so close. But I couldn't let go of the past. I was too afraid of the future.' Her voice dropped so he had to bend his head to hear. 'I will always love Robert but you loved him too, he's still part of our lives. No, my dear,' her voice became steady and sure again, 'there are no shadows between us, are there?'

'None,' he replied softly. 'So when do we start our marvellous project at Bargeddie, Doctor McBride?'

Peggy's face glowed with enthusiasm. 'Why not right away? That's what Elspeth wants.'

'Will Libby and Kirsten come here too, I thought you couldn't sell the house in Kilmarnock?'

'Och we'll let it out till Kirsten is old enough to decide what she wants to do with her life. Andrew can invest the income for her.' In her new mood of optimism the ideas poured out. 'Just think, I can show my lassie the places I played in as a bairn. Och it sounds good!'

'We must choose the best people to work here, Peggy, who understand the needs of the wounded souls we'll be treating,' Douglas added with his usual mixture of good sense and kindness.

'Kirkowen folk are canty and stout-hearted Douglas, and they sorely need work. There will be no shortage of willing labour. Libby will expect to be head housekeeper when Kirsten goes to Miss Lovat's later in the year. She and Louisa can come to Bargeddie at weekends and all the holidays.' Peggy danced a few steps along the heathery path like the happy child she had once been. 'And I've just thought of a good cook and assistant for her, a woman called Jessie Laird. I've heard she has four lads and a wee lassie called Margaret.'

'Margaret, like you? There's a coincidence, eh?' Douglas rejoined.

She slipped her hand in his and replied with an enigmatic smile, 'I've discovered there is no such thing as coincidence in this life, Douglas Munro.'

'There's something in that,' he agreed.

'Och, man, shall we go to Bargeddie this minute and tell Elspeth she's won after all?'

'Not till I've kissed you till your face is as red as that hair of yours. I've been longing to do this for years. Just never ask me how many!' He drew her to him and did as he promised.

Arms round each other they walked back, leading the horses and making their plans. Peggy felt her ghosts and ghaisties' retreat further with every step.

As they reached the rise above Bargeddie House, she saw the caretaker load the last of his belongings onto the cart. There would be a house free on the estate, a decent house with a stout roof and walls that did not run with damp.

'And I know just the man to become our new caretaker, Douglas. He lost half an arm in Flanders, but he still has the other one and a brave spirit. There's no reason why he can't look after the grounds and the beasts. But somebody else would have to stick the pig and wring the necks of the chickens, he hates killing!'

'Then how did he manage in the war?'

'Och, he did his bit like many another in the mud of Flanders. Are you willing to give him a chance?'

'Why not?' Douglas replied at once. 'It would be fitting for a real war-hero to have a job here. It takes courage to face what you're afraid of and still do it without flinching. But, lassie mine, who is the person you have in mind?'

'A local man. You met him once in Flanders, though you'll hardly remember. He should be out of hospital soon,' Peggy leaned her head on Douglas's shoulder. Hope and joy flooded into her heart. 'And I bet he still plays the mouth organ like magic, one hand or not.'

Curee, curee ... Above their heads a curlew swooped and cried across the moor, then wheeled back towards the heathery cliffs and the wild, free sea.

A SELECTION OF NOVELS AVAILABLE FROM JUDY PIATKUS (PUBLISHERS) LIMITED

THE PRICES SHOWN BELOW WERE CORRECT AT THE TIME OF GOING TO PRESS. HOWEVER JUDY PIATKUS (PUBLISHERS) LIMITED RESERVE THE RIGHT TO SHOW NEW RETAIL PRICES ON COVERS WHICH MAY DIFFER FROM THOSE PREVIOUSLY ADVERTISED IN THE TEXT OR ELSEWHERE.

Catch the Moment	*Euanie MacDonald*	£5.99
Bridge of Hope	*Anne Douglas*	£5.99
As the Years Go By	*Anne Douglas*	£5.99
Mile End Girl	*Elizabeth Lord*	£5.99
A Matter of Trust	*Mary A Larkin*	£5.99

All Piatkus titles are available by post from:

Bookpost PLC, P.O. Box 29, Douglas, Isle of Man IM99 1BQ

Credit cards accepted. Please telephone 01624 836000,
fax 01624 837033, Internet http://www.bookpost.co.uk
Or e-mail: bookshop@enterprise.net for details.

Free postage and packing in the UK. Overseas customers: allow
£1 per book (paperbacks) and £3 per book (hardbacks).